"What's wrong?" Trigger asked.

The softness in his voice made Ashley look up at him. Way up. The man was so tall.

She found her voice under the wave of fear gripping her. "I know you don't mean to, but you're scaring me."

"Look at me, Ashley."

She sucked in a breath, found a shred of bravery from the tatters of her will, and raised her gaze to meet his.

"I will never hurt you."

She fell into the depths of gray and flecks of blue in his eyes and drowned in the sincerity and promise she found there. Deep down, she believed him. Part of her needed to believe him, because she needed something real to hold on to before she sank any deeper into despair and the paranoia that everyone wanted to hurt her.

She nodded. "If he finds me, he'll kill me."

"He'll have to get past me first."

By Jennifer Ryan

Montana Heat Series
MONTANA HEAT: ESCAPE TO YOU
MONTANA HEAT: PROTECTED BY LOVE (novella)

Montana Men Series
HIS COWBOY HEART
HER RENEGADE RANCHER
STONE COLD COWBOY
HER LUCKY COWBOY
WHEN IT'S RIGHT
AT WOLF RANCH

The McBrides Series
DYLAN'S REDEMPTION
FALLING FOR OWEN
THE RETURN OF BRODY MCBRIDE

The Hunted Series
EVERYTHING SHE WANTED
CHASING MORGAN
THE RIGHT BRIDE
LUCKY LIKE US
SAVED BY THE RANCHER

Short Stories
CLOSE TO PERFECT
(appears in SNOWBOUND AT CHRISTMAS)
CAN'T WAIT
(appears in ALL I WANT FOR CHRISTMAS IS A COWBOY)
WAITING FOR YOU
(appears in CONFESSIONS OF A SECRET ADMIRER)

JENNIFER RYAN

MONTANA HEAT

ESCAPE TO YOU

AVONBOOKS

An Imprint of HarperCollinsPublishers

Excerpt from *Montana Heat: True to You* copyright © 2018 by Jennifer Ryan.

MONTANA HEAT: ESCAPE TO YOU. Copyright © 2017 by Jennifer Ryan. All rights reserved. Printed in the United States of America. No part of this book may be used or reproduced in any manner whatsoever without written permission except in the case of brief quotations embodied in critical articles and reviews. For information, address HarperCollins Publishers, 195 Broadway, New York, NY 10007.

First Avon Books mass market printing: September 2017
First Avon Books hardcover printing: August 2017

Print Edition ISBN: 978-0-06-264525-8
Digital Edition ISBN: 978-0-06-264526-5

Cover design and photo illustration by Nadine Badalaty.
Cover photographs: © fstop123 / Getty Images (fence and background);
© vectorbomb / Getty Images (tattoo).

Avon, Avon & logo, and Avon Books & logo are registered trademarks of HarperCollins Publishers in the United States of America and other countries.

HarperCollins is a registered trademark of HarperCollins Publishers in the United States of America and other countries.

FIRST EDITION

17 18 19 20 21   QGM   10 9 8 7 6 5 4 3 2 1

For Bella.
My furry partner in crime,
who sits beside me while I write all my books.
You never judge when I look up disturbing things that
surely have me on the FBI's, DEA's, and Homeland
Security's watch lists. You don't mind when I ask
questions like, "How should I kill this person?
Gun? Knife? Barbed wire?"

Best of all, you're always up for a snack,
even though you get apple slices and I get chocolate.
Thanks for always being by my side.

You're my friend, my confidant, one of the kids.
I love you, sweet girl.

CHAPTER ONE

Welcome to Celebrity Centerfold. *I'm your host, Sharon Waters. Tonight, we delve into the life, career, and mysterious disappearance of Oscar-winning actress Ashley Swan.*

Trigger sat in his recliner, drinking a beer, staring at the striking photo of Ashley on the TV screen and didn't care one bit about why some spoiled, rich, self-important movie star ditched her extravagant life. He rubbed his hand over his aching shoulder and the scar on his chest where he'd been shot. What did he care about some overpaid actress when two months ago he'd killed an innocent woman, and last month he'd avoided killing his brother's girlfriend by a mere inch, then killed the man who tried to kill his brother?

Next week marks the one-year anniversary of the last confirmed sighting of the mega movie star when she appeared on After Midnight *with Brice Mooney. The two shared an evident affection for each other that drew fans and jacked up ratings whenever she appeared on Mooney's show, but nothing compared to her appearance on his final show before he retired. Audience members, show producers, and Mooney himself said she was happy that night and enjoyed Mooney's celebration before he took his final bow and retired to his secluded ranch in Montana.*

Clips of Ashley Swan and Brice Mooney laughing together as she sat in the chair next to his desk during her appearances on the show played on the screen. Ashley Swan teased with coy smiles and sultry looks as Brice Mooney's adoration spilled out in his seductive comments and suggestive jokes. Ashley played along with the much-older man, striking the perfect balance between shy modesty at his praise over one performance or another, and joking away Brice's obvious infatuation and comments about her exceptional beauty with outrageous flirtations she overplayed for the live and TV audience.

Ashley Swan has not been seen since she left the after-party that night. Rumors have circulated from inside sources who claim Ashley complained for months leading up to her disappearance about her nonstop work schedule, the pressure to get the next Oscar, the paparazzi dogging her heels everywhere she went, and tabloid stories about the many men she dated.

With an open missing person's case with no evidence of foul play or her death, no ransom demands, and all reports claiming she was unhappy living her life in the public eye, many believe she simply walked away from it all. What would make her turn her back on fame and give up her lucrative career? The pressure? Drugs? A secret lover who swept her off her feet and took her away from the bright lights of sin city to live a quieter, peaceful life in seclusion?

Where has she been hiding this past year?

The bigger question remains: why hasn't anyone seen her?

Did she really walk away from it all without a word to her publicist, agent, manager, the studio, or even her hairdresser? Or did something darker claim her and we'll never know?

Trigger shut off the TV and stared out the windows at

the darkening evening sky, trying not to think of all the horrors that could have befallen her. Lost in his suffocating guilt and heavy grief, living with his nightmares, old and new, every second of the day, he'd locked himself away on his secluded property, hoping to find some peace.

God, he hoped he didn't have to shoot anyone this month.

CHAPTER TWO

Ashley's arms ached; her fingers tingled as the silk straps tied around her wrists and the carved bedpost cut off her circulation. Arms over her head, she stood beside the bed, her naked body stretched with her back pressed to the cold, hard wood. She didn't feel the crisp winter chill in the room from the open window anymore. Another small but effective means to torment and degrade her. Numb from the inside out, she stood before her captor, indifferent to whatever he did next.

After all this time, what did it matter?

Every escape attempt futile and foiled.

Every plea for mercy unheeded.

Every day another day of torture to endure.

She didn't know how long she'd been here. The days and nights blurred into one big never-ending nightmare. She stopped wondering if anyone was looking for her, or even cared that she disappeared. She didn't think about the life she'd lost back in L.A. She didn't dream of her future, or regret all the might-have-beens that would probably never be.

She endured each and every day with only one thought in mind: survive.

Some days, like today, she didn't know why she bothered. Last night, she'd made a mistake. Miscalculated her captor's tenuous hold on sanity. Or maybe more accurately, his need to inflict pain and have his fantasy play out just so. It had to be flawless, the illusion only he saw in his mind but expected her to play to perfection.

Illusion was her stock-in-trade.

She'd earned three back-to-back Oscar nominations, winning the third for making people believe the characters she portrayed.

Until now, she'd refused to become the character her captor demanded, wanted, craved.

And she'd paid dearly for it the many months she'd been here, but most especially last night. Her ribs and back still ached from the beating. Every breath felt like sucking in fire. Her cracked ribs would heal in time. She wasn't so sure about her fractured mind.

It had finally come to the point where she understood, believed she was his—to do with as he pleased.

She would never escape this hell.

"I hope tonight will be different." Brice pulled the ice-blue gown from the closet. The elegant dress swished as he draped it over his arm to show it off. She'd worn such beautiful things on dozens of red carpets. But the thought of putting that on *for him* filled her gut with dread and pushed bile up her throat, choking her with fear.

Not that one.

Not Aurora from *Flame in the Night*.

Any other character. Any other movie she could play out for him again and again, but this one only ended badly.

Last night's beating would seem like a trip to an amusement park. He wanted to punish her for holding out, holding back day after day, night after night. She'd reached the end of his patience and endurance.

He wanted what he wanted.

And he meant to get it from her, even by force, despite the fact that he knew the only way it would ever be perfect was if she gave in, gave up, and committed to giving him the dream: her, wholly and completely immersed in character and in love with him.

Before tonight her mind screamed *never*.

Now that voice sighed its last breath in defeat.

Until tonight, she could not pretend to be the woman he wanted, a made-up character on-screen, a woman who adored him with undying love. She could not pretend that she'd find a way out of here. She could not pretend this was all a terrible nightmare.

She could not do this anymore.

She won the Oscar with her portrayal of Aurora, a woman who falls for a rich and powerful businessman disillusioned with people and the world until he meets her. Aurora reignites his passion for life. The love they share is something neither of them expected.

A modern-day fairy tale set in New York. Duncan living alone in the penthouse of his skyscraper castle. Aurora living on the lower floor, taking care of her ailing aunt, wishing for excitement and a less lonely life.

The movie instantly became a classic romance, one that would probably stand the test of time and be adored by one generation after the next.

Brice wanted that love story to be his. He wanted Aurora to be his real-life lover. He wanted to have a love like no other. He wanted her to bring that fantasy to life.

But he didn't know how to love. He'd never felt that in his life. Within himself. Or from another.

She didn't think he felt anything at all. Not really. Which is why he tried so hard to feel something.

"You brought on what happened last night. If only you'd stop holding back, we could have the life we both want. We would be the envy of all of Hollywood. The world."

Yes, fans all over the world clamored for every scrap of information about her personal life. They devoured every picture and video of her on TV, the internet, and splashed across tabloid magazines. Didn't matter if the stories were true or not. Didn't matter if the man she was with was just a friend. People imagined an epic love story because that's what she'd given them on-screen.

Just like everyone else fantasizing about being a movie star and living the perfect life, Brice wanted to live the dream that she knew was nothing more than illusion.

The backhanded slap across the mouth brought her out of her head and made her present in the moment.

"I'd hoped last night taught you to respond when I talk to you."

Unsure if he asked her a question, or said something that even required comment, she stared at him, hoping for some kind of hint.

None forthcoming, her silence continued, and Brice's face contorted with anger at her perceived insolence. He tossed the beautiful gown across the bed and punched her in the ribs to get her attention. Her body bucked and contorted with the force of the smacking blow. Reflex made her try to pull her arms down for protection, but the silken straps held her arms above her head, her body unprotected. Flesh pounded into flesh as another fist socked her in the side, connecting with her already-screaming ribs. She didn't cry out at the sickening crack or the excruciating pain that followed. She focused on trying to get her breath, her back pressed to the post behind her, and the feel of the wood against her skin.

Instead of focusing on the roar of pain, she lost herself in her mind and the dream she'd created by the rippling river: the cool water flowing over her bare feet, the sun warm on her hair and shoulders, the sound of the wind whispering through the pretty green trees all around her. Peace.

A trick she'd taught herself weeks into her captivity

because she couldn't escape her gilded torture chamber, but her mind could take her anywhere she wanted to go.

Lately, a man joined her there at the river, his dark hair and narrowed eyes filled with pain and regret she recognized. Every time she reached out to him, he got farther away, but still she held her hand out and ran toward him, hoping to catch him and feel his strong, protective arms around her.

If only she could reach him.

"You will scream for me."

And with those words, her sweet illusion vanished.

Yes, she would scream. The beating wouldn't stop until she did. If she screamed too soon, he'd beat her for being weak. Too late, she might not be able to scream at all. The game had to be played. She knew the rules and the fine line she walked every second of the day.

She'd play her part, or he'd bring on the pain.

He liked to hurt her.

One day, she'd find a way to hurt him.

She'd find a way to escape.

She'd save herself.

And the boy he called son, but treated like an unruly dog that needed to be beaten into submission.

If only he'd make one mistake. Give her one small opening. She'd find a way to overcome the crippling fear of more pain and certain death, and take it.

But that day would never come. She knew that now.

The riding crop lashed across her bare thighs, once, twice, again and again as her body absorbed the punishment like a sponge does water, taking it in like memory. Bruises faded, cracked and broken bones mended, but every beating remained a part of her, darkening her mind and heart, leaving an indelible mark on her soul, never evaporating like water from the sponge.

Who would ever have guessed the guy everyone thought funny, charming, and warm was actually a cold-hearted bastard with a sick fascination with torture and pain.

His hand clamped onto her jaw, holding her face in his tight grip. She tried to stay in that place by the river in her mind, fighting to get to that dark-haired man with the reluctant grin he sometimes gave her, but Brice got in her face, demanding her undivided attention. With him this close, his body pressed to her naked one, she could only focus on him and the overwhelming fear twisting her gut. The anticipation vibrating through him rocked through both of them, dilating his eyes with a passion he couldn't fulfill no matter how hard he tried.

She paid dearly for his inability to fuck her. As much as he wanted her, without her devoted performance of his fantasy, he couldn't get what he needed to get it up and find satisfaction. So he found it in the excitement inflicting pain gave him.

She knew exactly what would happen if she finally gave in, gave him what he wanted and he still couldn't take her to bed and finish his fantasy. He'd kill her for giving him everything he wanted and blame her for his not being able to be the man, the lover, who fulfilled her every erotic need.

"The sacrifices I've made for you. The things I've done to please you."

He'd cut his thinning, graying brown hair short and styled it like the young actors and rock stars did these days. That messy bed-head look with an edge. He kept his beard trimmed short, though it didn't grow in evenly. Across his cheeks and jaw, the patches were varying shades of brown, gray, and white. It didn't make him look distinguished or youthful. He looked ridiculous.

Especially now, when he was dressed in a black skinny-leg suit, white shirt, and gray tie. He tried to attain the slim, ripped physique of the men she played opposite in the movies, but with his advanced age, his penchant for fine wine and decadently rich foods, he'd never have the physical perfection of some twenty-something man again. Thirty-six years her senior, he deluded himself into believing a young woman like herself would see a sexy, distinguished, worldly man. All she saw was a delusional old man, trying to be something he'd never been, even in his youth.

"You have everything you need here."

A beautiful room filled with antique furniture, thick carpets over gleaming hardwood floors. Priceless floral art on the walls. A plush bed with silk sheets. An all-too-inviting Jacuzzi tub in the marble bathroom. Velvet drapes over embroidered sheers.

Bars on the windows. Locks on the door. And the converted walk-in closet that served as her cell with its hardwood floor and heavy metal doors with the wood veneer to hide what lay behind on her side of them. No light. No window. An empty, dark box. A place to hold her until she gave him what he wanted.

The rest of the room a temptation she didn't dare want.

But she did, especially when she lay on that cold, hard floor aching from yet another lesson in pain and endurance.

His hand clamped over her breast in a punishing squeeze. She hissed out a pain-filled breath, but he took it for excited passion. "This is what you want."

She wanted it to be over. She didn't want to spend another minute in that black box. She didn't want to hurt anymore. She didn't want to feel anything anymore.

All she had to do was become his living fantasy and it would all be over.

What started as psychological torture and rare out-bursts of physical abuse had turned into increasingly dire beatings. The gnawing ache of hunger her constant companion. Every breath hurt. Every bone and muscle ached. Every second she spent alone and lonely and desperate and sad in her cell had become one too many. She couldn't do this anymore.

She wanted out.

She needed out.

One way or another.

Living in hell, she decided to walk right into the fire and end this once and for all.

"You know what I want."

He took her weary acceptance of the inevitable as breathless anticipation. "What, my darling?"

"To begin our special evening." She had his attention. She normally didn't speak unless spoken to first, or in reaction to Brice reciting lines to her movies and the part he expected her to play.

She cast her gaze toward the pretty, torturous dress on the bed. Despite the weight she'd lost since being held here, he had the dress altered time and again to always be one size too small.

He held it in front of her, down low. She stepped into the gown, spun on her toes to face the bedpost, twisting her bindings painfully around her wrists. She blew out all the breath from her lungs. Brice muscled the zipper up her back, taking his time and prolonging her pain as the too-tight dress closed over her bruised back and battered ribs.

His hands rested on her bare shoulders. She sucked in a shallow breath, needing the air, but hating the pain it caused as her lungs filled and constricted against the confines of the heavy dress that pushed her breasts up until they nearly spilled out the top. Just the way he liked it.

His fingers combed through her tangled mass of oily hair. He hadn't allowed her the luxury of a shower in three days. He mussed it more, letting it spill down her back and shoulders. His body pressed against her back, pushing her chest into the bedpost as he reached above her and lifted the strap off the metal hook, stretching her arms so high it felt like they might pop right out of the sockets. She endured the painful prickles and tingling as blood rushed down her arms and into her hands. She didn't move. Couldn't with his body smashing hers into the post.

He dipped his head to her ear. "Don't disappoint me tonight."

She leaned back into him. Despite the layers of satin and chiffon of the full skirt keeping her skin from touching him, dread shivered over her nerves no barrier could stop. His arm wrapped around her middle, squeezing her already-aching ribs until they screamed with pain. She held it together, even as his thin lips pressed to her cheek.

"Has the scene been set?"

He vibrated with anticipation. "Yes. Oh, yes."

"Then let's begin." A single tear slipped past her lashes and rolled down her cheek. She hadn't cried in a long time, having spent her many tears long ago. But something about reaching the end—knowing all was lost and that she just couldn't take it one more second—sent a wave of grief deep into her soul and shattered it.

Brice took her hand and raised it to his lips, kissing the back of it like some gallant knight in shining armor. He didn't mean to save her. The devil in him wanted to destroy her. She feared he already had, but tonight would be the end.

Finally.

Like the prince in *Cinderella*, Brice dropped to one knee, picked up the crystal-encrusted heels, and slid them onto her feet. He stared up at her with such worship. If she didn't know the monster behind those adoring eyes, she might actually believe he loved her.

She walked with him out of her beautiful cell and down the hallway, knowing she walked to her death like an inmate leaving death row for the last time.

At the top of the stairs, she stared past the living room to the beautiful dining room table laden with expensive white china and sparkling crystal glasses. Covered dishes held the fragrant food he'd never actually allow her to eat. The incessant gnawing hunger in her gut made her mouth water. She wanted to run to that table and gorge, but fear and painful memories froze her in place.

"Look at the beautiful garden, Aurora."

Without a window in her cell, she craved the outdoors, the pretty landscape. Even at night, she longed to be outside where she could smell the flowers, feel the wind and any sense of freedom. But he hadn't let her out in a long time and preferred to torture her with the gorgeous view.

At least that's what she originally thought, but over time she realized he had some strange fascination with the garden. A look came into his eyes when he stared at it, like he saw more than anyone else.

His eyes were filled with that overexcited look right now. "I'll go down first. Then you can have your moment and sweep down the stairs to me."

She glanced at him, his eyes sparkling with anticipation. "Of course."

Brice rushed down the stairs. She prayed he stumbled and fell to his death. He hit the landing in the wide foyer and turned to stare up at her. Dressed in the elegant suit, he appeared the picture of a successful businessman waiting for the only woman he ever loved.

I am Aurora.

She embraced the numbness, swept her tangled mass

of hair over her shoulder, put her trembling hand on the banister, and forced herself to take the first step to her death. She made her way down each tread with her head held high, the dress swept out behind her, her gaze locked on Brice just like in the film. She pretended this was Duncan's New York penthouse, not Brice's house of horrors. She showed him the regal woman while on the inside the pain and anguishing inevitability crushed her heart and soul.

Brice took her hand at the end of the stairs again. The triumphant smile made her stomach sour. He led her to the table, held her chair out, and pushed it in as she sat. She ignored the piercing pain radiating from the backs of her bruised thighs.

Just like in the movie, she held her wineglass out to him. "Let's celebrate." The words stuck in her throat, but she pushed them out with a breathy tone that had the anticipation in Brice's gaze flaring with passion that turned her stomach.

Brice filled her glass with red wine just like Duncan had for Aurora.

Duncan had set up the special evening to propose to Aurora. The first night of the rest of their lives.

This would be Ashley's last night on earth.

He held his glass up. "A love meant to be will find a way." The line from Duncan was meant to convey the love he and Aurora found when, after months of living in the same building, probably passing each other dozens of times but never seeing each other, Duncan discovered her struggling in the pool when a leg cramp made it difficult for her to get to the edge. He rescued her. Coming from Brice to her under these circumstances, the words made her skin crawl.

She held her glass out to toast her demise.

The doorbell rang behind her, halting her shaking

hand and sending a bolt of fear quaking through her body. She trembled, not knowing what to do or what this meant. Although people came and went from the house, Brice always ensured that when he let her out no one saw her. But Brice let her see them, the influential people who could help her if only they knew she was there. If only they weren't in Brice's pocket. He tormented her with their presence by making her watch them through the two-way mirrors in the secret passages he'd had built into the house. While they enjoyed themselves at the lavish parties Brice threw, she stood behind the glass and watched how Brice ensnared them in a trap they didn't see.

Just like he did to her.

Brice grabbed her by the throat, his fingers biting into her skin and cutting off her breath, and pulled her close. She dropped the wineglass, spilling red wine over the pristine white tablecloth.

He growled his frustration at her clumsiness.

She clawed at his hand at her throat, desperate for air.

"I don't know who would dare come here uninvited, but it must be important to drive way the hell out here at this hour. Be good. Don't make me punish you, my sweet Aurora. I'll find out what they want and send them away. Nothing will ruin our night."

He rose and drew her up with him, pushing her back and releasing her neck at the same time. She coughed and sucked in a much-needed breath, her chest constricting against the confining dress, her throat sore from Brice's grip. He took her by the arm and dragged her to the stairs and up. The frosted panes of glass concealed her and whoever was at the door.

"On my way. Be there in a minute," Brice called from the top of the stairs. He rushed her down the hall and into her room, past the luxurious bed, and shoved her into the converted closet turned cell. Weak from being unable to breathe with the constricting dress and the meager food Brice allowed her, she stumbled and fell to her hands and knees. Knowing better than to turn her back on a wild animal, she scrambled away and turned to face him.

"Don't worry, darling, I'll get rid of whoever dared disturb us and be back for you. We will have the perfect night, Aurora."

The doorbell rang downstairs three times. Brice lost the lover's look in his eyes and gave her one last fierce frown, turned, and shoved the heavy metal door closed, rushing off.

She hung her head and breathed a sigh of relief for this short reprieve. When she raised her head again, the sliver of gray light slicing across the dark floor didn't register at first. Then it hit her.

He made a mistake.

He left her an opening.

Literally.

He didn't push the door all the way closed, so the thick automatic bolts hadn't sprung home, locking her in.

No telling how long she had before he came back. She fought the instinctive fear that told her to stay put or face dire consequences that only meant more pain if caught trying to escape. Again.

Nightmares of her earlier attempts swamped her mind, but out of those gruesome images hope grew that *this time,* luck was on her side. She conquered her fear and moved to the heavy metal door, pushing it open an inch at a time, the muscles in her arms quivering with the effort. She listened intently for any sound of Brice's return. Not a floorboard squeaked or footstep sounded.

Her heartbeat thundered in her ears as she struggled to push the heavy door closed until she heard the familiar *thunk* of the bolts sliding into position. If Brice didn't open the door again tonight, distracted by his visitor too long to want to play with her again, she'd gain precious time to get away undetected. She didn't know where she was going, only that she needed to get away. Fast.

She crept out the bedroom door. Instead of going left toward the main staircase, she turned right and padded down the hallway past several closed bedroom doors to the back stairs. She tried not to think about what she'd seen people do in those rooms while Brice held her by the neck and forced her to watch through the two-way mirrors. At the end of the hall, she stood in front of the large window, staring at the rolling gray clouds darkening the sky and closing in fast. The last thing she needed was to get caught in a storm, but wet and cold was better than locked up or dead any day.

The urge to run pushed at her, but she fought the impulse and did the one thing sure to slow her down and put her in more danger.

She turned to the door beside her and quietly opened it. Adam sat on his bed, feet dangling off the edge, a picture book in his lap. His wide eyes met hers. She'd only seen the four-year-old a handful of times. She hadn't seen his mother in more months than she could add up right now. Too long to leave her son if she was coming, or could come, back to him.

Maybe it was crazy, but she couldn't leave him behind. "Do you want to go with me?"

Adam deserved a chance to make his own decision after his life had been decided for him, and she held part of the blame.

He nodded. Lucky for her, he was dressed with his shoes on. "We have to run. Get your coat and hat."

Adam disappeared into his closet and came back with a blue knit cap on his head and one arm stuffed into his red coat. She took his hand and pulled him with her down the back stairs. At the bottom, she unlocked the French door and opened it slowly, hoping it didn't creak and give her away. Taking the four-year-old might be the right thing to do, but it added a level of danger and consequence that might be her downfall.

After the way she'd been treated, knowing how the boy suffered, she had to do everything in her power to keep him safe.

She quietly closed the door, fighting every urge in her brain and body to bolt. No lights showed on this side of the house, but she couldn't take a chance Brice or his guest might spot them through the massive windows facing the beautiful garden and rolling land. She couldn't go around the front and to the road and risk being caught if they were out on the porch, driveway, or still standing in the entry. The only way to go would be the hardest path, but she'd take it and hope that she got them both away from this house of horrors.

Her heels clicked on the flagstone path along the veranda leading to the garden. She pulled them off and ran barefoot over the gravel to a huge tree. She ducked behind it, keeping Adam close. He didn't make a sound, but pressed to her side, his body trembling as even he understood the danger they faced.

She glanced back at the house. The only lights were from the dining room and kitchen. Another light went on in Brice's study. If she ran to the left, across the horse pasture, she'd hit the road in about a mile, but Brice could certainly see her scaling the split rail fence in her bright, light blue gown. Her only option was to go right across the back of the property. She didn't know what lay that way, but anything was better than the punishment waiting for her if Brice caught them.

She leaned down close to Adam's ear. "We have to run. Really fast."

Adam nodded, squeezed her hand, and ran beside her all the way across the garden until they crossed the manicured lawn and hit the dirt beltway that separated the ranch property from the vast landscape that made up the acres and acres of land Brice owned, giving him the privacy he craved and needed to keep his dirty secrets.

CHAPTER THREE

Brice slammed the study door and turned on his personal assistant. "What the hell are you doing here, Darren?"

"I'm sorry to show up unannounced, but you didn't answer any of my calls or return any of my emails."

"Didn't that tell you I wanted to be alone?"

Darren's eyes narrowed, but the playful smile didn't disappear. "I've missed you, Brice, but not your sharp tongue."

Right. Darren worshipped Brice. He'd practically stalked Brice for weeks to get a job and be close to him. Hypnotized by Brice's Hollywood life, the glitz and glam, even the darker side of things intrigued Darren. He craved being a part of Brice's larger-than-life world, knowing the inside scoop about people in the business, actors, and TV and movie projects. It made Darren feel important. The middle child of five, a nobody in his small-town high school, Darren grew up feeling invisible. Being Brice's assistant made him somebody. And Darren wanted to be somebody, no matter what it took. Brice used Darren's eager-to-please nature to his advantage. To keep Brice happy, Darren didn't mind using a little force or imagination to coerce others to do what Brice wanted on his behalf.

"What is so important you came all the way out here instead of calling?" Which Brice preferred, especially when Darren interrupted the most important night of his life.

"Ashley Swan."

Brice narrowed his gaze, hoping Darren hadn't put the pieces together. The downside of having someone privy to your personal life the way he'd allowed Darren to be—to a point—was that they knew things that if made public could hurt you. Darren had shown his loyalty time and again, helping Brice maneuver things in Brice's favor in business and personal matters, little things, really. But Ashley was his secret treasure.

"What about her?"

"You never speak about her, the loss of her in your life, nothing." Darren touched Brice's shoulder. "I know you miss her. It's been almost a year."

Far longer than he thought it would take her to become his everything.

"We don't have much time. I've got several requests for interviews next week and appearances on some of your favorite shows. They want your insight into her state of mind in the weeks and days leading up to her disappearance. You were one of the last people to see her at the *After Midnight* party. They'll show clips of the two of you on the show."

They wanted to share his memories of Ashley's appearances on *After Midnight*, the intimate conversations and dinners they shared in private—that had always been ruined by her manager, agent, friends tagging along after the show—but he'd hold on to the truth and how wonderful it had been to spend this past year with her.

Up until they got interrupted.

Darren had no idea how close he'd come to getting his head split open for showing up unannounced.

"They're hoping the publicity will generate new leads into her disappearance."

"They? Who is they?"

"Her lawyers, manager, agent, her mother—hell, everyone wants to know what happened to her."

"Ashley was nothing but a money machine for all of them. Not one of them understood her and what she really wanted and needed."

"You'll make people understand her in a way no one else can. You were her friend."

More than that. They were kindred spirits. One look in her beautiful eyes and he heard all she couldn't say, all the things she wanted from him but didn't dare admit out loud. She wanted him to take care of her, give her all the things she craved deep in her heart that she didn't want anyone else to know.

He saw it the first time she appeared on his show. He'd read her desires in her eyes. Her smile hid the truth that she wanted him to hurry up and take her away from everyone else.

She'd told him she wanted to get away from it all.

What she really wanted was to belong to him.

She didn't want the pressure, the demands. She didn't want to be Ashley anymore.

She wanted a timeless love story she'd never find in Hollywood.

She wanted to bring Aurora to life and feel the love and happiness Aurora found in Duncan's arms. Brice had transformed into her ideal Duncan. Tonight, the tenacious shreds of Ashley he'd helped her shed finally fell away, and Aurora emerged wholly and fully transformed forever.

Like a beautiful butterfly, she'd come to him tonight ready to be his forever. Perfect in her beauty and love for him.

Everything would be different now.

The thrill of anticipation rippled through him. He

needed to see her. He needed to touch her soft skin, feel her breath on his face a moment before they shared that perfect kiss, and revel in her body yielding as he finally loved her the way he'd always wanted but Ashley had denied him until now. Aurora would welcome her lover with open arms. She'd welcome *him*.

He'd give her everything she'd ever wanted.

Brice waved Darren over to the desk where he could set up his laptop and get to work. "Stay here. I need to check on something."

"I'm sorry I interrupted your dinner. Who's the lucky lady?"

"What?" Brice eyed Darren.

"The table full of food. The wine spilled on the tablecloth. You must have rushed whoever it is out of there pretty fast so I didn't see them. You know, you don't need to hide your affairs from me."

Brice ignored Darren, walked to the door, calling over his shoulder, "I'll be back soon."

Brice walked through the living room, biting back the string of curse words that red wine stain on his beautifully set table invoked. Dinner ruined. The rest of his night could be salvaged.

Anxious to see Aurora's beautiful face and have her back in his arms, he rushed up the stairs, ignoring the ache in his bum knee and lower back. Getting old sucked, but Aurora made him feel young and virile again. She was his fountain of youth, his chance for the life he'd given up for fortune and fame. For her. Now he'd have everything.

Adam's door stood open at the end of the hall. He'd told that boy a hundred times to stay in his room. He'd never had a child. His desire for one grew in his heart now that Aurora had finally reached the pinnacle of her transformation. She'd be a lovely bride and soon the warm and loving mother his child deserved but Brice had never had himself.

If Brice's mother had lived to see him finally happy, she'd find no fault in his beautiful creation. Aurora was everything he deserved. Everything he'd fought his mother to have one day.

She'd tried to change him.

Tired of her constant pressure to be someone else, or seek help for what she thought were his many faults and deviant behavior, he'd shut her up for good. She had no idea what drove a man like him. What might have been deeply hidden in her time had become part of the norm in many subcultures that were kept quiet, but not hidden anymore. Love came in many forms, even in pain that evoked a passion like nothing he'd ever felt.

Aurora felt it, craved it, wanted it from him. She understood his dark desires and how to play the game.

He missed Adam's mother. When he hired her on at the ranch, he expected her to cook and clean and nothing more. But alone out here together, he soon found himself drawn to her outgoing spirit. Jackie liked to play, too. She'd been a nice distraction before Ashley came to him, but Jackie had forgotten her role and had gone against him.

She shouldn't have done that and ended up like the others and left her child all alone.

He'd taken care of Adam, though sometimes it became tedious to remember the boy when all he wanted to do was be with Aurora. She'd taken longer than he expected, but he so enjoyed teaching her to be exactly as he desired.

And he desired her right now. So much so that his dick hadn't been this hard and aching in years. Everything was finally as it should be.

He opened the secret panel on the wall and punched in the code. The vault he'd had built into the room—"for storing his art collection"—had been a stroke of genius. Temperature controlled and built to keep things in and people out—ha ha—he'd found the perfect place to hold his treasure.

Time to let her out and make her a real and true part of his life. If all went as he expected, they'd reemerge in Hollywood as royalty. They'd be the talk of the town.

They'd be the love story to end all love stories.

People thought she'd disappeared. Some speculated she'd run off with a lover. He'd use the publicity next week to hint that's exactly what happened. And when the time came, everyone would see them together and understand why they'd wanted their privacy. A love like theirs couldn't be denied and needed time to allow their souls to merge into one.

He'd felt it the moment it happened tonight.

Now they'd come together as one, and nothing and no one would ever tear them apart.

The locks slid free and the door popped open slightly. Anticipation coiled in his gut. She'd been waiting for him and he couldn't stand to be away from her another moment. He hooked his fingers in the door and tugged the heavy panel open and stared into the dark—empty—room.

"Nooooo!"

He ran into the small space and checked every corner, up and down, all around, his mind not wanting to believe the truth turning his stomach and freezing his insides.

"Where are you?" he screamed, clutching both sides of his throbbing head. The blood pounded through his veins. His heart thrashed against his ribs. He brought his arms down, clenched his fists, and let the rage tighten every muscle. "Come back!"

Darren appeared in the doorway, his eyes lit with concern and worry. "Brice, what's wrong?"

"She's gone. Did you see her? Search the house."

"Who's gone?"

"Aurora. Find her."

"Who the hell is Aurora?"

Brice didn't have time to explain everything, but Darren would keep his secret. He'd do anything for Brice, which is why he kept his little pet around. "Ashley Swan."

Darren's eyes went wide. "She's here?"

Brice spread his arms wide. "Do you see her? She got out."

Darren gasped. "What do you mean, she got out?"

Brice didn't have time to explain. "Find her. We can't let her get away."

With those words, dawning understanding lit Darren's eyes. "Shit."

"She can't have gotten far. She's got to be here. Where would she go? How the hell did she get out?" He tried to think through the panic and pain.

She'd left him. After all he'd done for her she'd turned her back on him and escaped. He'd thought those days were over. Transformation didn't come easy. People instinctually fought change even when they wanted it. He'd helped her to find acceptance, and this was how she repaid him.

Well, he'd make her pay for abandoning him after all he'd done. She'd beg him to take her back so she could feel the connection and bond they shared again.

"Damn it, Brice. People are looking for her. I can't believe you put everything at risk taking *her*." The worry in Darren's eyes didn't hide the other thoughts he quickly put together about what would happen to them if they were caught. Brice made Darren his accomplice. "I'll search the house. You check outside."

Brice expected Darren to help him, but relief swept through him anyway, knowing Darren was now fully committed.

Brice rushed out of the room and checked the others down the hall.

Darren's feet pounded down the front stairs. The front door slammed behind him as he rushed to check the property.

Brice approached Adam's slightly ajar door, hoping to find her there, taking her place as Adam's mother. They'd raise the boy together with their own child. He pushed open the door. It swung wide and thumped against the wall. He held it open with his hand splayed on the wood and silently seethed, the rage boiling in his gut and spreading to every part of his being, pushing against his skin. But he held back the explosion. Barely. "If you're hiding from me, Adam, I suggest you come out now or you will never leave this room again."

Nothing. Not even one of Adam's pathetic whimpers. The kind Brice's mother used to despise and punish Brice for making as she educated him on the proper way to think or behave. Brice had learned to be silent and take the pain she'd inflicted. It made him stronger. It transformed him. Brice used pain to transform Adam and Ashley, though she'd taken much longer than the boy.

And now she'd taken Adam, too. She'd pay. Dearly. And never defy him again.

He ran down the back stairs and out the side patio door. She had to have gone this way. He stopped on the back patio and searched the area, trying to figure out what she'd do. The last time she tried to leave him, she'd gotten as far as the front lawn before he'd shown her there was nothing he wouldn't do to keep her here with him where she belonged.

Once he showed her no one would help her, she'd stopped trying to get away.

"Seems you didn't learn your lesson the last time. I can't wait to teach you again," he said to the night. He listened for any sign she cowered behind one of the large potted plants or raised flower beds. Nothing.

"Have you seen her?" Darren huffed in and out as he ran toward him from around the side of the house.

Brice stared into the night, then looked up at the dark clouds rolling in. He didn't need to see them to know they'd be buried in snow soon. The temperature seemed to drop by the second.

Overcome with the need to find her fast, he ran across the yard and into the night. He didn't have a clue to follow. She wouldn't have a plan or idea of where to go. He hoped to find her stumbling around in the dark, lost and ready to come home.

Darren followed on his heels. They called her name, following what seemed like the easiest path. How far could she go with Adam? She hadn't touched a bite of the lovely meal he'd set out for them to enjoy before they were so rudely interrupted.

Somehow, she always managed to foul things up before they enjoyed the delicious meals he spent hours planning.

"Ashley!" He used that name because he didn't want to explain to Darren what he'd been working toward and achieved this past year. Every time he used it, his frustration intensified until he felt it in every cell.

He stumbled over another rock and kicked it, sending it tumbling into the dark until it thunked against a tree. A stick snagged his pants and tore the expensive material. He thought he heard a sound to his left and ran toward it. Ten minutes later, his lungs burning, his breath sawing in and out, the cold air burning his throat and lungs, he'd found nothing. Not even a glimpse of her. For two hours

he chased every whisper, shadow, and divot in the ground
that might be a trail.

Darren spread out from him. Both of them frustrated
when the sound they chased was each other. Time grew
long and Brice's patience frayed to the point he stopped in
his tracks and screamed, "Where are you?"

Brice listened for any sound, any indication of her direction.

Leaves and brush rustled to his right.

Darren stepped out from behind a tree, his breath floating on the wind as he gasped for every breath. He closed
the distance between them, lumbering on his fatigued
legs. Brice's muscles ached with the desperation he'd put
into the search to find her as soon as possible.

Darren put his hand on Brice's shoulder. "We can't
keep doing this. We don't even know where to look.
There's no sign of her. It's freezing out here."

Brice turned on Darren, who stood with his arms
crossed over his chest to help ward off the shivers. "You're
giving up?"

"I'm being realistic. We're stumbling around in the
dark. We'd need a huge search party to find her out here."
Darren threw his arms wide to indicate the massive ranch.

"We can't call for help." His frustration came out with
the yelled words.

"Then we need to be smart. If she's hiding out here,
she might come back to simply get out of the cold. She'll
need food and water. If she manages to find help, you'll
need to spin this to your advantage. If she's lost out here,
well, then problem solved."

Brice didn't want it to end this way. He didn't want to
lose her. She belonged to him. But Darren was right—he
needed to face reality.

"If you come back now, I'll forgive you," he shouted
into the night. "This is your one and only chance."

Nothing. Not one damn sound. Not even one of her soft whimpers, telling him she'd do as he said.

He'd given her a chance and been generous with his offer. If she'd heard and ignored him, she'd pay. One way or another.

The dark clouds obliterated the full moon, sending them into deeper darkness.

If she knew what was good for her, she'd find her way home and beg his forgiveness.

If she stayed out and the snow hit, she'd freeze to death.

If she found help, she'd wish she was dead.

CHAPTER FOUR

Ashley and Adam came to a jarring halt. Brice's threat echoed across the land and in her ears. Her heart and lungs seized for one heartbeat, then two.

Is he close?

She wanted to believe he was too far away to catch them. But if he was close enough to hear, he was too close. He'd discovered her gone too soon.

She needed more time.

She needed to get away.

She needed help.

But the night didn't offer anything but ominous dark clouds closing in to curtain the nearly full moon, her only means of seeing the obstacles in front of her, and a spotlight on her bright dress. If Brice was close, he'd see her.

She tugged Adam's hand and ran away from the monster stalking them in the dark.

She wouldn't be a sitting target.

So she ran past trees and bushes, across an open field of grass until the forest swallowed her and Adam again.

Fast and slow, they ran. Through the pain radiating up and down her battered legs, she ran.

Brice's threat faded into the night long before Ashley stopped. Adrenaline and fear pushed her forward when all she wanted to do was stop and rest. With little energy and even less surety that she'd find a way out of this, her spirits dipped, but she pressed on, telling herself over and over again to just keep going.

They ran as fast as they could for as long as they could into the night, but they couldn't outrun the biting cold. Her cheeks and lips chapped. Her back and ribs screamed every time her feet pounded against the ground. Adam's energy sapped out way too soon. She stopped again to catch her breath and pray for a miracle, though all the other times she did so went unanswered.

Adam leaned heavily against her thigh, hurting her many bruises and sore muscles. She pressed her hand to his back, held him close, and tried to think through the still-rising panic.

They needed to get out of here.

For a split second she thought she saw a pinpoint of light in the distance. She second-guessed herself, thinking it too far away to see anything real. Too many obstacles stood in her path for her to have actually seen anything. But her heart pushed her to go forward toward that glimmer of light she could no longer see but which still called to her through the trees and over the rough landscape to that far-off place that promised nothing but a very long night of walking. Even then, she might not reach it by morning. She knew the road lay behind her past Brice's ranch, but a small voice inside her told her to go deeper into the open countryside.

Adam couldn't make it on his own. She wouldn't leave him behind, and they needed to keep moving. She bit back the pain and picked him up. She held Adam close to keep them both warm, ignored the pain slowly being concealed below the cold seeping into her skin and down to her bones, and put one foot in front of the other long into the night.

Thank God the storm held off. Just another ominous presence behind her.

Her head told her to quit, but her heart forced her to push on into hours and hours of perfect quiet.

Adam alternated between walking on his own and her carrying him. He fell asleep with his head on her shoulder, his sweet face buried in her neck for warmth she no longer felt. She forced herself to keep going, keep moving, desperately trying not to let every sound around her freeze her with fear that they'd been discovered.

This was her chance.

The one chance she had to get her life back.

She'd keep going, or die trying, because there was no way in hell she would stop and let that bastard find her. If she was going to die, she'd die trying to save herself, not meek and battered at the hands of a monster. She'd rescue Adam, even if it meant sacrificing her own life.

Light-headed, freezing, hungry, desperately in need of water, she continued on as the first touch of gray lit the black night. Her heel caught on yet another rock or root and was pulled off. Too weary to care about the loss of her shoe, too numb to feel the cold, jagged earth beneath her bare foot, she took two more uneven steps, her eyes drooping, the dizziness and darkness tunneling in her blurry vision. She stumbled and fell to her knees, sad she'd failed getting Adam to safety, but happy she hadn't died by Brice's hand, and resigned to the fact she'd done all she could, but she'd been right to believe she'd die tonight.

The light she'd seen before blinked on. So close, just past the trees and a wide pasture, but still too far and out of reach.

Adam jolted awake with a soft whimper. Her arms felt like lead weights. She couldn't hold on to him another second. "Whatever happens, Adam, don't let him find you."

He stepped out of her embrace and tried to hold her up, but as hard as she tried to keep the blackness at bay, i took her.

CHAPTER FIVE

Trigger woke before the crack of dawn, tearing free of another nightmare that followed him through his day with incessant bursts of adrenaline, anxiety, and frustration. He wanted to forget, but his mind replayed the shooting over and over again.

Paula, the woman he manipulated to get information on her boyfriend, Marco, had jumped in front of Marco during the drug bust in a naïve attempt to save the man she loved from the inevitable. Trigger's bullet, meant to take down Marco before he killed Trigger, slammed into her back. Horror filled her eyes as blood poured out of her. Marco's bullets slammed into Trigger's chest and side, leaving an agonizing pain that raced through him like lightning moments before the meth lab exploded. A searing wave of heat and flames hit Trigger, catching his leg on fire, shooting agony along its length.

The pain echoed through him now even after the burns had healed. He still walked with a slight limp, but the stretching exercises worked. The flexibility in his ankle got better by the day. He wished he could say the same about his mind.

He'd retreated to his secluded property, taking a leave of absence to heal from his wounds and figure out what the hell he wanted to do next. He wasn't sure he could go back to undercover work. Not when he'd become too comfortable living the lie rather than facing his real life. When you felt more comfortable surrounded by drug dealers and thugs than you did around your family, maybe it was time to get the hell out before you got sucked in so deep you became the thing you'd spent your life fighting to take down.

With the walls closing in and a storm about to dump a shitload of snow on his place, he headed out the door to settle the horses and secure the barn.

He'd asked his brother and sister to give him some space. It didn't stop them from dropping by—often. The storm and snow would give him the space he needed and the solitude he craved—most of the time.

Seeing his brother Caden with his girlfriend, Mia, happy and so damn in love, made Trigger think about the things missing in his life. A woman unlike the ones he usually met undercover: cynical, looking for an angle, out for themselves, and desperate for the drugs and money that ruled that scene. It had been a long time since he had a kind, sweet woman in his life. Someone with a genuine smile and a warm, open heart.

Trigger grabbed his jacket off the peg by the front door, pulled it on, and walked out into the frigid breeze, cursing himself for fantasizing about a woman he'd never find out here. He pulled the door closed against the biting wind and headed down the porch steps and across the yard to the barn. The open door stopped him in his tracks. He must not have closed it hard enough to catch. The wind blew the door open six inches, then pushed it back, bouncing the door in and out of its frame.

Caution and suspicion were his go-to modes, so he scanned the yard, every shadow and crevice around the barn, the surrounding pastures and trees. Nothing but the wind made a sound. He dialed down the shot of adrenaline, drew his gun from behind his back, and approached the barn with extreme caution, all his senses on alert for any threat.

No telling if one of the drug dealers he'd taken down had come for their revenge.

He threw open the barn door, stepped in, gun held out in front of him, and gave his eyes a second to adjust to the darker interior. Nothing but the horses stirred. His truck and Camaro sat to his left. The vehicles were exactly as he left them. He needed to finish taping and papering off the Camaro and finish getting it ready to paint. He loved the black, but the car was too recognizable. A few minor changes and maybe he could keep it and not alert every drug dealer in the state that he was the same guy taking everyone down.

He scrubbed his free hand over his full beard and shook his shoulder-length hair back and thought maybe he needed a shave and haircut before anyone believed he wasn't a drug dealer himself.

The horses swished their tails and nickered at him, giving him the sense that if they were okay and not nervous or spooked, then he should relax and stop looking for trouble where there was none.

He lowered the gun and slid the wide door separating the garage area from the stables all the way open. He walked down the aisle giving the three horses a pat and checked to be sure they had enough water. He'd clean their stalls, feed them, and make sure everything was shut up tight before the storm hit and they got too cold. Heading back to the tack room to grab the horse blankets, he stopped in his tracks, staring down at the two apple cores, the empty bottle of water, and the box of crackers he'd left behind the other day, now spilled across the floor. One of the horse blankets was missing, too.

The outer door slammed and this time it wasn't the wind. Trigger pulled his gun again and ran after whoever made it onto his property, past his security system, and sneaked into his barn. He bolted out the door, searching the yard for any sign of the intruder. Another half-eaten apple in the dirt gave him a direction. He ran toward the trees, ignoring the pain in his calf and ankle from the burns, slowing to a halt when he spotted the horse blanket draped on the ground as a small child tried to hide behind a tree with his entire backside sticking out. If the dark blue blanket hadn't given him away, the red coat made him a perfect target.

How the hell did such a small child get here?

Trigger tucked the gun away at his back. He didn't want to scare the kid.

He scanned the sparse forest, checking for anyone else trying to hide among the thin trees. He didn't see anything. Nothing moved, including the child.

"Come out," he ordered.

The child jolted, then took off at a dead run, halting only momentarily when the blanket caught on an exposed root, held, and the boy lost his grip. He turned momentarily, with a look of regret and desperation that surprised Trigger and told him how much the child needed that blanket. The boy must be freezing out here.

And where the hell were his parents?

"Hey, come back," Trigger called when the boy ran off again.

Unable to let the kid go without making sure he was okay and found his parents again, though how they got way the hell out here boggled the mind, he ran after the kid again. His burned leg protested the exertion, but Trigger ignored it and tried to keep track of the boy as he dodged trees, winding his way down a path only the kid knew. Trigger couldn't think of a single place out here that the boy and his family could squat and endure the cold.

Trigger rounded yet another pine and skidded to a stop, struck by the oddest scene he'd ever encountered. As an undercover DEA agent, he'd seen some weird shit and bizarre situations.

The woman lay facedown, sprawled in the dirt and weeds wearing an ice-blue evening gown and one sparkling crystal high heel. The other lay stuck between the ground and a thick root four feet behind her. Judging by the disturbances in the dirt and brush, either she skidded on her belly, or the boy had tried to drag her. He sat on the dress between her wide legs with a thick stick in his hands to protect her, the layers of fabric from her skirt bunched around him in a puffy cloud.

Trigger might have smiled at the heroic attempt to defend the defenseless woman, but the kid couldn't be more than three or four and about as tall as his thigh. Not much thicker than it, even in his heavy coat. No wonder the kid scarfed down the apples and crackers. He must be starving. Judging by how skinny his mother looked, he'd think they'd been living on the streets if not for her gown and the boy's clean clothes.

Something didn't add up. Lots of things—like the way she was dressed—set off all the alarms in Trigger's mind, but none sounded louder than her pale, gray skin. He couldn't see her face beneath the fall of thick, dark, greasy hair. Judging by her coloring, she was either freezing or dead. The tight top of the dress made it impossible for him to tell if she was still breathing. Hell, he didn't know how she breathed in that thing at all.

"Hey now, it's okay. I won't hurt you. Is she okay? Is this why you needed the blanket?"

The boy's bottom lip trembled, but he held it together and raised the stick higher to ward off Trigger.

"Let me check her out, see if she needs help." Or a coroner.

The wind kicked up and the dark clouds overhead dumped the first flutters of snow. By tonight, they'd be wrapped in a whiteout and enough snow to reach his knees, or worse. He needed to get these two squared away and out of the weather.

Trigger stepped forward, not stopping even when the boy shot out in front of the woman to keep him away. He swung the branch, but Trigger simply grabbed it and pulled it out of the kid's grasp. The kid wasn't done yet; he kicked Trigger right in the shin. Trigger bit back the pain flaring in his injured leg. He took the kid by the shoulders and held him up in front of him. A little intimidation to get the kid under control.

"I won't hurt you or her. She needs help. You wanted to get her warm."

Tears shined in the boy's eyes. He nodded.

"Okay, then let me see if I can move her and get her up to the house."

The boy eyed him, the woman, then him again. So much showed in the depths of his eyes, but one thing stood out—he didn't want anyone to hurt his mother.

Trigger set the boy back on his feet and held out his hand. "I swear to you, I will not hurt her."

The boy hesitated but took his hand and shook.

Trigger knelt beside the woman's head and gently touched her cheek, pulling her long hair back from her face. "Holy shit!" This scene took on a whole new level of strange. Not only should these two not be out here in the middle of nowhere, but the woman lying on the ground hadn't been seen by anyone in a year. Ashley Swan's face was all over the news and tabloids, and her name was mentioned on the radio every five seconds as the anniversary of her disappearance approached.

And he'd found her. On his property. Lying at his feet.

"Shit." His quiet solitude was about to blow up with

cops, press, and way too much attention for an undercover agent.

The boy stepped close and stared down at Ashley, reminding him he shouldn't swear in front of the kid. It hit him all at once. From everything he'd heard about Ashley over the last week and from past publicity of her movies, she didn't have a child. The silent boy was yet another mystery.

"Where did you come from?"

The boy pointed past Ashley at the trees and open land. Nothing out there but wide-open spaces.

Trigger bit the bullet and slid his hand over her freezing skin to her neck. The flutter of her pulse against his fingertips barely registered. If she stayed out here any longer, she'd be dead in hours. If she even had that much time.

"Did she hurt herself? Break a bone?"

The boy shook his head, held up his hand, his fingers pointed up, then let his hand fall forward flat.

"She fell."

He nodded, rolled his eyes back in his head, and pretended to faint, falling to his knees.

"She passed out?"

He held out his hand to her and frowned.

"Okay. How long ago?"

He held his hands out wide.

"A long time ago?"

The boy nodded, making Trigger's stomach tighten with dread.

"An hour?" Trigger kept going, watching the boy for any sign he hit the mark. "Two hours? Lunchtime? Morning? Was it still dark?"

Finally the boy nodded.

Shit. A hell of a long time to pass out and lay unconscious.

"You know this would go a lot faster and help me out if you talked to me."

He rushed over to Ashley and hid in her skirt again at Trigger's sharp tone. Those things not adding up started turning into dark thoughts and places in his mind Trigger didn't want to go.

"I'm going to make you a deal, little man. We made a deal that I wouldn't hurt her, right?" He got another of those repetitive nods. "I'll make you another deal. I will never hurt you. Ever." Trigger held out his hand.

The boy took it and shook again.

"Now, you have my promise. Want to tell me your name?"

"Adam," he whispered.

"Nice to meet you, Adam. I'm Trigger."

The narrowed, confused gaze wasn't hard to read.

"Strange name, I know. Let's take care of Ashley, okay?"

Another confused look.

"She's famous. I saw her picture on TV."

That seemed to frighten Adam even more.

"Don't worry. No one knows she's here."

Who the hell could find them out here anyway? Where the hell did they come from? The closest property to his had to be about ten miles away as the crow flies.

He needed to get her out of here. Fast. The snow fell in a light flutter, but in another hour he'd have a hard time finding his way back home.

"Move out of the way, little man. Let me roll her over." Trigger gave Adam a second to move to his side, then he took Ashley gently by the shoulders and slowly rolled her over. She didn't so much as blink, let alone make a sound. The dress constricted her chest so tightly her breasts nearly spilled right out of the top. Any other time he'd have appreciated such lovely things, right now he worried about her shallow breath. He hated to keep moving her without knowing exactly what ailed her, aside from the fact she was absurdly thin, but he had no choice. The woman could use another fifteen pounds to fill out her bird-like frame.

He rolled her to her side and tried to unzip the dress a couple inches to give her some room to breathe, but the dress was too tight to move the zipper. He grabbed hold of the edge with one hand and muscled the zipper down with the other. The small gap revealed deep purple bruises. He swore and slid the zipper all the way down revealing a disturbing array of purple splotches across her entire back. The second he freed her torso of the constricting garment, she moaned and sucked in a ragged and shallow breath. The stupid dress had made it impossible for her to breathe. If her back looked this bad, he didn't want to see the rest of her. Someone had taken out their rage on her in a calculated way that hid their dirty work on parts of her you couldn't see when she was dressed. It turned his stomach.

The sick bastard deserved the worst pit in hell and an eternity of pain.

Adam went to Ashley's legs and pulled up the thick skirt revealing the bruises he hadn't seen on her thighs.

How the hell did she make it this far in her condition?

Determination.

She wanted to get away.

Trigger practically tore off his jacket. He draped it over her, gently putting her arm down one sleeve, then maneuvering her so he could do the same with the other. He found the strength to go slow, but every one of her pain-filled moans made his chest constrict. He settled her on her back and zipped up the jacket, dreading the moment he got her home and had to undo this process. She needed a hospital. Now. But the falling snow thickened. The temperature had dropped another few degrees. And Trigger felt like hell when he picked her up and she yelped, holding her elbow to her side. He guessed cracked or broken ribs. He'd like to take the time to check all of her out, but he needed to get her out of the elements.

"S-stop. P-please stop."

Trigger didn't know what came over him, but he held her close to his chest, leaned down, and pressed his forehead to the side of her face and whispered into her ear, "You're safe. I won't hurt you. No one will ever hurt you again." He meant that promise with every fiber of his being. He'd taken the leave of absence from the DEA because he couldn't watch one more person get hurt or die. It was his job to protect the innocent, but so many times they got caught in the cross fire. Literally in Paula's case when he accidentally shot her during a raid. Accident or not, he killed her and that was another black mark on his soul.

The biting cold and snow pushed against his back as he walked to his house. Adam easily kept up with Trigger's uneven gate. Carrying Ashley put a strain on his healing leg and shoulder where he'd been shot, but he bit back the pain that didn't compare to what Ashley went through as he held her close, trying not to jostle her too much over the uneven terrain. He cursed every root and rut in his path. If he could fly her home, he would, but he had no choice but to prolong the agony by taking the least treacherous route.

He loved his place, but he'd never been this happy to see it any other time. The roof already had a thick coat of snow. His shoulders and head felt like he'd collected a couple inches himself. Freezing without his jacket or a hat, he needed to get inside, start a fire, get something hot to drink and eat, but he still had a hell of a lot to do before he took care of himself.

Adam huffed up the stairs to the covered porch. It took

Trigger concerted effort to get up the stairs. His arms ached from carrying Ashley, mostly due to the bullet wounds to his chest and side. He needed to step up his exercises. His thighs ached when he reached the porch. They'd walked a hell of a long way.

"Open the door, little man."

Adam bit his lip, stared past Trigger and up at Ashley, uncertain what to do. Go inside with a stranger, make a run for it, or get Ashley the help she needed.

"Remember my promise. I have something to show you inside. Trust me, you're safe here."

Adam opened the door and stepped into the house, holding the door wide so Trigger could carry Ashley in. He had to go sideways. Even then, he barely fit through the door with Ashley in his arms and the damn ridiculous dress with its thick skirt taking up the entire doorway.

He carried her through the wide-open living room to his bedroom. Adam trailed behind him, not letting Ashley out of his sight.

"Pull the bedcovers down. Let's get her warm."

Adam pulled back the rumpled blanket and sheet. Trigger laid Ashley down gently on her back, her head on the pillow, her arms falling to her sides like lead weights. He needed to get some water and food into her, but she was barely conscious.

First, he needed to get Adam settled in the other room so Trigger could get that damn dress off her and see just how badly she'd been beaten.

Frustrated and furious with no outlet for his anger, he scooped up Adam and carried him out of the room. The boy stiffened, then jerked back, ready to fight his way free. He took Adam's hand and held it against his own chest. "You're okay." He hated that such a small child didn't want to be carried and touched. Maybe he should take the kid's jacket and shirt off to see if he needed attention, too.

That sick feeling in his gut flared.

Trigger set Adam on the kitchen island counter and reached behind him. He handed the boy the leather case. "Go ahead. Open it."

Adam opened it and stared at his badge and DEA credentials. His eyes glassed over and his gaze shot up to Trigger's.

"That's right, little man, I'm a cop. You are safe here." He should have told the kid when he caught up to him in the trees.

"Good guy," he whispered.

Trigger may not look like it—maybe he really wasn't—but if it made the kid feel better, yeah, he'd do his damndest to be the good guy for him. And Ashley.

"Yes. I put bad guys in jail. Can you tell me about the bad guy who hurt Ashley?"

Adam pulled his feet up on the counter, wrapped his arms around his legs, and hid his face in his knees. His whole body trembled with fear.

"Okay, little man. You don't have to say anything." Trigger brushed his hand over the boy's head, pulling his icy blue cap off and ruffling his bright blond hair. "Let's take these soaking wet shoes off." The snow had saturated the thin material. He pulled off one shoe and the other before taking off Adam's soaking wet socks. He took the boy's feet in his warm hands and tried to rub some warmth and blood back into his pink feet. "Better?"

Adam nodded.

"Let's take off your jacket." Trigger unzipped it and pulled the sleeves off both his arms. "We'll put this and your shoes and cap out by the fire to dry."

Adam stared past him at the cold fireplace.

"Don't worry. I'll have a big fire going in just a minute. Your pants are all wet. We need to get you out of these clothes." And Trigger wanted a look at the boy to be sure he wasn't hurting like Ashley, too. "Wait here. I'll get you a shirt of mine to wear."

Trigger went back to his room, frowned at the sight of Ashley in his bed, uncomfortable in that dress, his coat, and with her injuries. He'd take care of her soon. Every minute he tended to Adam and not her wore on him.

Shirt from his drawer in hand, he headed back to Adam. He picked the boy up and set him on the tile kitchen floor. "Is it okay if I help you?"

Adam pulled the T-shirt over his head. Though not nearly as bad as Ashley, every new and fading bruise on Adam, such a small and innocent child, ate a hole in Trigger's already-battered heart. He could count every rib and bone in Adam's shoulders and arms.

"Do you hurt anywhere the most?" Trigger didn't think Adam's wounds needed anything more than time to heal, but he needed to be sure. The kid sure hadn't gotten some of those deep welts from playing in the yard.

Adam shook his head.

The T-shirt draped all the way to the floor and pooled at his bare feet. "Let's get those wet pants off. I'll get you something to eat and you can sit by a warm fire."

Adam's eyes lit up with the possibility of food. He hadn't been treated as poorly as Ashley, but he hadn't been treated well either.

Adam had to sit on the floor to maneuver the wet denim off his legs, but he managed.

Trigger gathered up the clothes and shoes and handed them to Adam. "Take those over to the fireplace and set them out on the side of the opening. I'll get you some food. Do you like peanut butter and raspberry jelly?"

Starving, Adam nodded vigorously.

"You got it. How about some chips and a glass of milk?"

The smile nearly undid Trigger. Choked up that such a simple thing as a sandwich and chips made the kid that anxious and happy, he stood and went to the kitchen, getting everything ready for Adam and Ashley. It didn't take long for him to put the meal together and carry the plate and glass to Adam, who sat on the floor in front of the fireplace. He'd done a decent job of spreading out his wet things.

Trigger handed Adam the plate and set the milk on the coffee table. Adam picked up one of the sandwich squares and stuffed nearly all of it in his mouth.

"Slow down, little man. You'll choke."

Adam chewed and washed the peanut butter down with half the glass of milk. Trigger turned his back on the ravenous boy, trying to contain the wash of fury sweeping through him. He used the poker to stir the coals in the fireplace, then tossed on a few pieces of kindling and a couple of logs. Some wadded-up pieces of newspaper got the fire burning hot. Trigger closed the screen and turned back to Adam, who had a mouth overflowing with potato chips. Several crumbs landed on the carpet between his knees.

"You're making a mess, little man." Trigger reached out to pick up the bits of food, but halted when Adam recoiled like Trigger meant to hit him. Apparently, he'd been trained to fear making any little mistake and anticipate a smack or worse for the slightest misstep. "Let's pick up the crumbs and set them on the plate." Trigger showed him that's all he meant to do and Adam joined in, cleaning up quickly, his gaze darting to Trigger every few seconds to be sure Trigger didn't ambush him with an attack. "There we go. Full?"

Adam swiped the back of his hand over his mouth, taking away the milk mustache that made him look adorable. He yawned so big Trigger could count all his tiny teeth.

"I'll get you a blanket. You can hang out here by the fire while I take care of Ashley."

Adam yawned again.

Trigger went to the linen cupboard and pulled out a thick comforter. He laid it in front of the fire and opened one fold so Adam could climb inside. Trigger took one of the pillows off the couch and put it under Adam's head, then tucked him in. Adam's eyes fluttered closed almost immediately.

Trigger sighed. One down. One to go before he could stop and think what to do next. He should call the cops. Ashley was a missing person. He had no idea about Adam. Something told him to wait, talk to Ashley, then blow the whistle on her whereabouts.

Besides, no one could get out here tonight with the snow coming down thick and hard outside.

Trigger steeled himself for what he had to do next. He went to the kitchen, grabbed his ID, the mug of warm water mixed with the dissolved pain pill from his gunshot wounds, and a bottle of water, and headed back to his bedroom.

He never thought the next time he had a woman in his bed he'd have to hurt her to make her feel good.

He set everything on the bedside table and carefully sat next to her on the bed. He took a deep breath and did what needed to be done. He unzipped his jacket, but left it closed over her bare chest. He had to stand to take hold of both sides of the dress and work it down her body all the while trying not to jostle her too much. He tossed the thing to the floor and pulled off the one shoe she still had on. He tossed it atop the puddled dress. One of her ankles was swollen. He went into the bathroom and found an old bandage and came back and wrapped her foot. He should ice it, but he wanted to give her time to rest and recover. Without the dress constricting her torso, she breathed steady and easy.

He leaned over and shook her shoulder. "Ashley. Hey, can you hear me?"

She raised her hand to his chest and tried to push him away, but her hand simply slid off him and fell back to her belly. "Stop. Go away." Her voice sounded stronger than the last time. She finally got some oxygen into her blood. Even her skin color had improved.

Who the hell would torture her with that damn dress? Someone had to have put it on her, because there's no way she got it on alone, not when he'd barely been able to get it unzipped.

"I'm going to take the coat off and check your ribs. I won't hurt you. You're safe," he assured her, though he didn't think anything he said or did would convince her after what she'd obviously been through.

He braced himself for what he'd see again and opened the coat, revealing her bare body. The dark bruises held his attention, but seeing her hip bones and ribs sticking out like she hadn't eaten in a decade soured his stomach.

Poor thing.

He gently removed the wet coat. Goose bumps broke out on her bare skin. He walked his fingertips along her ribs, checking for obvious breaks that might poke into her lungs. Aside from a couple of bad areas that made her moan and try to turn away from his touch, nothing appeared to be serious. Cracked ribs hurt like a bitch—he knew from experience. She'd be fine in a few weeks. Malnourished, battered and bruised, in need of a hot shower and several good meals, she'd heal, but he wondered about the injuries he couldn't see, the even more disturbing torture done to her mind.

He covered her with the sheet and blankets up to her

chin, lifted her head and shoulders, and held the mug to her lips. "Take a drink. It'll taste bad, but it'll make you feel better."

The second the water and pill liquid hit her lips, she drank deeply, thirsty for more.

"Hold on, let me fill it back up." He set the mug on the table, managed to get the cap off the bottle of water one-handed without laying her back down and moving her more than necessary. He filled the mug halfway, not wanting to overtax her system and make her sick. He held the mug to her mouth again. She drank more. He caught a glimpse of her green eyes intent on him. "You're safe." Her eyes fluttered shut.

"He can't find me," she whispered the moment he took the mug away and settled her back on the bed.

He wanted to reassure her he'd keep her safe, but she'd already fallen back to sleep. She needed it.

Trigger rolled her onto her more injured side so her free side could expand with every breath and the other side could take a rest. He adjusted the pillow to make her as comfortable as he could without knowing the true extent of her injuries and pain. He gently tucked the blankets around her to keep her warm. He glanced out the window again and cursed the snowstorm that trapped them here and prevented help from reaching them. The fact that she didn't seem in distress helped ease his anxiety. Some. But he still worried about internal injuries.

"The pain meds will kick in soon. You'll feel better." His need for her to feel better struck him hard in the chest. He hated seeing her suffering like this. Anyone, but especially her for some reason. Maybe because of the way he'd found her, lost in the middle of nowhere, and at the end of her endurance.

He pulled another shirt and a pair of sweats from his drawers and set them on the end of the bed. Neither would fit her, but if she woke up, he wanted her to have something to put on and feel comfortable. He opened his ID on the table beside the bed facing her. He stood there staring down at her face, looking for what, he didn't know. He couldn't take his eyes off her or convince himself that she was okay here for the time being. He felt the threat of danger infused in her plea that "he" couldn't find her and the unsettled way she slept, her body tense and ready to fight or flee, though she was in no condition to do either.

Nothing spooked him, but he'd had to be hypercautious working undercover and trust his gut. Something told him to keep her close and hidden, despite the fact he should call the cops and let them handle things and bust whoever hurt her.

Until she gave him some answers and he knew she'd be safe, he'd protect her here. The storm helped. If whoever held her all this time came looking for her tonight, he'd have a hell of a time surviving the dropping temps and increasing snow on the ground.

He tore his gaze away from her and went to the fireplace. He stoked the coals and rebuilt the fire to keep her warm. He didn't want her to wake up in the dark, if she even woke up before tomorrow morning.

Despite telling himself no one could get here tonight, he checked all the windows and doors. With his place locked up tight, he checked on Ashley one more time to ease the tightness in his chest, but seeing her so still and small in his bed renewed his anxiety. He reluctantly left her to add another log to the fire Adam slept peacefully in front of, grabbed a beer out of the fridge, settled into his recliner, and picked up the phone to call for the only help he could count on, no questions asked.

CHAPTER SIX

Trigger took a long pull on the beer bottle, hit the speed dial for his brother Caden, and tried to think things through and decide what needed to be done first.

"Are you okay?" Caden asked, concerned. He had reason to be. Trigger's injuries might be healing, but his emotional and mental state hadn't gotten any better. Look at the crazy thing he had done, bringing Ashley and Adam here instead of calling the cops and dumping what was sure to be a mess on someone else.

Still, not even a hello from his brother, so he got to the point, too. "I need your help."

"What's wrong?" Mia asked in the background.

"Is it Guzman?" Caden worried the drug dealer had discovered Beck's true identity.

"Not this time."

"Are you hurt? Did you take too many pain meds?" Caden's increasing concern touched and irritated Trigger.

"No," Trigger bit out. "But thanks for the vote of confidence."

"If you talked to me more often, I wouldn't be so worried."

Fine. Working undercover meant he sometimes had to do things he didn't like, things that he hated, including using the product he tried to take off the streets. He did it to stay alive, but every once in a while it became less about that and more of an escape. But Trigger loved his misery, so kept those escapes short-lived. Another reason he needed this break and time to get his head straight.

"Whatever. Listen, I found a woman and child on my property tonight."

"Did their car break down? We've got to have at least a foot of snow already."

Probably two out here where he lived. "Shut up and listen. She's in trouble. It's safer to keep her here, but I need you and Mia to bring me some supplies, including some clothes for her and the kid."

"Um . . ." Yeah, Caden never expected that.

"Have you seen the news about that actress who went missing a year ago?"

Caden swore. "Are you telling me you found Ashley Swan? *The* Ashley Swan. The actress. And she has a child with her?"

"Yes. But I have no idea who the kid is."

"You have Ashley Swan in your house?" The disbelief and surprise in Caden's voice annoyed him as much as his asking the question again.

"Yes. You can't tell anyone. I'm still trying to figure out what happened and how the hell she ended up walking onto my property."

"Wait. What? Your property is miles from anything. You sure she didn't have a car?"

"I'm telling you she walked. Or ran might be more accurate. Listen, I don't have all the answers right now, but I plan to get them before I let the world know she's alive. So can you help me, or not?"

"Yeah. Anything you need. You know that."

"Thanks, man." The relief in his ragged voice alerted Caden.

"Is she okay?"

"No." The single syllable held a wealth of worry, desperation, and fear.

"Beck, do you need me and Mia to come over now?"

"No. I've got them settled for the night." He hoped Ashley got the sleep she needed to erase the dark circles under her eyes and put some color back in her hollow cheeks. "I don't want anyone else out in this storm. I need groceries and clothes for her and a very skinny little boy."

"Okay. I'm sure Mia can help me with that. We'll be there tomorrow, or as soon as we can get there with the snow."

"Thanks, man." Pure relief infused Beck's voice.

"I've got your back. Always."

"I know you do. Call me tomorrow. I should have a list of supplies by then. This stays between us. Tell Mia, too. I need you to trust me on this, Caden. No one can know she's here. Please," he added, the desperation coming back into his voice and racing through his veins.

"You got it."

"Okay. Thanks. Oh, did you ask Mia to marry you yet?"

"How did you—"

"I know you. Soon as you figured out you loved her, it was only a matter of time. You like things all tied up nice and neat. I'm happy for you guys." Beck really was happy his brother had found a friend and partner to share his life, a woman who stole his heart and made him smile.

A spurt of jealousy hit Trigger by surprise. He wanted the best for Caden. And wished for a bit of that kind of easy happiness in his own life.

"Tell her I said welcome to the family."

"Thank you, Beck," Mia called out, overhearing their conversation.

"Are you sure you're okay?" Caden never stopped worrying.

"I got this." If Trigger didn't sound absolutely sure, he

couldn't help it. He needed answers. But those would have to wait until Ashley woke up and gave them to him. The storm would pass; he'd get her to someone who could help her. He barely took care of himself these days. Ashley and Adam needed more than he could give.

Trigger hung up without a goodbye, downed the rest of his beer, and lay back in the chair with his forearm over his eyes. He let the quiet settle around him and listened to the occasional spark and pop in the fireplace. The storm made its own monotonous sound outside the huge windows. He moved his arm and stared at the white haze outside—like watching static on an old TV.

It took a long time to settle the disturbing thoughts in his mind and give in to sleep. Instead of waking from his own nightmare, Adam woke him with his. The boy shot bolt upright, breathing heavily; his mouth opened to scream, but the sound never came. Adam barely spoke to him. Trigger didn't want to think about how he'd been taught to be quiet as a mouse.

Adam's gaze collided with his. Beck didn't move. He didn't want to startle the poor child, but Adam's tears tore at Trigger.

"It's kind of scary being in a new place, right?"

Adam wiped at his eyes and nodded.

Trigger took a shot at getting some answers. "Do you miss home?"

Adam's eyes grew wide with fright. He shook his head back and forth faster than a bobblehead in an earthquake.

He definitely didn't want to go home.

Ashley had taken him with good reason judging by the bruises on him and the nightmare that made Adam groan and whimper in his sleep.

Adam yawned and laid his forehead on his up-drawn knees, then looked up and shot his gaze toward the bedroom door.

"It's open. You can go see her if you want."

Adam eyed him, then rose and tiptoed over to the door and stared in at Ashley. Satisfied she hadn't left him and was safe and sound, Adam came back, but stopped at the edge of the carpet and shifted from one foot to the other.

Trigger got the message and pointed to the door behind Adam. "Bathroom is right there, little man."

Adam dashed off, flipped on the light in the room, and pushed the door shut, locking it. Trigger shook his head. The kid didn't speak, had nightmares, and locked doors. The kid took just about as much caution as Trigger.

The door opened with barely a sound. Adam tiptoed back to the living room without taking his sharp gaze off Trigger. He dropped back onto his blanket bed and glanced all around the room, the uncertainty and fear evident in his puppy dog big blue eyes. The boy didn't want to go back to sleep, knowing the only things awaiting him were more nightmares.

Trigger felt the same way. "Hey little man, you want to come sleep up here with me?"

He practically bolted up from the floor and ran over, his arms up for Trigger to pick him up and settle him next to him in the lounge chair. Squeezed up to Trigger's side, Adam snuggled in under Trigger's arm and against his chest, staring out the window at the snow. Adam pointed one finger toward the window.

"It's coming down pretty good. Supposed to last a couple of days. Ever made a snowman?"

Adam shook his head, a forlorn look coming back into his eyes.

"Well, we'll have to do that once the snow stops."

Anticipation filled his big eyes. Adam settled and gave in to the exhaustion still showing in the dark circles under his very expressive eyes.

Trigger held the boy close, letting him know he was safe and protected with no one and nothing to worry about tonight. The snow fell, Trigger lost himself in the nature show, the rise and fall of Adam's small chest tucked against Trigger's side, the pop and crackle of the fire, and fell into a deep sleep he hadn't enjoyed in too long to remember.

Adam startled awake with a piercing scream. This time, Trigger woke with a gun in his hand pointed at the last person he wanted to shoot.

CHAPTER SEVEN

Ashley woke with a start that jolted her right out of a nightmare and made her sit bolt upright in bed. In bed? A surge of adrenaline shot through her, masking the pain in her ribs from the sudden jarring. This wasn't her dark cell. This was someone's bedroom. Oh God.

Where was she? What happened?

She'd gotten away.

Where's Adam?

She sat on the bed, taking in her surroundings, the fire glowing in the fireplace keeping her warm, the snow falling outside the huge windows, the leather chair by the fireplace with a paperback on the small table beside it, and the orange glow coming from the bedroom doorway. She snatched up the shirt at the end of the bed and pulled it on. She ignored the pain in her sore legs and back and swung her feet to the floor, noticing at the last second the wrap someone put around her ankle. She braced her hands on the edge of the bed to push herself up and noticed the open badge on the table. She picked it up and stared at the picture of the dark-haired man. A flicker of a memory came back of someone hovering over her outside. The same striking blue-gray eyes as the man in the picture, but he sure as hell didn't have the same clean-cut look.

She stood on her wobbly legs and braced a hand on the

table and waited for the dizziness to subside. She needed: water, food, sleep, help, a chance to catch her breath and figure out what to do. She needed to find Adam and get them to safety, though right now she didn't know if anywhere would ever be safe for them.

The huge shirt draped off her shoulder and down her body, nearly to her knees. She tiptoed to the open door and pressed her body back against the wall, then sneaked a peek into the large open kitchen–living room combo. But for the soft glow of the fireplace it was dark, and she barely spotted the man lying in the recliner. Adam lay practically on top of the massive man with tattoos all down the arm he had over Adam's back. The boy's blond head and the way-too-big white T-shirt he wore stood out against the man's black T-shirt. She didn't know what to make of them sleeping together, but her heart sighed at the too-sweet, if not odd, picture they made.

Why did he bring them here instead of taking them to the authorities?

The thought of what she'd go through once people found out about what happened to her made her insides sour. The publicity. The questions. Everyone after her for information. The false news and outright lies they'd splash across every type of media.

It wouldn't matter what really happened. They'd make up their own truth.

Brice would put his own twisted spin on things.

They'd take Adam away from her.

She needed to get away. Find someplace safe where no one could find them. She'd protect Adam and keep him away from the monster who terrorized his so-called prize possessions.

Her hands shook and her body trembled with the fear she couldn't subdue, but she quietly tiptoed over to Adam. She didn't want to startle him, but she needed to get him away from the man and out of here as fast as possible. She slipped her hands around his bony sides and yanked him out of the man's light hold.

Adam woke with a scream. She scrambled back and away from the man who sat up with a gun in his hand pointed straight at her head.

Adam wrapped himself around her front. She held him tight to her chest, his face tucked under her chin.

"Stay where you are," she ordered the man. "Don't move. We're leaving."

He dropped his hand. The gun smacked against his thigh. He raked his fingers through his long dark hair and fell back into the chair. "You can leave anytime you want."

She backed up to the door, keeping him in front of her. She reached to the side and unlocked the dead bolt and lock on the handle, then swung the door open wide. A blast of frigid air and icy snow blew in, freezing her bare legs and arms. Her lungs seized when she sucked in the cold air. The wind had swept snow onto the covered porch and piled it two feet high against the door.

"I suggest you wait until the storm passes or you'll freeze to death." The man's matter-of-fact and calm tone turned the fear in her gut to roiling anger. "Either way, you're not taking the boy."

Stuck like she'd been in Brice's prison, she tried to think, but her slow mind couldn't process things as fast as she needed to form a plan and escape.

"Close the door before you freeze the boy."

She didn't have anywhere to go. She didn't know what to do. "I can't do this again. You have to let us go. I can't . . ." Her knees buckled and she fell hard to the floor, smacking her ass on the hard wood. The wind and snow blew against her back, turning her outside as cold as her inside.

The man leaned forward, folding up the recliner, and came up out of the chair. He slowly walked toward her. Though his movements seemed calculated to not appear threatening—his size, the wicked tattoos, and his dark gaze did that all by themselves—she thought he might also be sore or injured.

He walked past her and slammed the front door shut and relocked it. The sound of the bolt sliding home sent a shiver up her spine.

Locked in again.

The primal urge to run raced through her, but she barely had the strength to hold on to Adam.

The man crouched in front of her, his hair falling forward to cover most of his face, except for those penetrating eyes, and held up the DEA badge she must have dropped.

"Where is Agent Cooke?" Out of breath from exertion and lack of food and water, she barely got the words out of her dry mouth.

The man's gaze narrowed, then his mouth drew back in a half frown. He raked his fingers through his hair again, drawing it away from his face. "You're looking at him."

He must have read the disbelief she couldn't hide and turned the badge to look at the picture on it that looked nothing like him. "It's been a while since I had a haircut or shaved." He brushed his fingers through his thick beard, then turned the picture back to her. "Same gray eyes though, right?" The words were soft and coaxing.

"Same shape and color, but now they're filled with . . . too much," she said, unable to come up with the right words to describe the sorrow, regret, and ghostly nightmares that seemed way too close to how she felt inside.

"Yeah, I've had a rough year. Or two," he added with another of those half frowns that came way too often. "I am a federal agent. This is my place. You are safe here.

I know who you are, but I'm not holding you here. The storm is. As soon as it clears, we'll call the cops—"

"No!"

One dark eyebrow went up. "Why not?"

She shook her head, so many reasons running through her mind, but how could she make him understand. She needed time to think, to form a plan and do this her way. She needed to protect Adam.

"Agent Cooke, you don't understand . . ."

"Trigger."

"What?"

"Call me Trigger."

"I thought your name was Beck." She nodded toward the badge in his hand.

"Yeah, I work undercover—everyone just calls me Trigger now." He said it like the name left a bitter taste in his mouth. "And you're Ashley."

A well of sorrow rose in her chest. It had been a long time since she'd been called by her name and not one of the characters she'd played. *I'm Ashley.* Tears stung her eyes. She couldn't speak and just nodded.

"You look wrecked, Ashley. You need some sleep. Whatever happened to you can wait until morning."

"We need to get out of here. He can't find us."

"The storm isn't going to let up anytime soon. I proved to you a minute ago that I can protect you."

It took her a second to figure out he referred to the gun he'd pointed at her.

Beck—she couldn't think of him as Trigger—reached out and rubbed Adam's back and ruffled his hair. "Ready to go back to bed, little man?"

Adam pulled out of her arms and went right into Beck's. The big man scooped Adam up, stood, and carried him back to the blanket pooled on the floor in front of the dying fire. Adam settled in and Beck laid another log on the fire. The wood caught on the bright red coals and flames rose up, brightening the room. She wanted to lie beside Adam in that pool of warmth and find the peace and rest that had eluded her for so long she barely remembered what it felt like.

She pressed her hands to the floor and tried to stand up on her shaking legs. She made it to her feet, barely, and swayed from the dizziness she couldn't seem to shake.

When she looked up, Beck was there. Close. Too close. She didn't even hear him walk to her. She put her hand up to ward him off, though she was anything but steady on her feet and no match for him.

"Hungry?"

The persistent gnawing in her gut never went away, but she'd gotten used to it a long time ago. She nodded, trying to wrap her mind around the fact she was here, not there.

Beck swept his arm out for her to lead the way into the kitchen. She stood her ground, not turning her back on him for a second.

With a shake of his head and roll of his eyes, he walked into the kitchen and straight to the stainless steel fridge. She followed at a silly, but safe-feeling, five-foot distance behind him. He opened the door wide so she could look inside. She approached with a caution that made him give her another look that said, *You're being ridiculous.*

Maybe, but she couldn't help it.

"What do you want?"

The fridge wasn't full by any means, but it held more food than she'd seen or eaten in months. Immediately drawn to the fresh fruit and vegetables in the drawer she reached to grab an apple, but snatched her hand back and glanced over at Beck, afraid to take what she wanted and get punished.

How many times had she sat at the dining room table, craving the food set out before her, the smell as intoxicating as a drug, and not been allowed to have anything Brice didn't allow her to eat? He rarely was that generous, too often letting her go without anything, or simply tossing her a hastily slapped together cheese and bologna sandwich, a half-eaten container of leftovers, an almost-empty bag of cereal—not enough to make a bowl and no milk. Never anything hot. Never enough to satisfy her hunger. Never more than once a day, and often several days apart.

Beck pulled the drawer out, picked up the fattest apple from the three, and held it out to her. She snatched it from his hand and brought it to her mouth, biting in and taking a huge chunk out of the juicy flesh. She chewed and bit more off all at the same time, savoring the sweet, juicy fruit.

"I'm not going to take it away from you." Beck reached up to a cupboard beside her.

She jumped away, keeping him in front of her and escape at her back.

He ignored her strange behavior and pulled out a can of soup and held it up for her to read the label.

Beef with vegetables. She could already taste it on her tongue.

"Please." The desperation in her voice made him narrow his gaze even more.

"Go sit at the table and eat your apple one bite at a time before I give you a heart attack."

Guilt shot through her thrashing heart. This man hadn't done anything but . . . She really didn't know how she'd gotten here, but he'd taken care of Adam and her and hadn't asked anything of her. "I'm sorry, Beck. I'm a mess, and I've completely forgotten my manners."

"You said please," he pointed out matter-of-factly.

She backed out of the kitchen, limping on her sore ankle. Beck turned his back to her and went to the counter to open the can at the electric can opener. She glanced over to be sure Adam slept peacefully in front of the fire in the other room. The urge to back herself into the corner of the dining room and curl up in a ball and cry seemed like a good idea and a release she needed, but self-protection took over. She gingerly lowered herself onto the bench seat at the table with Beck in front of her and the front door to her left. Too far away for her to make a run for it before Beck caught her if he wanted to, but she couldn't help her instinct to run. Everything in her wanted to keep going and never stop. She had the will but not the strength. She didn't even really have an immediate threat.

Beck, a DEA agent, a man who upheld the law, had helped her and meant no harm. That should be enough to ease her worried mind, but it didn't, because Brice had seemed like a good man, a friend. A monster hid under that polished persona. She'd never look at anyone the same way again.

She took another bite of the sweet and tart apple, devouring it one bite at a time. The microwave dinged. Beck took out the bowl of soup. The rich scent of beef and broth filled the room and made her stomach grumble even more.

Beck pulled a box of crackers from the cupboard and set it on the counter. His sharp gaze shot to her. "Are your ribs broken?"

She stopped squirming and bit off the last morsel of apple from the core. She stared at him, surprised he'd been paying any attention to her while making her food. "I'm fine," she mumbled around the chunk of apple in her mouth.

He slowly walked over, set the bowl of soup and a sleeve of crackers in front of her, then stood a foot away—too close—glaring down at her.

"I took that ridiculous dress off you. You took one hell of a beating. Are your ribs broken?"

She bent her head and stared at her lap, unable to answer that simple question without remembering all she'd been through.

"Ashley." Beck's deep rich voice filled her with a warmth she didn't recognize but drew her in all the same. Maybe it was that he used her name and she longed to be Ashley again, even though she didn't know that naïve girl anymore. She only knew this husk of a person so filled with anger and pain and longing and loneliness.

"Ashley." The sharpness in his voice demanded an answer. She didn't question the lack of sympathy or concern. She'd lived without both for a long time.

"A few cracked ribs this time."

"This time." He bit out the disgust-filled words. Maybe under his stoic demeanor he did care. After living in Hollywood's superficial world and being held captive by a man without feeling or real emotion, even a glimpse of Beck's disdain for what happened to her went straight to her heart.

The longer he stood over her, staring at the top of her head, the higher her anxiety jacked up until she could barely breathe. Her hands remained gripped tight in her lap.

"What's wrong?" The softness in his voice made her look up at him. Way up. The man was so tall.

She found her voice under the wave of fear gripping her. "I know you don't mean to, but you're scaring me."

He planted his big hands on the table beside her and leaned down close. "Look at me, Ashley."

She sucked in a breath, found a shred of bravery from the tatters of her will, and raised her gaze to meet his.

"I will never hurt you."

She fell into the depths of gray and flecks of blue in his eyes and drowned in the sincerity and promise she found there. Deep down, she believed him. Part of her needed to believe him, because she needed something real to hold on to before she sank any deeper into despair and the paranoia that everyone wanted to hurt her.

"If he finds me, he'll kill me."

"He'll have to get past me first."

She believed that, too. Everything about this man spoke of restrained danger, but he meant those words. He'd never hurt her. He'd protect her. God help whoever got in his way or on his bad side.

Trigger backed off. Ashley needed time, space, and a moment to eat the food she'd been denied far too long. Every little glimpse he got of what happened to her turned his stomach. Her frail body, achingly beautiful face and eyes, and her deceptive fragility drew him in, but he saw the strength in her. The will she summoned to get through every second when everything in her wanted to give up, give in, let the pain and the horror she'd been through swallow her whole so she didn't feel anything anymore.

Been there, didn't want to go back.

Hell, honestly he was still fighting his way back from that black pit of hell.

The boy slept soundly in front of the fire like a well-contented pup.

Ashley tackled the soup and crackers at the table. Her starvation drove her to eat too fast.

"Slow down before you choke," he warned.

She didn't look at him. Didn't say anything, but she did take the time to savor the next bite and chew.

He didn't know what to make of her. He wanted to demand answers and get her to tell him exactly what happened. Who hurt her?

Scared to be within five feet of him, she'd shut down if he pushed too hard.

Starved. Beaten. He didn't want to know what else to

add to that ominous list. But he'd damn well get the story before he turned her over to the cops and put her life in jeopardy. He'd have the name of the man who hurt her and the bastard would be behind bars before he let Ashley out of his sight.

Any man who'd held her for nearly a year remained a risk to her and the population at large.

He had a duty to take the guy down.

It had nothing to do with the overwhelming urge building inside him to protect her.

Not his job. The last person he was supposed to protect he ended up shooting. Accident or not, Paula had trusted him to keep her safe.

As soon as the storm passed and the roads cleared, Trigger would get the cops involved and ensure they took down the asshole who hurt Ashley.

She'd go back to her glam life.

He'd go back to . . . whatever the hell he was doing these days.

Ashley shifted again, bent over the bowl of soup she'd annihilated over the last few quiet minutes. His T-shirt engulfed her small frame. The neckline so big, it slipped off one of her shoulders, exposing her bony frame. She pulled it up, but it slipped down again. Her feet shifted under the table, bumping his sock-covered toes, reminding him that she wore nothing but his shirt and probably felt very exposed.

"I can get you some sweatpants and socks to wear."

Her gaze left the near-empty bowl of soup and met his. She adjusted the shirt again. "I'm, um, not really used to wearing clothes, I guess."

He eyed her. "What do you mean?"

Her gaze dropped to her lap. "Other than the costumes he made me wear, I wasn't allowed anything else." She plucked the T-shirt out from her chest and stared at it.

"This is the most comfortable thing I've worn in—" Her gaze shot up to his. "What day is it?"

"Saturday. Well, Sunday at this point."

She checked the clock on the microwave to verify that at two in the morning, it had indeed become a new day.

He didn't want to overwhelm her, but thought some basic information might help her cope and assimilate to her new reality. "According to the news, the anniversary of your disappearance is next Friday."

Her eyes glassed over. "Is that what people think? I disappeared?"

"According to the news, no one really knows what happened to you after you left the *After Midnight* party. Did someone kidnap you?"

Her head shook. "No. Turns out I'm stupid and no one will believe me."

"Is that you talking, or the sick fuck who made you believe that?"

Her head snapped back like he'd slapped her. Good. He had her attention. Thanks to the food and glass of water she downed, he hoped she'd start thinking more clearly, too.

She propped her elbows on the table and held her head in her shaking hands. "His voice is in my head. Those damn lines from the movies he made me recite over and over like some robot. Always demanding I give him that perfect version of what he saw on-screen. They aren't real. I'm real. I'm Ashley." Her voice cracked on her name. "I'm not them. I don't want to be them anymore." Tears clogged her throat. She sat up and scrubbed her hands over her face and bright eyes, pulling herself together. "I'm done. Do you get that? I don't care what it takes, where I have to go, how long I have to hide, I won't do it again. I won't play the part and be someone's fantasy." She slammed her hands on the table. "You got that?"

He couldn't help the grin tugging at his lips. She might be down, but she wasn't out. "Loud and clear." In fact, he glanced past her at Adam. The little guy slept right through her shouting.

"Sorry. My mind is all over the place. I didn't mean to yell at you. I'm the one who walked right into a trap. I didn't see the bars around me until the cage door closed. Then it was too late.

"When a friend says, 'Come over. Stay as long as you like. Ditch the spotlight for the big Montana sky and the freedom you've been without too long,' all you want to do is get there as fast as you can. The first week is all about settling in to the vacation you've desperately wanted. You relish the quiet, the long days spent doing nothing more than sitting in the garden reading a book that came out last year but you never had time to read. The days fly by with easy conversation and good food. Then you realize the friendly jests are too close to being serious. The simple touch on your arm lingers a bit too long. You don't expect it from a man you'd never consider a boyfriend, and he plays it off as admiration and warmth between you because he understands you like no one else. It feels that way because he's manipulated you into believing it. Before you know it, two weeks have passed and the phone you promised yourself you wouldn't answer until you were ready to face all those demands and obligations again is missing. You must have misplaced it.

"But you haven't spoken to anyone but him. You haven't seen the news because watching movies in the screening room is so much more relaxing and entertaining. It's flattering he wants to watch your movies with you, hear the inside story about the filming, your thoughts on the characters, until you go to dress for dinner and he's left you a copy of the dress you wore in his favorite film. You wear it to thank him for all he's done, giving you this place to rest and find your head again. You come down to dinner and it's the scene from your film. He speaks the lines and you give him back your character's words because it seems like a silly joke.

"You ignore the warning ringing in your head that something isn't right. When he tries to seduce you with words and actions from that same movie and you reject him instead of playing along, the slap across the face is so unexpected and jarring, you don't know what to do. Your mind doesn't figure what to do until it's too late and you're locked in a room that's been turned into a vault. No windows. No light. No escape.

"You're trapped, and you quickly learn that if you don't live up to the fantasy you created on-screen, you'll pay dearly." She slid her hand around her side and held her cracked ribs.

"I thought he was my friend. It's still so hard to reconcile the man I knew and trusted hid the monster he unleashed on me. How could people look at him and not see it? I didn't see it until it was too late."

"People are very good at presenting that part of themselves they want you to see. Look at me." He held up his tattooed arms and pointed to his long hair. "I work undercover. I want people to believe I'm the guy who will cut them down if I don't get what I want. I'm the guy who sells drugs and doesn't care about anything but the money. I'm part of their deviant crowd.

"You saw the badge. It tells you I'm the good guy, but one look at me and you dismissed that I'm a cop, fighting to take that shit off the streets and put thugs behind bars where they belong."

Beck locked eyes with her. "Never believe what people show you, only the things they do."

He glanced over at Adam. "For a second there, you saw me with Adam and couldn't resolve my kindness to the boy with the way I look. I get that. My people skills are lacking these days. I don't trust anyone. I'm always looking for their angle, waiting to see if they're going to shoot me in the back."

Ashley sighed, her mouth dipping into a soft frown. "I'm sorry I thought the worst. You brought us here, took care of Adam and me. He's been taught to hide, yet he saw a protector in you. It took me a minute to see it, but I don't trust myself anymore, so if I hold on to my suspicions and paranoia, it's not you—it's survival. I guess you get that, too."

"More than you know." He'd been living in survival mode so long he'd alienated his family, lost friends, and isolated himself to protect himself and others.

Another tether connected him to Ashley. It started with him simply wanting to protect her and the child, but now he felt a real connection to her and their shared experience of having to play a part to survive. They'd done so for different reasons. Him for a righteous cause. Her to save her life. But they both ended up in the same place, unable to go back to who they used to be, forever changed by their experiences and longing to feel connected again, but too wary of others to reach out.

For all she'd told him, some big questions still needed answers. For him, one thing mattered more than all the rest. "Who did this to you, Ashley?"

Her gaze held his for a long moment that stretched with nothing but the crackle and pop of the fire breaking the silence. The indecision in her eyes told him she didn't think he'd believe her.

She leaned forward with her folded arms on the table, continued to look him right in the eye, and gave him a name he never expected. "Brice Mooney."

Images of her smiling at the late-night talk show host from the clips the news outlets hadn't stopped playing over the last few days ran through his head. He'd focused on her—beautiful and captivating, she held every man's attention—but now he thought of Brice in those clips. The way he stared at her, all adoration and devotion in his eyes. The flirting that seemed fun but held a wealth of meaning and intent for Brice. Knowing what he knew now, Trigger reevaluated the covetous look in Brice's eyes. What everyone else saw as idolization, he now saw as possessive. An unhealthy worship that went too far. It wasn't enough to be a part of her very public world. He wanted to keep her all to himself. Brice actually believed all those smiles she flashed for the camera were truly meant only for him.

"If you don't believe me, someone who can read people and see right through them, how am I supposed to convince anyone else?"

"I believe you. Where did he hold you? Did he move you around from one place to another?"

"I've been at his ranch the whole time."

Trigger thought about the ranches and properties around him. Spread out over vast amounts of open land, he knew two of his five neighbors. Chance meetings really, because he hadn't been inclined to announce his presence here or let it be known a DEA agent lived right next door. His undercover work necessitated that he keep a low profile when off duty. You never knew when a neighbor might recognize you because they had a friend or relative who liked to get their hands dirty in the drug world and would out you inadvertently or on purpose.

He stood to get his phone so he could pull up a map of the area. Even if Ashley couldn't pinpoint where she'd been held, maybe she could narrow it down before he called the office and got some computer geek to do some property record digging.

Ashley startled and slid down the bench when he

stood, putting more distance between them. She sucked in a ragged breath and held her arm to her hurt ribs.

"Easy. I'm just getting my phone." He bypassed the counter where his phone sat charging and went to the other side to retrieve his bottle of pain meds by the sink. He brought them, another glass of water, and his phone back to the table. He set the pills in front of Ashley's bowl along with the water. "Pain meds. Take one. You'll feel better."

She still sat three feet down the table. "As much as I'd like to check out and numb—everything, I'd like to keep some semblance of a clear head."

It stung she didn't trust him, but he got her need to stay in control and aware.

"Do you have some ibuprofen instead?"

He passed the phone with the map app opened to her. "Think you can find where you were being held?"

She reached out and took the phone, sliding down and back to her spot in front of him as he stood and went to the cupboard to find the medicine. By the time he sat back down, she'd fiddled with the map and turned the phone to face him. He handed her the bottle of pills and took the phone, studying it.

"This is pretty damn far from here."

"By road, yes. But I must have walked a fairly direct route right to you."

He checked the map key and calculated how far she'd come. "That's about ten miles, give or take a couple."

"Give a few, if you ask me. I carried Adam most of the way."

"In heels and that cinched dress? Are you kidding me?"

"I didn't say it was easy, but I knew it was my one and only chance to escape. All my other attempts failed." He read the nightmare in her eyes about what happened after those failed tries. "I had to keep going, get as far away as fast as I could and find help. Though to tell you the truth,

I'm not sure anyone can really help me. He'll spin this his way. It's my word against his."

"Adam will back up your story. There must have been others working on the ranch. Staff to cook and clean."

She shook her head at every guess he made to help her build her story.

"He kept me locked up. He only let me out when we were alone. The first few weeks I was there and everything seemed normal, Adam's mother cooked and cleaned. I didn't interact with her much, but she and Brice seemed close. I had the feeling she'd worked for him awhile. He seemed fine with Adam at his mother's side while she worked. In the past year . . ." Her words fell away. The disbelief that she'd been held for almost a year showed in her eyes. "I haven't seen her. I've only seen Adam a handful of times, mostly because he peeked out of one hiding spot or another when he spied on Brice and me."

"So you don't know if his mother is still there or not?"

"I don't think so. Adam wanted to leave with me."

And didn't that just say everything. He wouldn't leave his mother.

"Is he Brice's son?"

"No. Brice caught Adam sneaking into the kitchen while we were at the dining table acting out Brice's favorite scene." She closed her eyes, too overcome to speak for a moment.

"What did he do to Adam when he caught him?"

"He kicked him again and again, calling him a mangy dog who didn't know his place." Ashley held her arm like a baby.

Trigger notched his chin toward Ashley's telltale gesture. "You stepped in and saved the boy, but Brice paid you back for being disloyal to him."

"Adam escaped the rest of the beating, but I didn't. He broke my arm, stripped me of the pretty gown he so generously allowed me to wear, dragged me up the stairs by my hair, and dumped me back in that dark box to wallow in my pain and starve for God knows how many days."

Trigger swore, imaging the hell she'd been through.

He wanted her to stop. Shut the hell up. He couldn't take any more. But then she spoke again and his already-battered heart took yet another beating.

"In the dark, time is measured in endurance and the strength of your will. Mine didn't always last as long as I needed it to between that door closing and opening. There comes a point where you run out of tears. You forget who you are and used to be. You understand on an elemental level that it doesn't matter how famous you are, how much money you've made, the countless fans who cheered your name, the awards you've won, the admiration you received, and that in the end you are as vulnerable as everyone else. And when you run out of hope and know deep down that no one is coming to save you, you don't even blink an eye or shout for the injustice of it all. You give up and give in because you know doing so will finally be the end."

Trigger had known some truly sadistic people and understood exactly what she hadn't said. "Your not giving in to him saved you all those months. It kept the potential for his fantasy of you being his loving partner alive for him. Once you gave him what he wanted, what he thought he wanted but would never be real enough for him, you knew he'd kill you." She'd truly reached the end of her endurance and lost her will to live.

"If not for someone coming to the door and Brice making one tiny mistake, I'd be dead right now. Of course, if you hadn't found me passed out, I'd be dead right now, too."

"I don't know how Adam found me, but he led me to you."

"In my prison box I wished for a spark of light. In the dead of night, with a million stars overhead, a storm and Brice closing in, your light guided me to you."

His insomnia saved her life. Who knows how long she might have been wandering outside before someone, if anyone, found her? The storm would have killed her and Adam.

Trigger stared out the huge windows and thought about last night and the never-ending dark thoughts about what he'd done that kept him up, his attempts to resolve events that were out of his control and turned out so bad, and the one thing he wanted but felt he didn't deserve. A small piece of the happiness his brother found with Mia. A partner who understood him and wanted the same things he wanted: a quiet, safe life. Family. An unbreakable bond with a connection rooted in love.

That was something he'd never had with a woman, but seeing it between Caden and Mia, he couldn't help but want it for himself.

He wanted more than a life filled with work and other people's problems.

"You found exactly where you needed to be. I can help you." Surprisingly, he didn't have a single reservation about getting involved. For all his declarations that he wanted to be left alone out here to wallow in his misery, he actually wanted to make a difference in Ashley's and Adam's lives. Maybe if he helped them, he'd find some sort of redemption for his mistakes and the shady deeds he'd done in the name of good but which left a black mark on him anyway.

"While I appreciate your help tonight, calling the cops in the morning and getting them involved won't help the way you think it will. Brice knows I'm gone and that I took Adam with me. If the cops get involved, he'll kill me to shut me up. If he can't do that, he'll flee the country and never face justice, but I'll live the rest of my life looking over my shoulder, knowing he's coming after me again. If that's not bad enough, I'll be hunted by the media and paparazzi, all of them wanting to get the story and all the dirty details. When they don't, they'll make it up and turn my life into an exhibit for everyone to judge and blame me."

"Who the hell would blame you for what happened?"

She rolled her eyes. "Brice's fans. My critics. Anyone with an internet connection who wants to spout off about things they know nothing about and have even less care for how their words affect others. People like to put stars on a pedestal, but what they really love to do is watch them fall.

"You said the perception is that I disappeared to escape the Hollywood stress. Seriously?" She shook her head.

"People closest to you believe something happened to you, but yes, the media is speculating you ran off with a lover, or—"

"Great. The media has already supplied the narrative for Brice to use against me."

Trigger had to admit she made a good point. "The cops will prove what happened. They'll tell everyone the truth."

Disbelief filled her rolling eyes. "I'm famous. No one cares about the truth—they just want a good story."

How many times had a suspect, witness, or family member exaggerated or outright lied to change the narrative of a case? Too many to count. Even though he gathered the evidence and presented solid facts, the public still believed those accounts because they missed the follow-up, or simply didn't care about or believe what really happened.

"I'm not the princess in the story everyone wants to root for. I'll be made into the witch everyone wants to burn at the stake. You'll see. Look up on the internet any story written about me and you'll find a dash of truth mixed in with a bucketload of lies. That's why I'm not sticking around to find out how big and bad this turns out. As soon as the snow stops, I'm out of here. If I'm going to hide the rest of my life, I'm getting a head start and finding the most secluded and secure place I can for Adam and me."

"You can't just take him."

"Watch me." She stood and walked away.

"If he doesn't belong to Brice, he must have other family."

She turned and faced him. "Where the hell have they been? No one came for him. No one came for me." The unrestrained anger he understood all too well. "Adam needs someone to care enough to keep him safe. He stays with me." She glanced at the massive windows and the deluge of falling snow. "We need to get away as far and fast as we can."

She wrapped her arms in front of her to hold off the shiver that shook her body.

He understood her fear, but the thought of her leaving and on the run turned his gut.

Ashley needed someone on her side, someone who cared about what happened to her. He did. But could he make her the princess in the story when his knightly armor had tarnished long ago?

CHAPTER EIGHT

Ashley woke to blinding white light and a high-pitched screech. She bolted out of bed, ignored the searing pain that flashed through her side, and ran toward the heart-wrenching sound. Unsteady on her hurt foot, she rounded the doorway and entered the large open room on the run, only to stop short at the half-naked man hanging from a bar attached to a thick wood beam in the center of the room. He pulled himself up to raise his chin over the bar. Adam squealed with delight, his arms secure around Beck's neck, his legs hooked on Beck's lean hips.

Beck rose and fell two more times in an easy motion despite Adam's added weight. She took him in with one long sweep of her gaze. Big hands. Strong arms. Rippling muscles all down his chest and stomach. Black sweats ended in huge bare feet that hit the floor just as she snapped her gaze back to his face, then back to his chest once more before she met his dark gaze. His chest and everything else on display was worth a second glance.

Her heart thudded against her ribs, making them ache and stealing her breath. Dizziness clouded her vision. Her legs buckled with relief that Adam was okay, and she hit the wood floor hard on her bare butt. Pain lanced up her side. She tried to cover her legs with the too-big T-shirt and catch her breath, though it burned to suck in the tiniest amount of air.

Adam dropped to his feet behind Beck and ran to her, falling to his knees in front of her.

She reached up and cupped his face. "You were having fun."

A bright smile split his lips. He nodded, but didn't say anything.

Beck kneeled in front of her. Adam hooked his hand on Beck's massive shoulder, his tiny fingers landing just above a large scar on Beck's chest that looked healed but new. Beck stared down at her, his expression unreadable. One of the many things that probably helped him survive working undercover.

He held his hand out to her. "Come with me."

"What happened to you?"

"Bad guy took exception to being arrested. He gave me a matching set about a month ago." Beck used the hand he held out to her to tap the scar on his side. "Adam and I already had breakfast."

She followed Beck's gaze to the breakfast bar off the kitchen island and the empty glasses and plates still there.

"You slept in. I bet you're starving. Sit on the couch. We saved you some bacon and I'll cook you up some eggs."

Her mouth watered just thinking about it. "I'd kill for a cup of coffee." The lingering scent hung in the air battling with the bacon aroma setting off a new round of grumbling in her stomach.

"I don't think it will come to that, but you might try to dial down the fear that I'm a threat. Adam and I are buddies. Aren't we, little man?" Beck hugged Adam to his side. Beck didn't smile. That sort of thing didn't come easy to him. But Adam's mouth curved with a silly grin and his eyes were bright with joy.

Adam reached out and brushed his fingers down her hair, grabbing hold of a huge chunk near the end.

She poked him in the belly. "Did you steal Beck's shirt?"

Adam looked down at the shirt draping all the way to the floor and nodded.

"Help me out, little man. Go get the eggs out of the fridge and put them on the counter. Find a bowl and crack three eggs into it for Ashley."

Adam ran off, eager to do what Beck said.

Ashley recognized the diversion tactic and waited to see what Beck wanted from her.

"How bad does it hurt?" He stared at her hand on her thigh covering one of the larger, darker bruises.

She blinked back the sheen of tears filling her eyes. "I heard him scream . . . I've rarely heard his voice." She didn't know how to explain to him the overwhelming urge to get to Adam and protect him in that moment that blocked out everything, including the pain and her understanding of where she was and how she'd gotten here. "I didn't think. I reacted. Until I saw that he was okay and it was you, I don't know, it all came back." She glanced past him to the windows and behind her to the door. "Are we safe here? Is he coming? Have you seen anything outside? Heard anything on the news? We need to get out of here!" She tried to push herself up to get moving, but Beck laid a big hand on her shoulder to still her. The second her muscles relaxed, he removed his hand and the warmth that went with the touch felt oddly comfortable, not intrusive.

"Stop. Calm down. The roads are completely impassable. The snow is still coming down, though it's lightened up considerably. No one in their right mind would go out in this weather."

"That's just it. He's not in his right mind."

"Ashley, get a grip. If I thought for a second you and Adam weren't safe here, I'd take you away myself."

"We aren't safe. We'll never be safe."

His hand came up and cupped her cheek and the warmth came back. "Right now, you are. The snow covered any tracks you might have left. It's also preventing anyone from mounting a search for you or Adam. As far as I can tell, there are no new reports on you other than the ones that have already come out about the anniversary of your disappearance. I waited for you to get up before I called the police. Out here, the sheriff has jurisdiction. They'll probably call in the feds to help out because it's a high-profile case."

She hadn't stopped shaking her head throughout that last part. "No. No cops. The governor, a senator, any number of other people in a position to help him are in his pocket."

Beck's gaze sharpened. "What do you mean?"

"The house, the room he kept me in, it's not his only secret. There are secret passages, two-way mirrors, and cameras. He recorded them and took pictures. He made me watch." She shook her head. "Parties with underage prostitutes, drugs, or them just doing things others would find appalling. Drunken confessions," she added, trying to erase all of it from her mind.

Beck raked his hand over his head. "Shit."

"As soon as I can get out of here, I am."

"You can't just run. If you're right and he goes after you, you'll have no way to protect yourself or Adam. Do you really want to risk that little boy's life? Think, Ashley. The only way to get your life back is to stand up and fight. Take him down."

"Easy enough for you to say. You're not the one about to have your life explode on every form of media."

"What the hell do you care about your name and picture splashed across the internet and TV screens when there's a man out there who will come after you or someone else to feed his sick fantasy? Stop being his victim, get up off the damn floor, and figure out a way to make him pay for what he did to you. You're so afraid of what he'll make people believe, but what about your status? Your word. You make people believe you're someone else up on that screen. Make them believe you in real life."

She hung her head, knowing that what he said was exactly what she needed to do, but after everything, she didn't know if she had the strength to do it. "What if they don't believe me?"

"I believe you. Others will, too." He dropped his hand to the hem of her shirt and pulled it up two inches to reveal the dark edges of the bruise that throbbed with pain up and down her thigh. She flinched, but the instinctive fear washed away with his deep voice. "There is nothing he can say that will ever make me believe you asked for, or deserved this." His fingertips swept softly over her skin, sending another wave of warmth through her.

Comfort. Compassion. She'd gone too long without both.

"You trusted someone you knew, a man who called himself friend, who had treated you with kindness and never showed you any ill will. There's no fault in that, Ashley. He fooled you once, but he won't fool you again. Don't let him fool the world, too. You know the real man. You can take him down."

"Your faith might be a bit misplaced considering I can't even get up from this floor on my own."

He held his hand out to her and gave her what for him passed as a grin. "I'll help you."

She wanted to believe he meant more than helping her to stand up. But she shut down that delusion. Once she was back on her feet, she'd be on her own again.

Been there. Done that her whole life. She'd had to fight for everything she'd gotten, but Beck was right.

She hadn't asked for what happened to her. She hadn't deserved Brice's cruelty. She refused to stand back and take it anymore.

She hoped she had the strength to face what was coming.

CHAPTER NINE

Trigger slipped one hand under Ashley's knees and the other around her back and under her arm. Unable to lift herself, she allowed him to pick her up right off the floor. He held her in his arms against his chest, dismayed by how little she weighed, and surprised by how right she felt against him.

She gasped in pain and leaned into him to ease her ribs. "Put me down."

He adjusted her in his arms, carried her to the sofa, and gently set her on the cushion, her back to the side, feet spread out in front of her. He pulled the soft blue blanket off the back and draped it over her.

"Stay put. I'll get you some ice for your injuries, more ibuprofen, and food."

She gazed up at him, her eyes pleading. "Coffee. Please. I beg you."

He laughed under his breath at the drama she put into wanting a simple cup of coffee. He wondered how long it had been since she had one. "We need to have a serious talk about what happened to you. We'll need to file a report. Take pictures of . . ." He swept his hand in the air down the length of her.

She paled even more than her sun-deprived skin showed moments ago. "You can't be serious."

"Proof of his abuse can't be denied."

"Haven't I been subjected to enough humiliation?"

He wanted to ask what else she'd been subjected to, but held his tongue because Adam waited patiently for him in the kitchen.

"It's necessary. A female officer or nurse will take the pictures."

"Right. And sell them to the highest bidder at some sleazy tabloid."

Trigger sat on the coffee table, leaned forward with his forearms on his thighs, and looked her right in the eye. "I know you're scared to face what happened and tell your story. The cops will take it slow. They'll explain everything along the way about the process and where they are in the investigation and arrest."

"With the connections Brice has and the dirt he has on them, they won't arrest him. They'll simply find a plausible reason to dismiss my claims."

Trigger stared at her. "Your appearance can't be dismissed."

She scrunched her mouth into a pout and took a minute to think through what needed to be done. She didn't look at him, but said, "You do it."

"The cops will want to control the case. I'm DEA. They won't let me interfere, but I can make sure they're doing what they should for you."

She shook her head and wrung her hands in her lap. "No. You take the report. You take the pictures. I've already told you some of what happened. I can . . . I can try to tell the rest and put it in some kind of order."

"Ashley, I hunt down drug dealers and infiltrate and take down drug trafficking rings. I don't know anything but the basics of working a kidnapping, torture, and rape case." There, he'd said his worst fear that for the last year that piece of scum had not only held, starved, and beaten this beautiful, fragile woman, but abused her in another horrific way, too.

Ashley's whispered words barely registered to his ears. "He tried, but he couldn't. That's why he hurt me."

"Christ." Trigger raised his head to the wood ceiling and rafters overhead, pissed and relieved all at the same time. He didn't know if his gut or the heart that woke up again in his chest the moment he found her could take much more of this.

He'd shut the damn thing off for a reason. Caring got in the way of doing his job.

Here she was asking him to do a job he never signed up for and didn't want, but she trusted him to do it anyway.

"Once Adam eats himself into a food coma . . ." Trigger shook his head at the boy who'd made himself at home and gotten himself yet another handful of fudge stripe cookies from the pantry and his third glass of milk. The kid acted like he'd never had sweets. Trigger didn't want to let his mind go to that place where a little boy had never been given treats or hugs or any kindness in his short but precious life. "No matter what happens, we have to be sure Adam gets all the cookies he wants."

"We?"

Trigger tore his gaze from Adam happily chomping down his cookies to stare at Ashley. He didn't know what to say because while he'd spoken without thought, he really did feel like they were in this together for Adam's sake. Yes, that was it. For Adam. Not the woman he had a hard time keeping in the victim-who-needed-his-help zone in his brain.

"Kids should not be denied cookies." As covers went, that one sucked, so he got them back on track. "Once he takes a nap, we'll deal with the pictures, then you can take a shower."

She nodded her agreement.

"Great. I'll make you something to eat, take a shower, and find you something more suitable to wear."

Trigger stood and went to the kitchen, giving Adam a pat on the head as he passed him at the bar. Trigger made quick work of scrambling up some eggs and re-heating the bacon strips they'd saved from breakfast this morning. Adam found his way back to Ashley on the sofa and curled up with her. She gently brushed his hair over and over and stared at the fire Trigger built up to keep the place extra warm for them. Skinny, undernourished, Adam always seemed cold and tired.

Trigger plated up the food, buttered the toast that popped up from the toaster, added a generous amount of raspberry jelly, then carried it all over to Ashley, and handed her the plate and the cup of coffee she'd desired. She took one sip after another of the hot brew, then sighed when she satisfied that initial craving.

"I suggest you eat slow and eat it all even if you feel like you can't. You need your strength and your body needs the energy to heal." He stared down at Adam sleeping peacefully, his body tucked in the curve of Ashley's. "Are you comfortable?" Her ribs must hurt like hell every second of the day.

"I'm fine, Beck. Thank you."

"Want those pain meds now?"

She shook her head. "No, thank you. A good night's sleep helped. I feel better this morning. Plus, I woke up here and not there."

The relief in her eyes told him how much that meant to her. Freedom, even if the storm kept her here, meant a new day without crippling fear.

"I'm going to take a shower. Help yourself to anything else you want."

She stuffed half a strip of bacon in her mouth and

chewed, her eyes rolling back in ecstasy. "I'm good," she said around the other half of the bacon strip as she chewed.

"There's nothing better than bacon."

"Amen." She bit a smaller piece off the next strip.

He turned to head back to his room, but stopped when she called his name.

"Beck."

She never called him Trigger.

"Yeah?"

She glanced out the big windows, then at the front door. "Can I have your gun?"

"No." The last thing he wanted to do was walk out of his room when she got spooked and get shot because she lost her shit and perceived some threat that wasn't really there. Still, he understood her fear and desire to protect herself from ever going back to that hell she escaped.

He picked up the remote from the coffee table and pointed it at the flat screen. He quickly changed the channel from CNN to his security setup.

"Hey, wait, go back to the news. I want to see what's happening in the world."

"No."

She wanted to see what they were saying about her. She needed more time to settle into the fact she escaped and understand what came next.

"You're not ready to face the full scope of reality. Eat. Rest. Take the time you need to breathe before we have to begin the hard stuff."

He pointed to the screen. "Hidden cameras at the front and back of my place, in the barn—"

"You have horses."

The delight in her eyes made him grin. "Rocket, Gypsy, and Berry, short for Blueberry."

"Berry?" Ashley's eyebrow shot up in question.

"Named by a six-year-old girl who loved her gray horsie, but the horsie proved too spirited for a child."

"It's sweet you kept the name."

"The horse answered to it, so what the hell." He pretended it meant nothing. But really he kept it because every time he called the horse he thought of that sweet little girl. He had too few good things to think about sometimes.

"Monitors." He reminded her of what they were really talking about before she asked too many questions about things he didn't want to talk about. "You can see 360 degrees around the house. Motion sensors on the gate and spread around the property will sound an alarm." He pointed to the doorbell box over the door. "Normal doorbell for when guests arrive, which never happens, and a buzzer when the alarm triggers, which hopefully won't happen."

Ashley swiped her tongue over her bottom lip to clean away a dollop of jelly. "Uh, why do you have so much security here?"

He gave her the cold hard truth of his life. "Drug cartels from Mexico to South America would love to find and kill me. I've made it damn hard for them, but nothing is infallible. The alarms give me a head start if they actually get past all the security measures I've put in place."

"Wow. I'm not sure if I should feel safer here or more in danger."

"The best I can do to reassure you is say that this"—he pointed to the nine blocks of security feeds on the screen—"is better safe than sorry. My way of feeling relatively safe when I live in a very dangerous world." He spun around and headed for his bedroom, knowing she spotted the gun he had slipped in the back of his pants.

CHAPTER TEN

Shadows shifted on the screen. Ashley tracked them on one monitor then another, knowing nothing was out there, but driving herself insane with each obsessive stare-down of yet another imagined threat. Her stomach soured, yet she kept eating. She needed to get her strength back. She needed to be at her best to protect Adam. The food would help her physically, but what would help her to mentally prepare to face what was to come? Sooner rather than later, since Beck wanted to get all the facts on film, so to speak, and on paper. She dreaded having him take photographs of her battered body. She'd told him as much as she ever wanted to say about what happened to her. But the investigator in him would ferret out every last detail.

Would it really make a difference?

She didn't think so. She truly believed that in the world she lived in, Brice would use his money and celebrity to twist the story to his advantage and use the people who'd come to his home to rub elbows with celebrities but ended up trapped in his web to protect him from jail.

She rubbed Adam's back, reassuring him that she was there as he slept peacefully. She tried to shut off her mind, the overwhelming urge to run, the fear that at any moment Brice would bust down the door and take her again. She felt the walls closing in.

Something moved on the screen again. Her wandering gaze shifted to the horses in their stalls. While all the other cameras pointed to possible points of entry and hiding spots, one camera kept an eye on them. She wondered if sometimes Beck sat here watching them, lost in their simple lives, the sheer wonder of such large, magnificent animals. Graceful in their way. Strong. Capable. Yet sensitive to their environment and emotions. Or so she'd heard. She wanted to go out and see them.

She'd bet Adam would love to pet the horses. She'd give anything to erase the bad memories from his mind and fill it with nothing but happy ones from now on.

Berry. Who knew the all-too-serious Beck had a sensitive side?

It hit her that as paranoid and scared as she was about Brice coming after her, Beck lived with that kind of mindset every day, knowing that someone he'd gone up against in his work wanted revenge and might come after him. He did a noble job that put a target on his back. He lived in a world full of lies and betrayals. Not unlike her, but in a different way.

"Ashley, you okay?"

Well, her throat went a little dry when she looked up and spotted the tall, dark, and handsome man standing there in snug jeans and a black T-shirt that stretched across his wide chest and shoulders. The description almost made her chuckle, but his dark, intense gaze told her he was anything but the gentle sort. Everything physically and mentally about him was hard. At least that's what he wanted people to think, but he'd shared that tiny glimpse of a tender side in the story about the little girl who loved her horsie. She would never forget the sweet way he held Adam close to his chest as they slept together in the chair last night. Or the achingly soft way his fingers brushed her skin the few times he'd touched her.

She wondered if she'd ever take anyone at face value again.

She went with an honest answer. "I'm trying to contain my paranoid crazy by watching the horses and not my imagined ghosts lurking on the property."

Beck picked up the remote and clicked off the TV. "It gets better." He tried to reassure her, but the shadows in his eyes said better was relative and a long way off, especially if she kept feeding her fears.

He stared at her and raked his fingers through his long, damp hair. "Uh, are you up to taking care of some business?"

"No, but I'd rather do it this way than having a bunch of strangers staring at and dissecting me."

She didn't know what she said to make his gray eyes narrow with an intensity that stilled her under his sharp gaze. She didn't look away under his scrutiny. She couldn't. Instead, she fell into the depth of his eyes and found a connection to him she recognized on some level and felt deeply in that moment. She didn't know what it meant, but somehow that feeling of being utterly alone dissipated like smoke on the wind.

Funny how the man who saved her but she didn't know at all felt like much more than a friend. A friend she could sit beside, say nothing, and feel like he got everything about her.

Strange. The details of who he was and what he believed in didn't matter. She needed something deeper. Something more. And she found it in this dangerous-looking, stoic, quietly intense guy who had just as many nightmares locked inside him as she did.

A guy who'd recently been shot in the line of duty and hid away in the middle of nowhere alone.

"Whatever you're thinking, stop. I am a stranger and, more importantly, someone you don't want to know. I'll help you navigate the investigation and make sure that bastard pays for what he did to you and Adam, but that's it. I'm no good for anything else."

Ashley eased away from Adam, settled him in the spot she moved out of without waking him, and stood to face Beck, though she kept that same five-foot distance she needed less and less, but he seemed to want with those words he gave her.

"I'm not sure if I can stand to be locked inside this house for another second. I'm not sure I can stand this constant fear and feeling like any second my worst nightmare will show up at the door. I don't know if I can take speaking the words about what happened to me when it is so raw and suffocating. I don't know if I can endure you or anyone seeing the evidence of my stupidity."

"Ashley, no. It's not your fault."

"I'm not sure about that. But I am sure of one thing despite the fact I have little evidence or reason to believe it other than my gut and heart convincing me of it absolutely."

"What?"

"You are a good man. I don't know if I'll ever be able to say that about anyone again, but I can say that about you."

Beck sucked in a breath, ready to wind up and tell her all the reasons she was wrong, or just warn her away. She didn't want to hear it because, like him, she presented one thing with her distance and actions, but deep down in the part of her that couldn't stand the loneliness one more second, she wanted a connection to him. It mattered. It made a difference, even in its small, fragile way.

"So let's do the hard stuff, then we can go back to our easy silence where we're both mired in our shit swamp, hoping it doesn't suck us under completely, knowing that we aren't suffering alone even if we do it separately."

"I have no idea what you need."

"That's okay, Beck. I have no idea what I need, except what you've already given me. A safe place to stay, food, an honest assessment of what I'm facing, and more important than anything, you showed Adam not all men are bad guys."

"You give me far too much credit."

"I owe you my life and Adam's. I'm pretty sure I haven't given you enough credit or proper gratitude."

"I don't want either."

"I think it's more accurate to say you feel like you don't deserve it. Doesn't matter. You have both my gratitude and belief in you."

"Then you're doomed to disappointment."

"No one is infallible. No one is all good or bad. But it's how you treat strangers—taking them in, caring for them instead of dumping them on someone else—that speaks volumes about who you really are on the inside."

Ashley didn't want to hear another denial or excuse for why she should stop thinking of Beck as anything but a good guy, so she marched right past him—ready, though scared, to face taking the pictures Beck insisted she needed as proof against Brice.

Too mentally weary and physically exhausted last night or this morning to even think about a shower, she desperately wanted one now. Especially after smelling Beck's clean scent and realizing she could scare away a skunk with how bad she smelled. Even worse, she felt grimy and unclean in a way that went beyond skin-deep. She desperately wanted to scrub away the filth Brice left behind, that indelible mark he'd put on her, unseen, but felt all the same.

She smiled at the small pile of items Beck left for her on the bathroom counter. A towel, washcloth, razor—her furry legs needed one—and a brand-new toothbrush. The anticipation of being clean, silky smooth, and minty fresh died the second she caught her reflection in the mirror. Her hands gripped the edge of the counter. She leaned on her arms as her knees shook at the sight she beheld of a woman she didn't recognize.

Silent tears cascaded down her cheeks. She lost her breath as her chest constricted. She ran her hand over her pale face, her fingers brushing over her dull skin, the dark circles under her hollow eyes, her sunken cheeks, and cracked lips. The T-shirt fell off one bony shoulder, revealing her too-prominent clavicle. Her once-full breasts barely rounded under the draping material. She leaned back and stared at her stick-thin legs and feet that were bare but for the wrap Beck put on her very swollen ankle. What she thought was her uneven gait because of her injury had more to do with her utter lack of strength.

She'd once been touted as one of the most beautiful women in Hollywood. "They should cast me as a zombie in some horror movie," she whispered, tears clogging her throat. "No makeup or special effects needed."

Beck stood in the doorway, quiet and watchful as ever, and frowned at her assessment. He walked up behind her, standing more than a head taller than her. He set his phone on the counter, bent, planted his hands next to hers on the marble top, and leaned in close, his head at her shoulder.

Blocked in by his big body and arms, she didn't feel trapped. He'd let her out if she wanted him to. His nearness didn't disturb her but gave her comfort. Just like before, she welcomed the wash of warmth that went through her. She wasn't alone. With him, danger seemed faraway, unable to touch her.

"Look at that woman again. She's a shower away from having shiny, silky hair. She's a few days' sleep away from losing the dark circles under her gorgeous green eyes. She's a dozen good meals away from filling out her beautiful face and building back the muscle and curves every man admires." His deep voice rumbled at her ear as his soft beard barely brushed her cheek. "You will get back to what you used to be, but look deeper and see that the woman you're looking at right now is a survivor. She's filled with strength and courage and a determination that defies limitations. Your will alone made you walk out of hell. You carried Adam through the night and across some damn rugged land in heels headed for nothing more than your freedom. He tried to break you, Ashley, but all he did was make you stronger.

"Don't for one moment think that you are anything less than amazing."

She closed her eyes and leaned her head against Beck's face. She needed the contact and a moment to drink in his words, said with such sincerity and warmth she couldn't help but believe he truly meant them.

One of his arms hooked around her front. His hand settled on her side. Her body trembled at the contact, echoing with the anticipation that a soft touch would turn mean and hurtful. But this was Beck, not the monster who didn't see her but a distorted fantasy.

She wrapped her arms over Beck's against her stomach and held tight to him. He stood tall behind her, wrapped his other arm across her chest, his hand on her shoulder, and pulled her against the hard wall of his chest. She leaned her head against his arm and felt safe and protected and let it all go. The dam on her emotions broke and the tears flooded out. She cried like she hadn't allowed herself to cry in months. She felt the grief, the sadness, the loneliness, the anger, and fury for all the injustices and humiliation she'd suffered. The overwhelming emotions racked her body along with the tidal wave of tears. Knowing she had so much more to face, she allowed herself this moment to release it all and let it go as much as she could.

Beck didn't say a word, just held her through the worst of her breakdown. He held her until she wound down and found her footing again. She hadn't realized at some point her knees buckled and Beck held her up and close. As much as she wanted to stay in his strong arms, suspended in this state of safety, she needed to stand on her own and not expect Beck to make it all better. Though he had with his kind words and solid presence.

She hugged Beck's arms tight to her body, then let loose. "Thank you. I'm okay now. I'm sorry I lost it on you." She tried to step away, but Beck held her still. He gave her a soft squeeze to get her to look up at him in the mirror.

He held her gaze for a second, then said, "You're going to be okay."

Funny how she needed to hear that from him to believe it. Maybe he needed the same thing, because she saw far too much of what she felt in him.

"You will be okay, too?"

His mouth flattened. "We're not talking about me."

Easier to talk about him, think about what he'd been through, than to think about herself. "Maybe you need someone to talk to about why I'm not the only one hiding out here."

He gently set her away and reached for his phone. "Let's get this done."

Right, he wanted to focus on her, not himself. They should both do something else. "Can I avoid this the same way you're avoiding your problems?"

"My only problem right now is a feisty movie star who wants to avoid doing the hard stuff by turning things on me."

"Movie star," she scoffed. "He stole that from me. The

only thing I'll ever be famous for now is being the woman Brice Mooney kidnapped and tortured. They don't give out Oscars for that."

"What happened doesn't change the fact you're a damn good actress."

She rolled her eyes. "Please. You're the last person I would say watched my movies."

His mouth tilted in a lopsided frown. "I may not have seen them all, but *Dark of Night* was my favorite of the couple I did get a chance to see. You really made me believe you were two different people. You played each role so well."

She dropped her head. "Thanks. I appreciate that you said it and you meant it. A year ago, I was so tired of everyone kissing my ass. It all seemed so shallow and calculated. Over the last year, I'd have given my right arm to be mired in the Hollywood illusion—glitz and glam and everything is nothing more than surface with no depth—just to avoid another criticism, the verbal abuse, the beating for forgetting a line or not delivering it just the way he wanted."

Beck touched his finger to her chin and made her raise her gaze to meet his. "You know nothing you ever did would have been right and the second you gave in he'd have turned on you. You said so yourself." Beck poked the end of her nose. "Now stop stalling and let's get this done."

She dropped her head again and stared at her feet. "How do you want to do this?" She didn't have anything on beneath the T-shirt. She'd spent countless days, weeks, and months naked. Punishment. A way to degrade her even further. A means to keep her from trying to escape yet again. She'd become comfortable in her skin, but stripping down now made her shudder and feel exposed.

"We'll do this in . . . sections, I guess. Let's figure out

how to do this with a thought that these photos might be leaked. We want to document the bruises and how thin you are because he starved you." Beck sighed. "Um, the sight of you is enough to convince anyone you've been terribly mistreated."

"Stray dogs are fatter than me." She tried to think how to do this without humiliating herself. She sat on the toilet, tucked the T-shirt between her thighs and close to her crotch, showing her wrapped sprained ankle and exposing the bruises all up her legs.

Beck bent and gently unwrapped her foot. Her ankle was swollen, but didn't hurt as bad as her ribs.

"Look straight ahead. I'll get a few shots of your legs, but I want your face in the frame so there's no doubt it's you."

"Just do it." She'd done a Nike commercial decked out in a cute workout outfit showing off her ripped abs and toned thighs. She'd been a running and Pilates fanatic. It seemed a long time ago. Now she could barely keep her eyes open after only being up for a couple of hours.

Beck made quick work of taking the photos. He even snapped one of her face as she zoned out.

Knowing what she had to do and dreading it, she stood and turned her back to him. Her hands shook when she took the hem of the shirt and pulled it up and over her head. She held it down the front of her to cover her breasts and private parts, but it didn't make it any easier to stand naked in front of a man she barely knew.

She held her breath while he took more pictures. Her ribs ached. Her heart hurt. Her mind wanted to shut down and go to that riverbank in her mind.

"Ashley, I'll turn my back. Sit back on the toilet with the shirt draped over your hips. Cover your chest with one arm. I'll take a few of the bruises on your neck, chest, and running across your ribs."

She glanced at their reflection in the mirror. Sure enough he'd turned his back. Only the side of his face was visible and the pulsing muscle at his jaw. His free hand hung clenched at his side against his thigh. This wasn't easy for him either.

She positioned herself on the toilet seat as he instructed with the shirt covering her and one hand covering one breast, her forearm covering the other. She used her free hand to hold on to the seat and help her sit as straight as possible to relieve the pain in her ribs.

"Ready?"

"Not really," she admitted, her eyes filling with tears she thought had dried up.

"Take your time."

"Hurry up and finish it."

Beck spun around and raised the phone to take the pictures. She didn't look at him. She couldn't. Not sitting here completely exposed and vulnerable. She couldn't hide what Brice had done to her. She couldn't help but remember how she got every bump and aching bruise.

Beck turned his back the second he finished. "I'll leave some clean clothes on the bed. I know it's been a while, but I'm sure you can resurrect that high-maintenance movie star and be that girl who takes forever to get ready."

Beck left her, if not with a grin on her face, than lighter for his small attempt at a joke and teasing her.

Ever considerate, he closed the door, but left it ajar, understanding her need to know she could escape, even if it was unwarranted.

Desperate to wash away the past year, she stood, letting the T-shirt slide to the floor, turned on the shower beside her, grabbed the washcloth and razor, and stepped into the spray. She didn't care that the water took a minute to heat and steam the wide tiled stall. The blessed sluice of water over her skin sent a wave of relaxation through her.

The soap smelled like Beck, simple and clean. She used it and the washcloth to scrub her skin pink. It didn't take away the echo of Brice's hands on her body, but it made her feel better. She put the razor to good use, then lathered and rinsed her hair twice before she cleaned away all the oil and grime and mud from her tumble in the weeds on her mad dash to escape. She stood under the spray, letting the hot water ease her tired and sore muscles. Who knew she still had a few more tears to shed, but in the quiet with the monotonous beat of the shower spray over her head and body, she gave herself one more chance to grieve what she'd lost, rage for what had been done to her, and find the strength to keep going.

She shuffled out of the shower just as the water cooled. She dried off and wrapped the thick, lush towel around herself. She took Beck's advice and took her time combing out her long hair with his brush. She brushed her teeth and blow-dried her hair.

She stared at the reflection of yet another version of herself. Not the movie star she used to be. Not the beaten down woman of yesterday. But a survivor who still faced several hurdles and obstacles before she could live her life again. She didn't know how that new life would look or what it would include, but right now she told herself to take it one day at a time. That's about all she could manage.

With Beck's help, she'd been able to endure one of the hard things facing her. She hoped she had the strength to complete the rest.

She hoped she didn't have to face them alone.

CHAPTER ELEVEN

Trigger walked out the front door and into the cold, needing an escape. He'd done some pretty shitty things in his life, and putting Ashley through that torment ranked among the worst in his book. He had a picture in his mind of her on-screen. The woman he just photographed resembled a starving refugee, not the gorgeous actress paparazzi chased for a photo to splash across magazine covers. It made him sick and angry and heartbroken.

Not even the falling snow cooled the fury running through him. He wanted nothing more than to get his hands on the bastard who hurt her. To think of all she'd endured . . . Days, weeks, months of abuse and torture. The long periods of time she spent locked in a dark room with no food, water, light, clothes, dignity, or hope. His gut soured. His chest ached. He'd seen some terrible things, things he tucked away, but he feared he'd never stop seeing the image of Ashley's battered, bruised, and emaciated body.

Frustrated by the piling snow still coming down and his inability to do something productive to help her—like killing the bastard so he never hurt her again—Trigger slid open the barn door and stepped in to check on the horses. They nickered their hello and poked their heads over the stall doors to greet him. Despite the freezing temps outside, the interior of the barn remained comfortable, the horses made even more content with their blankets. He checked each one of them to be sure they had enough water and food.

He spent a few extra minutes with Gypsy. Her sweet affection eased his troubled mind and heart. Over the last weeks of being home and healing, he'd spent a lot of time with her. He planned to bring Adam out here to see her.

The child's silence disturbed him. Little boys should be loud, boisterous, energetic to the point you wanted to strap them down. He stopped that thought because he didn't want to think about anyone hurting that innocent boy. One bright spot—if there could be one in this situation—was that the boy hadn't been as badly abused as Ashley. Skinny, but not starved. Bruised, but not hurt so badly he had any broken or cracked bones. Adam had suffered, but he'd bounce back physically a hell of a lot faster than Ashley. Especially if he kept eating like an NFL defensive tackle. But mentally, time would tell.

And what happened to his mother?

Beck brushed his hand down Gypsy's long neck and rubbed his head against hers. "Keep these guys in line," he ordered the chestnut mare. "I'll be back in a couple of hours."

The blast of cold hit him the second he stepped out of the barn and muscled the door closed behind him. The lingering storm gave him time to think about how to handle Ashley's and Adam's situation. Ashley's reservations and outright fears about taking this public weighed on him. The last thing he wanted to do was announce what happened to her only to have her hunted by the press and locked away someplace to keep her privacy.

The last thing he wanted to do was make her a prisoner again.

He scanned the yard and as far as he could see through the falling snow. He didn't see anything out of place. Not one track in the pristine snow that he hadn't left himself from the house to the barn. Though he had state-of-the-art security and monitors around the property, in these temps and weather conditions he couldn't rely on them to work properly. The threat of Brice showing up, or someone from his past, remained ever present in his mind. Guzman wanted his revenge after Trigger killed his cousin Marco. Didn't matter that Marco kidnapped Caden and Mia to uncover Trigger's true identity. Marco never got that information. As far as Trigger knew, his identity remained a secret. It wouldn't stay that way long. He couldn't hide and help Ashley at the same time.

He needed to make a choice. While the easy way kept him safe and tucked away here at the ranch, the hard way put Ashley, Adam, and his life in danger on two fronts.

The storm provided security in one sense. Who the hell would be out in this for long? But on the other hand, it provided the perfect cover. No one would expect anyone to use the storm to conceal their approach to the house and take them by surprise.

Trigger had some fucked-up thinking to worry about such things, but that was how he stayed alive in a dangerous world where threats were serious and one misstep meant death.

He didn't take protecting Ashley and Adam lightly. They needed someone like him to keep them safe. Because once the storm passed, Brice would come after them, hell-bent on getting them back or shutting them up. For good.

The cops worked by the book, and that could put Ashley in more danger. Because to take down a man who played without any rules, you sometimes needed to play dirty. He'd lived that life, and knew what they were up against. She needed him. He didn't know if he was up for the task after everything he'd been through lately, but he couldn't bring himself to turn his back on her. Or Adam.

The steps to the porch had already disappeared beneath another thick layer of snow. He'd shoveled the porch and them on his way out. He jumped the steps, leaving the pristine snow. The burned skin on the back of his leg, though healing, pulled and ached with the impact when he landed. He needed to put some more ointment on the wounds. Thanks to his workout this morning with Adam, his shoulder and side ached, but in a good way. He was getting stronger and feeling more like himself. Physically. Mentally, well, he hadn't really had time to think about his problems when Ashley's seemed far worse than his.

She'd probably call him out for not dealing with his shit and focusing on the plan forming in his head to help her. What the hell. Maybe helping her would help him. He needed the distraction.

And she was one hell of a distraction.

He couldn't think of another woman he'd liked the way he liked her. He admired her strength and perseverance and even her spunk. She'd been hell-bent on saving Adam from him last night. If not for the storm, she would have taken that boy and run with him again even in her poor condition.

She knew what she faced. He did in some respects. He'd spare her the whole ordeal if he could, but running wasn't the answer. No one should get away with what Brice did to her. Celebrity and blackmailed officials wouldn't save him from paying for what he did. Trigger would make sure of that. He'd take them all down if that's what it took.

He stomped the snow off his boots, trying to be quiet and not spook Adam or Ashley. He walked in the door and pried off his boots, setting them in the metal tray at the side of the door. He glanced to the sofa but didn't see

Adam sleeping there. The boy stood at the back of the room by the massive windows.

"Hey, little man, what are you doing?"

He stepped to the side, revealing Ashley sitting on the floor leaning back against a large pillow she'd propped against the wall, sound asleep wearing the black sweatpants and white T-shirt he put out for her. Her toes peeked out the too-long ends. Color had seeped back into her pale face. Her hair softly waved over one shoulder and down her chest. Soft, full, a temptation to run his fingers through the silky strands. The shower transformed her appearance but sapped her energy. She'd barely gotten through the peanut butter and jelly sandwich he left on the counter for her. The third of a sandwich she couldn't finish sat on the floor beside her with the empty glass. She drank all the milk. The food would give her some energy, but what she really needed was sleep and time to heal.

"Is she okay?" he asked, just to be sure she'd nodded off and not passed out from something more serious. Her injuries and malnutrition were still a huge concern. He needed to get her checked out by a doctor.

Adam nodded.

Trigger walked over and kneeled beside Ashley. He reached to slide his hands under her to take her back to bed to sleep, but stopped when Adam tugged on his shoulder.

Trigger glanced over at Adam, who stared out the massive windows.

"Nice. Bright."

Trigger looked back at Ashley. Her head rested against the pillow, her face turned to the luminous outdoors. Nothing much to see but the snow falling and yards and yards of white-covered landscape and trees.

"Pretty," Adam said, his tiny hand steady on Trigger's shoulder.

Yes, a pretty view, nice and bright for a woman who'd been held in a dark cell. "Maybe we'll let her sleep a while longer." Trigger turned to Adam. "Want to watch cartoons?"

Adam stared blankly at him.

Everything can get worse. What four-year-old didn't know about cartoons? "You're in for a treat."

"Cookies?"

"No more cookies until after dinner. Come here." Trigger stood and guided Adam to the couch. He turned the TV on and flipped through channels until he found a *Scooby-Doo* rerun.

Adam smiled up at him and settled back into the couch.

"Cartoons, little man. Enjoy. I need to make a call."

Trigger went to the spare room to grab his laptop, a pad of paper, and a pen. He started out of the office to keep an eye on Adam and Ashley, but turned back at the last second, rounded the desk to his printer and pulled out several sheets of blank white paper. He dug through his desk drawer and came up with half a dozen colored pencils. He liked to use different colors on his case files to organize things for each suspect. He stacked everything on his laptop and headed back to the living room. Adam giggled, completely lost in Scooby chasing after more Scooby Snacks.

Trigger set the colored pencils and paper on the coffee table in front of Adam. "In case you want to draw or color."

Adam's gaze shot from the TV to the table and back. Cartoons won out over everything else again.

Trigger left him to Scooby and took a seat at the dining table facing the living room. He stared at Ashley, sound asleep, light shining on her hair and pale face. She looked better after the shower, but he wondered if he'd set her back making her endure those pictures.

Better the stranger you know than the one you expect to sell you out.

At least she trusted him that much. He still needed to convince her to stand and fight and that running away solved nothing and might make things worse.

To that end, he called a friend, hoping she could help him out. After all, she'd saved his life once.

"Hello." The sweet voice came on the line, taking him back to one of the nightmares that haunted his sleep. A knife plunged toward him and Sadie laid herself out over his chest and saved him from being stabbed right through the heart. He'd never forget the sight of her blood oozing out of her shoulder, or discovering that she was pregnant at the time, too.

"How's my favorite guardian angel?"

"Beck. How are you?" Funny, she always called him by his name, too. Never Trigger.

"I've been better." He told her the honest truth. "How's that baby boy? Big as his father?"

"If John keeps eating the way he does he'll be as big as Rory by Christmas. Thank you for the baby gift. John loves his stuffed horse.

"What's going on, Beck? Are you okay?"

Because she'd been through hell with her brother cooking meth on her husband's ranch and trying to kill her in a drug-hazed rage, she understood a little of what he faced undercover on the job. Hell, she'd saved his ass when she figured out he wasn't with her brother and his friends, but trying to take them down, and she stayed quiet.

"I ran into some trouble several weeks ago. I got shot and burned when a drug lab blew up."

"Oh God, Beck, why didn't Caden call me? I'd have come to see you. What can I do?"

"The injuries have healed. For the most part," he added. "But I've taken a leave of absence to clear my head."

"You should have done that after the business with Connor here."

Yes, he should have. Instead, he'd found himself easily infiltrating a branch of the same cartel Connor got mixed up in and everything went to shit and an innocent woman lost her life. Because of him.

"Beck?" Sadie coaxed.

"Listen, Sadie, I'm mixed up in some other stuff and thought maybe you could help me out."

"Anything you need. You know that."

Rory Kendrick lucked out when he hooked up with Sadie. If a guy as guarded as Rory could win the heart of a sweet, kind woman like Sadie and the kind of love he found with her, then maybe there really was hope for Trigger. Maybe. Someday.

His gaze strayed to the woman across the room he vowed to protect.

"The situation I have on my hands is tricky. I need someone at the sheriff's office I can trust to keep his mouth shut. Someone who can handle something by the book but do it with an eye for the victim." He hated calling Ashley that because, although she'd been Brice's victim, given a chance to fight, she took it. He may have stripped her down to her last shred of strength and endurance, but she found her reserves. Tired now, she'd bounce back. She'd be a force. He sensed it in the way she snapped at him and instinctively came out with the claws to protect Adam. "The deputy who kept after Connor. You said once that he'd looked out for you and your father and even tried to massage things to help you get Connor the help he needed."

"Not that Connor ever cooperated, but yes, Mark saw Connor got caught up way over his head. He gave Connor several ultimatums. In the end, Connor chose not to take the lifelines offered to him."

"Do you think he's objective enough to bend the rules to protect a victim?"

"Bend, yes. Break, no. No matter what, Mark meant to take Connor down. How, he gave Connor a choice. The easy way, or the hard with many more consequences."

Exactly the type of guy he needed on his side and inside the investigation. And he hoped a guy not in Brice's pocket. "How do I get in contact with Mark?"

Sadie rattled off the phone number. "If you need anything else, call me."

"I keep calling you, that big man of yours will knock my head off."

Sadie's soft giggle eased his heart. She'd been through so much with the loss of her father and arrest of her brother after he tried to kill her. "Come by the ranch anytime. Rory would love to see you. I'll put little John in your arms and you'll feel some of the best of life."

Trigger stared at Adam smiling at the TV, enjoying another episode of *Scooby-Doo*. The little boy took him out of his head and made him forget his problems. He had a new focus, to make it safe for that boy to smile every day for the rest of his life.

"Thanks for the help."

"Beck, there's more to life than the dark side you infiltrate. There is so much good in the world, too. You just have to open yourself to it. Take this break and find some of it. Seek it out the way you hunt down the bad."

Not bad advice, but right now he had another bad man to find and put behind bars. "I've got a different kind of mission right now."

"I'm worried about you, Beck. You sound too close to the way you did when we met."

He'd been desperate to get out from undercover. He'd been in too long and saw the danger closing in and knew it would all end badly. It almost did. If not for Sadie, he'd be dead.

"I need to take care of this, then everything will be fine."

Sadie's soft sigh told him even she didn't believe that empty statement. One misstep and he could put Ashley and Adam in danger again. Hell, the bastard who hurt them was still out there, free to do as he pleased. Trigger worried about what he was planning even now.

CHAPTER TWELVE

Brice stared out the window at the thick blanket of snow on the ground and the millions of flakes still coming down and cursed the storm, his luck, his life. He'd barely slept for the nightmares and questions plaguing him.

Where is she?

What happened to her?

Is she still alive?

Is she out there freezing and begging for me to come for her?

With her strength and determination, and just pure stubbornness, he knew she could make it. She wasn't dead. She couldn't be. He'd know. He'd feel it.

He needed to find her and bring her home where she belonged.

"Brice!" Darren called his name like he'd said it several times already.

Brice turned from the wall of white out his windows to his pet assistant. "What?"

"Any news?"

"Nothing," he bit out, wanting this agony to be over. Without her, he felt incomplete. If only he could find her, he could set things right again. She didn't know what she was doing. The connection they formed overwhelmed her. She needed time to accept. Once she did, she'd want to come back to him.

Brice turned the laptop on his desk around to show Darren the map he'd pulled up. "We know she didn't take the road." They'd driven up and down the road in the early morning light despite the treacherous icy conditions. They'd put the four-wheel drive to the test. The hair-raising experience left him reasonably sure she hadn't gotten to the road and flagged down another car. "There's a property on either side of my land."

Darren pointed at the phone. "So, call the neighbors."

"I want to see their faces in case they try to lie."

"You're exposing yourself by going out and looking for her, alerting people that she's been *hiding* here. We'll use the boy. Where is Jackie? With her help, we can call the cops and say Adam went missing and get local help. Find Adam, find Ashley. Then spin the story about Ashley to our advantage."

Brice glared at Darren. "Jackie is gone because she didn't know her place or when to keep her mouth shut."

Darren sucked in a breath understanding what Brice meant.

"If you don't help me fix this and find Ashley, you'll be *gone*, too."

CHAPTER THIRTEEN

Trigger took a breath and a minute before he made the call to Deputy Mark Foster. This one call opened up the can of worms Ashley wanted to keep sealed. As much as he'd like to keep her and Adam hidden away here co-cooned in safety, he needed to stop the madman who wanted them back from getting close to them ever again. Trigger couldn't afford to hold on to hope that they had any more time before Brice started looking for them close to home or worse, went to the press and spun some story that ruined Ashley's life even more. He couldn't risk that bastard getting his hands on Adam. Trigger still didn't know if the boy had family looking for him or were unaware the boy was seemingly on his own with only Ashley and him as protector and caregiver.

He needed to call in the troops, but he didn't like it. Could he trust anyone? He assumed everyone was under Brice's thumb.

If he was honest, he didn't want the sheriff's depart-ment and possibly the FBI swooping in, taking over, and taking Ashley and Adam away from him. He didn't know how they managed it, but in a short time, he'd gotten used to them being here with him. The house didn't seem so big and empty anymore. A beautiful woman in his bed made him think of things he shouldn't. It got harder and harder to see Ashley as just a woman who needed help and not a woman he wanted.

After all she'd been through, she wasn't someone who needed or wanted something casual. If she wanted him at all. The way she looked at him sometimes . . . He shut that line of thinking down and ordered himself to get to work.

Trigger picked up his cell and dialed the number Sadie gave him.

"Who is this?" Deputy Foster demanded to know.

"You first," Trigger answered, wanting to be sure he got the right guy. Plus, he didn't much want to say who he was to the wrong person.

"This is a private number. I don't know you, or how you got this number, but—"

"Sadie Kendrick," Trigger interrupted.

"Then she gave you my number for a reason."

Trigger gave him a hint. "I'm the guy she saved during the drug bust that took down her brother Connor."

Silence. Then, "What do you want?"

Trigger had been arrested along with Connor during the takedown to make it look like he was one of the other drug traffickers. Appearances had to be maintained even if Connor's friends and the guys he took down thought he was really working undercover. The game had to be played. These days, Trigger hated the game, but he was damn good at playing it.

"I need to know if you're a guy who can be trusted."

"Sadie trusted me enough to give you my number even though I arrested her brother more than once and threatened to put her ass in jail along with him if she helped him again. Other than that, I can only give you my word that if you ask me to keep a lid on something I will, so long as it's this side of legal."

"Will you ride the line if it will keep someone safe and alive?"

"I will venture into the shadows, but if things get too shady I'll fall back on the book and play things straight."

Exactly what Trigger needed. An ally working the case. "Fair enough. Here's the deal. I'm not a drug dealer. I'm undercover DEA. Special Agent Beck Cooke. I need you to open a Jane Doe kidnap report. The woman has been held against her will for nearly a year. She's been repeatedly starved and tortured. I found her and a child who doesn't belong to her or the kidnapper. I want the boy kept quiet for now. I need to figure out who he is and how he's connected to the kidnapper. If he is at all."

"Where are they now?"

"Safe."

Deputy Foster would probably guess he had them at his place, but Trigger didn't want to say outright. Deputy Foster could read between the lines that Trigger wanted to keep some information confidential for now. Like not giving him Ashley's name.

"Does Jane Doe need medical attention?"

"Yes, but that can wait until the storm passes. I've got her and the boy squared away. I've got pictures of her and the boy's injuries." Trigger hated it, but he'd snapped a few photos of Adam while he slept. He didn't want to put the kid through the ordeal the way he'd done with Ashley. The less intrusive and probing he could be with Adam, the better for the kid to move forward and forget any of this ever happened. Ashley didn't have the luxury of being a four-year-old with a mind that would fade these memories until he either didn't remember at all, or the things he did remember felt like they'd happened to someone else.

"She will need X-rays to show her current and past cracked and broken bones for evidence. Later, we'll order her past medical records for comparison and corroboration that the injuries were sustained during her captivity." That word left a bitter taste in his mouth. He tried not to let the images of her condition now turn into a dark story in his mind that spun out of control with one scenario after another of what she'd been through.

"That bad, huh?"

"Worse." Broken bones healed. Mentally, Ashley would never be the same again. Even now, she slept, but her body shook with whatever nightmare plagued her. She mumbled and whimpered. Her pain and anguish twisted his gut. He wanted to pick her up off the damn floor, hold her in his arms, and find a way to make it all go away. He understood those dark dreams' effect on the mind, the way they lingered even when you woke, the way they tormented when you let your guard down and couldn't hold them off in sleep. The way they sapped your energy and will to do anything, like if you sat still long enough everything would finally stop. But it doesn't. Your mind won't rest and your body twists into a mass of tension that coils tighter, suffocating you.

"I'll need to talk to her, get all the facts so we can make an arrest."

"It's not that simple."

"Not simple as in high-profile suspect or victim?"

"Both."

"That explains Jane Doe, but we need to get this guy in custody before he hurts someone else or finds her and the child or skips on us."

"The storm is helping me with that. Now I need to set things up so we play this smart and things fall in her corner and not his."

"We can put her in protective custody."

"I want to avoid taking a woman from one prison to another. Right now, she's coping. I'm not sure how she'll deal once word gets out and the investigation heats up."

"What the hell do you want me to investigate?"

Trigger understood the deputy's frustration. He'd asked for help and tied Deputy Foster's hands at the same time.

"Open the case. Send me the case file. I'll fill it out and take her statement. We'll get it on record before this guy comes forward with his own version of events. And he will. I'll send back the report, then we'll move forward with you arresting him. This guy has the goods on some high-up people in power." Beck didn't think Brice targeted a sergeant in the sheriff's department. "Someone like that tries to shut you down I want to know about it."

"Shit. Okay. Give me your email."

Trigger rattled off the information.

Ashley screamed and startled herself awake. She sat bolt upright and stared right at him. The second her eyes locked with his, she relaxed and took a painful breath. He didn't want to read too much into her immediate relief at seeing him, but damn, the connection he tried to ignore flared in his chest. He gave her a nod to let her know everything was all right. He wanted to do a hell of a lot more than give her a look. His need to touch and comfort her nearly made him stand and go over to her. Instead, Adam jumped off the couch and went to her, sitting in her lap and hugging her close. Ashley held the little boy, though it probably cost her to have his weight on her bruised legs and leaning into her battered body.

"What the hell was that?" Deputy Foster asked, over-hearing Ashley's scream.

"Nothing." His deadpan response made it clear he had no intention of explaining. "I've got to go. Send the report. I'll get back to you, and we'll figure out the best way to move forward. And I mean it, keep this quiet." The longer he kept the secret, before the powers that be found out, the better.

"Beck."

He looked up at her beautiful face and still-haunted eyes. He held his finger to his lips to ensure she didn't say anything else.

"Holy fuck, is that Ashley Swan? I'd know that sultry voice anywhere."

Beck swore and glared at Ashley. People recognized more than her face. It was like hearing Anthony Hopkins, Liam Neeson, or Morgan Freeman. You just knew that voice.

"One word leaks out, I'll know who did it, and that person won't see the light of day again."

The deadly tone got through to Deputy Foster. "Dial down the threats, man. I'm on your side."

"I don't threaten people—I make promises. Now get to work. We need to move fast."

"On it."

Trigger hung up and stared at Ashley's confused eyes. "Who was that?"

"When I'm on the phone, you stay quiet. Unless you want the world to know you're alive and staying here."

"Did you tell someone?"

"No, you did with just my name."

Her eyes went wide and her hand covered her open mouth. "I have to go." She took one step back before he snagged her wrist and pulled her to a stop.

"Relax. He won't tell anyone. Deputy Foster is about to make a preemptive strike by opening a case file on you."

"With my name. It'll be out"—she looked at his phone, then back at him—"now."

"Can you do two things for me?"

"What?" Her voice trembled on that one word.

"Breathe. And trust me."

She sucked in a steadying breath, her eyes narrowed and filled with concern. "I'm trying."

"Hungry?" Trigger read more in her soft touch on his

arm than he did in her eyes. He released her wrist, not wanting to make her feel trapped. He definitely didn't want her to think anything else was going on.

But Ashley didn't let go of him. Instead, her gaze dipped to his arm and the tattoos weaving their way up under his sleeve to his shoulder. "This is really interesting." Her fingers smoothed over his skin. Electricity shot up his arm, making everything in him still. "The two sides of you."

Trigger glanced at the intricate tattoo with the sharp-edged green vine and single red rose in bloom with the skull in the center. "How so?"

"Lethal and fighting for life."

That got his attention. His heart beat faster. "I just thought it was cool."

She didn't believe him. "You thought the skull would warn people away. You like to do that."

"It keeps me, and them, alive."

"Yet you left one side of the leaves soft." She traced her finger over the rounded edge of one of the leaves on his forearm.

He tried not to tense at her touch, or feel the warmth spreading up his arm and into every cold, dark corner inside him, or acknowledge the way his heart beat faster with every brush of her skin against his.

"The other side is razor sharp. Another warning that if you get too close you'll get cut down. But the rose . . ."

Drawn in by that voice and her insight, he reluctantly asked, "What about it?"

"A red rose. A symbol of beauty and love."

"It blooms with death," he pointed out.

"You too often see the bad in what appears on the surface as benign. But you spend your life trying to erase the malevolent so beauty and love can bloom. You take death off the streets." She touched her finger to several of the leaves weaving up his arm. She tapped another wicked leaf. "As each new threat appears, you follow the path and take that one out. No matter how hard you try, that vine of death keeps spreading." She traced one stem until it came to a sharp end on his bicep. "It spreads until you cut it off." She held his gaze. "You'll keep hacking at it, knowing it will continue to grow and the best you can do is slow it down because others feed it and all you want to do is choke it." She spread her fingers wide over his forearm like the vine wrapped around him and squeezed.

"You see a hell of a lot in a simple tattoo." She saw too much on him and inside him.

"There's nothing simple about you. *Beck*." She emphasized his name, reminding him of how she'd repeated to herself, *I am Ashley*. A way to remember who she was at the core.

He had yet to dig deep enough to find Beck under Trigger's mound of shit.

"I see you, Beck. You can't hide from me beneath Trigger. He's a character you play, a defense against the world you infiltrate but don't belong to. The role has gotten harder to shed. You've played him so long he's become comfortable. Maybe it's easier to stay Trigger than be Beck. He's the bad guy who did all those things you can't reconcile. Beck's the good guy who suffers the consequences. You've lost touch with him while you punish yourself for whatever is eating you up inside."

Unable to go there, he denied, denied, denied. "You have no idea what you're talking about."

"You know I do, but you don't want to hear it." Her hand slid down his arm to his hand. She traced her fingers over the back and gripped it in hers. "You saved me, Beck. I'm just trying to repay you. You took this break, this time to get your head straight again, but how can you do that when every time you look in the mirror you see

Trigger." She tilted her head and stared right at him. "The best way to get into character for me is putting on the costume. The hair. The makeup. The clothes. I fall into the part. I look in the mirror and see the person I'm playing." She reached out and took some of his long hair between her fingertips. "You needed to play the part, so you transformed yourself into Trigger. Maybe if you transform yourself into Beck again, you'll remember that he's who you really are and you'll feel like him again."

He raked his fingers through his long hair. He really was tired of it. Sometimes he caught his reflection and wondered who the hell that thug was staring back at him.

"What do I know? I could barely remember my own name when you found me and I've made a living, won an Oscar, and saved my life pretending to be someone else."

She walked away.

Damn the woman for knowing exactly what to say and daring him to look long and hard at his life and decide if he wanted to continue to wallow in self-pity, regret, and recriminations for what he'd done, or remember why he'd done those things and that forgiving himself meant accepting responsibility and choosing to move on with his life.

He didn't need to decide what Trigger was going to do. He needed to figure out what he was going to do, because Beck was a DEA agent and the man he'd worked damn hard to be, pushing himself through school with top grades, applying to the DEA, making it through the rigorous training and qualifiers to become one of the best. He worked undercover because his superiors trusted him to do the job with integrity. He never meant for anyone to get hurt. He'd have given his life to save Paula.

Mistakes were made. Things happened beyond his control. He needed to stop thinking of all the bad that happened and remember he did important work. He made a difference hacking away at the drug distribution chain. He put bad people behind bars. He took dangerous drugs off the streets. He'd saved countless lives.

That mattered.

What he did mattered.

Who he was mattered.

Maybe he couldn't go back to working undercover. Not now. But that didn't mean he couldn't still make a difference in people's lives.

He'd made a difference in Ashley's. And Adam's.

He picked up his phone and got back to work. "Hey, it's Beck."

Ashley stared at him over the glass of milk she chugged. She pulled the glass away from her lips and smiled at him with an adorable milk mustache.

One side of his mouth cocked up in a half grin he couldn't stop. He nodded, giving her that small acknowledgment that she'd indeed nudged him enough to make a change in him, but not to gloat.

Caden, on the other hand, remained silent on the line, taken by surprise that he'd used his real name. Caden knew from caller ID that he'd called, but Beck wanted to let him know in this way that something was different now. Beck was different, because of the woman standing in his kitchen, wearing his T-shirt and way-too-big sweats, devouring yet another apple. She shouldn't look that damn sexy, but she did. He didn't know how she did it, or how she'd so easily worked her way under his skin, but damn the woman had really gotten to him.

"Hey, man, I've got a problem. I'm nearly out of clothes. Ashley looks ridiculous walking around holding up her pants so they don't drop to her ankles and trip her."

"Uh, are you okay?" Caden asked, surprised by Beck's teasing tone.

"I'm good." For the first time in a long time, he meant

that. The tension in his shoulders eased. The constricting band around his chest let loose. He breathed easier and actually felt comfortable in his skin. For the most part. The outside needed a little work. He'd get to it soon. "Snow's letting up. Forecast calls for clearer skies tomorrow. Where are you on getting the supplies I need?"

Since Caden and Mia lived closer to town, where the snowplows worked a hell of a lot faster than out here, and they got a lot less snow than he did, he hoped they'd been able to get some of the shopping done.

"I checked—the snowplows are out and clearing the roads and headed your way. We've got the truck packed and ready to go. Any last-minute things you need?"

"Were you able to get all the food, multivitamins, and supplements?" Beck had looked up everything he could about malnutrition and boosting your immune system. The last thing he wanted was for Adam and Ashley to get sick in their weakened conditions. While their energy levels increased with the sleep and food they'd gotten over the last two days, they still had a long way to go to good health. When he took them to a doctor, Beck would make sure to ask what else they needed. For now, he'd do his best to give them the best he could provide.

"Everything on your list, or as close to it as I could get."

Ashley stood over him, her brows drawn together. She mouthed, "Who is that?"

"Hold on, Caden." Beck held the phone away, his thumb over the microphone so Caden didn't hear them. "It's my brother. He's DEA, so he'll keep his mouth shut. He's bringing us supplies, including new clothes for you and Adam and more food, since you're eating me out of house and home," he teased.

She stuck her tongue out, then took another big bite of her apple.

"Is there anything you want?"

She tugged her pants up again before they fell down her hips. He could barely make out her shape under his too-big clothes draped over her thin frame. She scrunched her lips into a thoughtful pout. The hand holding the apple shook. "I can call my manager or my bank and get them to overnight me a new credit card. I can order what I need online." She glanced around the room, unease building in her fidgety body and worried eyes. "I can find us a place to stay. We'll need a car. I don't even know if I still have my place in L.A. What happened to all my stuff? Is everything just frozen in time?" Her whole body shook now. Her voice grew quiet and shaky. "You've done so much. We've stayed too long. I'll just . . ." Overwhelmed, she didn't know what to do.

Beck stood and wrapped her in his arms. "Shh. Stop. You don't have to do anything but tell me if there is anything you need right now. We'll figure out the rest soon."

She burrowed into his chest and held tight to the back of his shirt with one hand. She sighed so big he felt the warmth of her breath penetrate the cotton T and seep into his skin.

"I need to know what to do and how to make this right. I don't know what I'm supposed to do. I mean, there's no rules or guidelines to follow when someone steals a year of your life."

Beck held Ashley and put the phone back to his ear and told Caden, "Come as soon as you can. Bring what you have. If we need anything else, we'll get it later." He hung up, dropped the phone on the table, and encased Ashley in both his arms.

Beck leaned down and kissed the top of Ashley's head for no other reason than that he wanted to comfort her. "You don't have to do anything right now, except breathe. You want to control how this plays out. I get that. He took away your choices and forced you to bend to his will.

This investigation and making this right means others are going to make decisions that affect your life. It will take on a life of its own. You want to find your footing and take control of your life again, but you're going to have to fight for it. Let me handle the investigation part. You concentrate on getting healthy again. Take a breath, find your head, and think about what you want for your future.

"In the meantime, you can stay here as long as you want and as long as it's safe." Until he said it, he didn't realize how much he meant it. He didn't want her out of his sight until he knew 200 percent that she was safe. The longer she stood in his arms, the more right it felt, the more he didn't want to let her go. Dangerous territory. She didn't belong here. She had a life in L.A. Friends. Family.

The thought of someone waiting for her, missing her, wanting her back sent a bolt of jealousy through his gut, but he asked the hard question anyway. "Is there anyone you want to call? There must be a lot of worried people out there who want to hear from you."

She stepped out of his arms, anger flaring in her eyes. "Is there a missing person's report on me?"

"I'm not sure." He'd seen the reports on TV, but he hadn't seen a single cop asking for information about her disappearance.

"Has anyone been on TV or in other news holding up a picture of me with a number to call, asking for information on my whereabouts?"

"Uh, not that I've seen, but that doesn't mean—"

"Right. People don't think things apply to you when you're famous. There is no such thing as privacy and personal space. Nothing in your life is off-limits. People think you asked for it when someone does something to you that they'd never do to a normal person. They think they can insult me to my face and it doesn't bother me.

'You're so much prettier on-screen.' 'Is that really your voice? You sound so much better on TV.' 'I thought you'd be taller or thinner,' or 'I thought your boobs were bigger.'"

"Seriously?"

"They say all kinds of stupid things. They put you on lists. Best Dressed. Worst Dressed. Sexiest. Most Beautiful. Who wore it best? As if there isn't enough judgment in the world.

"Do you have any idea how hard it is to have a genuine friend? A guy who's interested in you and not who you can connect him to in the business or just wants to be seen with you to advance his own agenda?" She rolled her eyes.

He didn't want any part of that kind of life and understood she wanted to stay as far away from it as possible right now. "So you don't want to go back to L.A.?"

"Don't get me wrong, I love acting and making movies. Everything else, not so much. But you can't have your passion and not accept that all the rest comes with it. I have—had—a good team of people around me, but I am always aware they're paid to be there. Maybe I'm more aware of it because of the way I grew up having to fight for everything I wanted. My mother raised me on her own. She didn't have time or the desire to give me anything more than a roof over my head, food on the table, and the necessities of life. She lived her life. I lived mine. I wasn't abused or neglected, but I didn't get a lot of support either. I was expected to go to school and stay out of trouble. Anything else I wanted, I had to figure out a way to get it. My life wasn't good or bad, it just was, and that wasn't enough for me. The more I wanted, the more my mother resented that I didn't appreciate what she gave me. She was satisfied with her ordinary life. I wanted a big life. She didn't get that, until I achieved something she never thought I would. She expected me to fail like so many other dreamers do, but I worked hard. I didn't take the setbacks as defeat. I used those experiences to feed my ambition.

"The more success I achieved, the more she wanted to benefit from it. Our relationship was never warm, but I wanted it to be despite understanding she just didn't have it in her. But to watch it deteriorate to the point where I no longer felt like family but a means to an end . . ." Ashley frowned and shook her head. "With success, you gain so much, but you never expect to lose the things you do. It's very lonely at the top."

Beck sympathized and opened his mouth without thinking. "It's lonely undercover. To have success, you give up everything to become something else. The relationships you have are all superficial. You're using them. They're using you. In the end, you'll take down a guy who's been your friend, maybe even saved your ass, because he's breaking the law."

"I bet you never thought you'd have so much in common with someone like me."

In fact, he'd seen the reports on TV and thought some spoiled, self-centered movie star didn't deserve his consideration. He had more important things to think and care about than a woman who'd run away from her glamorous life. Ashley changed his mind. He appreciated her strength, determination, her thoughtfulness to consider him and see that he was hurting, too, when she had every reason to focus on herself and what she'd been through. For whatever reason, she'd gotten through to him when his family and coworkers hadn't made a dent in his determination to remain locked in his head, mired in his regret and guilt, and living alone in exile. The woman he'd found nearly dead had breathed new life into him.

He still had a ways to go in reconciling his past, but he actually felt better about his future. One where he moved forward and didn't stay mired in his nightmares. He could finally see the light.

"I'm glad you're here, Ashley. I needed you." Not an easy thing for him to admit, but he'd told so many lies, he liked that she forced him to own up to the truth.

"This from the guy who warned me away."

"Be careful," he warned her again, letting her in even more. "I'm having trouble thinking about letting you go."

CHAPTER FOURTEEN

Ashley stood in front of the window, the light shining on her face, her eyes closed, and breathed through her warring emotions. She fought the urge to hide so no one, especially Brice, saw her basking in the bright, white day, and tried to enjoy her freedom. Beck's warning that he might not be able to let her go initially set off a bolt of fear. But that quickly got swamped by the warmth that spread through her system and the thoughts of staying here with the intense man who surprised her with his honesty and depth of emotion when he tried to hide everything behind a wall of indifference. She saw past the facade to a man with a kind but battered heart. And a smile that made her belly flutter when he let one loose, which wasn't often enough.

She hadn't had anything to smile or laugh about in a long time, but she found herself daydreaming of a day when, held in Beck's arms, she smiled up at him and something made them laugh together. As much as she wanted that kind of joy back in her life, she wanted to see Beck happy, too.

If she got the chance.

She glanced back at the laptop on the table. Before Beck disappeared into his room, he'd sat her down, put his hand on her shoulder, and asked her in his gentle but firm way to tell her story. She tried to boil down what happened to the bare facts in the report, but the more she entered and filled in that empty space the angrier she got until she couldn't stand to think of it one more second. She felt the tick of an imaginary clock in her mind counting down to Brice coming after her and counting up the seconds Brice took up in her life.

She wanted this to be over.

But it was far from done.

As much as she wanted to run, Beck was right, she needed to stand and fight. To do that, she needed to find her feet again.

She wrapped her arms around her middle and stared out the window at the snowy landscape. Three months to Christmas. She'd missed spending the holiday with her friends, the dinners and cocktail parties held by friends in the business in gorgeously decorated Beverly Hills homes, and even the strained call with her mother they shared each year. She didn't miss the loneliness of spending Christmas morning alone trying to make herself believe she wanted the peace and quiet. She didn't even have a dog for company. She didn't want the responsibility or guilt for leaving it every time she had to go on location for work for long periods of time.

She missed her simple house with the beautiful view of the hills. She loved sitting in the backyard, the flowers blooming in the Southern California sunshine year-round. She'd drink her coffee or favorite tea and stare at the view soaking up the sun.

The dark clouds parted and a sliver of sunlight beamed through, bounced off the crystalline snow, and shined on her face. She closed her eyes and soaked up the warmth. Her heart lightened as some of the fear she'd felt trapped in the dark fell away.

A hand settled on her shoulder, pulling her back into that nightmare. She jumped and swatted the hand away.

Her back hit the glass as her hands came up to protect herself. She yelped, cutting off the scream that rose in her throat when she saw the man standing before her, familiar but different.

"Beck?" She stared in amazement at his transformation. He'd shaved the beard and cut his thick, long hair short along the sides and back, leaving it longer on top to fall back in a soft wave.

He slid his hand along his bare jaw and up along the side of his head. "It's been a while since my face saw the sun. The hair wasn't easy to cut with the clippers, but it's a hell of a lot better than having it falling in my face all the time."

She didn't know what to say. She'd never seen a more handsome, rugged man in her life. Those penetrating gray-blue eyes stared at her. At first she was tongue-tied, then words tumbled out her mouth before she thought of them. "You're gorgeous." So much so that her stomach fluttered and her fingers tingled with the desire to reach out and touch his strong jaw and slide through his thick, silky hair.

His eyes narrowed, then dipped, scanning down her face and body, all the way to her toes and back up leaving a trail of heat in their wake.

Beck reached out, took the side of her face in his big hand, and swept his thumb over her cheek. "If you keep looking at me like that, I'm going to have to—"

The alarm went off, buzzing incessantly, cutting off whatever Beck intended to say and her hope that he meant to kiss her. After all she'd been through, she couldn't believe her mind and heart reached out to Beck in that way, but she craved his touch and the sweetness and light it shined into her desperate heart. For a split second there, she'd felt like a real person again. A woman, not some possession.

Beck swore, gave her one long regret-filled look, then went to the coffee table, picked up the remote, shut off the alarm, and changed the channel to check the cameras.

Ashley gasped. The unfamiliar white truck made her heart thunder. "Someone's h-here." Her voice cracked, fear clogging her throat.

Adam bounded off the couch and ran to her, wrapping his little arms around her hips. She held him close, looking from the front door to the back for a means of escape.

Beck closed the distance between them in a few long strides. With Adam between them, he cupped her face and made her look up at him. "It's my brother. You're safe. Don't bolt." A trace of a plea sounded in his deep voice, despite the order in his eyes.

With his hands on her face, the warmth from his palms sinking into her skin, the total awareness she had of him this close, she couldn't do anything but fall further into the depths of his eyes that convinced her he'd protect her no matter what. The urge to run dissipated, but the frantic need to hide lingered in her gut.

The knock on the front door made her jump. Beck held on to her, leaned in with his cheek pressed to hers, and whispered in her ear. "No one will ever hurt you again and get away with it." His lips pressed to her temple in a soft kiss, then he let her go all at once, turned, and walked to open the door for his brother.

Beck held the door only wide enough for him to look out. A man's deep voice boomed with, "Holy shit, you finally cut your hair," then, "You look damn good, man." Relief laced those words from Beck's brother. He cared deeply about Beck. That eased her a bit more about meeting strangers.

Beck said something under his breath that sounded like, "Take it slow and easy," then opened the door and a near-duplicate version of himself walked in behind a golden-haired woman carrying a box filled with cup-cakes.

Adam buried his face in Ashley's leg and held her tight, hurting the bruises on her legs, but she held him close anyway and tried to breathe and soothe his fears at the same time.

The woman stopped in her tracks when she spotted them. "Oh my God, it's really you. I knew that, but you're here." She smiled nervously like a lot of fans did when they saw her in person. "I loved you in all your movies, but *Flame in the Night* is my absolute favorite. The love story between you and Duncan is so romantic."

Memories of the past year flashed through her mind. Bile rose up her throat and soured her mouth. She covered her lips with her fingers hoping she didn't throw up as every ounce of blood drained from her head down to her feet with a punch to the gut that stopped her breath and her thrashing heart.

"Ashley." Beck snapped out her name, drawing her attention and reminding her she wasn't Aurora. She didn't need to speak her lines for a madman, or anyone, anymore.

She found her breath again.

"This is my soon-to-be sister-in-law, Mia. Lord knows, we question her sanity for agreeing to marry Caden, but we're happy to have her join the family."

Mia held up her hand, showing off a huge diamond solitaire. The smile, love, and happiness on her face warmed Ashley's heart, but made her wonder if she'd ever feel that kind of love and joy in her own life. Her gaze slid to Beck. Their eyes locked and the connection she couldn't deny between them tugged against her chest, making her want to close the distance between them and tell him she got it. He didn't think he'd have that in his life either. But maybe that look he gave her meant *with her* it might be possible.

She wanted to cup that possibility in her hands, protect and hold on to it because everything seemed so out of control or lost to her and she wanted to have something, someone that made her feel good and hopeful again.

Ashley found her voice. "Congratulations."

"Thank you." Mia beamed, though at one look from Beck she dialed down the vibrant joy Ashley had a hard time feeling even a tenth of these days.

"I'm Caden." The big man gave her a nod. "Whatever you did to transform this one back into my brother, thanks."

She tilted her head and studied Beck's new look. Though his appearance changed, he was still the same handsome man she saw under the disguise, but seeing the darkness fade from his eyes had changed a lot about him. He seemed more open, less guarded with her. Maybe because she saw right past all the barriers and fronts he put up to keep people away.

"Sometimes the character you play takes over. All I did was what he did for me and remind him who he really is." She sucked in a steadying breath. "I'm Ashley." It still felt weird, but she tried to embrace her true self and not stay locked in a part she hated but played to stay alive. "It's nice to meet both of you. Thank you for picking up supplies for us. Once I've got my life back and squared away, I'll pay you back for everything."

"Already done," Caden said, nodding at Beck. "That's all the thanks I need." He openly stared at Beck. "This is the best I've seen you look in two years. More."

Beck gave Caden a dismissive half frown, but the shrug acknowledged Caden's words and the concern that went with them. Caden didn't mean the haircut and shave. He meant the ease that settled over Beck, though maybe not as comfortably as Beck hoped, but he'd get there.

She hoped she did, too.

Caden held up several large plastic bags. "We brought you both some new clothes and stuff."

Mia crouched and held the box of cupcakes out to show Adam. "I heard you like sweets. I made these for you, Adam. I'm a chef and love to bake. Want one?"

Adam glanced up at Ashley, looking for approval and assurance that it was okay to approach the newcomers.

She softly brushed her thumb over his cheek. "If you don't eat them, I will."

"Share," he said. One of the few words he'd spoken to her. He seemed to find it easier to open up to his idol, Beck.

"Now that sounds good."

Ashley took Adam's hand and walked him over to Mia. She hated how he hesitated the closer they got to the strangers. But she couldn't fault him when she discovered she'd slowed her own pace, keeping Caden in her sight. Beck kept his steady gaze on her. He didn't miss anything. She took a deep breath, let it out, and tried to relax so Adam could relax.

Adam stared down at the cupcakes with their thick white frosting.

Mia smiled softly, not moving an inch. "Do you like chocolate with vanilla frosting?" she asked Adam.

He looked up at Ashley.

She ran her hand over his head. "Do you, sweetheart?"

He nodded, but didn't reach for one.

Ashley took one of the fat cakes, peeled the wrapper down, and took a huge bite. She rolled her eyes back and said around the sweet confection, "Oh, that's good. You don't want to miss out on that, sweetheart."

Adam eyed Mia one last time, then grabbed a cupcake. He took three steps back and licked the frosting. That one sweet taste was all it took for him to stuff half the cake in his mouth without peeling the paper.

Mia laughed. "Slow down. You can have as many as you want."

Adam's eyes went wide. He chewed and glanced at Beck to be sure he could indeed have more.

"It's your lucky day, little man." Beck gave Adam a nod to let him know he wouldn't get scolded or worse for taking the cake.

Adam went to him, leaned against his thigh, stared way up at Caden, and pointed his finger at him. "Good guy?"

Caden handed off the bags he held to Beck and crouched in front of Adam. He pulled his wallet from his back pocket and held it up to Adam, showing Adam his badge and credentials. "I'm a good guy, just like Beck."

"I don't want him to do it again."

Caden narrowed his gaze on Adam. "Do what again?"

Adam ran back to Ashley and buried his face in her belly. She held him close with one hand at the back of his head and brushed her fingers through his bright hair to comfort him. Beck's, Caden's, and Mia's gazes all went to her.

She met Beck's hard stare. "He can't find us." She didn't have to say anything more. If Brice found them, he'd kill them.

Caden stood and planted his hands on his hips. "The roads are icy but clear. A few more storm systems will move through over the next few days, but nothing like the last storm. We need to move forward on this."

Ashley held up her hand to stop him.

She glanced down at Adam and brushed her hand through his hair. "Want to watch TV and finish that yummy cupcake?"

He nodded and took another bite of the treat. While he licked his lips, most of the frosting remained smeared on his mouth. And her shirt.

"Looks like you need a change of clothes," Mia pointed out. She traded the box of cupcakes for the bags in Beck's hand. "It's not designer, but it will fit a hell of a lot better than the giant's clothes." She cocked her head toward Beck.

Ashley used to love trying on new clothes, experimenting with different styles, and transforming into yet another character. Now Beck's oversized clothes felt like armor. Or just a comfy way to hide the evidence of her ravaged body. She hated to admit how much she used to relish her lithe frame with just enough curve to draw attention. She prided herself on being sexy, but not audacious. Classic, romantic with a hint of flirtation in the fashion she loved.

She checked on Adam sitting on the sofa, watching TV, and devouring his cupcake. Beck and Caden watched her. She didn't mind Beck's intense gaze. She'd grown used to it and the warmth and tingle it sent through her. She'd recognize that ripple of awareness the rest of her life and miss it when this thing blew up and she had to leave here or subject Beck, her very private rescuer, to her very public life.

"Ashley."

Drawn back to Beck, she stared at him, wondering if he or anyone understood how something as simple as new clothes paralyzed her. She could almost feel Brice here, waiting for her to comply, to be his vision in whatever costume he chose. She wanted to tear off all her clothes and stand in her own skin. Naked, she was just Ashley. No polish. No covering up who she was from the inside out. No way to pretend she was someone else.

Beck walked over, took the bags of clothes from Mia, took Ashley's hand, and gently drew her with him to his bedroom. Inside, he shut the door, released her shaking hand, and went to the bed. He upended the plastic bags

on the bedspread, dumping pants, shirts, packs of socks
and underwear, and a couple bras that got tangled around
a sweater. Beck sorted out the jumble of clothes and laid
them out so she could see everything.

"What do you want to wear?"

She stared at him completely at a loss.

"Mia picked out things in the colors you like," he
pointed out.

The long-sleeved tunic-length shirts in raspberry, dark
purple, and a pretty sky blue were indeed some of the
colors she favored. The cream sweater looked soft and
warm. The leggings and jeans would be comfortable. She
had a thing for cable-knit socks.

"Pick something," Beck coaxed. "These are your
clothes, Ashley. You decide what outfit suits you today."

"What do you like?"

"You. I don't care what you wear."

Tears stung her eyes. "How do you know exactly what
to say?"

"The truth is simple."

And a bit complicated due to their circumstances. She
couldn't deny the attraction between them. Beck didn't,
in his way. But neither of them was in a good place. Two
broken people coming together didn't make a whole.

She tore open the plastic-wrapped bikini panties and
chose the white with pink roses and satin trim. She added
the pretty pink lace-trimmed bra to her hand, hoping it fit
and didn't hurt her ribs too badly. Opting for comfort and
the potential for the best fit, she chose the black leggings
with the raspberry top.

Beck tore the plastic ties off the pack of socks and
handed her one of the white-and-black-speckled pairs.

"Come out when you're done. They brought you some
shoes, a few more sweaters, and a coat." He turned to
walk out and give her some privacy to change, but stopped

short and turned back. He stared at her with her hands clutching the clothes she picked out to wear. He took two steps to her, reached up and took her face in his palms, and kissed her on the forehead. She leaned into him, savoring the feel of his warm lips on her skin, the softness of his touch on her face, the steady presence of him in front of her. "It might not ever go away, but it will get easier." He kissed her forehead again, then released her. He headed for the door, saying, "I'll get Adam dressed in his clothes, then we'll need to come up with a plan for what to do next."

He closed the door and she dropped onto the edge of the bed, wondering how he did this to her. One minute he made her feel present and in the moment and she fell under his spell of protection, the next he asked her to face her past and future. If she could, she'd freeze time and spend an eternity standing in Beck's sweet embrace, his lips against her skin, his warmth wrapped around her, and the feeling of being truly cared for filling her heart and every dark corner in her soul.

Ashley went into the bathroom, set the clothes on the counter, stripped, and dressed, trying not to make a big deal out of something so stupid and simple. But the panties that hugged her bottom and stretched across her hip bones leaving a small gap between the band and her too-thin belly startled her. The bra, one size and cup smaller than she normally wore, sagged a bit against the top of her breasts even after she adjusted the straps. She reminded herself she'd fill out once she got a few more good meals.

The leggings hugged her legs and hips even if the waistband remained a bit loose. The tunic hung down her torso, showing off her bony structure. The bright color highlighted her pallor, hollow cheeks, and dull eyes.

"You just need some food, vitamins, and some more sun." She silently scolded herself in the mirror for being so petty and superficial. She enjoyed wearing clothes that fit better and made her feel a little more like herself. She pulled on the socks, wiggling her toes in the soft material and the warmth that enveloped her cold feet.

"Ashley," Mia called through the mostly closed bathroom door. "Did you find something that fit? Can I get you something else to try on?"

Ashley brushed her hand through her hair, sucked it up, and let go her worries about how she looked to herself and what she'd look like to others. She opened the bathroom door to the woman who'd gone out of her way—at the tail end of a massive storm—to help Ashley.

Mia smiled softly, standing back to give Ashley some space. "Oh, you look great. It's probably not what you're used to wearing, but I hope it will do for now."

Ashley smoothed her hand over the pretty shirt. "Thank you. The clothes are great. All my favorite colors."

"Well, there are so many pictures of you. It wasn't hard to figure out what you might like. The sizes were my best guess and Beck's suggestions based on your height and approximate weight."

"I'm approximately half my size," she tried to tease.

Mia smiled, helping ease Ashley's nerves a bit more. "They're a little big on you, but a few more cupcakes will take care of that."

"I appreciate your thoughtfulness for the clothes and for making Adam's day. He's been through so much."

"You've been through a hell of a lot more," Mia pointed out. "If I can help you feel better, even in a small way with the clothes and supplies we brought you, then please, let me know if there is anything else you need."

Ashley stared past Mia and out the huge windows,

feeling the walls closing in on her again. "I want to go outside, but I'm afraid to leave this place."

Mia put her hand on Ashley's shoulder. "I know how you feel. After Caden and I were kidnapped and we got away, I had so many bad days where I had to force myself to leave the house."

Ashley's gaze zipped from the snowy landscape outside to Mia's face and the pained look in her eyes. "What? You were kidnapped?"

"By a drug dealer who wanted revenge and tried to use Caden to find out Trigger's true identity."

"Good lord." Ashley had some idea about the dangers Beck faced on the job, but to have someone come after your family to get to you. She understood even better how that would tear Beck apart and the guilt he must carry because of it.

"We got away. I'm alive because Beck helped save me. I've seen him falling faster and deeper into this dark place where even Caden and their sister, Alina, can't reach him. Somehow, you did. I can't tell you how relieved and hopeful you've made Caden. He's been really worried about Beck. So thank you for giving Caden and me some peace of mind." Mia gave her a playful grin. "I never thought I'd see him without that long hair and beard. I knew he was as handsome as Caden, but damn he's gorgeous all cleaned up, right?"

Ashley couldn't help the smile or the lightening in her heart. She missed this. Girl talk. Connecting with someone, talking about men and clothes and just having fun. "He doesn't even know it."

"He spends his life trying to look and act tough, but he's got such a good and big heart."

"He's been very kind and patient and steady."

"He won't let anything happen to you or Adam. He

and Caden are working on the best way to handle this and keep you and Adam safe."

"I don't know if anyone can keep us safe."

"If anyone can, it's Beck."

Ashley didn't need Mia's assurance. Beck was that kind of guy. If he made a promise, he kept it.

Ashley followed Mia out into the living room and stopped short when she spotted Beck and Caden leaning over the laptop reading her account of what happened in the early days she'd been held by Brice.

"We're going for a walk," Mia announced.

Beck and Caden both jumped and turned to face them. The sorrow and anguish in their eyes tore at Ashley's heart.

Mia pulled the tag off a brand-new thick black coat. She handed her the jacket along with a pair of black boots. Ashley didn't take her eyes off the two men staring at her, knowing exactly how she woke up one day and realized that she was well and truly trapped. She wrote down the how, but in their eyes she saw the understanding of how desperate she'd felt and the endurance and will it had taken to get through all of Brice's punishments. They'd seen too much in their work not to see in her all she didn't capture in that report.

CHAPTER FIFTEEN

Beck's stomach soured with every gut-wrenching sentence he read in Ashley's account of what that bastard put her through. She had a way with words. Direct. To the point. The facts in brutal honesty.

I woke up alone, swallowed by a darkness I couldn't escape in an empty cell with no windows. Nothing but the terror eating away at me as I struggled to understand how my friend turned into my captor. I tried to convince myself it was a misunderstanding, a mistake. He'd let me go. Hours I spent trying to convince myself he'd never hurt me. He wouldn't leave me here alone and terrified. Those hours turned to days and even my worst nightmares about what he might do to me didn't come close to the horrors I faced when that door opened again. The light poured in and revealed the evil that overtook my friend and turned him into the monster in my living nightmare. He beat me with a purpose. To cause pain. To make me understand that without my compliance in his twisted game I would endure more pain, more punishment, more humiliation than any person, animal, or thing should endure. He transformed me from one to the next until I felt nothing and became his possession to do with as he pleased. And it pleased him to torture me with his fists, with starvation, by withholding basic sanitary and biological needs, with his indifference, with devotion

*distorted by love that was nothing more than delusion
and executed with exacting precision to create an illusion
that broke me down to the point I knew giving in meant
my death and I welcomed it.*

If she ever took the stand against Brice, he wouldn't
stand a chance. No way a judge or jury heard her account
and didn't think that Brice deserved the maximum punishment for all his many twisted sins.

He'd like to get his hands on the bastard.

Brought out of his dark thoughts by Mia's statement,
he stared at Ashley as she mechanically put the jacket
and boots on. She intended to leave the house and go for
a walk. He understood how his place must feel claustro-
phobic after all she'd been through, but the hesitation in
her movements, the way her gaze darted to the windows,
and her teeth gnashed her bottom lip, he didn't think she'd
get far before her nerves got the better of her and she ran
back to the relative safety she'd found here.

He didn't want to think too hard about how it made
him feel to know she wanted to stay here. He hoped with
him, but understood most of her need to do so was a protection mechanism. No one would look for her here. He
hoped. But knew inevitably Brice would come looking
for her. It was only a matter of time, because the man
Ashley described in her report needed his possession
back. Without her, he'd never feel whole. He'd never feel
anything. And the evil inside him needed to be fed or
it would destroy Brice. And Brice would do anything to
keep that evil happy so he could endure and feel alive.

If they were going for a walk, he'd tail them and make
sure they remained safe. He stood but sat back at the table
when Mia shook her head and warned him off with a
narrow-eyed look.

She walked to Caden and held out her hand. Caden
pulled the gun from the holster at his side and handed

it to her. She tucked it down the front of her jeans and pulled her jacket closed, but didn't zip it, ensuring she could get to the gun in a hurry if she needed it. Caden had trained her well after the trouble they faced hardly more than a month ago. Mia didn't like guns, but Caden insisted she learn to respect and use one in case she ever needed it again. In their line of work, threats against them and their families were expected and sometimes carried out with dire outcomes. As Mia and Caden almost found out before Beck ended that threat with a bullet.

"We'll be back soon." Mia stood with her back to Ashley and pointed to the kitchen, sweeping her finger in an arc to the back of the house and around the property to indicate the route they'd take. Just in case.

All the bells and whistles went off in his mind and gut. He wanted to keep Ashley close and safe. He couldn't do that if she was out of his sight.

Mia read his unease. "She needs this, Beck. I got it covered."

Which meant Mia was prepared to do whatever was necessary to keep them both safe.

Beck still needed Ashley's go-ahead. "Do you want me to come with you?" He wanted her to know he'd take her out if she needed to go and stay by her side if she needed that, too.

The indecision showed in her eyes and the way she opened her mouth to answer, closed it, then said, "We'll be okay."

"I want to come," Adam said from the sofa. He looked so cute in his new jeans and blue monster truck T-shirt.

Ashley hesitated and so did Mia.

"I need your help, little man. We need to put together this puzzle Mia brought for you."

Adam glanced back and forth from him to Ashley and back.

"How about after my walk we go down to the stables and see Beck's horses?"

Adam's huge smile was all the answer Ashley needed before she turned and rushed out the front door like if she didn't do it now, she wouldn't be able to do it at all.

Beck stared at the closed front door and fought the urge to go after her.

"I see why you're attracted to her," Caden commented. "Every man on the planet probably is, but Beck, after all she's been through, getting involved the way you are, it's not going to end the way you want. She'll get through this and go back to Hollywood and make movies and get back to her glamorous and very *public* life. Your life depends on you staying deep undercover and off the radar."

"What if that's not the life I want to live anymore?"

"Can you live without the action, the danger, the adrenaline rush you've been chasing from the military to the DEA?"

Instead of answering, Beck asked, "How is life with Mia?"

"Great. I'm happier than I've ever been."

"What if instead of an adrenaline rush I wanted a steady dose of happy in my life?"

"If the DEA isn't what you want anymore, I support you a hundred percent. You'll save me several hundred gray hairs."

Beck didn't want to play pretend undercover anymore, but he still felt the pull of duty and desire to help others just as strongly as he ever did. "I'm thinking the DEA can use my expertise and skills in another way."

"If you'd use your knowledge to train the up-and-coming guys for undercover work, your knowledge and uncanny instinct would be invaluable to them. You'd make a great team leader. Your tactical expertise alone would save lives in countless ways on both sides. You know how those guys think, the extremes they'll go to to escape arrest. At this point, the DEA will practically let you write your job description. You know that. You've known that for a long time, but you never wanted to come in. You thrived being in the game."

"The game is kicking my ass and messing up my head. I want to have a life and a family before I'm too old or dead to do it."

Caden smiled. "You like her that much."

"She's so much more than I ever thought when I saw her in a movie. That's just one side of her. I like all the others a hell of a lot more than just the image she plays on-screen. I didn't expect this, her, to hit me the way they did. She's the first woman in a long time who made me think more about her than myself."

"Well, that's something, especially with all you're going through right now."

"Exactly. I don't want to pass up a chance that could mean something in my life because the timing sucks and it's hard. Maybe it turns out to be nothing. But maybe it's something."

"I think sometimes about the two times I stood up Mia and what I'd have missed in my life if she hadn't agreed to, and I hadn't shown up, that third time for our date."

"It was a hell of a first date."

"Don't remind me. The point is, if you want her, if you want this to work out, show up, Beck. Don't let the past hold on to you so much so that you aren't here right now."

"I am here, man. She cut right through all the bullshit I've been shrouded in and found me. Maybe that sounds stupid."

"No. It doesn't. I've been trying to find the brother you buried for a long time."

"I still have a lot of shit to deal with and resolve, but for the first time I can look at it without reliving it or feeling like I'll never feel anything but how I felt in those dark moments."

"Let them go, Beck."

"Maybe I'm . . . no, I am hoping for more than I deserve or she's capable of right now, but for a chance with her, I'd put it all away and try to be the man she deserves."

"Beck, man, I don't know what to say to that. What she's facing . . . it's a lot to deal with. You don't even know if she feels the same way about you."

"I know she does. What I don't know is if she feels it for me, or just because of all she's been through I'm a lifeline and a safe place to hide."

"I can see why she'd think that. You're a cop. You can protect her."

"She needs that, but I think it's more."

"I hope it is." The worry lines across Caden's forehead deepened with the concern in his eyes.

Adam crawled up into Beck's lap with the puzzle box. "Is she coming back?"

Beck kissed Adam on the head and held him close. "Yes, little man. She'll be back soon." He missed her already, too.

"Mom isn't coming back."

Beck met Caden's intense gaze. Unspoken questions bounced back and forth between them. They were both wondering the same thing. What happened to Adam's mom?

"Are you sure?" Beck held his breath, hoping Adam knew something about his mother and that what he thought happened to her wasn't the truth.

Adam didn't answer, just dumped out the puzzle pieces on the table in front of them. He handed a corner piece to Caden.

"Tomorrow." That's all Caden had to say to tell Beck that with the end of the storm came the end of their secrecy—they would have to reveal that Ashley hadn't given up her celebrity life and gone into hiding away from the public eye all this time. They needed to move forward and arrest Brice before he had a chance to make a move on them.

CHAPTER SIXTEEN

Brice and Darren drove the snowmobiles into the court-yard between the large ranch house and one of the many barns on the huge property that bordered his. Snow piled on the roof in a thick blanket to match the layer on the steps leading up to the door. Brice surveyed the surrounding land, the tracks leading from a back door and across the yard to the barn, tire tracks leading from the barn to the hilly pasture where black cattle huddled together, their backs coated in a thin layer of ice as they fed from two racks holding hay and grass.

The two men tending the herd hopped in the truck and headed back down to meet him and Darren.

Only a single light showed in the house. No drapes or shadows shifted. He didn't see anyone peeking out a window. He didn't see Ashley or Adam. He didn't feel her here, but had to tamp down his frustration and anxiety. He needed to be sure.

The truck pulled up and both men got out, eyeing them. Brice took off his helmet and raked his fingers through his hair.

"Well shit, look who we have here. I never expected to see the likes of you in these parts." The driver smiled, recognition dawning easily in his eyes.

Brice was used to everyone knowing him on sight. It got old, but in this case he hoped it worked to his advantage. He went with the same good ol' boy neighborly charm. "I hope you don't mind my stopping by unannounced. My property borders yours."

"I thought that big ol' house belonged to some celebrity."

Brice smiled and nodded. "It's mine, but let's keep that between us."

Both men grinned and nodded, their eyes narrowed with understanding that they'd been let in on the secret.

The other man stepped forward, his hand extended, "Joe Gordon. This is my place."

Brice shook the man's hand. "Brice Mooney, but I guess you knew that."

"What can I do for you, Mr. Mooney?"

"Oh, just call me Brice. All my friends do."

Joe stood a bit taller, thinking Brice had let him in the inner circle, letting him call him by his first name and in on the secret that he lived next door.

"I'm hoping you can help me out. Have you seen a young woman with dark hair and a boy with light blond hair last night or this morning?"

"What were they driving?"

"I'm embarrassed to say the lady and I argued and she ran off with the boy. I'm terribly worried about them."

"You think they ran off on foot in this weather?" Joe glanced around at the deep snow covering everything for miles. His heavy sigh came out in a cloud of white that quickly disappeared on the persistent wind that seemed to suck the heat right out of Brice's face. If not for his thick coat and gloves, he'd be a frozen Popsicle by now.

He didn't want to think about Ashley, cold and lonely and missing him out in the frigid temps and frozen landscape.

"My hope is that she found a kind rescuer and they took her and the boy in for the night while she calmed down and thought better of doing something so foolish.

Petty arguments always seem less important after one calms down."

Joe and the driver nodded.

"I hate to think her impulsive act has caused her any harm."

"I'm sorry to say we've had no visitors. My wife and two little ones are up at the house, a couple of the other guys are staying out at the bunkhouse farther on the property. I spoke with them both a little while ago. They had a quiet night and didn't report seeing anyone. I can give them a call to be sure if you like."

Brice knew they'd have said something if they found Ashley. No way they kept their mouths shut about finding her.

"As you said, they'd have said something if they saw them. I'm not even sure she came this way."

Darren handed over his card. "If you see them, or hear anything about them, please give us a call."

"Have you contacted the authorities? They can help you search." Joe's mouth drew into a grim line. "If they were out in the weather last night and this morning . . ." He shook his head in dismay, knowing they would never have made it.

"I don't believe things are that dire," Brice assured him, though it wasn't easy to pull off the unconcerned tone. "My guess is we'll find her safe and sound in a cozy warm motel drinking hot chocolate." He hoped that pretty little picture eased Joe's and the driver's mind. He walked a fine line trying to find her and not get caught up in an all-out search and rescue with the cops where he'd have to answer questions that were no one's business.

Joe held up Darren's card. "I hope you do. We'll keep a lookout for her and the boy as we check on the cattle and property today."

"I thank you kindly," Brice said, giving the men a

bright smile like he didn't have a care in the world. They didn't have her. They didn't know anything. They were of no use to him now.

He pulled his helmet on, seated himself on the snow-mobile, started the engine, and with a friendly wave drove back down the mostly plowed driveway.

He stopped near the road, out of sight of the ranch house and the two men they left behind.

Darren stopped beside him and flipped up his helmet visor. "She's not there." His words echoed Brice's thoughts.

"We'll check the other neighbor, then we'll need to alert the authorities and follow through with tracking down the boy to get to her."

"I think that may be the only way to find her." Darren's eyes filled with a gleam of mischief. "Asking the judge to declare you Adam's legal guardian was a stroke of genius."

Brice hadn't asked. He'd ordered the judge to do his bidding, knowing the judge had to comply or risk his job and reputation if the pictures of him with an underage prostitute snorting coke off her nipple were *leaked* to the press. Now Brice had the legal authority to claim Adam as his responsibility and find him and get him back. Which meant he'd draw Ashley out and right back to him.

CHAPTER SEVENTEEN

Ashley stood on the porch under the overhang wanting to step down the stairs and explore the beautiful property, but fear gripped her whole body like a vise and froze her in place. Mia stood beside her. She didn't move, just stared out at the yard like she had all the time in the world and had no intention of going anywhere. Her attention to every little sound and sight eased Ashley enough to make her take that first step to real freedom.

She stepped down the first tread, then the next, and all the way down to the path Beck must have shoveled clear while she'd taken a shower this morning. She stood in the cold and sun, her face raised to the sky more blue than gray clouds now. She stared at the massive expanse, sucked in a lungful of crisp air, and just breathed.

This was the first time she truly felt free.

"How long's it been since you were outside?" Mia's gentle tone coaxed her to open up.

The account she typed into Beck's computer took everything she had to put into words how devastating her experience had been, but talking to Mia about the more mundane things that took their toll on her seemed easier and harder at the same time.

"A long time." She breathed through the pain that admission caused her. So many simple things taken away from her. "He mostly only let me out at night. I have a feeling he had people at the house, the cleaning people, gardeners, others tending to the horses and cattle during the day. I never saw anyone after he made me disappear, except for the people he wanted me to see from the secret passageways. But I know the workers were there because of the fresh-cut flowers and the beautiful meals laid out on the table."

"Meals you never got to eat," Mia guessed, nodding toward Ashley's stick legs.

"Sometimes. But I had to earn it. And even then, I barely got a few bites down before he took it away or dragged me back upstairs for . . ." She couldn't choke out the words. The humiliation and punishment he subjected her to tasted bitter and vile, turning her stomach.

"Did Beck tell you Caden stood me up twice for our first date?"

Ashley appreciated the change of subject. Mia started down the path, her gaze straight ahead as she went on, expecting Ashley to follow. She did, because she wanted to know . . . "Why did you give him another chance after that?"

Mia glanced over, a sweet grin tugging at her lips. "Our aunts are a couple."

"That complicates things, I guess." Ashley knew many gay couples, but her friends Sophia and Lara made her jealous. Their connection and love so deep, you couldn't help but acknowledge how special and rare it was for others. She'd wanted something that extraordinary in her life, so deep and true, she couldn't live without it, or the man who gave her that kind of peace, connection, and love.

The familiar tingle danced over her skin. She turned to the house and spotted the outline of Beck standing in the window watching over her, sending a wave of warmth through her heart.

She warned it to stop hoping for impossible things.

"The aunts begged me to understand Caden's work sometimes took over his life and it really wasn't his fault. They conspired to get us together, but even they were exasperated with Caden's deplorable behavior. He made up for it though. Even though the date ended with our kidnapping and Beck almost shooting me, then shooting a drug dealer dead—it started off so good."

Ashley couldn't help the smile that came with Mia's soft giggle.

Mia gave her all the details from dinner to disaster, including Beck's heroic sniper shots that helped Caden save Mia's life. "We haven't spent a day apart since."

Ashley struggled to trudge through the deep snow. "And he asked you to marry him within weeks?"

"He asked me to move in and gave me the ring to let me know that it didn't matter when I said yes or we got married, but our being together was forever no matter what."

"You don't need a ring and a piece of paper to tell you that," Ashley agreed.

"Which is why I didn't care what anyone thought about how fast or slow we took things. As long as I have him, I have everything. After what I went through with him, almost dying, I didn't want to waste a single day. Not when I knew in my heart I loved him, he loved me, and that's all that mattered."

Ashley felt that way, too. She'd lost so many days. She tried not to think of all Brice cost her. It wasn't the movie roles she missed, the covers she didn't grace. What if she missed meeting the love of her life? What if she died and never knew that kind of love, or never had a child of her own? She had that chance now.

She'd spent the last five years working nonstop. She had her own home, money saved up, a few good friends, her mother for the most part, and not much else going on in her life. She loved her work, but in the end was the legacy she wanted to leave behind her image on-screen or the family she wanted more than anything?

"You're quiet." Mia stood beside her.

Ashley hadn't realized she'd stopped trudging through the deep snow and lost herself in thought in front of a winding creek. The water cascaded over rocks and swished around the next bend. Bare-limbed trees, heavy with snow, hung over the water and concealed them in this slice of pristine Montana paradise.

"It's like we stepped into a photograph."

"Beck found a great place to escape."

"He's hurting." *Just like me.*

"He's tired and disillusioned and sad and angry and feeling guilty for things that were out of his control and not his fault." Mia sighed. "You know how he feels, don't you?"

"More than you know." She thought of how they'd played a part and forgotten who they were and what they wanted. "I feel like I'm still waking up from that nightmare. Part of me is still in it while the other part is struggling to come to terms with my new reality. I'm not the woman I used to be. I'm not the woman he made me be. I don't know the woman I am right now, but I know I want him to pay, and I want something better for my future. I deserve that."

"Yes, you do. So do the first, so you can have the second."

Damn straight. "How did you get past it?"

"I was kidnapped and terrorized for one day. I have no idea how you survived for nearly a year. The second attack lasted about five minutes and felt empowering because I took the guy down with a pot and saved Caden."

"Really?"

Mia nodded. "The threat is real, but I'm not giving up what I have with Caden for anything."

Mia tilted her head. "It took great strength to overcome my fear. You'll need that now. I had Caden to see me through the rough days."

"Beck has been amazing," she admitted. His steady presence and direct manner pushed her to move past the fear and face what came next. "I guess I'll have to find some of that strength to face what comes next on my own."

"Oh, you won't be alone. Beck's in this with you now. He won't stop until the man who hurt you is dead or behind bars. You can count on that."

"I can't ask him to do that."

Mia smiled. "You don't have to ask him. But you already know that. Let me tell you the one thing I know for sure about the Cooke brothers. They don't fall easy, but when they do it's hard and fast. The way Beck looks at you"—Mia pressed her lips together and nodded—"it's the same way Caden looks at me. He's all in."

Ashley didn't know what to say to that. The thought both thrilled and scared her.

Mia stared at the vast landscape spread before them. "You found the perfect place to escape to."

"What do you mean?"

"Beck named this place Hope Ranch. When all else is lost, hope endures, just like this land."

Ashley didn't know what to say, but the name fit.

"Come on—he's probably prowling the house waiting for us."

Ashley took one more look around the pretty creek, then sucked in a surprised gasp.

"What is it?" Mia pulled the gun and expertly held

it in both hands sweeping the area, ready to face any threat.

"Nothing. No one is here. It's me. I'm sorry to scare you. It's just this place reminds me of something." Her perfect escape by the river in her mind. Where her hope for survival and finding something better endured.

Mia let her hand fall to her side, the gun bouncing against her thigh. She let out a relieved sigh. "Oh. Sorry. I guess I'm a little jumpy."

"All the more reason to stop stalling and do what needs to be done." Ashley gave one last, forlorn look at the creek that looked so much like the special place she'd dreamed up in her head to escape to when things got really bad.

She walked back to the house with Mia in the lead. Fatigued by the hike through the snow, her thigh muscles ached, but it felt like progress. She needed to build her physical strength back. She hoped she had the mental strength to get through what came next.

A surge of relief, a flutter of awareness, the pull she fought but wanted to give in to, and a sense of determination swept through her all at once when they came into view of the house and there stood Beck on the porch waiting for them. Reassuring and scary at the same time.

Mia easily made it to the house and up the stairs, smiling at Beck as she passed him and went into the house, closing the door and leaving them alone as Ashley approached at a much-slower pace.

Beck walked down the steps and met her on the shoveled path. "Tired?"

"Sore. Tired. Frustrated. Ready to move on, but stuck in some ways. But I'm good."

One side of his mouth cocked back in a half grin. "Sounds about right." He got it.

She liked that she didn't have to explain the complex

and convoluted emotions she didn't quite get herself but made sense nonetheless in a way.

She didn't know what possessed her to say it, probably the way Beck looked at her with that intense stare that saw everything and didn't judge, but she blurted out, "Caden really loves Mia."

Beck's head tilted and his eyes softened and filled with understanding. "Yes, he does. He's a lucky man. They're lucky to have each other." Those words told her so much more than what he said out loud.

"Are you ready?"

She meant a hell of a lot more than taking the next step to put Brice behind bars and letting everyone know she was alive and a survivor, not a runaway movie star. Beck had been through a lot, had spent the last many weeks hiding out here, trying to figure out his life. Neither of them were coming into this thing from a good place.

His sharp, intent gaze never left hers. "I don't think anyone is ever ready for something like this." He held his hand out to her.

She took it and walked into his arms. She stared up at him. With his face inches from hers, she saw the flecks of light and dark blue in the gray of his eyes and the redness in his cold cheeks, and smelled the coffee on his breath. Their bodies pressed together, heat and need rushing through her system.

"Despite the dangers we face, yes. I want this thing we both feel."

They had a hell of a lot to overcome. Brice. The drug cartel after him that also put her in more danger. But like him, she felt it was worth it to have something good come out of all this bad.

"If you want *me*, Ashley, not the star, not some character I've played, I'm in."

"None of that matters. I want *you*."

With those heartfelt words, he lowered his mouth to hers. She lost herself in the sweet, soft kiss that didn't demand, but lingered, warming her from the inside out, telling her he wanted her, but more, he wanted her to want him.

With her whole scarred and battered heart, she did.

CHAPTER EIGHTEEN

Beck tried to go slow, ease her into his arms, the kiss he desperately wanted, and his life, but one touch of her lips to his and he wanted to sink in and devour her. Her initial sense of testing the waters melted away with the heat neither of them expected. The tip of her tongue tasted his bottom lip and set him off. He dove in for more, sweeping his tongue along hers. Tempting and sweet, it left him wanting more, but a second before Caden opened the front door he heard the alarm blare.

He broke the kiss and held a dazed Ashley away from him. "We're not done." He took her hand and pulled her up the stairs behind him.

"Two men at the gate on snowmobiles," Caden said the second Beck hit the porch.

Beck handed Ashley off to Caden, took the gun his brother held out to him, and ran for the snowmobile he'd left in the driveway.

"Beck, no, stay here." Ashley's worried voice pierced his racing heart. He hated hearing the fear in her plea. He wanted to stay with her, but no way would he let Brice on his property or anywhere close to Ashley ever again.

"Stay with Caden." He pinned his brother with a sharp look. "You keep her safe." Caden gave him a nod, letting him know he'd do whatever it took to do just that, and probably in understanding that he knew how much Ashley already meant to Beck.

He jumped on the snowmobile, started the engine with the key he left in the ignition just for this reason, and took off down the long driveway to the gate.

He'd hoped for more time, but knew the minute the storm broke Brice would come looking for his prize possession. The guy had brass balls for taking chances like this. Celebrity made him arrogant and led him to believe he'd get what he wanted without any consequences. Not this time. Beck would never let him get away with what he'd done to Ashley and Adam.

Whatever he'd collected to blackmail people in power made him bold. Why else would he still be here and not hiding overseas?

Only a very dangerous man with connections would disregard how stupid it was to stay here and risk getting exposed and caught. A man obsessed with his target and with a plan to get out of any trouble that threatened to stop him.

Men like him, willing to do anything to get what they wanted, needed to be stopped because all they did was hurt people without remorse.

Beck rounded the bend in the driveway and approached the gate down the long straightaway. They saw him coming. He meant for them, or anyone trying to get on his property, to see him coming. They couldn't see the house or land beyond the curve. It gave him a place to scout those stupid enough to approach from the front.

The two men hopped the four-foot fence instead of trying to climb over the six-foot-tall metal gate, ignoring the NO TRESPASSING signs posted on both. Beck pegged the pudgy shorter one as Brice. The taller, leaner one trailed after him, his gaze darting back and forth between

Beck's approach and Brice, the man he obviously followed like a puppy dog.

Beck stopped the snowmobile ten feet in front of them, cut the engine, stood, flipped his visor up, pulled the gun from his back, and aimed it straight at Brice's head. "Turn around and get off my land. Since you can't read, I'll give you one verbal warning—you're trespassing."

Both men held their hands up in front of them.

Brice raised one to his helmet and pulled it off, smiling like an idiot. "Hey now, we don't want trouble. We're looking for some friends."

"You don't have one here."

Brice raked his fingers through his helmet-head hair. "You probably recognize me. I'm Brice Mooney."

"I don't give a fuck who you are. Get off my land."

Brice ignored the warning, showing how stupid he could be and walked a few more steps closer. Beck fired, kicking up snow an inch from Brice's left big toe. The man stopped in his tracks and glared.

The other guy whipped off his helmet and let it fall to the ground as he ran forward, put his hands on Brice's shoulder and chest and studied him to be sure he was okay. "Oh my God. You shot at him. What the hell is wrong with you? Don't you know who this is?"

"I don't care."

"Shooting at people is dangerous," the guy warned.

"One warning is all you get." Beck kept the gun trained on Brice, their eyes locked. Beck recognized a sociopath when he saw one. The gun, even death, didn't mean much to a man who liked causing pain and torturing people. The threat Beck posed appealed to Brice, where anyone else, the man standing beside him for instance, would be scared shitless.

Brice eyed him back, then cocked his head, put on a

grin that fooled most people. Not Beck. "Do you know Ashley Swan?"

"Should I?" Beck wanted to know where he was going with this.

"Oh come on," the other guy scoffed. "She won an Oscar for *Flame in the Night*."

"The girl in the new Bourne movie?"

"That's Alicia Vikander."

Beck tilted his head, still baiting the guy. "The one in that vampire series?"

"No, not Kristen Stewart."

Beck shook his head. "Not her, the other one who sees the future."

"Ashley Greene?" the guy asked, falling into Beck's trap of making them, or at least him, believe Beck had no clue.

"She's gorgeous." Beck only irritated the guy more by not getting it right again.

"She played an assassin in *Anarchy*," the guy suggested, trying to get Beck to figure out who they were talking about but missing the point completely that if he had her on his property he'd know who they were talking about.

Brice's patience snapped. "Long dark hair, green eyes, about five-eight. She left the other night—"

"I suggest you check the roads to see if she got in an accident."

"She was on foot," the guy blurted out.

Brice's gaze narrowed on the guy for giving away that information.

"Then she's dead. I suggest you contact the authorities and send out a search team for her body."

Brice eyed Beck again. "She's a resourceful woman. Strong. Remarkable."

"She'd have to be to survive the freezing temps."

"Or she'd have had to find shelter before the worst of it hit."

"Out here?" Beck looked around at the expanse of open land.

"Maybe in one of your outbuildings," Brice suggested.

"Not likely." Beck nodded to the security camera overhead, pointed straight at the gate. Another warning to keep off his land.

Brice followed his gaze, looked back at the formidable gate, and then at Beck again. "That's a lot of security."

"Which is how I knew you were here and she's not. So be on your way."

"Why all the security?" Brice asked, even more suspicious.

Beck didn't like questions or giving this guy a reason to look too closely at him. "Privacy."

An answer Brice could relate to. He'd come out here to the middle of nowhere so no prying eyes saw what he liked to do when he was alone and in control. Or so he thought. Because no one likes to be under someone's thumb. They fight back. They find a way to leave. Brice found that out when Ashley escaped.

He didn't just want her back. Beck read in his eyes what Brice could hide from most—he needed her back. Bad.

Brice understood the threat he'd put into that single word and the glare Beck sent his way. Brice backed away, but stopped short when his phone rang.

CHAPTER NINETEEN

Brice dug his cell phone out of his pocket and frowned. "What is it?" He'd left instructions for the cleaning woman to contact him if anyone came to the house, hoping Ashley and Adam found their way home on their own. His heart pounded waiting for her to answer him.

"The police are here to talk to you."

His heart stopped. Had they found Ashley? Did she betray him? "About what?" *Please God, don't let her be dead.*

"Mr. Mooney, this is Sergeant Mark Foster with the sheriff's department. Where are you?"

He dismissed the sergeant's question and asked his own. "What can I do for you?"

"One of your neighbors called in that you'd stopped by his home earlier and reported that a woman and child left your home on foot during the storm and are missing."

Damn nosy neighbors. Brice tried to think fast. He went with the most logical escape.

"Have you found him?" Brice put all the desperation he felt missing Ashley into those words. "I've been out most of the night and early this morning looking for him. Please tell me you found him and he's okay."

"I have reason to believe they are alive and safe." The sergeant's words eased his mind. Now all he had to do was get them back.

The guy with the gun and the deadly stare cocked his head, eyeing Brice even more for saying he was looking for "him" and not *her* like he'd told the man.

"I've been frantic wondering what happened to him. She didn't hurt him, did she?"

If Brice hadn't been watching the man as close as he watched him, he'd have missed the near-imperceptible twitch in his eyes of understanding exactly what Brice was doing. Damn, he knew about Ashley and Adam.

"Let's discuss this in person," the sergeant said.

"I'm on my way. Seems she was able to find help in the storm after all. I can't wait to have Adam back, safe and sound, where he belongs."

The guy had closed up even tighter than before, but he might not be so indifferent. His finger ever so slightly squeezed the gun trigger even though he kept the gun pointed at the ground.

"Please wait for me. You have no idea how happy I am." He hung up and turned to Darren. "They've been found."

"Thank God."

His neighbor cocked his head. "I thought you said you were looking for a woman."

"Yes. She kidnapped my boy."

"You have a son?"

"Well, it's not public knowledge, but I'm his legal guardian. His mother used drugs and ran around with some disreputable men. She worked for me. I did all I could to help her out and put her on the straight and narrow." Not exactly true, but Jackie had a thing for dangerous men and the finer things in life. She'd found both in him. But you play with fire, you get burned.

"You were very kind to her," Darren said, backing him up.

"I'm sure you were." The stranger's words didn't hold a trace of belief.

"When things were at their worst and she knew she was beyond help from escaping her terrible addiction, she asked me to always look after her little boy. I've tried to do so as if he was my own."

"Get out of my sight." The deadly tone and death glare weren't feigned.

Nothing scared Brice. He had the clout and resources to get out of anything.

But he did as ordered, knowing if he didn't leave now, he'd be dead and he'd never get Aurora back.

CHAPTER TWENTY

Ashley ran to Beck the second he stepped into the house. She launched herself into his open arms and hugged him tight, her body vibrating with fear and relief. He kissed the top of her head. Adam rushed over and wrapped his arms around one of Beck's legs.

"We watched on the monitor. You shot at him." Ashley's words got muffled in Beck's thick coat. Her heart stopped the second she saw Beck fire, thinking Brice would pull out a gun and kill Beck. She held him tighter, wishing she could keep him safe forever.

"Just a warning. We have a big problem. That call he took, I think it came from the sergeant I spoke to earlier. Brice knows you've been found. He claims you kidnapped Adam from him. He says he's Adam's legal guardian."

Ashley stepped back, outrage curling her fingers into a fist. "No he's not. That can't be."

"He'll have to prove it, but he's done exactly as you predicted. He's made you the bad guy."

"Call the sergeant. Tell him it's not true."

"I have a feeling he already knows what's going on. He'll have to play it by the book. Brice is about to use his trump cards."

"Just like I told you. I can't fight him and win when he's got politicians and people in authority who will cover up what he did to save themselves." Ashley turned and raked her fingers through her hair, feeling every bit as inadequate to stop Brice as she had all those months as his prisoner.

"We have all the evidence we need to prove he hurt you," Beck reminded her.

But was it enough? Brice thought he could use his celebrity, his money, to get out of this. But she had both, too. And she knew how to use them when it suited her. She didn't want to be a spectacle, but if it kept Adam safe and put Brice behind bars, she'd do whatever was necessary to accomplish both those things.

She'd do what had to be done to keep Beck safe and out of the spotlight, too, even though the thought of leaving him made her heart ache.

She turned back to Beck, resigned to the reality of her life and the inevitability of what came next. "We can't wait and see what happens next. We need to stop him before he muddies the waters so much that the real story is buried."

"What do you have in mind?" Mia asked.

"I need a phone." She glanced around the room.

Beck pulled out his cell and handed it to her. "Who are you calling?"

"Someone who can make sure everyone sees exactly what Brice did."

"Ashley, we need to control the situation as much as possible."

She gave him a sad smile. "It's too late for that. I wanted to run. You told me I needed to fight if I wanted my life back. You were right." She dialed her old friend and put the phone to her ear. She tried to organize her thoughts and find the strength to tell her story even as she wanted to forget it ever happened.

"Hello." The familiar voice brought tears to her eyes and made her think of happier times.

"Stuart, I need your help." She blinked away tears.

"Ashley." Her name came out choked with emotion.

"Yes, it's Ashley."

"Where are you? Are you okay?" Stuart wound up to ask a dozen more questions, but she cut him off.

"Listen, I'll explain everything later. Right now, I need to do that thing I hate more than anything." She closed her eyes and sighed.

"You've been gone without a word for months and now you want me to call the paps for some photo op?" The absurdity of it came out with his words.

She felt crazy for doing it. "Yes, call the press and let them know I'm being taken to—" She put her hand over the phone and asked Beck, "What hospital are you taking me to for the exam and X-rays?"

"There's a clinic in Crystal Creek."

She shook her head. "No. It's got to be a hospital emergency room. Somewhere we can make a big circus out of this."

"Ashley . . ."

"We either play the game against him or we'll lose because the only story anyone will hear is his whether it's true or not." She sighed. "A picture is worth a thousand words and can be interpreted a hundred different ways, but live video will show the truth."

"Bozeman it is. It'll take more than an hour to get there, maybe more depending on the roads."

"We'll need that time for Stuart to get everything set up." She put the phone back to her ear. "Sorry, Stuart. I'll be taken to the hospital in Bozeman. I won't make a verbal statement. My appearance will be statement enough. Leak to the press that rumor has it I was found near death in the middle of a snowstorm, beaten and starved."

"What!" Stuart gasped.

She went on, unable to explain anything more right now. She wanted to get this done and over with as soon as possible. "I barely survived and am being taken to the emergency room for medical attention."

"Christ." Stuart swore.

"The information came directly from the Crystal Creek Sheriff's Department from an unnamed source. The more photographers the better."

She listened while Stuart, ever the professional under fire, outlined his plan to make a spectacle of the trauma and cruelty Ashley suffered. She made these plans with a calculating mind, but her heart wasn't in it. Her heart wanted to hide and heal and stay here with Beck.

She hoped they could control what came next, but feared now that they'd opened Pandora's box this would take on a life of its own.

Ashley's trembling hand went to her forehead. Her voice shook with her next words. "No matter what, no matter how hard he'll deny it, the headline needs to remain that Brice Mooney kidnapped, tortured, and starved Ashley Swan, holding her in a windowless room at his Montana ranch home for nearly a year."

Ashley held the phone away from her ear as Stuart yelled a string of obscenities and death threats that ended with hanging Brice from his tiny pecker.

She might have laughed and enjoyed the imaginative insults any other time, but she didn't have it in her when her life was about to explode.

She yelled into the phone. "Get it done. I'll call tomorrow." She hung up, let a single tear slip down her cheek, sucked in a deep breath, and dialed another number. She put the phone to her ear and held her breath, thinking how many times she wished to hear this person's voice one more time. "Mom, it's me."

"Ashley," her mother gasped.

Just her name and she lost it, letting the tears come in a torrent.

Beck came to her, pulled her into his chest, took the phone from her trembling hand, put it on speaker, and explained for her. "Mrs. Swan, this is Special Agent Beck Cooke with the DEA."

"Oh my God, has my daughter been arrested for drugs?"

"No, Mrs. Swan, your daughter was kidnapped and held hostage for nearly a year." He didn't provide the horrible details.

Grateful, Ashley didn't want to frighten or worry her mother more than she'd been this past year not knowing what happened to her daughter. They may not have a close relationship, but Ashley loved her mom even when they disagreed or her mother did things Ashley didn't like.

"What? No. She couldn't handle the pressure. She ran away. That's all."

"I'm sorry, but that's not what happened. I found her after she escaped. She's hurt and too thin, but her injuries aren't severe enough that she won't make a full recovery. As you can imagine after all this time, she's scared and traumatized. It's difficult for her to talk about what happened to her. I'm taking her to the hospital shortly. The press will find out what happened. She wanted you to know she's alive and okay."

"Can I talk to her?"

Beck looked down into Ashley's upturned face. She'd regained her composure and strength once again.

"Here she is."

Ashley found her voice again. "Hi, Mom."

"Is what he said true?"

"Yes."

"Are you really okay?" Her mother's voice cracked.

"I will be."

"Where are you?"

"Montana." Ashley didn't want to give too many details about Beck and his place.

"You said you were going to stay with that talk show host. Brice, right? We all thought you'd run away to escape the pressure."

"I thought Brice was my friend. He wasn't. He did terrible things, Mom." The memories flooded her mind, but she fought them back and held on to Beck.

"Okay, honey, you'll get through this. You always do."

"It's so hard," Ashley admitted. "I can't stop thinking about it."

"Are you going back to L.A.? Do you want me to meet you there?"

As much as she wanted to see her mother, she didn't want to drag her into this mess. "No. I'm not sure where I'm going to end up."

A bolt of fear shot through her. Going through with this meant letting Beck go. For now. As hard as she'd fight to take Brice down and regain her freedom, she'd fight even harder to get back to Beck.

"I appreciate that you want to come, but this is going to turn into a media circus in a few hours. I just wanted to tell you myself, so you didn't find out on the news."

"I'm sorry, Ashley. I should have known something was wrong. I felt it, but dismissed it, thinking you'd run away from that life and me because you felt you had no support. We're two very different people and that means we sometimes have trouble understanding each other, but, honey, I love you. No matter what, you can always come to me. I'm sorry if it seems that the only time I come to you is when I need something and all we do is argue our differing opinions. I want you to be happy, honey, and I am so sorry this happened to you," her mother choked out.

Ashley's tears ran nonstop down her face. It had taken this terrible thing to bridge the gap between them and bring them back together. A silver lining that touched her deeply. She'd really missed her mother. "I love you, Mom. I hope Matthew has been taking care of you while I've been gone."

She'd always wanted to be able to take care of her mother. But even from the beginning when things were good but not yet great financially, her mother had made demands and laid on the guilt. Angry and sad, the resentment built until they barely spoke. To change the tone of their few phone calls from money to simply catching up, she'd instructed her accountant Matthew to pay her mother an allowance. She hoped they could put all of it aside now.

"The payments never stopped, which is why I assumed you instructed him to keep making them."

"I'm glad. How have you been, Mom?"

"Aside from worried about you, you know how things are—nothing much changes here."

"It's actually comforting to know that." Ashley sniffled back the last of her tears and sighed. "I need you to do something for me."

"Anything, honey."

"I'm going to send you a photograph. When the tabloids start calling you, and they will soon, take the highest bid—"

"No, I promised you I'd never do that again."

She appreciated more than words could convey the conviction in her mother's voice.

"This time, I'm asking you to do it. I need the photo to go out with your assurance that you've talked to me, you believe that Brice Mooney is responsible for my kidnapping and torture, and you have proof. You want him arrested and sent to jail for the rest of his life for hurting me."

"I do, honey. I want him to pay for what he's done. Come home," her mother added, her voice pleading.

"I will soon. I promise."

"Will you be okay? Are you safe now?"

"I'm as safe as I can be." She hugged Beck close. "I'll call you soon. Love you, Mom."

"Love you."

Ashley hung up, handed Beck back the phone, grabbed the front of his coat and pressed her forehead to his chest for a long moment. She soaked up his warmth and strength and the sense of ease that ran through her when he was with her. She wanted to hold on to him forever, but had to take the next step on her own.

She stepped back and looked up at him. "Call the sheriff or police department and tell them to come pick me up and take me to the hospital."

"I'll take you."

She shook her head. "You've done so much. I can't ask you to risk your life and put your face out there for the world to see and know who you are. I won't be the reason those drug dealers come after you."

Caden stepped forward. "She's right, Beck. You go with her, your face will be all over the news. People will want to know who you are and how you got involved. It won't take long for them to have your name and that you're DEA. Guzman will know exactly who you are and he'll come for you."

"It's a risk I'm willing to take. With the press and police around, he'll have a hard time getting to me."

"You'll put Ashley and Adam at greater risk." Caden didn't need to state the obvious, but maybe Beck needed to hear it.

"We need to keep Adam out of this." Ashley brushed her hand over the boy's head, then turned to Mia. "Will you take him someplace safe?"

Beck touched her shoulder, sending that familiar electricity through her system. "Ashley, the police will put him in protective custody. I don't like it, but we have to follow procedure."

"They'll put him in foster care with strangers. If they don't arrest Brice right away, he'll use his contacts and find Adam." She left off saying that Brice would kill the boy to silence him from talking about what Brice did to Ashley. And what about Adam's mother?

"Please, Caden," Ashley begged. "I can't keep him with me during all of this, but I can't lose him either. I promised I'd keep him safe. You can protect him. Please," she said again.

Caden exchanged a look and a silent conversation with Mia, who gave Caden a firm nod. "I'll make some calls. I can't promise anything, but I'll do my best. I'll also try to make sure his location is kept secret and off the books."

Caden pulled out his phone and stepped out onto the porch to get the ball rolling.

Mia took Adam's hand. "Come on, sweetheart. Looks like you get to have a sleepover with me and Uncle Caden."

Ashley liked the sound of *Uncle Caden*. She caught Beck's eye and saw her thoughts reflected back. Before they thought about that kind of future together, they needed to stay focused on the here and now and what happened next.

"Send one of the pictures you took of me to my mother's phone."

"Ashley, I don't think that's a good idea."

She appreciated the concern and how much he wanted to protect her from any kind of harm, but this needed to be done. "They'll leak anyway. This way, my mother adds to her retirement nest egg and we control the narrative."

"I hate the way this is turning into a means for people to make money off of and talk about you, missing the fact that you were hurt and deserve justice. They're going to take what happened and use it to hurt you more."

"I told you, Beck, this is out of my control. The best I can do is steer things to go my way and not let Brice turn things so he looks like the victim. Which he will if I don't get ahead of this."

"Look at you. No one will believe he's the victim."

"You'd be surprised what people will believe if they see it on the internet or TV. I've been pregnant like ten different times a year and been engaged to five or six guys I never even dated. Shall I go on?"

"No." He got the point.

Mia held Adam's hand; his things were packed into two plastic bags in her other hand. Adam held a paper in his free hand and held it up to Ashley.

She kneeled in front of him and took the drawing. "Is this me and you?" Ashley pointed to the yellow-haired boy standing next to a taller brown-haired woman.

Ashley held back a laugh that they appeared to be wearing Beck's clothes. Adam had a talent for capturing reality in his way. The figures stood in front of a grassy hill with large boulders and flowers. A big orange sun and bright blue sky completed the picture.

"It's all of us," Adam confirmed.

He may be good at creating a picture, but he still spoke like a four-year-old.

She hoped one day the picture included Beck, too.

"I love it." Ashley held it to her heart. "I know you're going to have so much fun with Mia and Caden. I will miss you so much."

"I want to stay with you and Beck."

"I know you do, honey. I want you here, but I'm afraid for you. I want you safe. I know you'll be safe with Mia and Caden."

"He's coming." Adam's bottom lip trembled.

"I'm going to make sure he gets what's coming to him."

Adam nodded just as Caden came back into the house with a blast of cold air through the front door.

"Good news. Since the phones started ringing off the hook with reporters wanting confirmation that Ashley Swan had indeed escaped her kidnapper, they feel it's in Adam's best interest to be kept out of sight and in protective custody while they investigate Brice's claim that he has legal guardianship, whether or not Ashley kidnapped him, or if she saved him."

Ashley rolled her eyes. "We'll clear that up with the hospital visit and my giving a formal statement to the police."

"That's what I told the sheriff, who agreed to let me keep Adam. He's the only one in the department who will know where Adam is, so it can't be leaked. He agrees that keeping your kidnapping case separate from Adam's and handling his quietly will ensure Adam's case doesn't muddy the waters."

Ashley asked the obvious question. "What if the sheriff is working with Brice?"

"He seemed genuine and appears to be doing what I'd expect on a case, but I will operate under the assumption that we can't trust him. If Brice comes after Adam, we'll know it's because of the sheriff."

Ashley pressed her lips together, but nodded, knowing they had few choices right now. "It'll be tricky to keep Adam's name out of things. Brice will go to the press to try to push back on me." Ashley held Adam to her side.

"He's already doing it with the sheriff's office. He's filed his report. They're questioning him about your kidnapping. This is going to start moving really fast now."

"Then we better get moving." Ashley leaned down and kissed Adam's cheek. "Be good. Eat lots. I want to see you grow an inch by the time I see you next. Which will be very soon."

"Promise?" Adam's huge round eyes filled with tears.

"Yes. I swear." Ashley hugged him close and stared up at Caden. "Keep him safe."

"I will. Mia will fill him full of sweets," Caden added to reassure Adam that although things seemed dire, he'd be spoiled and taken care of well.

ADAM RAN OVER to Beck and wrapped his arms around Beck's leg. Beck picked him up and held him close. He turned and whispered into Adam's ear, "I will keep her safe for you. We'll be together again real soon." Beck squeezed Adam tight again, his heart already missing the boy that wasn't his but felt like it.

He handed Adam off to Mia and gave Caden a look that said everything. *Be safe. Be smart. We got this.* Just like old times. Beck was back in the game. Though the game may be different, it still came down to truth and lies, justice, life and death.

Mia and Ashley took Adam and his things out to Caden's truck.

Beck handed Caden back his gun. "You might need this."

"I hope I don't. You know that by doing this you'll never go undercover again. Your face will be known not only in this state but across the country. Hell, everyone in the world is about to know who you are."

"I know."

"You'll give it all up for her."

"I gave it up after what happened to you and Mia—I was just letting it settle. But you already knew that."

"I did, but I wanted to know it really is your choice."

Beck nodded that it was the choice he made. He needed to make it to save what was left of his soul. "For her"—he nodded out the door at the beautiful woman fawning over Adam—"I'd lay down my life."

"You hardly know her."

"What if I said that to you the day after that bastard took you and Mia and held a gun to her head? What would you say?"

Caden scrunched his mouth, then admitted, "That the only thing that matters is being with her."

"She matters." That's as close as he'd come to talking about his feelings. Where Ashley was concerned, he had no words to adequately describe how she made him feel, or how important she was to him.

"Have you warned her about Guzman and the very real threat he'll be to her? Is she willing to face that with you and possibly be put in harm's way again the way Mia has been not once, but twice?"

"She knows. Maybe I don't deserve her trust, but I'm going to work damn hard to earn it and keep her safe."

Caden nodded, understanding that while Beck didn't like putting Ashley in more danger, she'd accepted it and him—the same way Mia had with Caden.

"She and Mia get along. Wait until Alina finds out you're in love with Ashley Swan."

Beck didn't confirm or deny. "She won't believe you."

"Only because we can't believe any woman would want your sorry ass," Caden teased.

"I hope she does. After all she's been through . . ."

"She looks at you like she wants you. It's muddled with all the pain and trauma, but those will fade with time and allow her to feel happy again. She trusts you. That's a good place to start." Caden clamped his hand on Beck's shoulder and squeezed. "Take it slow. Keep in touch."

Beck grabbed Ashley's coat and walked out the door behind Caden. The goodbyes went fast and Caden drove away with Adam and Mia. Ashley pulled her jacket on and stared at the back end of Caden's truck until it disappeared around the bend in the driveway.

"You'll see him again," Beck assured her because she looked like she was about to face a firing squad.

"I will see him again. He's going to be mine. If he has to grow up without his mother, I'll make sure he knows he's loved the rest of his life."

"Brice said she was an addict and liked to sleep around."

Ashley shook her head before he even finished his sentence. "I've seen people strung out on drugs and thinking no one notices. It's rampant in Hollywood. She wasn't like that. As for sleeping around, she wouldn't have jeopardized her ticket to Easy Street and a place like Brice's ranch for her son to grow up in by screwing other men. Brice wouldn't put up with that."

"No, he wants to be a woman's everything and thinks he is." Beck stared down the driveway, thinking about Adam. "Do you know what happened to her?"

"No. I didn't see anything, but I know he killed her. She wouldn't leave Adam."

Beck didn't think so either.

CHAPTER TWENTY-ONE

Brice resented Sergeant Foster insisting he come down to the police station to not only file his kidnapping charges against Ashley, but to answer questions about her charges against him. He needed to discredit Ashley before this spun out of his control. He should have known she'd betray him. After all he gave her, everything he did to transform her into her true self, she slapped him in the face with these lies.

This would go his way. He'd make sure of it once he spoke to the sheriff.

Brice didn't open the door when Darren parked the car outside the sheriff's department and Sergeant Foster waited for him at the curb. "Don't come in. Stay close in case I need you. My lawyer will be here soon. Until then, see what you can find out. If they want to question me, that means Ashley is either here or close. I want to know where she is."

"I'll start making calls. If she's going public, my sources will know when and where."

"She can't speak to the press."

"It's the cops you need to worry about." Darren nodded toward the officer waiting for him.

Brice kept his features neutral, but he wanted to growl and hit something.

Brice stepped out of the car, trying to pull his thoughts together and not slip on the icy road as he stepped up and over the piled snow. No way she got the better of him. He hated to expose himself more and use the information he'd gathered to force others to get him out of this mess. But he'd do whatever he had to do to get Aurora back.

The sheriff was a worry. The man had a conscience. This could go either way. Brice didn't like walking in not knowing the outcome.

Thankfully very few people were on the street or in the sheriff's office. The cold and snow kept the town nearly deserted and people home.

Sergeant Foster escorted him past three officers sitting in their cubicles in the open room, past several offices, only one occupied by another officer, to a conference room with a long table, six chairs, a coffeemaker and paper cups on a cart in the corner, and a bank of windows overlooking the street out front, the blinds open and layered with dust. Brice hated the stares. He was used to his celebrity, but didn't like people scrutinizing him so closely. He liked his privacy.

"Take a seat, Mr. Mooney."

Brice did so, playing Mr. Congeniality. "I can't wait to get Adam back. Where is he?"

"In protective custody."

"Where?"

"I don't know. The sheriff is the only one with that information."

Annoyance narrowed Brice's gaze. "Are you keeping him from me?"

"Until we clear up a few matters."

Brice raised an eyebrow. "I assume you've called the judge who signed the guardianship papers."

"We did. They're legit, but we have questions about Ashley Swan. How did she take Adam?"

"She snuck him out of the house while I was downstairs in a business meeting with my assistant, Darren."

"So you've said, but how did she come to be at your home?"

"She's been living with me for the past year."

Sergeant Foster's eyes narrowed. "What is the nature of your relationship with Miss Swan?"

"We were friends at first, but now we're more."

The sergeant stood over him and studied him. "Is she your girlfriend?"

"She's more than just that."

"She claims you held her against her will."

"Lies." Brice leaned in. "I want to see Adam."

"He's not here."

"When will I get him back?"

"That's undetermined at this time. Let's get back to Miss Swan."

"I hate to see her in trouble for her impulsive actions, but she can't just take Adam."

The sergeant tilted his head. "Why would she take him?"

"To hurt me, of course." After all they shared, he truly couldn't believe she'd do this to him.

"Why would she want to do that?"

He didn't answer, keeping his options open for how he wanted to play this out. "Is Adam okay? He must be frightened. Has he eaten? Where did he sleep? Was he out in the cold long?"

"Mr. Mooney, I assure you he's fine."

"How do you know? Have you seen him?"

Sergeant Foster shook his head. "I know the man he was with and he took good care of him."

Well, that was nice of the sergeant to let Brice know.

Sheriff Willis walked in, his gaze locked on Brice. "Give us a minute, Sergeant."

Sergeant Foster's gaze bounced from Brice to the

sheriff and back again. His eyes filled with anger and suspicion, but he left the room and closed the door behind him.

"Shut this kidnapping business down," Brice ordered the sheriff.

"Which kidnapping? Adam's? Or Ashley's?"

"Give me back Adam. Tell everyone Ashley and I had a fight, she took the boy, and this is nothing more than a domestic dispute."

"I don't believe that," the sheriff stated.

"It doesn't matter what you believe or can prove. I've got you by the balls. Do what I want, or I'll trash your career and your life."

The sheriff pinned him with his sharp gaze. "Go ahead."

Brice shook his head in disbelief the sheriff would dare go against him.

"I wasn't the only one at that party. There are people in your pocket higher up than me. I'm sure you'll use them to get what you want, but I won't be the one who helps you. What you have is circumstantial at best, and it probably will destroy my life and career, but I'd rather that than allow you to hurt that boy and woman again."

Frustrated by the sheriff's nonchalant attitude and defiance, Brice slammed his hands on the table. "I want Ashley and Adam back. Now."

"I won't help you. In fact, Sergeant Foster will handle the case. I will keep my hands clean and out of it so the case sticks no matter what you do to me. If I was you, I'd shut up and do exactly what your lawyer tells you to do when he gets here. Ashley is at the hospital right now. You can't explain away her injuries. You will be charged with her kidnapping and torture."

"My lawyer will tear your case apart. She's mine. This is nothing more than a domestic dispute, where my live-in girlfriend kidnapped Adam to get back at me after a fight."

The sheriff shook his head, his eyes filled with recriminations. "You're the only one who believes that. Once people see what I've been told you did to her, you won't convince anyone else that bullshit is true. Anyone who backs you up on that story will look like a damn fool."

Brice couldn't believe this man would ruin his whole life over this. He didn't need the sheriff. He had people with more power who would make the sheriff do what he wanted. If they didn't, he had a way out. But the longer he sat there, the more he felt the walls closing in and his freedom slipping away.

CHAPTER TWENTY-TWO

Ashley sat beside Beck in the truck, both of them quiet after he'd finished his call with Sergeant Foster.

"He's in custody." She really couldn't believe it.

"They haven't charged him yet. He refuses to speak without his lawyer about anything other than having you arrested for kidnapping."

"Are they going to do that?"

"You didn't kidnap him. You rescued him. The cops know that—now they need to prove it. Sergeant Foster has the statement you started on my laptop. He's got the pictures, including the one you made me send to your mother." Beck's mouth drew back in a tight line. He'd hated doing that for her. "She should get an Oscar for that interview she gave about your chilling phone call, telling them how scared you were, how broken you sounded."

"Beck, I know you don't like this part."

"I hate it, Ashley. You shouldn't have to do this to get justice."

"The hardest thing about being a celebrity is the moment you realize that, although you still feel like everyone else, no one thinks you're like everyone else. Brice will use that to his advantage. No one wants to believe the guy who cracked jokes and played with celebrities on his show is a monster. He's the guy who got to hang out with Matt Damon, Chris Hemsworth—"

"And you. I get it. People related to him because Brice felt like a regular guy who got to rub elbows with the elite."

"I'm not part of the elite," Ashley scoffed.

"The public thinks you are. I think you're exceptional."

"Beck." She stared at him.

He reached over and softly brushed her cheek. "He won't get away with it. You'll have your exam, X-rays, and give the rest of your statement at the hospital. They'll arrest and charge Brice right there at the station. He's not going anywhere."

"I can't believe it was that easy."

Beck stopped at a red light a block from the hospital and stared out the windshield at all the white news vans with their satellite dishes.

"You can still back out. I wouldn't blame you." Ashley's stomach soured just thinking about walking through that crowd of reporters, the flashes going off in her face, all of them staring and judging and pitying her.

Beck's hand settled over hers on the seat between them. His warm hand engulfed hers and squeezed. "I won't let you do this alone."

Ashley swallowed back the bile in her throat and looked Beck in the eye, speaking her heart. "I'm not sure I can do this without you."

"Yes, you could. But you don't have to. Not anymore."

Drawn in by his sweet sincerity and the promise that he'd be by her side, she leaned across the seat and kissed him softly, lingering over the soft, sweet kiss. She poured everything she couldn't find the words to say into the press of her lips to his. "Thank you."

Beck's lips drew into a tight line. "Don't thank me for putting you through this."

"This is necessary and not your fault. It's going to suck, but with you beside me, I'll get through it."

He leaned in and kissed her again. They lost themselves in the quiet moment, stopping only when the car behind them honked to get them to go through the green light.

She sat back in her seat, took his hand, and squeezed. "Whatever happens next, please don't leave my side."

He held on tighter. "Never."

She released him, raked her fingers into her long hair, and messed it up. "As ridiculous as this may seem, we need to act this out just like we planned." Which meant she needed to look the way she felt when she woke up terrified, dazed, and bedraggled in Beck's bed.

"I don't think we need all the dramatics. The facts are enough to get him arrested, charged, and locked up for life."

"That's what you need for court—we need this for the court of public opinion. I don't like it any more than you do, but if he's going to turn the tables on me, I'm going to make sure no one believes him."

"They won't. I read what you wrote in that report. Your words, the account of what happened to you was chilling and you didn't even finish it. What you went through, Ashley . . ."

The despair and anger in his voice, for her, touched her deeply and told her how much he truly cared. Not just because it was his job to protect the innocent, but because he cared about her.

"It's over, Beck. I'll never let him hurt me again."

"Except that because of him, you have to do this." Beck slowly drove through the throng of photographers up the driveway to the emergency room doors. Flashes went off incessantly, blinding them. After spending so much time in the dark, her eyes still ached in the bright lights.

She curled in on herself as much as she could without making her ribs scream with pain. Actually, they were getting better. Everything seemed better since she ended up at Beck's place. She put her hand over her eyes and tried to hide, not wanting to give the photographers too good a picture. They'd get one, but she didn't have to make it easy. She didn't want it to appear obvious she'd set this all up even if they understood the game as well as she did.

Beck sighed, not wanting to go through with this at all. "Here we go." He got out of the truck, slammed the door, and pushed his way past all the reporters and photographers shouting questions. He came to her side of the truck, opened the door, scooped her into his strong arms, and pulled her out of the truck. Like Kevin Costner carrying Whitney Houston in *The Bodyguard*, he held her limp in his arms, her hair a mass of tangles, her face buried in his neck, right up the path. People crowded in around them with microphones held out. Their overlapping voices and questions a roar in her ears.

Reality set in and she held Beck tighter. She didn't want them to see her like this. She didn't want her pain and nightmare on display, so she hid in Beck's embrace and held on hoping he got her safely inside the hospital fast.

"Back up," Beck ordered, getting everyone to leave a not-so-easy one-foot circle around them. It didn't stop them from shouting her name and ordering her to raise her head and turn their way so they could get the best picture. She didn't comply, just held tighter to Beck as he jostled her through the crowd and into the emergency room where security guards let them in and held back everyone else.

Beck set her on her feet, but held on to her like she couldn't stand on her own. He turned just enough to let the photographers get a few shots of her, too thin and frail to hold herself up. The leggings showed her stick-thin legs. The short-sleeved top she'd changed into revealed her bony arms and skeletal hands. She kept her head down as a nurse and doctor took her arms and helped her sit in the waiting wheelchair. She leaned to the side, curled up on herself, and held her head in her hand, letting her hair spill over her face just enough to hide her eyes, but not her too-pale skin and sunken cheeks. She had been sleeping better, but the nightmares still woke her every few hours. She hoped that improved as her body healed, time passed, and she found some peace.

She wouldn't get any today.

Beck stood beside her and took her hand.

"Let's get her into an exam room," the doctor ordered. "Tell X-ray she's here and we'll be up soon." The doctor bent down to her. "Don't worry, Miss Swan, we'll take good care of you. I'm Dr. Bell Bowden. Beck's friend Sadie asked me to be here for you. I'll try to get you through this as painlessly and quickly as possible. I won't leave your side."

Ashley looked up and into the doctor's soft gaze. "No matter what, Beck comes with me."

"Unless you say otherwise, he can stay with you."

Beck squeezed Ashley's hand, but addressed Dr. Bowden. "Thank you for doing this. She's been through so much."

"We'll get her through this. Let's get her out of the lobby, settled in an exam room, and we'll go from there. Slow and easy. We'll start with some blood work, then do the exam, and head to X-ray after that."

The nurse pushed her down the hall. The shouted questions from the reporters faded behind her, easing her mind on one front, but her anxiety amped up when they entered the private room and the nurse pointed to the gown on the exam table.

Dr. Bowden stood in the doorway after the nurse left.

"I'll be back in a minute. Put the gown on, opening in the front, then we'll get started."

Alone with Beck, she looked up at his grim face. "Getting through the reporters was easier than this."

"Sadie assured me Dr. Bowden is the best. She's had a difficult life, so understands your need for her to be kind and gentle, and she's aware of how hard it is for you to face what happened to you."

"Sadie?" she asked, trying not to show the jealousy eating away at her. They hadn't really talked about their personal lives. She didn't much have one because of her circumstances, but she guessed the gorgeous, smart, kind man had to have a woman, or women, in his life.

"She saved my life a while back when I busted her brother for cooking meth and took down a drug ring he was working for. She's married," he added, giving her a knowing grin that said he'd guessed her little green monster had poked his head out to embarrass her. "I thought a woman doctor would suit you in these circumstances and asked Sadie if she had a recommendation. Her husband's family is close to Dr. Bowden's husband, Dane."

"It's really true—everyone knows everyone in a small town."

"Everyone in the world knows you," he pointed out.

"Does it bother you that I'm famous?"

"It bothers me that I can't bring you to the hospital for the care you need and not have at least four people on the staff sneak a photograph of you as we walk down the hallway."

"That's why you wanted a doctor you could trust to take care of me."

"If anyone comes into this room and thinks they can invade your privacy, they'll find themselves fired or locked up at best."

The unsaid death threat and his clenched fists brought

on a smile even though she didn't feel much like smiling at all.

"Stop stalling, Ashley. The doctor will be back any second. Let's get this done so I can take you home."

She pressed her lips together, then admitted, "That sounds really good."

He held his hand out to her. She took it and he helped her up from the wheelchair. "Then let's do that."

"You know what would be even better."

He stared down into her upturned face. "What?" His indulgent tone said he'd do anything to make this better for her.

"If you bought me a burger and fries and a chocolate shake on the way back."

He finally smiled. This wasn't easy for him either. "Deal. Now strip and put that gown on." His teasing tone relaxed her a tiny bit. She didn't have to ask him to turn his back. He gave her the privacy she needed despite the fact he'd already seen her naked and covered in bruises. "You're still stalling."

Instead of taking off her clothes, she wrapped her hands around his middle, clasped them at his taut stomach, laid her head on the back of his shoulders, and held him tight.

His warm hands settled over hers. "You can do this, sweetheart."

She slid her hands around his sides and up his strong back and pushed away from him. She took a deep breath, squeezed his shoulders in a kind of thank-you for giving her the nudge she needed, and replaced her comfortable clothes with the hospital gown that made her feel as exposed as if she had nothing on. She didn't underneath the thin fabric. She slowly stepped up on the platform in front of the table and sat down, pulling the gown over her bruised thighs and holding it closed at her chest and lap.

Beck turned back when she got settled on the crinkly paper covering. "Okay."

"I'm scared." She didn't know why, but her whole body trembled and all she wanted to do was run.

Beck stood in front of her and wrapped her in his arms, protecting her and blocking her from the door as Dr. Bowden knocked.

"Come in," Beck called over his shoulder, but never let her go.

The door swung open. "Do you need a few more minutes?" the doctor asked.

Beck leaned back, cupped her face and tilted it up so Ashley looked at him. "She's ready." The words answered the doctor and were meant to encourage her.

Ashley gave him a nod that she was indeed as ready as she'd ever be under the circumstances.

With the door closed, Beck stepped to her side. Ashley faced the doctor, nurse, and the next two hours of poking and prodding of her body and memory of what happened.

"We'll start with the noninvasive stuff. The nurse will draw some blood. Then, I'll take down the details of what happened to you and your injuries. We'll do a physical exam, including a gynecological one. Beck can wait outside during that if you'd like."

"He stays," Ashley ordered, holding Beck's hand in both of hers.

"Okay. Then we'll go up for X-rays and possibly an MRI depending on your injuries."

Ashley nodded, extending her arm to the nurse, who quietly and efficiently tied a band around her bicep, stuck a needle in her arm, and drew at least ten vials of blood.

Dr. Bowden waited for the nurse to leave them alone before she asked her questions. "I understand Beck's already photographed your injuries, so we can skip that part here. Let's start with your most recent injuries. Where do you hurt right now?"

"Everywhere." Ashley admitted to the throbbing pain that ebbed and flowed the more she used her muscles and exacerbated her actual injuries. "My ribs and back the most."

"What about this wrapped ankle?" Dr. Bowden pointed to her foot.

"It's just a slight sprain. It barely hurts anymore. It's a bit swollen, but I can walk on it."

"Let's have a look." Dr. Bowden unwrapped the bandage.

Ashley let out her breath. Starting with her barely hurt foot helped ease her into the exam and allowed her to relax before she had to show the really bad stuff.

"This doesn't look bad at all." Dr. Bowden flexed Ashley's ankle. "Does it hurt when I do this?"

"A little. Not bad. It's the side to side that hurts the worst. I got it caught on a root and twisted it when I fell."

"In four-inch heels," Beck added, his frown showing his disgust at what Brice forced her to endure to save her life.

Dr. Bowden glanced up at him, one eyebrow cocked. "You ran across miles of open land in heels?"

"Yes."

"Carrying a four-year-old," Beck added.

Ashley bit her lip, her mind taking her back to those dire hours, hearing Brice's voice shouting at her in the night, the fear rising up and choking off her breath and making her heart gallop faster than her feet could carry her away.

"Breathe," Beck ordered, brushing his hand over her hair.

She came back to the present, sucked in a breath, and looked up at Beck to center herself again.

"Keep the foot wrapped a few more days. Ice it, prop

it up when possible, and stay off it as much as you can. That should give it time to heal without reinjuring it." Dr. Bowen rewrapped her foot, then stared up at her. "We'll weigh you before we go up for X-rays, but I'd guess you're about twenty pounds underweight. Before you go, I'd like to do an IV with some vitamins and minerals. How is your appetite?"

"Coming back slowly. It's hard to eat."

"She does best with small meals. Her cravings are coming back. She asked me for a burger on the way home."

"Good. Increase your calories a little at a time. Don't go more than two hours without something to eat until you're able to eat more at each sitting. Though I recommend the burger, try to get as many varied and healthy foods as you can. I'll narrow down what you're lacking once your blood results come back, but my guess is that you're anemic and missing vital nutrients across the board. Red meat, dark green leafy vegetables like spinach and kale, and broccoli will help. High-protein meals to build back muscle. Complex carbs to help with energy."

"At first, she could barely stay awake. Now she fatigues easily, but it's much better." Beck touched Ashley's back to comfort her.

Ashley enjoyed the contact, but flinched when he hit a sore spot.

"Sorry, sweetheart."

"It's okay."

"Let's have a look," Dr. Bowden took the opportunity to move on from the easy stuff to the hard and stepped to her side and waited for Ashley to drop the gown down her back, holding it over her chest.

"Okay." Dr. Bowden's voice held a note of alarm. "Have you been taking anything for the pain?"

"Beck gave me a Vicodin the first night, but since then nothing but ibuprofen."

"Are you against taking something stronger?"

"I need a clear head to get through this."

"I'll prescribe something that will help with the swelling and pain but no narcotics." Dr. Bowden did a visual exam of her back. "I know you've been through a lot, Ashley. I don't want to add to it, but I'll need to touch you to complete the exam. Is it okay if I touch you?"

Ashley appreciated the doctor giving her a choice when she'd had none living with Brice. "Go ahead."

"I'll be as gentle as I can. If you are uncomfortable, it hurts, or you just need a minute, let me know and we'll stop until you're ready to start again."

Ashley endured Dr. Bowden's gentle pushes and prods down her back, flinching when it hurt, and trying to point out areas that hurt now and had been injured in the past. Dr. Bowden took note of everything in the chart, circling areas on a human diagram on the paper in different colors to show her injuries now and from the past.

Beck helped her lie back on the table so Dr. Bowden could examine her torso and especially her aching ribs. Beck did what he always did and kept his gaze averted from her naked body. He never stopped holding her hand, even when she yelped in pain when Dr. Bowden pressed on the very worst bruises and swelling along her side. Even Beck flinched.

"I'm sorry, Ashley. Did he hit you with an object or his fists?"

"His fists on my back and ribs. Riding crop on my legs. He likes the different sounds they make. He likes to put his hands on me. He wants me to scream. But I can't scream too soon, or it ruins his fun. If I do, he'll punish me more. I have to hold it in and go to another place in my mind. I have to go to the river, where I can't hear his taunts and how much he loves me. All I want to do is hear the river, see the pretty trees, feel the sunlight warm on my face." She left off the part about the dark-haired man who always seemed out of reach. The man she'd hoped would save her.

Beck swore and squeezed her hand, bringing it to his lips.

She opened her eyes, and there he was, leaning over her, his gray-blue eyes filled with rage and sorrow and something she hoped was real and not just her imagination.

Dr. Bowden gave them a minute.

Ashley stared into Beck's eyes, seeing so much without him having to say a word. She hoped he saw the same thing in her eyes for him.

Sometimes you just didn't have the words to tell someone how much it meant for them to stand beside you and comfort you through one of the worst moments in your life.

Beck closed the front of her gown. Not because of the terrible injuries, or to keep her from being embarrassed about him seeing her, but to offer her some protection from being exposed like this. She felt open and raw and violated all over again even though this was necessary and required to help her. He got that.

"Finish up, Doc."

"I'll need you to move down the table." Dr. Bowden put the stirrups up.

Ashley's whole body shook uncontrollably. Beck remained leaning half over her, his gaze steady on hers.

Ashley got into position, though it took all her courage and strength to put her feet up.

"I'm sure you've done this before, but I'll talk you through each step so nothing is a surprise and you expect each touch." Dr. Bowden did just that, completing the exam as quickly as possible and making her notes for the official record.

"Everything looks fine, Ashley, including the strings from your IUD." Dr. Bowden pulled off her gloves with that rubbery snap echoing through the room. "Go ahead and scoot back."

Ashley did so, rolling to her side, facing Beck, and tucking her legs up to her belly. She stared at Beck's shirt, tears sliding down her cheeks. She didn't know why she cried anymore.

"Can you tell me approximately how many times or at least how often he raped you?" Dr. Bowden's whispered words didn't lessen the impact of what they meant.

"Does it count if he never actually achieved that particular brutality? Do all the times he put his hands on me, rubbed his body against mine, forced himself between my legs but never got it up, make any difference if he didn't actually do the act?"

Beck leaned down, his hand braced at her back, the other holding her hand at her chest. "Yes. Every ugly thing he did to you counts. He will pay for all of it."

Ashley recited the terrible things Brice did to her in a remote voice that didn't sound like her at all. Dr. Bowden wrote them down to add to the assault charges against Brice.

Beck stood beside her, a vibrating ball of barely contained rage.

She went numb.

"Let's head up to X-ray, then we'll do the IV. While that's being done, Ashley, for the official record and your well-being, I'd like to have a psychiatrist talk to you. It's not that I don't think you're coping well, but I think you'll want an evaluation for your case and a chance to talk about what happened."

"I have Beck." Though maybe it wasn't fair to dump her shit on him when he had so much of his own to deal with.

"Is there a female doctor available?" Beck asked, knowing she didn't want to talk to a man who might inadvertently feel like a threat to her. A woman might relate more to her than a man in these circumstances.

"I've made that request. If there's not, we can find someone and do it later, but I'd like her evaluated soon so it's on record."

Beck helped Ashley sit up and slide off the table. He held her arm to steady her as she sat in the wheelchair. Her ribs and back ached more after the exam.

"Do you have a blanket or sheet?" Beck asked Dr. Bowden.

"Behind you in the cupboard."

Beck pulled out a sheet and draped it over her. She clutched it to her chest and settled back into the chair, exhausted already.

Dr. Bowden touched her shoulder gently. "We're almost done."

Ashley wondered if this whole ordeal would ever be over.

CHAPTER TWENTY-THREE

Brice sat next to his high-priced lawyer, bored out of his mind and pissed off that the sheriff left without doing what Brice wanted. These people didn't know anything. They didn't get it. He resented them keeping him waiting in this small room that reeked of burnt coffee and other people's desperation. The officers outside the inner wall of glass stared at him. Some with nervous smiles, overcome with their excitement at seeing a celebrity. He felt like an animal caged behind glass. His sense of freedom faded with every second that ticked by and they built their case against him for something they didn't understand.

Ashley wanted to be with him. She wanted to be transformed.

"Brice, we need to come up with a better plan than accusing Ashley of kidnapping a child who doesn't actually belong to you. The cops are going to ask about his mother, his father, other family members. Do you even know?"

"The boy doesn't matter. The only thing that matters is that I walk out of here."

"That's not going to happen. They want to charge you with kidnapping, multiple attempted rapes, assault, and attempted murder if they can get it because they think you starved that woman near to death over the last year," Arthur W. Carroll III emphasized.

"Then it's your job to convince them none of that happened. She's a messed-up movie star with a self-image problem that manifested itself as an eating disorder. I tried to help her."

Sergeant Foster walked in overhearing Brice's last words. "You tried to help her?" He pinched one side of his mouth back in a derisive scoff. He pulled a photo out of the folder he carried and placed it on the table in front of Mr. Carroll. "Does that look like your client helped her in any way?"

Brice touched Ashley's beautiful face.

Sergeant Foster pulled the picture away and held it up in front of Mr. Carroll, but addressed Brice. "You don't even see her skeletal frame, the bruises you left all over her body, or the devastation in her eyes."

"She's a troubled woman." Brice sat back in his chair, tired of trying to explain to everyone what he'd done for her. "I tried to love her enough to make her happy."

"You love her," Sergeant Foster spit out.

"Sergeant, my client and Miss Swan were friends, who became lovers."

"Not according to Miss Swan. Mooney can't get his tiny pecker up even for the so-called love of his life."

Mr. Carroll interjected. "If that's true, and that is her statement, then you see, he never raped her."

"No, but the number of sexual assault charges alone stack up to a life in prison." Sergeant Foster sneered. "He didn't want to fuck her—he gets off on the pain he inflicts." The sergeant leaned in close. "One hand on your dick, the other slamming a fist into her ribs." He pulled another photo out of the folder and held it up.

Mr. Carroll gasped and fell back in his seat, his face turning green. He looked away from the red, purple, and blue splotches covering Ashley's perfect body. Brice felt his manhood stir as he relived the last night they were together.

"Wipe that disgusting look off your face," the sergeant ordered. "How can you look at that and get off on it?"

"You don't understand the connection Ashley and I share."

"Their relationship was tumultuous. Their lovemaking unconventional, but consensual." Mr. Carroll tried to defend him again. That's what Brice paid him to do, but Brice felt the reasonable doubt he'd built with his story slipping away.

"You think she wanted him to break eight of her ribs over the last year? That she liked it when he broke her arm because she stopped him from kicking a child? You think she got off on him hitting her so hard that he tore her muscles to shreds? Or that she liked it when he snapped her finger like a twig when she tried to get him off but he couldn't get it up and blamed her?" He pulled another photo out. "Do you really think she liked being whipped with a riding crop until her thighs and back were striped like a tiger?"

"What we have here is nothing more than a domestic dispute." Mr. Carroll tried to put things into perspective.

"He kept her locked in a windowless cell."

"She had a beautiful room if she wanted it," Brice pointed out.

His attorney grabbed his arm, a silent command to shut up. They didn't get it.

Ashley needed the isolation to become that which he knew she could be. The person she wanted to be for him.

"She wanted to escape. And she finally did when you didn't close the door all the way."

Brice seethed. One mistake. She betrayed him. Now she wanted to see him behind bars after all he'd done for her.

"We have a warrant to search your house. Call it whatever you want, but we'll find the evidence to prove you are the monster Miss Swan claims. Then, you'll never see the light of day without looking through a set of bars or barbed wire. That's more than you allowed her."

Sergeant Foster turned to the commotion in the outer office, where two officers wrestled a drunk and belligerent man through the front door. The man slammed one officer into a desk, toppling a lamp and sending papers floating to the floor. The officer stumbled back. The one still holding the guy got a kick to the gut that sent him into a bank of filing cabinets.

"Stay put." Sergeant Foster ran out the door, pulling it closed behind him, and ran to help the other officers wrangle the out-of-control man into submission.

Brice took this opening and headed for the door.

"Where are you going?" Mr. Carroll demanded.

Brice didn't stop. With the officers intent on wrestling the drunk to the ground, he didn't have much time to make his getaway.

Mr. Carroll tried to stop him. "You'll only make things worse if you leave."

"Then I guess you'll have to earn the ungodly retainer I paid you."

Brice left the sputtering attorney at his back and dashed around the corner and down the hallway that led to the restrooms and employee parking lot. The officers were all on their knees, subduing the drunk on the ground wrestling to get free. All the officers were inside, their attention diverted, as he walked out the side door while they were dealing with the man yelling that his wife was a cunt and he'd never laid a hand on her.

Brice didn't think he'd get any further with that explanation than Brice had gotten trying to make them believe that what he'd done for Ashley had been her wish and her will. He'd do anything for her. And once he had her back, he'd finish what they started.

CHAPTER TWENTY-FOUR

The short ride down the hall and up the elevator went by in a blur of people staring and whispering. Though there were many X-rays to cover the old and new breaks in Ashley's bones, they went by fast, or so it seemed as she completely zoned out and went numb. She could do so with Beck a constant presence by her side or standing sentry outside the X-ray room.

Dr. Bowden settled her in another room and a more comfortable bed while they set up the IV and gave it time to slowly work its way into her system. The pain meds she added didn't make her loopy, but lessened the pain and helped her relax after the day's ordeal.

They helped loosen her tongue, too. She'd spent the last twenty minutes answering Dr. Lanning's questions. She'd never seen a shrink. Didn't know what to expect, but it felt more like talking to a new friend than someone trying to pry secrets out of her head.

"Is being in the hospital difficult?"

"It makes what happened to me seem even more real." She didn't know if that made sense. Of course what happened to her was real.

"Now everyone will know," Dr. Lanning spoke Ashley's thought.

"Yes. Not just the people who've seen me here."

"Fans are swarming outside with the reporters and

photographers. Your celebrity will ensure the story is spread far and wide."

"There will be no escaping it."

"Is that what you want to do? Escape?"

"Wouldn't you? I wanted to be famous, but I didn't want this. I wanted to be known for my work, the characters I played."

"He took what you wanted and turned it against you."

"He took the greatest thing in my life and made it ugly. I make people forget who I am and show them someone else. He twisted that around on me. And when I couldn't convince him, he punished me."

"Because you aren't those characters, Ashley. You're real. They are an illusion. One that you created, but that is different to each and every person who sees it because their perception is different from everyone else's. Your version of that character takes on a life of its own in their imagination outside the story you show them on the screen. You'd have never gotten it right because he still saw himself as he is, but he wanted you to play the character who fell for the man sharing the screen with you."

That made more sense than anything she'd ever thought to justify Brice's behavior and how no matter how perfectly she played the role to match the movie, she'd never gotten it right for him, when it should have been perfect.

The same sense of frustration and defeat filled her.

Dr. Lanning glanced over her shoulder at Beck, who Ashley stared at nonstop. He centered her. He never took his gaze off her, but still caught both of the guys who walked by pretending to check their phones, but really snapped photos of her. He'd simply snagged the phones from their hands and tossed them to the security guard by the door, who erased the photos and escorted the people away.

"Is it hard for you to be around men?" Dr. Lanning

asked, noting that Beck wasn't the only one outside her window. Doctors and nurses worked at the station just past her room.

"I don't know. I've only really been around Beck and his brother."

"How does it feel to be around Beck? He's a formidable man."

For the first time all day, Ashley smiled softly, making Beck narrow his gaze on her, wondering what made her smile. Him.

"The first time I saw him, he had long hair, a full beard, tattoos up his arm, and an angry glare and scowl on his face. He pulled a gun on me. If I'd met him out in my old life, I'd have crossed the street to avoid him."

"That must have scared you to see him like that with a gun in his hand."

"It did. At first. But I couldn't get the image of him with Adam sleeping in his arms out of my head. That big man held that little boy safe and sound. He told me I could go, but I couldn't take Adam with me. He knew I needed to know I could leave, but he still wanted to protect Adam, even from me because I was out of my mind. Then he took care of me. He wasn't gentle. Not in a way that he coddled me. He nudged. He pushed. He gave it to me straight. He never treated me like I'd break. That made me feel stronger. When I faltered, he held me up. For all Beck has had to do on the job, all the things he's seen and done that weigh on him, I would bet my life that man would never hurt me."

"You've formed a deep connection to him."

"Maybe all a broken soul needs to heal is for another broken soul to see the whole of you and accept you, flaws and all."

"He saved you. It's normal to feel grateful, even beholden to that person."

"I feel both those things for him, but I feel something much deeper, like without him in my life I'd be missing something truly precious."

"Ashley, I should warn you that after what you've been through forming this kind of attachment won't shut off the bad feelings and emotions you need to deal with."

"That's just it. I still feel all those things. I can feel them right out in the open with him. He understands. He gets it in a way others can't because of the things he's seen and done in his life. It's not one-sided either. I see his pain, the torment he's in, the way he's had to play a part and forgotten what it's like to be himself."

"Don't you think that two people who have similar experiences and things to work through and overcome might make it hard to give the other person what they need?"

"You have that wrong, Doctor. We're the perfect people to help each other out because we can't hide from each other."

"What happens when you've both had time to heal and come to terms with your past?"

"I hope we'll be better for each other. Whether that's as friends or something more, I don't know, but I will forever hold him dear. That's just the way it is. I've never had that, or felt this way about anyone. I can't explain it. I don't even feel the need to analyze it or put it in terms that make sense to you or anyone else. After all I've been through, all he's been through, I can only say that I deserve a friend like him in my life. I will be the best I can be for him and hope he feels the way he makes me feel."

"Where do you go from here?"

"I don't know what's going to happen in five minutes, an hour, or days from now. I can't seem to think like that right now. It overwhelms me. I know this thing will spin out of control. I don't want to go with it. I want to find the calm in the storm and breathe. When I'm with Beck, it's so easy to find that place." She sighed, wishing to be back at Beck's place, the snow falling outside, a fire in the hearth, and her safe with him. "I'm tired. I don't want to talk anymore."

She kept her gaze locked on Beck even as the doctor rose and went out to talk to him.

BECK TURNED TO face the doctor as she came out of Ashley's room. Dr. Bowden joined them for the meeting. Beck made sure no one was close enough to overhear their conversation and kept his voice low. "How is she?"

"As expected, traumatized, suffering from PTSD, but holding strong considering all she's been through. She wants justice. She wants her life back, but she's not sure what that will really look like. She has no real idea what she wants anymore except for this to be over."

"She doesn't need to know every detail right now," Beck pointed out.

"No. I wouldn't expect her to, but she's got a sense that everything will be okay. That's good. She understands that she won't be allowed to cope and deal with this privately. Not like someone unknown would. It weighs on her that the life she chose has made her life infinitely more difficult in this situation where privacy and peace are necessary for her to heal."

"I'll find a way to give her those things the best I can, but under the circumstances we'll have to fight for it."

Dr. Lanning smiled at him. "She found the right man for the job. I have a feeling there's nothing you wouldn't fight for, for her. The bond she's made with you is extraordinary."

"If I can be the calm in her storm, I'll do everything I can to protect her and make her feel safe again."

Dr. Lanning narrowed her eyes. "How did you know . . ."

"Reading lips in my line of work comes in handy when you're watching a suspect across the room and they think you can't hear them."

"What did you think about what she said about you?"

"That I feel exactly the same way about her. I can't explain it either." Two days ago he didn't want to be around anyone. Now he couldn't stand to be ten feet away from her. The impact of her words to Dr. Lanning made his heart ache with wanting her even if it was only exactly what Ashley said, two friends who held each other dear. He wanted more.

"You are important to her in a way that is tied to her recovery. Do you understand what I mean by that?"

"That if I let her down it'll be detrimental to her." He wasn't just talking about hurting her feelings or breaking her heart. Those things were already damaged. He had the ability to devastate her even more. The thought of hurting her in any way made his own battered heart bleed. "I won't let her down."

Dr. Bowden interjected. "Can I release her, or do you think she needs to stay for observation?"

"As long as she's staying with Special Agent Cooke, I see no reason to keep her. Her mental state is shaky, but she's making reasonable and positive decisions." Dr. Lanning directed her attention to him. "Keep things simple right now. Don't ask her to make too many decisions about the future all at once. Keep her focused in the present to help her cope with the nightmares and memories that drag her into the past. Whatever you've been doing, it's working for her. She told me she feels steadier than she has in months because of you. She may suffer bouts of being quiet or withdrawn. Try to pull her out of them, but don't push too hard. She needs time to reflect and put things into perspective. If you feel that her attitude is shifting to destructive thoughts or she feels no sense that good things will happen or she'll ever be happy again, we may need to medicate her and reevaluate her."

"I'll keep a close eye on her."

"She wants to go home, but she's afraid to also. It's normal for her to want to do things, but be afraid of them. Coax her to try, especially when it comes to going outside. She's been locked away—don't let her do that to herself."

"Now that Brice is in custody, I think she'll want to spend more time outside and her fear will fade. She'll lose that sense that he's out there trying to get her."

Dr. Bowden jumped back in. "I'll sign her release papers, but the press and a horde of fans are still camped outside."

Beck glanced over at Ashley, sound asleep in the hospital bed. "I'll let her sleep a couple of hours, then sneak her out."

"The staff is prepared to help you do that," Dr. Bowden assured him.

Dr. Lanning handed him her card. "I'll leave her in your capable hands. If she needs me, give me a call. After all she's been through, talking to a professional will help."

"When she's ready," he assured the doctor. He didn't particularly like his sessions with the psychologist the DEA made him see after the shootings, but he had to admit they helped when he participated.

If Ashley wanted and needed the help, he'd make sure she got it.

"Take care of each other," Dr. Lanning said, shook his hand, then left.

Dr. Bowden gave him a knowing smile. Yeah, he got it—everyone could see how much he and Ashley cared about each other. He'd get used to it. Right now, he wanted to take Ashley away from all the prying eyes. He didn't much like everyone looking so closely at him either. It made his skin itch and the hairs on the back of his neck stand up. The warning that something was about to happen stirred in him but he didn't know why. Then his cell phone beeped with a text message.

Sgt. Mark Foster: Brice Mooney walked out before being arrested. He's in the wind.

Beck swore.

"What's wrong?" Dr. Bowden asked.

"Brice is on the loose. Tell hospital security to be on the lookout. Any reason someone from the staff needs to see Ashley again?"

"I'll remove her IV myself. Otherwise, no."

"No one but you comes into her room."

Beck went to the security guard, gave him the heads-up about Brice and keeping everyone out of Ashley's room, then he went in, took a seat next to her, held her hand, leaned in and kissed her good-night, and stood guard so she could sleep in peace until she woke up.

CHAPTER TWENTY-FIVE

Brice poured the last of the gasoline across the beautiful bed in Ashley's room. He hated to lose the precious art, but had to cover his tracks and didn't have much time. The cops would be here soon to execute their search warrant. All they'd find was the charred remains of the home he shared with Ashley.

He missed her. But he'd get her back. And he knew exactly how he'd find her and Adam. He had an inkling of where he'd find Ashley, but first he needed Adam. The boy could talk about what he'd seen between Brice and Ashley the few times he'd defied Brice's order to remain in his room.

Did he remember more?

Brice couldn't take the chance.

"Everything is set downstairs." Darren held the over-stuffed briefcase in both hands against his chest. Everything from Brice's office, the cash from the safe, and Brice's passports. One in his name. One in a name no one knew.

He had an escape, too. Someplace no one knew about. But first, he needed to collect Adam and Ashley and get them on the plane he had on standby. They'd go to his hideaway and everything would be back to normal.

"I'm done here."

"We need to hurry. We can't get caught here." Darren

checked out the barred windows yet again for any sign of someone coming up the drive. Brice had closed and locked the gates. It would take them a while to bust through and give him time to get away if they arrived too soon.

"Let's go." Brice tossed the empty gas can on the bed and pulled out the gold lighter Snoop Dogg left in his dressing room after sparking up before the show. Brice lit the lighter and tossed it on the four-poster bed that held so many sweet memories of him with Ashley. The flame sparked the fumes seconds before it landed in the puddle of gas and burst into a ball of flames that spread quickly.

Too quickly. He and Darren ran down the stairs. Thick, noxious smoke following them.

The place would burn to the ground before the fire department arrived.

Brice burst through the French doors and ran across the back patio. They fled across the open pasture filled with the horses he'd ordered Darren to release from their stalls in case the stables went up in flames with the house. He wasn't inhuman like that asshole sergeant thought.

Darren stashed the rental car on the dirt road that ran along the edge of his property. They got in and sped away, smoke and flames pouring out of several exploded windows on the second level of the house. No way the fire department made it out here before the fire gutted the place and left only a charred stone facade.

Darren drove the speed limit. Only two other cars passed them on the road. Brice didn't even hide. He planned what came next.

They pulled into the lot behind a deserted office building on the outskirts of town and parked beside the second car Darren rented for Brice. The cops would have a hard time tracking him if they didn't know what car he was in. He'd left all his vehicles at the ranch.

"Go back to your hotel and wait to hear from me," Brice ordered. "I'm going to pay that asshole sergeant a visit and repay him for all the vile things he said to me. He'll tell me where Adam is or wish he did."

"It's too risky. You know where Ashley is. Get her and let's get out of here."

"No. I need Adam, too." Getting past the asshole with the gun and all that security would be dangerous. But if he had Adam, she'd come to him.

"Let me go. I'll find out what the guy knows, get Adam, and bring him to you. You know I can do it."

Darren had seduced a very well-known playboy who didn't want anyone to know all those gorgeous women on his arm were nothing but window dressing to hide what and who he did behind closed doors. Danny Radford refused to appear on Brice's show when ratings were declining and Brice needed the boost. After Darren got the goods, and the pictures to prove the kinky shit he liked, Danny Radford happily appeared on Brice's show. More than once. Every time Brice demanded it.

Brice liked making people bend to his will. He wanted the pleasure of watching that asshole cop squirm, go against his protective instinct, and give up the information Brice wanted but he'd be hell-bent on keeping secret. Brice couldn't wait to break him.

"I need you to be ready to go once I have Ashley and Adam back."

"Let me help you." Darren wanted to prove his love and loyalty to his idol.

Brice would normally use that, but he wanted to be the one to put his family back together. "Do as I say. I'll be back soon." He needed to prove to Ashley that he had what it took to keep her and Adam and be everything she needed and wanted.

CHAPTER TWENTY-SIX

Earlier today Ashley Swan entered a Bozeman hospital emergency room carried by a man identified only as a DEA agent who found her passed out and near death on his property two days ago during a massive snowstorm.

Video of Beck carrying her into the emergency room and her in the wheelchair played on the side of the TV while the ten o'clock news announcer continued.

Ashley escaped a house of horrors miles away. Sources say the house belonged to Brice Mooney.

The video switched to the house going up in flames earlier tonight. Ashley's stomach soured even as she inwardly cheered the destruction of the place that had become her living hell.

The retired After Midnight *talk show host is believed to have set the fire to prevent investigators from serving a search warrant and gathering evidence against him.*

He moved there after Ashley appeared on his final show. Speculation is that Brice kidnapped Ashley and has been holding her there as his prisoner for nearly a year. While everyone in Hollywood suspected she'd run away from the limelight, her closest friends and business associates believed foul play, but their pleas for an investigation went unanswered, despite the L.A. police department stating unequivocally they'd looked into the matter but found no evidence to corroborate their claims or lead them in a direction to locate Ashley Swan.

Now the Oscar-winning actress actually is in hiding while police hunt for Brice Mooney after he walked out of the Montana sheriff's department before he was arrested for multiple counts of kidnapping and assault charges that may put the once-beloved superstar interviewer behind bars for life, if they find him before he flees the country to avoid answering the heinous charges against him.

Coming up, with warmer weather temps expected over the next few days, we'll see clearer skies and runoff filling creeks, steams, and rivers, so be aware of rising waters and flooding in some areas. Let's go to Allan with the full weather forecast.

Ashley sat up from leaning against Beck's shoulder while they watched TV after he snuck her out of the hospital and brought her home. But not before he stopped and got her the promised burger and fries she didn't really want anymore. Her hospital visit left her drained and anxious after bringing up so much of the past. Beck let loose the arm he'd gently draped over her shoulders to hold her close. She should feel safe, but didn't with Brice on the loose again.

"I spent the day getting all the evidence I could gathered up for the cops and Brice walks out of the station without anyone trying to stop him and destroys evidence."

"They don't need the house to prove what he did to you." Beck spoke softly and gently, sensing her rising anger and panic.

"Don't need it? I wanted them to see, to understand, that inside that beautiful house with all the pretty, expensive things, he hid me away in a room built to destroy me from the inside out."

"He didn't destroy you."

"He tried. Again and again and again."

"You survived. Again and again and again."

"He's out there. Free. Able to hurt me or someone else. That's not right."

"The cops have doubled their efforts. They want to find him just as much as we do."

"Yeah, to save their pride for letting him get away." She knew that wasn't fair, but her anger ruled her tongue right now.

"He'll go down for what he did to you," Beck assured her in that same soft, definite tone.

Deflated of her anger and filled with a sense of uselessness because she couldn't do anything to find Brice, she hung her head and sighed out her frustration.

Beck's hand settled on the back of her neck and squeezed her tight muscles. The warmth and his restrained strength unknotted the tension in her neck and belly.

Beck shut the TV off with his free hand, gave her one last squeeze on her shoulder, then stood and held his hand out to her. "Come on, sweetheart. You're beat. You need to get some sleep."

"I'll take the couch. You can have your bed back."

Beck shook his head, his hand still out to her, palm up, his patience infinite where she was concerned.

She took his hand and stood when he tugged her up gently. "You can't be comfortable sleeping in that recliner or on the couch. You're too damn big."

Beck stood with his back to the fire, his features dark in contrast to the bright glow behind him. He looked just like Dr. Lanning described. Formidable. "Does my size bother you?"

"The opposite. It comforts me. I feel like nothing can get past you. You make me feel so safe," she admitted.

He slipped his hand beneath her hair at the back of her neck and pulled her into his chest. His cheek pressed against the top of her head. His heart beat slow and steady against her ear, though it sped up when she wrapped her arms around his middle and snuggled in close to him.

"You are safe with me, Ashley."

The way he said that hit her heart like a love bomb that sparked a thousand stars and lit up her soul. Whimsy. Happiness. She'd missed feeling this way. And Beck brought it back to her.

Beck stepped back, took her hand, and led her to his bedroom. He let her go beside the bed and went to the cold fireplace. She sat on the edge of the mattress, glanced out the huge windows at the millions of sparkling stars, and felt the wonder of all that big open sky. She'd missed the sky, the beach after a storm, a quiet morning under the trees in her backyard, walking down a crowded street unnoticed as she window-shopped, lunch with friends, and flirting with a sexy man. She actually had a hard time thinking of the last time she'd done the last. Now she found her gaze and heart only went to one man.

Ashley stared at Beck's back as he stuffed wadded newspapers into the crevices between the kindling and logs he'd laid out in the bedroom hearth. His wide shoulders blocked most of the fireplace. The muscles in his arms bunched as he worked. His back tapered to a really nice ass in jeans. He sat on his heels, but rose up on his knees to light the fire, giving her an even-better look at his ass and taut thighs. A soft glow highlighted him in the dark, and while the fire's warmth spread through the room, another kind of warmth spread through her.

Desire.

The need to connect with another so deep and consuming you wanted to heed its call even when things seemed really bad. Here was a chance for something pure and good.

Beck scratched at the back of his leg. She caught him

doing it all the time. That and rubbing at one of the healed gunshot wounds on his chest and side. He needed comfort, a distraction, someone to be kind and loving, just like she did.

"Is your leg bothering you?"

Beck glanced over his shoulder at her, then back at the fire. "No. It itches when the skin stretches. I'm fine, sweetheart."

He used that sweet name more and more when he spoke to her and it made another spark of joy burst in her heart each time.

"Can I see it?"

Beck twisted and studied her watching him. "Sure." He sat on his butt, the fire glowing hot and wild beside him. He pulled off his sock and dragged the hem of his jeans up his leg to bunch at his knee. He turned his leg so she could see the burn scars, red and white, puckered and smooth all up the back of his leg.

She slid off the end of the bed and crawled over to him, sitting on her knees between his feet. She reached out, but pulled her hand back.

Beck met her gaze. "You can touch it. It doesn't hurt. Some of it I can't feel at all."

She smoothed her fingers and palm up the back of his leg, her gaze following her hand over the smooth but rough skin. She met his steady stare. "Are your chest and side better?"

"The exercise helps my shoulder. My side aches a bit when it's really cold, but they're both healed."

"Show me."

Beck's eyes filled with heat, hotter than the blaze in the fire. "What are you doing, Ashley?"

"Being brave." She swept her hands up over his knees and down his corded thighs. His breath stopped with hers. She scrunched the hem of his shirt in her hands and dragged it up his lean body and over his head when he raised his arms. She tossed the shirt away, her eyes locked on Beck's massive chest and the scar from a bullet that ripped into him. The thought of him hurt froze her heart and sent a chill up her spine.

She leaned in and kissed the scar. Beck braced his hands on the floor slightly behind him, leaned back, and let her kiss the scar on his side. "Ashley." He choked out her name.

"I'm safe with you, Beck. You're safe with me. I won't hurt you. I just want to make you feel good. *I* want to feel good." She kissed her way up his chest and found his hungry mouth. He slid his tongue along hers, but didn't touch her. He let her lead, let her hands roam over all the tense muscles in his chest, shoulders, and arms. She lost herself in the feel and taste of him until he vibrated with all the need he put into kissing her.

She leaned back just enough to look him in the eye. "Touch me, Beck. I want you to."

And just like that she let him loose to love her the way she desperately needed him to love her. He wrapped his arm around her shoulders, his big hand on her head, his lips fused to hers as he rolled, gently laying her on the rug beside him, his body half covering hers as he kissed her again and again. She settled back and sighed out her pleasure as her hands rubbed over the muscles in his back and down to cover his ass.

Like following a map in his mind, Beck touched every place on her that sent ripples of pleasure spreading through her system and never once touched any place that might cause her pain. She wallowed in the desire Beck fanned inside her with every stroke of his hand, every touch of his lips against hers, down her neck, and over her chest.

Like before, he waited for her to ask for more. Dissatisfied with the barriers between them, she peeled off her shirt. Beck helped her with the bra, replacing the soft cup with his urgent mouth and tongue sucking at her taut and so-sensitive nipples.

His hand slid down her belly and back up. On the next descent, she rocked her hips toward his hand and called, "More." He slipped his fingers down her leggings, over her mound, and between her legs, his fingers softly brushing her already-wet folds. "More." She sighed out the word.

Beck sucked hard at her nipple until it pulled free of his lips. He pressed his fingers to the seam between her legs and stared down into her eyes. "Ashley, if you're not ready . . ."

"Do you want me?"

"More than I've ever wanted anything in my whole damn life."

She rose up and kissed him, pushing him onto his back. She sat beside him and showed him how much she wanted him, undoing the button on his jeans and sliding the zipper down over his hard length. She spread the denim wide and slid her hand over his thick, boxer-covered shaft, having a moment's hesitation before she found the need for him far outweighed the past that wanted to steal even this from her. She wouldn't let it and dragged the jeans and Beck's boxers down his legs. She boldly took him in her hand. Warm, hard, smooth. She felt his need in the pulse against her palm and the ragged breath he let loose when she stroked him up and down.

His hand smoothed up her thigh and down to her knee in the same rhythm she used on his hard cock.

Unable to endure her pleasuring him, he rose up, took her breast in his mouth again, dragging her over his chest as he lay back down. She sighed and arched her back, pushing her breast into his mouth. One arm held her in place; the other hand dragged her panties and leggings down her legs. She kicked them free when Beck couldn't manage, too distracted sliding his hand up the back of her leg, over her ass, up her back, then back down over her rounded bottom until his fingers found her wet center and one finger sank deep inside her and stroked in and out as her hips rocked against his hard length pressed to her belly.

"Condom," Beck said, laying a trail of kisses from one breast to the other, trying to hold on to her and set her away so he could get up for what he'd said.

She held him close, pulled his hand away from her slick center, shifted and sank down an inch on the head of his hard cock. She stared down at him, felt his whole body vibrate beneath hers wanting to join them together. He knew she had birth control. He didn't have to worry about getting her pregnant. She didn't have to worry about anything with Beck. In all things, he'd protect himself. He didn't need to protect himself with her. She didn't want anything between them.

"Me and you and nothing but what is real between us."

Beck thrust into her, drew her down, kissed her softly as his body moved inside her, against her, around her. Their lovemaking was raw and open. No barriers. No hesitation. No taking without giving everything. She lost herself in him and the moment. He went under with her, and when they rose to the pinnacle and found that pure bliss, she collapsed on his chest wrapped in his arms and knew true peace and heaven for the first time in her life.

CHAPTER TWENTY-SEVEN

The fire died an hour ago. Beck could barely make out Ashley's beautiful face on the pillow next to him as she slept in his arms without a single nightmare disturbing her rest. She needed it after they made love in front of the fire. His body stirred just thinking about it. She was everything he wanted in a lover but never found. Open. Honest. No trace of self-consciousness. No hesitation to take what she wanted or give herself over to him, knowing he only wanted to please her. After all she'd been through she found it within herself to give him that gift.

What they shared went deeper than two people needing a distraction or release. It wasn't just mutual attraction or lust. He'd had that and found it felt good in the moment, but never lasted long after it was over. Even now, he wanted more with Ashley. Not just to feel her body move over and against his again, but to feel the connection they shared even now flare to life and take them both to a place that only existed for them.

He loved her. It surprised him how quickly and completely it came to him. He never expected it. Never thought he'd be blessed to have something this good and right in his life. But here she was, lying in his arms. And even though he didn't think he deserved her, he'd spend the rest of his life trying to be worthy of all she offered him or die trying. He'd wished to find the kind of love and companionship Caden found with Mia. He had it. Now all he had to do was hold on to it. Her. For the rest of his life.

The thought didn't even make one nerve twinge with anxiety. Thinking of the rest of his life without her, this kind of happiness, made his future seem bleak.

He brushed his fingers over her cheek, hoping he didn't wake her but needing to touch her. She snuggled in closer to his chest and tossed her leg over his, pulling him close so not even a breath of air was between their bodies.

She read him so well. Better than anyone. Caden got him, but Ashley saw right into him, found all the broken pieces, and with her words and hard-to-come-by smiles and the way she loved him with an open heart that she had every reason to protect, she healed him.

He wanted to heal her, but the best he could do right now was hide her away. "I'll keep you safe," he promised, hoping nothing and no one made him break that promise.

The quiet finally settled into him as he listened to Ashley's soft breath whispering across his skin. Nearly asleep, he jolted when his phone vibrated. Ashley bolted upright in bed, her hands up to ward off an attack as she gasped for a breath.

"You're okay," he assured her, putting one hand on her thigh and grabbing his phone off the bedside table with the other. He might have spoken too soon.

King: One on foot North two o'clock out back door

Beck rolled out of bed, grabbed his jeans off the floor, and dragged them up his legs before Ashley even spoke. "What is it?"

"Someone is on the property."

"How do you know?"

I have a sniper on the roof. He didn't think she'd like hearing that. "Someone is watching over us."

"A guard?"

"A friend from the DEA. Get dressed." He tossed her the pants and T-shirt he found on the floor. She dressed quickly while he checked the clip in his gun, pulled two more out of the bedside drawer, and stuffed them in his back pocket. He took her hand, pulling her along after him through the house to the kitchen. The fire in the living room had died to embers leaving the house in total darkness.

Ashley's hand trembled in his as he pulled her through the kitchen to the pantry door. "I need you to be brave. I hate to do this to you, but I need to know you're safe."

"Beck, please don't leave me." Her voice cracked. "Stay. I don't want anything to happen to you."

"It won't. I promise. I need you to get inside the pantry."

Her eyes went wide with fear. He hated panicking her, but he needed to move and make sure the asshole who dared trespass on his land and came after his woman didn't make it within a thousand yards of her.

"If he's coming, you have to get me out of here."

"It could just be a reporter, a fan, or some photog hoping to get a picture of you. I don't have time to find out and get you out of here. Please, sweetheart, I need to protect you and this is the only way I can do what I have to do without being distracted that you're not where I put you." He didn't need to say anything more. He was so proud of her for conquering her fear. She opened the door and stepped inside. "The door is steel and locks from the inside."

Her eyes narrowed with that bit of news. Yes, if someone got in, he had his own safe room with food, water, and a bulletproof door to give him time to call for help and survive until it got here. He lived a pretty fucked-up life to need something like this to make him feel safe, but right now he thanked his paranoia for a means to keep Ashley alive and safe.

"Do not open this door unless I tell you to, or a man named King comes for you. He's six-two, blond, has a scar on his left bicep that looks like a lightning bolt. We shoot together. He beat me last time with a shot at a green apple dead center at a thousand meters. If the guy can't answer all that for you accurately, don't open this door." He kissed her fast and hard, putting everything he wanted to say in the brief kiss. He shoved her in the door and pulled it closed. He didn't move until he heard the click of both locks. "Good girl. I'm coming back for you," he promised, stomping his feet into his snow boots, tying them off, and grabbing his jacket. He went through the house to the window in his office with the huge bush growing in front of it. Anyone watching the house might see him come out of the doors, so he'd use the cover of night, the shadows the bush cast on the house and window, and sneak out that way.

As quiet as he was, King chirped like a bird to let him know he was clear to run for the target. Beck took an indirect route, King sending him texts to give him the location of the man still working his way through the deep snow toward the house.

Only one man. Beck didn't think Brice would be this stupid to come looking for her here after the news reported that she was with a DEA agent. His boss threatened every news station that if they let out his name they'd find themselves in deep shit. Luckily, all of them complied. So far. Beck wasn't under any illusions he'd keep his identity a secret. They may not have his name, but everyone saw his face. It wouldn't be long before those who knew Trigger figured out the DEA guy and him were one and the same.

The dumbshit walking straight across his land to the house didn't even try to conceal his tracks, hide in the shadows, or be quiet. Beck circled around, drawing closer to him. With a ski mask covering his face, Beck couldn't ID the guy, but he was the right height. With the bulky coat and snow pants, Beck couldn't guess accurately at his weight. It could be Brice. Or some paparazzi asshole, although Beck didn't see a camera with a telephoto lens, or some other recording device. The guy could have something in his stuffed backpack.

Beck snuck up behind the guy, leveled his gun, and put a stop to amateur hour in the woods. "DEA. Stop right there and put your hands up."

The guy didn't follow directions and spun around, his eyes wide. Beck caught a glint of metal a second before he fired, hitting the guy in the chest, and another bullet ripped through his back and exploded out his shoulder, making him drop the gun before his knees even hit the ground and he fell face forward gasping for a breath.

Beck waved his hand over his head to let King know he wasn't hit despite the close call.

The guy sputtered and tried to roll over. Beck took hold of his good arm and dragged him over so he fell on his back beside the bloodstained snow. Blood seeped out of the hole in his shoulder. The guy grabbed his chest where Beck shot him and pulled his hands away and held them up, blood dripping down his fingers.

"You sh-hot m-m-me." The words came out stilted with pain.

Yeah, looks like he didn't get through the month without shooting someone.

"You pulled a gun on me, idiot. I told you I'm DEA. What did you think would happen?"

He sat up and grabbed the front of Beck's coat in both his bloody hands and pulled Beck close, getting in his face. "You took her from him. He's coming for you. He'll kill you for taking what is his."

"Let him come. He'll get exactly what you got and

worse." Beck shoved the guy back to the ground before King took another shot at him. He snatched the black ski mask off his face, confirming he wasn't Brice Mooney, but the same guy who came with him looking for Ashley. Some thirtyish guy with light brown hair, thick brows, and a baby face that made his feral frown seem petulant instead of mean. "Who are you?"

"He will come for her. She belongs to him."

"He'll have to get past me and that's not going to happen."

"He will."

"You didn't," Beck pointed out.

The guy let loose a hysterical laugh as blood spewed out of his mouth. They must have hit a lung. He'd die if they didn't get him medical help in time. King would have called in the troops by now.

"He'll get you, and then he'll take her back." The guy sputtered, gasped for a breath that ended in a watery-sounding gurgle, then he died.

Beck swore, turned toward the house, stood and waved his fingers across his neck a couple times to let King know the guy didn't make it.

If Brice sent this guy, who was he? Not a professional hit man, that's for sure. Beck pried the backpack off him, unzipped it, and pulled out the contents one by one, his gut tightening and his rage intensifying with each item. Duct tape. Rope. A knife. Apparently, the gun was to take Beck out, so he could take Ashley.

He wanted to keep this from Ashley, but he'd have to tell her. Maybe she could ID the guy. He needed to go and get her, but first he had to make sure no one came with this asshole. If Brice was waiting for the dead man to bring Ashley to him, he'd find hell came looking for him instead.

The tracks led straight back through the woods to a fire road that bordered his property. He had security set up in that direction. Either the guy saw it and avoided it—not likely—or, as he'd feared, the cold temps disabled it. He'd checked everything himself, but with temps dropping at night some of the sensors were bound to go out. Either way, he'd posted King on guard as backup.

Beck took a winding path back to the road and spotted the rental car. He discreetly circled the area, checking to be sure no one was around. With no other tracks in the snow, no sight of anyone else hiding in the vehicle, Beck approached and breathed a sigh of relief that Brice wasn't out there trying to get to Ashley and frustrated he couldn't take the bastard down right now.

Beck went through the front of the car and found a gas and hotel room receipt, but nothing else. He popped the trunk and went to the back to take a look. Among Brice's legal and financial papers he must have cleaned out of the house before he torched it, Beck found several other interesting files, confirming Ashley's account that Brice liked to take pictures of his guests, unbeknownst to them until it was too late. He grabbed the whole lot, stuffed them inside his jacket, and because his guilt over leaving Ashley in the pantry ate away at him, he ran back to get her.

He needed to see her. He needed to be sure she was okay. Hurting her like that, stuffing her in a dark room, killed him. He'd make it up to her. He couldn't ease her mind about her claustrophobia, but he could eliminate the thing that caused her nightmares.

He'd find Brice and make him pay for making Beck do this to her.

CHAPTER TWENTY-EIGHT

Ashley huddled on the floor with her knees up and her arms wrapped around them. The crack of gunfire pierced the quiet with two sharp pops, then everything went quiet again. She wanted to run to Beck, but stayed put, knowing there was nothing she could do to help, but getting in his way would put him in danger.

She made herself breathe, slowly and evenly as she listened to every tiny sound, any sign that Beck, or someone else, had come for her. The silence terrified her. Her mind tried to take her back to the days, weeks, months she was kept in that awful cell. But she fought off those memories with her fear for Beck's safety.

Please be okay.

Her one and only prayer.

She thought about him out there trying to take down her enemy and protect her. Memories of them making love in front of the fire, his gentle hands on her body, making her feel warm and safe and loved, and all the while she felt his strength in every hard muscle pressed against her. He'd use that strength and his training to stay safe.

He had to be all right.

"Ashley, open up."

She didn't recognize the voice. It wasn't Brice, or Beck's deep voice either. She didn't answer, but held her breath and her knees tighter to her chest as her heart slammed into her ribs over and over again.

"Beck sent me. You probably heard the shots. He's okay. You can come out." His voice was soft and gentle, but she still hesitated.

"I'm King. I work with him at the DEA. We're old friends."

She found her voice. "Who won the shooting match?"

"I did." The triumph in his voice told her the rivalry meant a great deal to him.

"How far?"

"A thousand meters, dead center. I kicked Beck's ass." Pride made it sound like he smiled when he said that.

"What was the target?"

"An apple."

"What color?"

"Green," he said without hesitation.

Ashley rose from the cold, hard floor, unbolted the door, and opened it slowly. The man stepped back, giving her room to come out and enough space not to seem threatening.

"Show me the scar on your arm."

He pulled his thick black ski jacket down his arm and his sleeve up. A lightning bolt scar zigzagged over his bicep.

"You can put the rolling pin down now."

She found the solid piece of wood on the shelf and thought Beck left it there more as a weapon than a means to make a pie. He definitely wasn't the pie-making kind of guy.

"Where is he?"

"He'll be here soon and so will reinforcements. I checked the perimeter and inside the house already. We're safe here, but I'll stay with you until Beck gets back."

She spotted the rifle with a scope propped beside the back door. "The shots?"

"One man down. Beck is not hurt," he assured her again.

"Brice?"

"I don't know."

"I want to see him." She ran to the front door and grabbed her jacket and stuffed her feet in her boots.

"We need to stay here."

"No." She needed to know if they shot Brice, if he was really dead. Her need to see Beck and make sure he was okay became an urgency that drove her right past the big man trying to block her from running out the back door. She hit the yard and ran toward the dark figure coming out of the wooded area to her right. King's footsteps sounded behind her as he ran with her to Beck. She didn't slow when she got close, but launched herself into Beck's open arms.

He crushed her in a hug and held her tight, letting loose a second after he kissed her head two times fast. He held her face and leaned down and kissed her hard. "I'm sorry I put you in that dark room." He kissed her again. "I'm sorry."

She pressed her forehead to his and looked him in the eye. "I'm okay. Are you okay?"

"Fine. It wasn't him." Disappointment filled his eyes. "I don't know who the guy is but I think Brice sent him for you."

"Where is he?"

"You don't want to see him, sweetheart."

"Maybe I can tell you who he is."

"No." Beck didn't want to traumatize her even more.

"I can handle it, Beck. If I can tell you who he is, it will save you time trying to figure it out and why he'd help Brice."

"She's got a point." King added his agreement.

Beck's face pinched into angry lines on his forehead and around his mouth, but he gave in and turned toward the direction he came from earlier. He didn't walk in that direction, just waited for her to make the first move.

She took Beck's hand and walked forward. He fell in step and directed her where to go. The white snow turned red as she moved closer to the body splayed out on the ground beside the open backpack with a roll of tape, rope, and a huge knife beside them. A gun lay in the snow several feet away.

It didn't take much imagination to put the scene together and act it out in her mind and see what this guy intended and how he'd ended up dead. It took her a minute to bring her gaze to his face, and when she did, she sucked in a surprised breath and covered her mouth with her hand.

"Do you know him?" Beck asked, squeezing her hand.

"His name is Darren. He's Brice's assistant. Brice treats him like crap, but Darren thinks Brice walks on water. He's obsessed with making sure no one treats Brice as anything less than a god. It's weird, but you see it in the business. I've had lots of people want to work with me who claimed to be my biggest fan and would work hard to get me everything I wanted. He's a people pleaser to the extreme when it comes to Brice."

"Do you think Brice ordered him to come and get you?"

"I think he'd do just about anything to get Brice's attention and earn the appreciation Brice would never show him."

"Asshole." King spun around and walked back toward the house.

Beck called after him, "Did she make you prove who you were?"

"And then some, I had to strip down to prove it." King gave Beck a wicked grin, taunting him.

Beck eyed her.

"He's got a huge . . ."

Beck's eyes narrowed dangerously.

"Frame. You were right, six-two."

Beck growled his frustration and pulled her into his side.

"And a scar on his bicep just like you said." She hugged him close. "I did just what you said." She tapped his belly in a playful punch, but hit something hard instead. "What is that?"

Beck unzipped his jacket and pulled out the folders. "Hold on to these. I want to go through them before the cops get here. Maybe we can use something in there. I saw the guardianship papers for Adam."

"I have the file on Adam's father," King added.

"What?" Ashley couldn't believe they'd found him. She stopped walking back to the house and looked up at Beck. "You've been looking for Adam's father?"

"King used tax records for all the people working at Brice's ranch. We made an educated decision on who might be Adam's mother based on the time she worked there and when she stopped getting paid. Once we had Jackie Howard's name and social, we found Adam's birth certificate. If Adam has a family, he should be returned to them."

"I know, but . . ." She didn't know what to say, except she'd promised to take care of him and hadn't thought about having to give him up. Sadness swamped her heart. She missed him already. She wanted to keep him.

"His father is a piece of work. He's in jail. Will be for the next twenty years," King told them. "The only other family Adam has is a grandmother raising two other grandchildren in a trailer park in Florida on her public assistance and not much else. Adam's cousins are ten and twelve and headed for a life of crime according to their school rap sheets and their many detentions for stealing and fighting."

Ashley shook her head in dismay. "How do you know all this?"

"King has a love affair with his computer."

"And beautiful actresses," he flirted, making Beck pull her to his other side and farther away from King, who snickered like a teenage boy.

"Get your own. She's mine."

Ashley's heart expanded with that sweet sentiment. It didn't feel possessive in the way that Brice made her feel, like some object he coveted. She felt wanted and cherished.

"I've got an op that will take me inside the prison where Adam's father is incarcerated." King's eyes narrowed as he got lost in thought. "I'd like to use him to get to the guys I need to get close to, and if we play our cards right, maybe he'll sign over custody to you, Ashley. Otherwise, I see Adam living in squalor and on the same path as his cousins in a few short years."

"That can't happen." Ashley didn't even want to think about what would happen to Adam's fragile psyche if he was put in yet another volatile home. He needed a place where he felt safe and protected and loved. The grandmother might be doing the best she could, but Ashley could do better. She had the resources to do a hell of a lot better. And she would.

They entered the dark house, and Beck and King made her wait in the kitchen while they checked the place top to bottom again, making sure Brice or anyone else hadn't snuck in while they were out back looking at that poor man who lost his way when his admiration for Brice turned down a dark road. Literally in this case, as that dark road led him to his death.

Ashley spread the files Beck had given her on the table and sorted through them, discarding the financial records along with the property and vehicle papers. She opened the file containing the guardianship papers and read them, frowning that they seemed legit and in order. As she turned the last page over, she gasped at the photographs beneath. One after another of an older gentleman with a very young girl. She slammed the file shut, unable to look at the disturbing pictures anymore. She understood now how Brice got guardianship of Adam.

She set the folder aside to use later. The next folder she opened contained more explicit photographs and an SD card from a digital camera. She recognized the famous actor immediately. She'd never worked with him, but he was on her short list of actors she'd kill to work with on any project. The other man in the photos lay dead in the snow out back.

She didn't know why Brice had these photos, but understood he'd use them as leverage against the A-list actor for something. If he hadn't already.

She went through other folders, stacking the ones Brice could use for blackmail with the one with the guardianship papers. Brice had dirt on a lot of influential people. Some she recognized from the times he forced her to watch them commit their crimes, so she'd know that if she went against Brice he'd have leverage over her. She didn't know all their names or their positions, but she'd sort it out later and see what she needed to take Brice down.

She turned the last folder toward her. Worn and wrinkled more than the others, the seams were a bit torn and ragged. A rubber band held the whole thing together. She pulled it off and opened the cover, then slammed it shut. The rage and panic that seized her heart, squeezed her chest, and made her head feel like it would explode pressed against every cell of her body.

She opened the folder again and faced the past in graphic detail. One picture after the next of the hell she'd endured. A plastic bag filled with SD cards. A hidden camera the only witness to her living night-mare. Unable to bear the memories that played out from seeing the still images, she slammed the folder shut and pressed both hands on top of it. Her head hung as she tried to find her breath and ease the panic and sorrow that washed through her.

"Ashley." Beck's soft voice held so much concern it brought tears to her eyes, but she fought them back. She'd shed enough tears for what happened to her. "What is it, sweetheart?"

King reached for the folder with the photographs of the famous actor. She slammed her hand down on it so he couldn't see or take it. No one should ever see them.

No one should invade another person's privacy in that way.

"You can't have that." She didn't look at either of them, just kept her hands pinned on top of both folders.

"It's evidence," King pointed out.

"No. It's not. It has nothing to do with my case. It's vile and inhuman and will never be seen by anyone." She turned and pinned Beck in her gaze. "I will not let him hurt anyone else."

"Is someone else in danger?" Beck needed to know if they had to help someone else escape Brice's hold or twisted adoration.

"No." She scooted the folder close to her. "This is blackmail. Pure and simple and ugly." She picked it up and tucked it under her arm. "I need to use your phone."

Beck handed it over without asking anything more.

She could keep these photos from ever seeing the light of day. She could allow a man to keep his secret and choose when and if he ever wanted others to know.

She didn't have that luxury. Her file was indeed evidence.

She turned her focus back to the thick folder under-neath her hand.

"What is that one?" Beck asked, touching her shoulder softly.

"It wasn't enough to have the reality of his dream come true. He needed a way to relive it over and over again."

"No." Beck wanted to deny what he knew was in the folder.

"Still shots from the videos he taped. The SD cards with God knows how many videos. Proof beyond a doubt of what he did to me." And when they got out, they'd go viral and everyone would see the humiliation and torture he inflicted on her. She didn't say the last part, but she read the fear in Beck's eyes that he'd thought the same thing.

"I will save this person from that humiliation even if I can't save myself." She handed the folder to King, hoping he gave it to the right people and Beck never saw what was in that folder.

"These are the folders of the others Brice is black-mailing, though they actually committed a crime or got caught doing something immoral. *We* will decide what to do with them later. So don't give them to the cops."

Beck nodded his agreement. "You know what this means—he's lost his leverage."

"Which makes him even more dangerous if he's stupid enough to stay here and not flee the country." King pointed out what they were all thinking.

She walked away from both of them, straight into Beck's room, and slammed the door. She checked Beck's phone and found he had Skype. She didn't have the actor's user name, so called the one person who could get her anything.

"Hello," the sleepy voice whispered.

"Wake up, Stuart, I need your help."

"Ashley. My God, is that really you? How are you? Are you okay? The press has been hounding me. They said Brice got away."

"He did. Darren just got shot trying to kidnap me for Brice, so it's been a crazy night. The cops will be here soon and I need to take care of something before they arrive."

Her publicist yawned but got down to business. "Anything you need? Anything at all. Do you want me to spread the word about Darren?"

"No. I need you to get Danny Radford to Skype me at this user name right now." She read off the odd sequence of letters and numbers Beck used for his profile.

"No one just calls Danny Radford at this ungodly hour."

"Stuart, I know you know him and can make this happen. I need to talk to him now, before it's too late," she added, hoping Beck and King didn't change their mind about letting her walk away with the folder. If the cops arrived and discovered she had it, they'd want to see it. She couldn't take that chance. "Make this happen, Stuart. I'll be waiting, but if it takes too long, I won't be able to save him. Please." She needed to save him for her own peace of mind.

"You got it. I'm on it."

The line went dead. While she slowly went crazy waiting for the call, she stacked pieces of kindling on the dying coals, a few wads of newspaper in between that caught quickly and flared to life, then added a log to start the blaze rising in the hearth. She sat on the floor, the folder held protectively against her chest and Beck's phone in her hand. It dinged with a request to accept a request to be added as a contact. She accepted and waited for the call to come through.

An odd ringtone sounded. She accepted the call and turned on the video on her side so Danny, one of Hollywood's biggest stars, could see her.

"Hello, Mr. Radford." Though they were close in age,

she gave him the respect he deserved as an elite actor in the business. "I assume Stuart told you who I am."

"No one needs to tell me who you are, Ashley. Please, call me Danny." He turned on his video and his sleepy face and bed head hair appeared on her screen.

"I apologize for waking you. Do you know why I'm calling you?" She hoped he had some idea since news broke that Brice kidnapped her.

"Are you alone?"

She held the phone in front of her and moved it around Beck's room so he could see that she was indeed alone. "This is between you and me and will remain so," she promised.

"And what is this, Ashley?" The skepticism and anger in his voice warned her that he expected the worst.

A man in his position, with as much clout as he had in Hollywood—she didn't doubt he expected her to do exactly what Brice had done to him.

"I'm sure you've seen the news."

"Yes. I'm very sorry about what happened to you. I saw the footage of you at the hospital, the way you looked . . ." His mouth pressed in a grim line and his famous blue eyes filled with sorrow. "I can't imagine what he did to you."

"He hurt me," she stated simply. "He hurt you, too. Maybe not in the same way, but that's what he did."

"My fault for trusting the wrong person," Danny admitted, talking about Darren and how he'd probably thought their relationship would remain secret.

"I trusted the wrong person, too. I know how it feels to think one thing, open yourself to that person, and then find out they used and betrayed you. That's why I called to tell you Darren was shot and killed not even an hour ago trying to kidnap me. And you are safe now."

Danny's eyes widened with surprise and hope.

She moved the phone so that he could see the folder sitting on the hearth. She opened it and he swore when he saw the first picture. She picked it up and set it on top of the flaming log. It caught, shriveled, and disintegrated into ash. She set the others in the fire to burn, allowing Danny to see that all of them were destroyed. Then she untaped the SD card and tossed it into the flames. It flared and sparked and melted into a completely destroyed piece of plastic.

She turned the phone back to her.

Danny stared at her, silent tears streaking down his face. "What do you want?"

"The same thing I want for myself. For you to be free and happy. Brice took those things from us. I swear to you, no one else has seen this, and I will never say a word about what was in that folder. That is my promise and my bond with you. I will never break either under any circumstances. You have my word. I hope you believe it."

Danny raked his fingers through his hair and stared back at her. "I believe you. Thank you, Ashley. I don't know how to repay you."

"You don't owe me anything. I'm not asking you for anything. I'll end with this—I admire you and your work. Live your life however you choose, but never stop doing what you love."

Danny nodded, understanding that she truly didn't want to take advantage. "I'm overwhelmed. When you're back in town, I'd love to see you and thank you in person."

Ashley smiled. "I'd like that."

"I'll feed you. You're too skinny, beautiful." A touch of the charm that earned him his fame and countless fans showed in his grin.

"Oh, you're definitely buying."

"What the hell is going on?" Beck's demand held a hint of jealousy that melted her heart. He peered over her shoulder. "Is that . . ."

"Danny Radford, meet my boyfriend, Special Agent Beck Cooke."

"Amazing job saving Ashley," Danny said, by way of hello.

"What is going on?" Beck asked, completely confused and off-kilter by her calling him her boyfriend.

She had to admit, it rolled off her tongue so easily.

Ashley tossed the folder in the fire to let Beck know the reason for the call was the contents she'd already destroyed.

"Danny invited me to a meal when I return to L.A."

"Keep her safe," Danny ordered. "I have a feeling I'll be seeing her a lot in the future." Danny winked at her. "Bye, beautiful."

Danny's face disappeared as he ended the call.

She tilted her head way back to look up at Beck.

His gaze narrowed on her. "Do I have competition?"

"I'm not his type."

Beck gave her a look like she was every man's type. She cocked her head and eyed him, hoping he got her meaning.

His eyes went wide with understanding. "Oh."

"That stays between us."

Beck nodded. "Okay. I assume that has something to do with whatever was in that folder."

"What folder?"

"Right." He crouched and brushed his hand over her hair. "You're a really good person."

"I did the right thing. He needed to know Brice can't hurt him anymore."

"The cops are here and they want to get my girlfriend's

statement." This time, the smile he gave her lit his eyes with a happiness she'd never seen in them.

She gave herself a second to bask in the joy filling her heart that they'd found each other and something wonderful despite all the bad in their lives.

"Can I stay in here with you and relive our evening by the fire instead?"

His eyes darkened with need and a hunger that matched her own. He leaned in and kissed her softly, lingering over the sweet task, letting her know how much he wanted that, too. "No. But the sooner we get these people out of here, the sooner I can be alone with you again."

"I like the sound of that."

He stood and pulled her up with him and straight into his arms. "This will soon be over for you, too." Beck understood exactly what she'd done tonight and what she wanted for herself. She'd ended Danny's torture. Now she wanted it to end once and for all for herself.

That would only happen with Brice behind bars, or dead.

CHAPTER TWENTY-NINE

Brice's patience wore thin the longer he spent waiting for that fucking cop to come home. If the sheriff wouldn't help him, Sergeant Foster would. The hours he spent in this little hovel of a home with the cold congealed bacon grease from yesterday morning stinking up the kitchen were about to be rewarded. As night turned to dawn turned to a morning spent eating stale cereal while he waited, his fury rose that the fucking cop slept in some lover's bed while Brice had forced himself to stay awake for just this moment.

Sergeant Foster walked in the front door and headed straight for the table, where he tossed his change and keys in the bowl Brice spotted earlier, anticipating the man was a creature of habit. That routine allowed Brice to gain the upper hand on the armed cop. He stepped out of the office on the other side of the wide foyer from the kitchen and swung.

The bat hit Foster in the back of the head with a sickening crack. The sergeant crumpled like a demolished building. Brice snatched the gun from his belt and tucked it behind his back in the waistband of his black trousers. He stared down at the unconscious man with a smug, satisfied smile.

"Take that." Brice used to play on the *After Midnight* softball team. They faced off with the *Marked* cast. A bunch of tough guys who played SWAT team members on a popular TV show. Brice might not look like a jock, but he could hold his own.

Brice clamped his hand around the big man's wrist, dragged him into the office, and rolled him to his back. He pulled his hands together and tied them with the rope he found in the garage.

Foster's eyes squinted with pain. He groaned as he regained consciousness. Brice worked fast, using Foster's disorientation to pull him up and into a chair. The man tried to fight, but the head injury made his movements slow and ineffective against Brice's steady head and speed. He had the man's ankles tied to the chair legs in less than a minute. Foster struggled more. Brice took the bat in hand and jabbed it hard into Foster's sternum to get his attention.

Foster coughed and tried to catch his breath, sucking in air that didn't fill his lungs at first, but then he regained his breath and his head and glared up at Brice.

"There now. I have your attention."

"What the fuck do you want?"

"An answer to a simple question. Who has Adam?"

Foster shook his head. "I don't know."

Brice punched him.

Foster's head snapped to the side. Blood dripped out of his cut lip and down his chin. He worked his jaw, then spit blood, hitting Brice right in the face. The goopy spittle rolled down his cheek. He wiped it away with the back of his sleeve looking at the bloody mess. He hit Foster again, breaking his nose and sending a gush of blood out his nostrils. This time when Foster's head snapped back, then forward he had the sergeant's full attention. And hopefully his cooperation.

Brice sucked in a breath, riding the rush of adrenaline and pleasure racing through his veins. "Didn't Ashley tell you how much I love to cause pain?" Brice set the end of the bat on the wood chair between Foster's widespread legs and nudged the tip right into his balls. "Who has Adam?"

Foster tried to breathe through his open mouth. His head hung forward, his eyes closed. Blood dripped onto the bat between his legs.

Brice grabbed him by the hair and yanked his head up. "I know he's not with the DEA agent who was with Aurora . . . oh, I mean Ashley, at the hospital. The one who thinks he can put his hands on my woman."

Foster's eyes opened and the man glared daggers at him. "You don't want to fuck with him. He killed your buddy Darren early this morning. You even think about going near Ashley, he'll kill you, too."

Brice pushed Foster's head, pulling his hair, and released him. "No. You're lying. Darren isn't dead."

Foster gave him a gruesome bloody grin. "He tried to sneak onto that DEA agent's property to kidnap Ashley back for you. For all his wanting to please you, he ended up dead."

Brice jabbed the bat into Foster's balls. "No! He's not dead."

Foster grunted in pain and folded over, trying to ease the excruciating pain and hide his nuts from another attack.

Brice seethed. "That stupid fuck. I told him to stay put and wait for me. He defied me and got what he deserved."

"You will, too." Foster found his breath and the ability to spit words through his clenched jaw. "They found your files in Darren's car, including the one with all the video cards of the recordings you made of all the twisted things you did to Ashley . . . Aurora . . . no, Ashley." Foster's narrowed, fury-filled gaze sharpened with the promise of death if he got his hands on Brice.

No. They took all his precious recordings.

All his allies would fall.

He'd have no help.

He was on his own.

They knew his secrets and what he'd done to help Ashley transform into her true self. They didn't understand. No one but Ashley understood why and how hard he'd worked to help her become her true self.

He swung the bat wide, whacking Foster in the head and putting him out, hopefully for good judging by the blood oozing out of the wound on the side of his head.

He didn't need Foster's help to find Adam. Once he got Aurora back, she'd know where to find Adam. They'd be together again. All he had to do was bide his time, find the right opportunity, and he'd have her back in his arms. They'd finish what they started. She'd finish her transformation and be his. Finally.

CHAPTER THIRTY

Ashley stood in the driveway in front of Beck's silver truck staring at the burned-out shell of Brice's once-beautiful home. No less than five sheriff's deputies stood around them, watching for any sign of Brice. No one had seen him in four days. While Sergeant Foster recovered in the hospital from his near-death encounter with Brice, she'd spent the last few days holed up at Beck's answering more questions about Brice and Darren and making plans for Adam. The nights she spent in Beck's arms were some of the best of her life.

In the dark, they lit each other up with so much passion and love—she'd never thought two people could share that kind of close connection.

She felt lucky to have something in her life so good and pure when all the bad still hadn't gone away. She still had to face things like today.

"As you can see, the place caved in on itself as the fire consumed the top floor and roof." The lieutenant taking over for Sergeant Foster stood beside her ready to take notes.

She stared at the charred remains of the house she'd once thought a lovely place to vacation and relax in the beautiful Montana landscape.

"Miss Swan? Can you tell me approximately where he held you?"

Beck stepped in front of her, blocking her view. "We can come back and do this another time."

"From the second-floor window, I could see the front gardens. They were lovely. White rosebushes. Lights pointed up at the canopy of the small trees and high-lighted the stone walls. The trimmed hedges' leaves were deep green and glossy. I remember thinking when I looked out at the beauty of it all that I felt like a princess in the tower." She sighed, angry at herself for such foolish thoughts. "Turns out there was no prince coming to my rescue. Only the devil hell-bent on transforming me into his puppet until he killed me."

"In your story, Ashley, the princess saves herself."

She finally looked into Beck's eyes. "Notice the oddly missing window on the facade of the house where you'd put one to make the front look uniform? That's where the 'safe' room was built. A vault within the house on the second floor." She pointed to the debris blocking the lower blown-out windows and the odd corner of something sticking through the crumbled stone wall.

Beck and the lieutenant nodded, understanding what they were looking at now.

She walked around the house, pointing out where the French door she snuck out with Adam used to be. Nothing was left of his room at the top of the back stairs. She followed the path along the back patio like a robot, showing them the path she took into the open field and land beyond. "I'm not walking that route to Beck's place again. All I can tell you is that I went that way with nothing but a prayer I'd find my way to safety, but really I just wanted away from here. Beck's light drew me to him."

"You must have been close to his place when you saw the light," the lieutenant guessed, jotting down notes in his book and on the diagram he'd drawn.

"No. It was nothing more than a pinpoint, but something in the dark to guide my way to someone I hoped would help me." She placed her hand on Beck's chest and smiled up at him. A silent thank-you to him and God for answering her prayer.

He smiled back, and said to the lieutenant who shook off her notion that she saw the light from that far away, "On a dark night, even a candle can be seen miles away."

Beck and the lieutenant wandered closer to the house to get a better view of the layout and the collapsed metal walls that had been her home far too long.

She stuck to the perimeter of the patio, enjoying the few hardy plants that withstood the snowstorm. Most of the snow had melted over the last few warmer days. She wandered the path toward the edge of the landscaped yard, enjoying the garden Brice took so much pride in, and stopped, staring at the small hill surrounded by large boulders with dead plants mixed between them.

She stilled, trying to figure out why that hill meant something to her. She closed her eyes and thought of all the times Brice made her stare out here from the wide windows. Something familiar about it nudged at the back of her mind, trying to come forward.

Then it hit her.

She tore her purse off her shoulder, unlatched the flap, and dumped it over, spilling the meager contents on the ground. She picked up the folded paper, sending the lip gloss Mia bought her rolling down the stone path. Her compact smacked against the stone and fell open. A pen rolled and slipped into a crack. She unfolded the drawing Adam made her and held it up. A perfect match to the hill surrounded in stones.

She stared at the picture of her and Adam standing next to it. "It's all of us." She repeated his words.

"What's all of us?" Beck asked.

"Get a shovel." She turned to him, her heart racing, her words quickly stumbling out her mouth. "You have to dig right here." She pointed to the grassy center of the hill.

"Why?" Beck's voice held a gentle tone to try to calm her down.

"There used to be small rosebushes here. Now it's grass."

"So? The gardener relandscaped."

She grabbed his arm. "No. Don't you see? He buried her here." She held up the picture Adam drew. "He said, 'It's all of us.' Not it's *both* of us. He was trying to tell me his mother is in the picture, too."

Beck swore, then yelled, "Lieutenant, get the forensic team over here. And tell them to bring some shovels."

The lieutenant ran toward the men sifting through the ash in the ravaged building.

Beck took her by the shoulders. "What do you know about Adam's mother that you haven't told me?"

"Nothing for sure. She worked here when I came for my getaway. I suspected they had a thing. She didn't like the way Brice flirted with me. But at that point, it was still just this thing we did, like people saw on his show. Nothing serious. Fun between friends. At least on my part. When Brice's advances turned serious, Jackie warned me to leave before it was too late. I thought she wanted me out of the way so she could be with Brice.

"He couldn't stand it when someone defied him. I thought it was just the perfectionist in him snapping at people to give him their best. Then I saw what he was really like when I defied him in those early weeks. She was still here when he allowed me out in the beginning. She served us dinner and tried to appear like everything was normal, but every once in a while I'd see this look in her eyes that she didn't think what he was doing was right."

"It wasn't. She should have called the cops."

"On her own out here, no place to go. If Brice discovered what she'd done before she got away with Adam . . ." Ashley shook her head. "I think, in the end, she tried to do the right thing and he killed her." She stared down at the patch of grass. Her gut soured and her heart sank. "It's my fault."

Beck took her shoulders and turned her to him. "No, sweetheart. If she's there"—he nodded toward the grass— "it's on Brice. All of this is his fault."

She wanted to believe that, but still felt responsible because she'd been naïve, too trusting, and never saw the trap before it was sprung. "If she's there, we'll finally know what happened to her."

"Yes, and we'll nail him for murder. There is no way he will ever be allowed out of jail. Adam will have some justice."

"Adam deserves more than that." Ashley had an idea of how she'd get Adam everything he deserved. Beck probably wouldn't like it, but sometimes you had to fight dirty.

"You both deserve more than that bastard gave you, and you'll get it once Brice is behind bars."

"That day can't come soon enough."

"For you and me both."

"If it comes to it and you have a chance to take Brice, don't hesitate because of my safety. No matter what, you take him down. He can't ever be allowed to hurt another living soul."

Beck wrapped one arm around her back and placed his hand on the side of her head. "Sweetheart, I will never put you at risk for anything. I know this might sound a little too close to the things Brice said to you, but without you in my life, it's just not worth living." He leaned in and kissed her, showing her just how much she mattered to him.

He held her face cupped in his warm hands and stared down at her.

She smiled up at him. "Nothing you say or make me feel is anything like what I experienced with Brice. I know the difference because you make me feel everything good people hope to have in their lives." She placed her hand over his heart. "All I want to do is spend more time with you."

Surprised, his eyes narrowed. "You don't want to go back to L.A.?"

"Why? You're here."

Beck grinned, wrapped her in his arms, and held her as they watched the forensic techs dig and sift through the partially frozen ground. It took nearly an hour before one of the techs held up his hand to halt digging again. Another tech took a soft brush and dusted the dirt away. Everyone stood back. Beck released her, but took her hand as she walked forward and stared into the hole at Adam's mother's remains. A tear slipped past her lashes and fell down her cheek. That poor, poor woman. Another one of Brice's victims.

One of the techs leaned down and brushed away the hair from Jackie's face revealing the jagged wound on her forehead.

Beck hooked his hand around her middle and gently pulled her away. "Enough, Ashley."

The farther he pulled her away from the garden and onto the patio, the wider her view of the yard. That strange feeling came over her again.

"Beck."

"Yeah."

"There are five more hills." She swept her hand out to indicate the five mounds she'd walked past when she reached Jackie's grave. She turned back to the house and around again. "That's what he wanted me to see from the windows. His view. His garden. His victims."

"Ashley, are you saying . . ."

"There are more of them." Deep down, she knew it. She couldn't have been his only victim. But she'd do whatever it took to ensure she was his last.

"Wait here." Beck ran over to the lieutenant and spoke to him. The man turned and stared at the other hills, then directed the forensic team to start digging up the next one.

Beck came back to her. "They'll get to work and let us know." Beck took her hand and pulled her around the patio toward the front of the house and away from all that death.

"They'll run a DNA test to confirm it's Jackie," he assured her.

"It is." Though badly decomposed, Ashley recognized the dark hair and one other thing. "They'll find Adam's baby picture in the silver locket around her neck. I want that back when they've finished with her. It should go to Adam."

"It will."

"Do you think they'll let me have him?" Ashley worried that he'd go to his grandmother in Florida and that a court or his father would never grant her custody.

"One step at a time. He'll stay with Caden and Mia in protective custody until Brice is found. You talked to him. He's happy there. Mia said he's gained five pounds, he's reading every book he can get his hands on thanks to Mia's tutoring, and Caden says he actually let go some of his apprehension about Caden being a stranger, a man, and so big, and played with him last night. He talks more and more each day. The pediatrician said he's healthy, and despite not having anyone really looking out for him this past year, he's nearly met all his milestones. Given a few more weeks with Mia, or us—"

"Us?"

Beck helped her into his truck and stood in the open door staring at her. "Yes, us. What did you think—that you and I ended when Brice got caught?"

"No." Raising Adam together was a big step to ask Beck to take with her. It would change everything. For both of them. It meant a commitment to Adam that required a commitment between them, too. She wanted that, but didn't want to ask for too much too fast. She didn't want to push Beck for more than he wanted to give. She didn't want to waste another day of her life, waiting for things to happen. But that didn't mean Beck felt the same way. "I haven't had time to think. All I know is I want you and Adam and a real life."

"Great. We're on the same page."

"Just like that?"

"I guess I need to take you home and show you again how much I mean it."

"By *home* do you mean the place I've kind of taken over?"

"I rue the day you ever got your credit card back and started ordering online and having things delivered overnight." He smiled. "If the worst thing you do is take over my closet and make me never want to leave our bed, I'm okay with that."

"You'd like my place in L.A. It's in the hills. Lots of flowers and trees. Private. Like your place."

"Our place." He corrected her again. "Do you miss home?"

"I miss having what's mine, but I love sharing what's yours. Does that make sense?" After Brice took everything from her, she missed the simple things, like picking out an outfit, drinking tea from her favorite mug, doing what she wanted to do when she wanted to do it, and saying what she wanted, not those damn scripted lines.

"Yeah. It makes perfect sense. Let's go home. And don't worry about Adam. He's in good hands right now. We'll give him a good life. The one his mother wanted for him."

She hoped she'd be a good mother. "I'll try to love him as much as she did."

"If you make him feel as loved as I feel from you, he's going to be the happiest kid on the planet."

"Aw, Beck."

"I know. Since I met you, all kinds of nice things come out of my mouth. What will all the drug dealers think?"

She smiled, because he'd made the joke to ease her mind about finding Adam's mother and possibly more victims.

A chill went up her spine that she could have ended up planted out there with the roses.

"What will you do now that you can't work undercover anymore?"

"Right now, I'm your full-time bodyguard as long as you need me."

She tilted her head, sad she'd taken something from him that he'd loved and done so well. "Beck, you can't give up your job."

"I can take a longer leave of absence. Believe me, I've earned it."

"You'd do that for me?"

"I'd do anything for you. Including putting up with a dozen paparazzi with long lens cameras watching my house."

"At least no drug dealers will sneak up on you and try to kill you."

His derisive chuckle didn't convince her that threat wasn't as real today as before he met her. More so now. "Don't remind me. We need to work on our security setup."

"Maybe we need to loosen security a bit."

He pointed a finger at her face. "Don't even say it. I'm not using you as bait."

"Beck—"

He slammed the door, cutting off her words, rounded the truck, opened his door, and slid into his seat. "I'm not listening to any plan that involves putting you within sight of that bastard. It's not going to happen. No."

"He might have already left the country."

"I don't think so. Not without you." Beck drove down the driveway and waited for the electronic gate to open and the sheriff's deputies to push the reporters and photographers back so they could drive through without running over anyone. It didn't stop them from shouting questions.

Is it true Brice held you in a safe room?

Did he only call you Aurora?

That sent a chill up her spine.

Did he beat you daily?

Did it matter if it was daily, weekly, monthly? Once? Ten times? A thousand times? He did it.

How many bones did he break?

Twelve. Some more than once.

Are you pregnant?

Are you engaged?

She turned to Beck. "Are they asking if I'm engaged to Brice or you?"

"Is the baby mine?"

She found she could laugh at the ridiculous. "The tabloids will probably say it's an alien's."

"Lucky bastard."

She glanced over at him. "Do you want to have kids?"

"Does that surprise you?"

"Actually, no. You're not the guy I met those first few days. You changed."

"You reminded me of who I really am and what I wanted but thought I couldn't have—not doing the job I was doing. We both have a chance to have a different kind of life than what we had before we met each other."

"Boy or a girl?"

"Yes."

She smiled again. Even after what they discovered at Brice's ranch, it was easy to smile when she was with Beck.

"I like that answer." She settled back in the seat, linked her fingers with Beck's, held his hand tight, and enjoyed the pretty ride back to his place, dreaming about a future with Beck, Adam, and their children running over the grassy pastures and woods at home. Yes, their home. Here. A place where the kids could grow up without her crazy life interfering in their lives. Beck would find a new place in the DEA. She'd find a project that sparked her passion for acting again when she was ready. Stronger. With Beck beside her, she'd get there. They'd have that new life they both wanted.

All they had to do was find and arrest Brice.

CHAPTER THIRTY-ONE

Brice expected a bull riding competition or football game on the country bar TV. Instead he got tabloid news. Nothing but gossip overlaid with country music in this neon-beer-sign place. The done-me-wrong songs went well with the juicy lies being told on TV. That bitch Sharon Waters from *Celebrity Centerfold* droned on as a beautiful picture of Ashley in front of his burned-down home came on the screen beside Sharon's surgically enhanced face.

While Ashley Swan remains under protective custody on a Montana ranch, speculation mounts that the gorgeous DEA agent protecting her is much more than a bodyguard. Rumors circulate that her sexy rescuer is truly a knight in shining armor who swept her off her feet.

Brice fisted his hand, trying to control the rage that swept through him at the thought of that man putting his hands on Ashley. The image of her being carried in his arms into the hospital burned in Brice's brain. He'd pay for touching her.

Sharon Waters dropped her voice, enticing people to believe the budding romance story. *Why else would the DEA be involved in a kidnapping and murder?*

Brice nearly spit out the single malt eighteen-year-old Talisker. He refused to waste the only decent drink he could get in this shithole bar.

Murder? No fucking way. Unless . . . No, they couldn't know.

The body of a woman was found at Brice's private ranch estate this afternoon as Ashley Swan took the sheriff's team on a tour of the house of hell she'd been held in for nearly a year by the once-beloved talk show host. Authorities are searching for more graves.

Oh God, they know.

The body has been identified by authorities, but her name is being held from the press until next of kin can be notified. An unidentified source close to the case reports the woman once worked for Brice at the property. Could she be another victim of Brice's sick and twisted games that turned deadly? Time will tell as the investigation continues and we learn more about the depraved acts Brice inflicted on Ashley Swan and possibly the woman who worked for him. Did she die when Brice's torture went too far, or did she try to help Ashley and paid the ultimate price? Maybe Brice will give authorities the answer when they finally arrest him. If he hasn't already fled the country and gone into hiding, though authorities believe he is still here as they have all routes out of the country on guard for any sighting of the famous and very recognizable Brice Mooney.

Brice's hand clamped onto the cold glass. The ice clinked and dissolved into his single malt scotch, the only extravagance he had right now. If they found him, he'd never have a taste of the finer things in life behind bars. He needed to get out of here before they caught him. He should be out of the country, sitting on a white sand beach somewhere that didn't extradite. He had money. Fame. Infamy, though he'd rather not have it for the crimes they wanted to pin on him because they didn't understand what he'd done. He'd helped Jackie, the others, and Ashley become who they truly were meant to be.

He downed his drink, welcoming the sting down his throat, tossed a twenty on the bar for the bartender who actually knew and stocked good scotch, and stood from the torn vinyl stool. A hand clamped onto his shoulder and shoved him back down. Brice looked down at the dirty hand on his last clean shirt. Being on the run sucked. He either needed to buy new clothes, or find a place with laundry service. Out here, in the middle of nowhere, not likely.

"Someone wants to talk to you."

"Not interested." He pulled the Dodgers cap low, ducked his head so he wasn't recognized, and tried to swivel and get off the stool the other way. He ran straight into another beefy man in a biker vest blocking him in.

Shit.

"It wasn't a request, Mr. Mooney." The low deep voice didn't carry, but if they knew who he was, it wouldn't be long before everyone else in this dive would, too. For all his trying to blend in with his unshaven face, jeans, simple black T-shirt, and jean jacket, he stood out among the work-roughened men.

Brice turned to face the men around him and had a moment to contemplate he might never see that beach or have his freedom if these four, no five, leather-, denim-, and tattoo-clad men took him out and shot him. For what, Brice didn't know, but it seemed a real possibility.

"Now," the tall white-haired man ordered. Premature gray was one thing for a guy in his . . . early fifties, Brice guessed. Sixties? Who could tell with that *white* hair? Brice had never seen anything like it. Except for maybe Betty White, but she was in her nineties.

"What do I call you?"

"Iceman."

It fit. The hair. The cold attitude. Brice didn't want to

think what else it stood for. Certainly not a love for Val Kilmer's character in *Top Gun*.

He grabbed one of Brice's arms. Another guy with a dragon tattoo flying up his neck clamped his fat fingers around Brice's other arm.

"Where are we going?" They led him out of the bar, not a single other soul bothering to look their way. One of the reasons he'd picked the place in the middle of nowhere. He'd hoped people would mind their own damn business. Getting noticed would get him arrested or killed at this point, so he went along with the men hoping to find an escape—from whatever this was.

"What do you want with me? There's no reward for turning me in. I'll make it worth your while to let me go."

"Shut up and get in." Iceman patted him down, took the gun from under his shirt at his back that Brice had taken from Deputy Foster, then shoved him toward a black Mercedes.

The wall of brute force behind him didn't bode well for him if he disobeyed, but it grated to be ordered around like some menial gopher.

Brice opened the door, bent, and peeked inside. He'd never seen the man sitting on the plush, pale-gray leather backseat, but his dark brown skin and jet-black hair spoke to his Mexican heritage. The exquisite black opal on his pinky said money just as loudly as his designer suit. Brice didn't need more than one guess to know how this man with the biker gang entourage made his money.

"Have a seat, friend."

Brice did as he was told again. The door closed with a respectful click, leaving him and his new "friend" in quiet peace.

"I don't believe we are acquainted."

"The enemy of my enemy is my friend. You know this

saying?" the man said, his words heavily tinged with his Hispanic accent.

"I do. But who is our common enemy?"

"Special Agent Beck Cooke of the DEA. He is known to me as Trigger."

After Trigger shot at him on his property missing him by a mere inch, Brice understood why he'd been given the nickname.

"He's caused me a lot of trouble and cost me a great deal of money. He is also responsible for the death of my cousin Marco." The man squeezed his hand into a fist on his thigh, the black opal sparkling blues and greens in the dome light overhead. "He took my family. He took your woman. This is a man who needs to be taught a lesson about loss."

Brice couldn't agree more. "While we have a common interest in seeing this man put down, he's out of reach. So is my Aurora."

"She is Ashley Swan, no? The famous actress. Such a beauty."

"Yes, but to me, she will always be Aurora."

The man's lips dipped into a frown of understanding, if only to appease Brice. It irritated him.

"You, my friend, were too easy to find. It is a wonder the police have not found you yet."

Brice didn't comment. He'd taken a calculated risk going into the bar. He was tired of hiding out in dingy motel rooms, and his own company, and wanted a decent drink.

"But you see I have resources they do not. I am a man who knows things and makes things happen."

"How can you get to someone who has proven that anyone getting close to that house will be shot and killed?" It's why he'd curbed his need to go after her himself, though he'd been racking his brain for a way to get to her. He wouldn't be impulsive and stupid, like Darren.

"You will get your Aurora back and I will get my money and Beck."

Brice doubted it, but played along. "And how will that happen?"

"He will come to us. This, I can promise and make happen." The guy's vague answer with no substance or details sounded like every politician promising voters results with absolutely no plan to back it up.

Brice narrowed his eyes. "That's all well and good, but he'll be armed. Reporters will follow them."

"My men will take care of all that. It should spike the news ratings, no? You get this, yes?"

"Yes." The photogs would get an up-close view of Beck's takedown and Ashley being captured by a group of unidentified men. They'd speculate that Brice hired them to kidnap her. "So what, you take them—how do I get Aurora back?"

"I'm a businessman. This is a business deal. Trigger cost me two million dollars during the raid he executed on Marco's land. If you want your Aurora, you will pay me two million dollars to get her back."

Brice had to admit, he hadn't seen that one coming. Anxious to have her back now, he asked, "When and where?"

The man handed over a black business card with a gold scorpion on the front and two sets of numbers handwritten on the back.

"Tomorrow. My man will meet you here at three and take you to the meeting place. If the money is not in that account by the time you arrive, you will be of no use to me, and I will kill you and keep the girl. I'm sure others will pay for her safe return."

"You'll have your money. Mr. . . . ?"

"Guzman. Do not forget it, for if you cross me, you will know the man who will see you dead."

Brice felt a chill of fear race up his spine along with the danger and excitement this man evoked in him. "You'll have your money. I will have my Aurora." He couldn't wait. Tomorrow seemed so far away.

"If you come through, I have a shipment leaving the country on a private plane to Mexico. Perhaps you would like to take your lady on a trip?"

"Yes. Thank you for your generosity."

"I have a soft spot for lovers. Another reason I want Trigger dead. He killed Marco's girlfriend during that raid. If not for that, I'd have gotten him out of jail, and Marco would be alive today."

"Sounds like the sooner I have Aurora away from Trigger the better."

Mr. Guzman handed him one of the small snifters of brandy set on the narrow bar in front of them. He held his glass aloft and toasted with, "Tomorrow, we will both have what we want."

Brice downed the shot. Two million was a small price to pay for his most precious treasure. The police would be watching his accounts. They'd see the transfer and probably figure out his location. By the time they tracked him and the money, he'd have Aurora back and they'd be out of the country.

CHAPTER THIRTY-TWO

Ashley held the peppermint out to Berry. He took it and nudged his nose in her palm for more. She smashed the plastic wrapper in her hand and stuffed it in her jeans pocket.

"Stop giving him so many of those," Beck called from the other side of the barn where he worked on his Camaro.

"I don't know what you're talking about." She held her finger to her lips in front of Berry. "Shh. It's our secret."

"Your secret is making him ornery. Every time I try to feed him, he nibbles at my pockets looking for those things."

Ashley gave Berry one last pat and headed down the aisle to the wide door that separated the horses from Beck's garage and workshop. Berry nickered, calling her back so he could have another candy.

Beck eyed her as she leaned against his car. "You're spoiling him."

"I'm happy to spoil you, too."

Beck finished prepping the window frame for painting and winked at her. "You did last night."

"And this morning in the shower," she added, her voice husky.

Beck set aside the roll of tape and came to her, planting his hands on the car door on either side of her. She thought he'd lean in and kiss her, but his head dipped,

missed her lips, and he kissed a path down her chest to the
V in her sky-blue sweater. His lips settled warm and soft
on the swell of her breast, his tongue sliding against her
skin before his lips pressed another light kiss and moved
on to the next oversensitive spot. She held his head to her.
Eyes closed, her total focus on the feel of his mouth on
her, she let her head fall back with the passion-filled sigh
she let loose.

Beck nuzzled her neck, kissed behind her ear, and
smiled against her skin when he said, "We keep this up,
there's no telling how long it will be before we make it
back up to the house."

"I don't have anyplace else I need to be but right here
with you." She cupped his face and pulled him in for another searing kiss.

Beck growled low in his throat, lifted her onto the side
of the car, and swung her around to the front. He moved
around the fender and right between her legs. She hooked
her feet around his hips and pulled him close, losing herself in his taste and heat as his body pressed down on her
and her back hit the hood.

Beck's big hands smoothed over her shoulders, down
her chest, and covered her breasts, kneading them in his
hands and driving her crazy. His hands trailed down her
sides. She giggled when he hit the sensitive curve above
her hips. Nothing deterred him from his mission as his
hands rubbed down her thighs and legs to her feet. He
pulled off her boots, smoothed his hands up her legs to
the button and zipper on her jeans. He hooked his fingers
in the denim and dragged the pants and her panties down
and right off her feet.

Her bottom settled on the cold hood. Goose bumps
rose on her legs, but Beck warmed her, rubbing his big
hands up and down them as he kissed her belly. One hand
swept up the inside of her thigh. She rocked her hips into

his hand as it settled between her legs, his thumb rubbing against her soft folds, up and down as she rocked her hips to his rhythm.

As desperate for her as she was for him, he undid his jeans, clamped his hands on her hips, and rubbed his hard cock against her slick core until she moaned, greedy for him to be inside her. His fingers clamped tight and pulled her down on him. His warm body settled over her as he thrust hard and deep into her wet center, filling her and making her want more.

She stared up at him, his eyes intense and locked on hers as he held her hips gripped in his strong hands, pulling and pushing her as he thrust into her again and again. Harder. Faster. He didn't relent until her body locked around his. She shattered right there on the hood of his car while he watched her, but he didn't let her go alone. His gaze stayed steady on her as he buried himself deep and his body bucked against hers and he lost himself in her.

His gray-blue eyes filled with intense emotion. Love. Possession. Raw desire. Longing. Neither of them said a thing. Words weren't needed. Nothing they said would accurately convey what they both felt in this moment. They stared at each other, locked together, her heaving breath a match to his. Her body rippled with aftershocks as he held her hips tight against his. The connection they shared surrounded them like a living thing; she felt like a warm blanket wrapped around them. Her heart and soul pulsed out of her chest, captured the piece of Beck he sent out to her, and fell back within her, a piece of him now a part of her. No matter what happened between them, she'd carry that piece of him with her the rest of her life.

"I love you. You know that, right?" Beck's passionate gaze never left hers.

She didn't understand what came over him. Why he

needed her to convince him that she did know how deeply he cared for her. But she knew those words and the emotion she saw in his eyes to be wholly true and indestructible. That's the way Beck loved.

"I know it. I feel it. I believe in it and us, Beck. I never thought I'd have someone like you as a part of my life. I feel lucky and unworthy, but I will love you with my whole heart until the day I die and hope that you feel the way you make me feel."

He fell onto her chest, his head pressed to her breasts, his ear over her heart. His arms circled around her back and held her close, their bodies still joined.

"I don't want to ever lose you."

She brushed her fingers through his dark hair and wrapped her arms around his head, holding him tight. "You won't. I promise you, Beck, the only place I want to be is with you."

He leaned up and stared down at her. "Don't you want to go back to Hollywood, your job, the fans waiting to see you again, all those people you've missed and are waiting for your return?"

"Yes. When I'm ready. But that doesn't mean I leave you. While I want to be with you here, I'll never be content to give up acting. I love it. The way you love your work and would never give it up even if you do it in a different way. We can make this work, Beck."

"We will make it work."

"There is nothing from my old life that pulls me so hard it will tear me away from you," she assured him.

"Do you think you could be happy living here?"

She placed her hand on his strong jaw. "I am happy living here."

Beck turned his face and kissed her palm. Satisfied with her answer—and getting what he wanted—he held her legs, stepped back, took her hand and helped her sit up once she unwrapped her legs from around his waist and planted her feet on the car bumper. He handed her the jeans and panties he'd tossed on the hood beside her earlier.

"You're a beautiful hood ornament," he teased.

She gave him a pinup pose and made him smile, his eyes filling with renewed heat as he stared at her. "Should I give up the big screen for doing car shows in my bikini?"

"Not enough of a challenge in that for you, sweetheart."

He was right. She loved creating the characters she played. She smoothed her hand over the hood. "I'll miss the black, but I can't wait to see this thing once you've painted it."

"What do you think, red with black racing stripes?"

"Silver with black stripes."

"Really?"

She shrugged, not really caring what color he painted it, more concerned with the fact every drug dealer in the state probably knew the car belonged to a DEA agent. A paint job wouldn't change the fact the car stood out just as much as her tattooed boyfriend. "Aren't you nervous about being seen in this car?"

"My face has been splashed all over the news and tabloids as your bodyguard lover." He shook his head and pinched his lips with distaste.

"You know you're more than that to me. That's all that matters. But people are interested in you because you saved me."

"Yeah, I get it. *DEA Agent Saves Oscar-Winning Movie Star* is a great headline."

She pulled on her pants over the panties she'd already shimmied up her legs and hips. "That's *Sexy DEA Agent*," she teased, punching him in the gut, his abs tightening under her fist.

He rubbed his hand over his rock-hard abs. "Nice jab."

"I've had some training on set for a few of my roles."

"Yeah, what other skills are you hiding from me?"

"Aside from boxing, I've had some martial arts and weapons training."

"Weapons?"

"Knives and guns. I played an assassin in one of my movies."

"Anarchy."

Happy and a little self-conscious he knew which one and had seen her movies, she smiled. "We should go target shooting sometime. I'm out of practice, but I wasn't half-bad."

"I'd like to keep you away from guns and anything else that puts you in harm's way."

"I'm as frustrated as you that Brice is still on the loose. But I can't say I'm surprised. He's probably left the country and will remain a ghost in my life, always out there but unseen."

Beck narrowed his gaze and handed her the shoes he'd dropped on the ground. "They'll get him."

"You're mad you aren't out there hunting him down."

Beck planted his hands on his hips. "I'm pissed off as hell they let him walk right out of the sheriff's department."

If not for that fight that allowed Brice a way to escape custody, he'd be in jail now.

"Any news on how Sergeant Foster is doing?"

Beck swept his thumb over her cheek. "Better."

She leaned into his palm. "I hope he's able to shake off what Brice did to him."

"You're still having nightmares. He probably will too for a little while."

"Mine are better. So are my ribs. I just want Brice found and for this to be over." Her cell phone rang in the jacket she'd taken off earlier and draped over the stool by Beck's workbench.

"Your manager again, wanting you to say yes to that media tour."

"I'm not doing that." She refused to put herself on display. For all she'd talked to Beck about what happened, and the cops, she wasn't ready to bare her soul to the public. If she could keep this private, heal in her own time and way, maybe she'd be able to talk about it someday without feeling like it was happening to her all over again.

She dug her phone out of her jacket pocket and checked the caller ID. "It's the sheriff's department."

Beck's eyes narrowed. "How'd they get that number?"

"Maybe they wrote it down after I called the office yesterday to make sure they received the file you sent with the rest of my statement."

"You didn't use the house phone?"

"No." She swiped the screen and answered her ringing phone before it went to voice mail. "Hello."

"Miss Swan, Deputy Kent from Crystal Creek Sheriff's Department."

"Yes, Deputy Kent, what can I do for you?"

"We have Brice Mooney in custody. We'd like you to come down to the station to assist us with verifying his answers while we question him."

Her hand shook as she pressed it to her mouth.

"What is it?" Beck asked.

"They caught him. He's in custody. They want us to come down to the station." Her voice shook with the relief coursing through her system. She spoke to the deputy. "We'll be there as soon as we can."

Beck's eyes narrowed. "How did they find him?"

"He didn't say. They want me to verify whatever Brice says when they question him."

Beck still didn't move to leave. "Why? They have the pictures and recordings."

"I guess they want me to verify the details that aren't in those things." She hesitated to leave now that Beck's radar had gone up. "What is it?"

"I don't want to put you through listening to him lie about and distort all the things he did to you. I can't imagine the sheriff wants to put you through that either."

Underlying Beck's concern for her was the fact he didn't want to hear all the things Brice did to her. While he'd read the beginning of her statement, he couldn't bring himself to read the rest. He couldn't read it dispassionately as a victim's statement and not feel anything, not when he cared so deeply, not when he loved her so much.

That alone made her love him even more.

"If I can't handle it, we'll leave, but I need to see him. I need to know that he's locked up and will never come after me again."

She needed to look him in the eye one last time and let him know he hadn't broken her.

CHAPTER THIRTY-THREE

Just like every other time they left the house, Beck approached the front gate with trepidation and all-out disgust and anger that the vultures were still there. Fanatical fans, reporters, and photographers poured out of their vans and cars into the cold. He'd never particularly liked snowstorms, but he found himself praying for another one so these guys would find some good sense and go home. Instead, they set aside their thermoses of coffee, pulled their scarves over their mouths as their breath drifted in puffs on the wind, and made sure their jackets were zipped to their chins.

"Why don't they just leave?" Beck hit the control for the gate, thankful it opened without him having to get out and do it manually.

The vultures stayed on the other side, thanks to his warning that he'd shoot them if they entered the property and rushed the truck like they did the first time he left with Ashley.

Since Darren's shooting, no one tried to sneak onto his land.

That didn't stop him from being paranoid about everyone still watching his property. One of these people could be a potential threat, either sent by Brice or the drug cartel that still wanted to take him down.

King briefed him the other day as they scouted the

property to be sure all the sensors were working. Whispers circulated that Guzman was out for his blood, especially now that Guzman had ID'd him as Trigger, thanks to his face showing up on every news outlet across the country.

It was only a matter of time, but Beck wished he'd gotten more of it. This added another layer of danger for him and Ashley.

The target on his back could shift to Ashley if he didn't put down Guzman and eliminate the threat against him. He'd been worried from day one that Guzman would use her against him. As much as he wanted to keep her here, sending her back to Hollywood might keep her safer, but he couldn't bring himself to tell her to go. In fact, he'd needed her reassurance that she wanted to stay with him. That the risk was worth it to her. That she loved him as much as he loved her and being apart wouldn't solve anything. The threats still existed. He couldn't protect her if she was away from him, and he didn't trust anyone else to do it.

She needed him to feel safe and protected while she healed. She'd done so well these last days, even after they discovered Brice's gruesome garden of bones.

He hated driving her to see the devil who'd tormented her for nearly a year. A man who still tormented her.

But not for long.

He'd spend the rest of his life in jail. A cell. Better than the one he kept Ashley in because he'd have light, three square meals a day, a small semblance of dignity to hold on to even if he didn't have his freedom. It's more than he gave Ashley.

Or the others.

"Beck, what are you waiting for?"

He shook off his thoughts and studied the faces of every fan, reporter, and cameraperson. The usual crowd. He and King had checked each and every one of them out. So why did he have this creepy feeling dancing up his spine telling him this was a bad idea? Nothing but his need to keep Ashley as far away from that sick and twisted bastard? He hoped so.

But if anything happened, Beck had his gun and backup.

He pulled out past the vultures, letting them take their pictures of Ashley as she covered her face with his flannel shirt. He pulled onto the road, hit the button to shut the gate, and drove away as the reporters and paps scurried to their vehicles like roaches when the lights came on. Beck watched in the rearview mirror for one particular vehicle and spotted it amongst the ones that turned to follow them.

"Everything okay? You seem on extra-high alert."

He did the speed limit, shaking his head at those behind him speeding to catch up and see where he and Ashley were going. He had no way to shake them on this two-lane straight road, so curbed his frustration that he had no choice but to lead them.

The closer they got to town, the more he wondered why the sheriff would want Ashley there while they questioned Brice. It didn't make sense. They could ask her to clarify and corroborate things after they got some answers.

"Something isn't right." He pulled out his phone and called the sheriff.

"Beck?" The anxiety in Ashley's voice matched the rising dread in him.

The sheriff answered, but Beck didn't even say hello. "Did you ask Ashley to come down to the station?"

"No."

No sooner than Beck heard his worst fears confirmed, they approached a four-way intersection and a truck and van peeled out in front of him. Another truck pulled out behind him. Needing both hands to drive, he stuffed his phone back in his pocket.

"Beck!" Ashley screamed as the truck and van in front of them slammed on their brakes, blocking both lanes. He wanted to go around them, but the ditch was too steep. He'd either nose-dive into it, or end up flipping his truck. He couldn't risk Ashley's life like that and stomped on the brakes. His truck skidded to a stop, the back end swinging sideways. The truck rocked to a halt two feet from the other vehicles.

The second truck pulled in sideways next to him, blocking him from backing up.

The van's side door flew open and two men wearing black ski masks jumped out, guns drawn on him.

He reached for his gun and pulled it out a split second before the side door opened and two other ski-masked men dragged Ashley from her seat.

"Beck!"

He made a grab for her, catching her leg. He held on for dear life and shot one of the men who had hold of her right arm. The guy on the left kept tugging on her.

Ashley screamed and squirmed, trying to get free, hitting the guy holding her in his head with her free hand, even though she was thrown off balance when the guy Beck shot dropped dead in the street beside her.

The driver's door swung open behind him. Another shot rang out, this one a report from far back where the reporters' vehicles had probably stopped, King hidden among them in his own car. King's expertly placed bullet hit the guy dead center in the back and took him down. But as soon as he'd fallen another guy crouched in the open doorway with a gun pointed right at Beck's back.

"Let her go, Trigger, or my partner will shoot her." The guy had cold, ice-blue eyes. Beck believed him. A glance in Ashley's direction showed him she'd gone still. The man held a gun to her head.

Beck wanted to fight. He wanted to shoot both these

men, but knew they had him by the balls. There was nothing he could do.

King didn't have a shot or he'd take it.

"Toss the gun out."

Beck looked back at Ashley. Her horror-filled eyes locked on him. For her, he tossed his gun toward the guy with ice-blue eyes, hoping he did the right thing and got another chance to take these guys down.

They weren't here for her.

They knew who he was.

They were here for him.

Beck locked eyes with the guy beside him. "Let her go. Guzman doesn't want her."

"That's where you're wrong. He wants both of you."

The guy holding Ashley with her back to his chest dragged her away even as she struggled to get free, fighting hard but getting nowhere because the guy stood six inches taller than her and outweighed her by forty pounds. He hauled her to the van, picked her up, and tossed her inside. She wasn't done fighting. She stood bent at the waist in the van, swung her leg back, and kicked the guy right in the nuts. He bellowed as all the air went out of him, his knees buckled, and he hit the ground hard, his hands covering his balls. Excruciating pain turned his face red. Ashley tried to get past him, but he planted his hand on her chest and shoved her back into the van wall. Her head bounced off the metal and she swayed and sank down to her bottom.

Beck slid across the seat, jumped out of the truck, and went after the guy. He shoved him back and tried to grab Ashley's outstretched hand. A gun bashed into the back of Beck's skull, sending him falling forward. Fireworks went off on his eyelids as he caught his weight on his arms on the van floor. Someone grabbed his feet and shoved him inside.

Busted-balls guy and ice-blue eyes jumped in after them, shutting the door. The driver stomped on the gas and drove away. With Beck's truck stopped in the intersection, blocked from behind by the other vehicle and two dead bodies, King couldn't possibly follow without first clearing the way.

Beck panicked. His heart stopped. "No. Let her go."

Ice-blue eyes leaned down, grabbed Beck by the coat, hauled him up six inches, and got in his face. "You don't have a say in this. You cost Guzman a lot of money. He wants his payday and you dead."

Oh fuck. They meant to ransom Ashley. And God knows what else. And to who. And for what purpose. The infinite possibilities tormented him.

Ice-blue eyes dropped him back to the floor of the van. Beck rose up, ready to fight, but didn't get anywhere in the cramped space. Ice-blue eyes punched him in the jaw and sent him back on his ass. Strong as an ox, despite his age, he muscled Beck onto his stomach, pulled one of his arms up his back, nearly pulling his shoulder out of the socket. Ashley tried to shove ice-blue eyes away, but only ended up getting shoved back into the wall again.

"No, Ashley, don't." He didn't want her to get hurt trying to help him.

"Let him go," she pleaded, her eyes glassy and her voice rough with emotion.

"Move again and I break his arm."

Ashley gasped and stared down at Beck, her eyes pleading with him to stop this.

He wished he could, but they had him and it didn't look good for him or Ashley.

The only thing on his side was that King and Caden would track his and Ashley's cell phones. Though Ashley didn't know it, he'd put a tracking device on hers, as well.

Beck stopped fighting the second the rope tied around

his hands. Ice-blue eyes took his cell from his back pocket, but thanks to his bulky jacket, the guy missed his knife. Beck rolled as the guy shoved him over, sat up, and scooted back into Ashley, sitting between her legs, keeping her protected behind him, and his knife pressed to her inner thigh. Ice-blue eyes patted down his legs, found the gun at his ankle, and disarmed him. Ashley slid one hand around his shoulder and rested it on his chest. The other she slid down his back to his belt. She unhooked the knife and stuffed it down the front of her pants. He leaned back into her, so the guys didn't see what she was doing.

Broken-balls dude sat in the other corner, holding his nuts, rocking back and forth, cussing under his breath, and glaring daggers at Ashley.

Beck didn't say anything. Neither did the men. He wished they'd say something to tell him where they were going and how long he had to figure out a way to get him and Ashley out of this dire situation. He'd been in some deep shit before, but this time it just might bury him.

CHAPTER THIRTY-FOUR

Brice sat between the two men in the backseat of the SUV, his heart pounding with anticipation. He had his bags packed, a private jet waiting to take him and Aurora to a private island after Guzman's plane dropped them in Mexico, and soon he'd have his precious treasure back. Two million seemed a small price to pay for his heart's desire.

He'd lost so much. His home. His beautiful garden. Tonight, he'd get back the one thing he couldn't live without. Maybe they wouldn't have Adam, but they'd make their own family. They'd go to his secret getaway, out of the States, and away from prying eyes and this mess. Once he completed Ashley's transformation and she truly became Aurora, they'd have a child of their own. A beautiful little girl. A handsome boy. The next generation to carry on his legacy.

They pulled into a parking lot in front of what appeared to be an abandoned warehouse and drove around to the back of the building. There, a small plane waited in the field.

"I see my ride is here."

Neither the driver nor the men on either side of him responded. They stopped the SUV near a wide set of roll-up doors. Two men who could be the poster models for gang members with their tattoos, bandanas, and too-big pants loaded a large produce truck with boxes of apples.

At least, that's what they looked like. Brice had no idea what was in the boxes. He didn't want to know.

The men got out of the car. The dark-haired guy on the right waved Brice to follow him. Brice doubted the guy spoke English, so followed without comment, but stopped midway to the door and turned to the guy following him with a gun pointed at his back.

"My bags?"

"Will be loaded on the plane along with the shipment as soon as Señor Guzman gives the order."

Which meant he wasn't going anywhere until Guzman got paid.

He walked into the warehouse, empty but for the fifty or so remaining apple boxes being loaded onto the truck. In another fifteen minutes, the place would be empty. Except for the wood chair sitting below a low-hung light next to the wall splattered with red and brown splotches Brice recognized as dried blood.

Guzman had his own playroom.

Soon, Brice would be at the house he and Aurora would call home.

Guzman came out of a small office at the back of the warehouse and walked toward him crossing the blocks of light and shadow on the floor from the high windows. Nearly sunset; it would be dark soon. He and Aurora would have a beautiful view on their flight. They'd reach Mexico with the stars shining and enjoy a late dinner on the private plane he had waiting for them in Mexico City to take them away. She'd love the extravagance and adventure of it all.

He couldn't wait.

"I told you that if you did not deposit my money, I would keep your Aurora."

Brice held up his cell. "As soon as I see her, I will finalize the transfer I've already set up."

"You do not have long to wait. Here she comes."

A white van pulled up outside the roll-up door and parked next to the produce truck. Iceman climbed out of the sliding door after two of his men exited the front. Another man gingerly stepped out of the back and stood next to the van, his legs wide, his body tense. Brice guessed he'd been hurt in some way.

Iceman reached into the van and dragged out the man who'd dared put his hands on his Aurora. Trigger. What she saw in him, Brice didn't know. His glare and feral look only made the man look mean.

The hurt man reached into the van and pulled Aurora out by her arm. She stood next to him and the man shoved her forward, making her fall to her hands and knees. Trigger pulled out of Iceman's grasp and ran head-down right into the injured man's stomach with his shoulder, sending the man to the ground. Trigger kept his feet and kicked the guy in the nuts. Hard. Right between his widespread legs. Direct hit.

Brice flinched, his thigh turning in toward his balls in sympathy. Every man knew how much it fucking hurt to be hit in that most vulnerable place.

"Don't fucking touch her again," Trigger ordered, kicking the wailing man in the ass as he rolled to his side to cover his balls.

Iceman grabbed hold of Trigger again by his elbow and swung him around to face Brice and Guzman. Even with his hands tied behind his back, Brice felt the threat this man posed in his deathly stare.

He tried to get away from Iceman and come after Brice. "I'm going to fucking kill you."

Brice ignored him and focused on the beauty standing to Trigger's left. The woman he'd never lose again. "Aurora, darling. I've missed you."

CHAPTER THIRTY-FIVE

Bile rose up Ashley's throat at just the sound of Brice's voice, but hearing him call her Aurora again sent a wave of anger through her system. She looked behind her, then around the wide-open space, and finally settled her gaze on Brice.

"My name is Ashley. I am not your puppet anymore."

Brice narrowed his dark gaze and he gave her that smile she hated and feared because it meant pain. "I see you've forgotten all I've taught you. We'll have to begin your lessons again. We'll start with scrubbing that man off you and getting you something more appropriate to wear." His eyes traveled over her simple tunic sweater and jeans to her black snow boots.

"Run, Ashley. Get out of here," Beck ordered.

She wanted to, but found she needed to stand her ground and claim her life back from this man. To do so, she needed to outsmart and outmaneuver him.

She turned to the dark-haired man standing off to the side wearing an expensive suit, his dark eyes on Beck. He exuded confidence and control. His eyes held the promise of death for Beck. He wanted his revenge.

She hoped to appeal to him on another level.

"I don't believe we've met," she addressed the man. "I'm Ashley Swan."

The man stood a bit taller, though she was taller than

him, and addressed her in the same polite tone she'd used to introduce herself. "Señor Guzman, Señorita Swan."

"Please, call me Ashley." He nodded to acknowledge this. "How much is he paying you for me?"

Her blunt question made the man's eyes widen with surprise and maybe admiration for her boldness.

Beck swore. "Ashley, don't."

Guzman nodded toward the white-haired man holding Beck. He immediately punched Beck in the side, sending him to his knees, bent over with pain.

Guzman turned back to her. "Two million is what Trigger cost me. Mr. Mooney has agreed to pay the debt to have you back."

She cocked her head and studied him. "I take it you're not inclined to abide by what I wish."

"While I love pleasing beautiful women such as yourself, in this case, Trigger has wronged both of us and needs to pay. He killed my cousin Marco and his fiancée, Paula."

Ashley glanced at Beck. He stared down Guzman, not giving the man one ounce of his fear or regret for what he'd done in the line of duty.

Ashley tried again. "You're a businessman, Señor Guzman. A good one, or you wouldn't be so successful in the enterprise you've built. I wish to make you a proposition."

"Beautiful women proposition me all the time." He smiled and laughed.

The seven men around them laughed with him.

Brice's mouth pulled into a tight line and his eyes promised her she'd pay for not cowing to his will. That if she tried to offer herself to Guzman he'd kill her. She already envisioned the punishment she'd endure after he did exactly what he'd promised and scrubbed her raw for allowing another man to touch her. She didn't want to know how bad things would get after that, but her body echoed with the fear and pain she remembered all too well.

"I'll pay you two million to let me go and one million to give me Beck. I can have the money transferred to you as soon as possible."

"Aurora, shut your mouth."

She ignored Brice, but couldn't help glancing at Beck, who stared at her dumbfounded. He didn't see that one coming, but what was she supposed to do? She couldn't fight her way out of this, but she could buy her way out. And his.

"You are right, Brice. She is a woman worth keeping."

Brice puffed up with pride.

She rolled her eyes. "This is business, Señor Guzman. Do we have a deal?"

"I must say, I never expected this. I like you. In your movies, you play women who have a vulnerability about them but are strong. Powerful. I see that in you now. But I'm sorry. I have made my deal and I am a man of my word. As you said, it's business."

"I implore you, Señor Guzman, please reconsider. He will kill me."

"A great loss. Perhaps you will find some of that strength and save yourself."

"That is what I am trying to do while I make you an even richer man," she snapped.

Guzman simply smiled and turned to Brice. "Complete the transfer, or I will take her up on her offer."

Brice pulled his cell phone from his pocket. "Look at that, cell service and Wi-Fi." The sneer he sent Ashley only made the fury building in her gut flare.

"We aren't savages," Guzman teased. The man had a sense of humor despite the fact that he planned to execute Beck.

She needed to get him out of here. She needed to get Brice's phone and call for help. The white-haired man had taken Beck's. Hers was still in her purse in Beck's truck. He'd told her to keep it on her at all times. She should have listened.

"The money should be in your account." Brice held up his phone so Guzman could verify he'd entered the right amount and account information.

Satisfied, Guzman walked to her, took her hand, and kissed her knuckles. "I enjoyed meeting you."

She smiled sweetly. "I'll enjoy seeing you behind bars."

He laughed at her boldness and dropped her hand. "You should leave with Brice so you don't have to see what I am going to do to your lover."

Terror squeezed her heart. She couldn't even think of a future without Beck.

With six men spread around them and Brice closing in on her, she ran past Guzman and launched herself into Beck, wrapping her arms around his neck and holding him tight as she kneeled between his knees. The tears came, but she didn't fall apart. She pressed her lips to his ear. "Tell me what to do." She'd run out of ideas.

Beck kissed her neck, then turned his face into her ear. "Go now. When you have a chance, take that knife and use it. Do whatever you have to do, then you run. Promise me you'll get away from here."

Brice hooked his hands under her arms and ripped her away from Beck, tossing her sideways, so she slid on the concrete floor and knocked her head.

"Take what you came for," Guzman ordered. "Our business is done. I have other matters to attend to."

Brice came after her again.

Beck rose to his feet and ran for Brice, knocking his shoulder into Brice's side and sending him to the floor ten feet away from her. "Leave her alone."

The white-haired man held Beck back from going after Brice again.

"All you're doing is making things worse for her," Brice warned.

Beck's gaze shifted to her. His eyes held the frustration, rage, and resignation she felt building inside her. He struggled against the man holding him back. "Don't you fucking touch her."

Brice pulled her up from the ground. Her back pressed to his chest, his hips against her bottom. He rubbed himself against her, his hand sliding up her side, over her breast, and up to her neck. He wrapped his fingers around her throat and squeezed, cutting off her air.

"Let her go," Beck ordered.

She didn't panic. He'd held her like this a hundred times. She'd let him, knowing fighting only meant more pain. But this time she didn't stand passive. She pulled the knife from her pants, flicked open the blade, and with her gaze locked with Beck's, she held it in her fist and plunged it into Brice's thigh.

Brice screamed, released her neck, and made a grab for the knife. She pulled it out, turned, and shoved him backward.

She didn't exactly know what happened next, but one of Guzman's men dropped two feet behind her, blood spreading across his back. The white-haired man held Beck in front of him, a shield against the unseen threat.

King. He had to be the one shooting. Another man fell.

DEA agents in black head-to-toe gear, guns drawn, yelling, "DEA! Hands up," rushed into the building.

The white-haired man shoved Beck to the ground and made a run for the produce truck with another man. She ran to Beck and used the knife to cut the rope binding his hands. Almost through the rope, someone grabbed her from behind and pulled her back. She turned and plunged the knife into Brice's chest.

He bellowed and fell back, taking her down with him. She landed on top of him and lost her grip on the knife as blood seeped out of the wound, covered her fingers, and made them slide free.

Brice's eyes went wide and filled with pain, then narrowed with rage. "You bitch. You'll pay for that. I'll teach you a lesson you won't forget."

"Never again." She kneed him in the nuts and struggled to get up and out of his grasp.

In the chaos, Guzman snagged her wrist and dragged her away from Brice, and Beck, who got caught up taking one of Guzman's men down. Her last glimpse of Beck before Guzman dragged her outside was of him with his knee jammed into the guy's spine as he pinned the guy's hands behind his back.

Guzman dragged her toward the plane at a dead run. Ten feet from the open door and being taken hostage by a drug dealer, she tugged hard on her arm, hurting her shoulder, but effectively stopping Guzman from dragging her one more step toward the plane and God knows how long living as his hostage until he ransomed her, or did even more terrible things to her.

He pulled her forward two more steps before she planted her feet and leaned away, stopping him again. "Come. Now. Or you will be shot."

The familiar tingle went up her spine and danced over her skin. She felt Beck behind her.

"You're going to be shot." She stepped to the side. A split second later, Guzman's head snapped back with the impact of the bullet that hit him between the eyes and exploded out the back of his head. He dropped dead at her feet.

CHAPTER THIRTY-SIX

Beck stared through the scope, his sight set on the man in the open plane door who pulled a gun from his back and aimed it at Ashley. Caden ran across the field toward her, his gun up, but no shot with Ashley in the way. He wouldn't get to her in time. Beck fired, taking down the pilot a split second after he fired and Caden tackled Ashley to the ground.

Beck handed the rifle back to Agent Bennett and ran for Ashley, knowing Bennett would make sure that fuck Brice remained in custody until the ambulance arrived. Beck ran as fast as he could, his thighs aching from the exertion, his mind screaming at him that Ashley couldn't have been hit. He killed the bastard and messed up his shot. She had to be okay.

Caden rolled off her, stood, and took her hand, helping her up. The second she hit her feet and spotted him, she ran to him. He caught her in his arms and held her close for two heartbeats, then held her away so he could check her out and make sure she wasn't hit. He didn't see any blood except for Brice's on her hand and pulled her back into his arms.

"Are you okay? Are you hurt?" He held her tight, his heartbeat jackhammering in his chest with relief and disbelief that she was really okay.

"I'm fine. Are you okay?" She held him tighter, pushing against his sore ribs.

He didn't care about the pain, only that she was alive and back in his arms. He'd never let her go again.

"As long as you're safe, I'm good."

Caden came to stand beside them. "That bullet whizzed right past my head. I got her just in time," he assured Beck.

"Thank you." Beck didn't stop holding Ashley close, but gave his brother a look that said so much more than he could get out right now.

Caden brushed his hand down Ashley's shoulder. "I hope I didn't hurt you, Ashley."

She shook her head against Beck's chest. "I'm fine." She trembled in his arms. "Is Brice dead? Did I kill him?"

Beck kissed the top of her head. "No, sweetheart. He's alive." Despite the fact Beck wanted to shoot him, too. He'd eliminated one threat by killing Guzman. He no longer had a man gunning for him or his family because of what he'd done. But Ashley still had to live with the threat of Brice making trouble in her life even if he did end up behind bars for the rest of his.

But she didn't have to live with killing him.

Beck cupped her face in his hands and leaned down and kissed her softly. "You scared the hell out of me." His heart thrashed against his aching ribs just thinking about the risk she'd taken stabbing Brice and cutting Beck's bonds. If she hadn't set him free, he'd have been almost helpless when Guzman's men moved in to take him out. Luckily, he'd broken the ropes Ashley almost cut through and took down the guy hell-bent on killing him so Guzman could get away with Ashley.

"I thought I'd lost you." She pulled him close again and buried her face in his chest.

"Let's get you both checked out." Caden pointed to the

ambulance pulling into the parking lot between all the cop cars.

Officers swarmed the building and were bringing out the remaining men who worked for Guzman. Beck spotted Bennett standing over Brice just inside the roll-up door. Brice yelled for help, his hand outstretched to an indifferent Bennett and the other hand locked around the knife sticking out of his chest.

"Maybe I should go retrieve my knife." Beck would like nothing better than to pull it out of Brice's chest and let him bleed out. It would save him and Ashley a hell of a lot of headaches as his arrest, sentencing, and jailhouse interviews went on for months. Beck had no doubt Brice would bask in the limelight and his infamy as long as he was allowed. The media would eat that shit up and broadcast it far and wide.

Ashley would have no peace.

He wanted that for her. Somehow, he'd find a way to give it to her.

The paramedics went to help Brice. Another ambulance pulled in. Beck led Ashley to that one, wanting to get her checked out just in case. She'd gone quiet on him. After all she'd experienced and seen today, he didn't blame her for retreating into her head and maybe that quiet spot by the river she'd used as a means to cope while in Brice's house of hell.

"Beck, really, I'm fine. I'm not hurt." Ashley didn't want to let go of him.

To get her to let the paramedics check her out, he sat on the edge of the back of the ambulance and pulled up his shirt, showing off the bruises already spreading across his side. "If I let them check this out, will you let them check you out?"

"Beck! Oh my God." Ashley touched his face. "I'm sorry."

"Why? You didn't punch me. Sit next to me. Let these guys do their thing and take a minute to catch your breath." He tugged her hand to get her to sit beside him. One of the paramedics started poking at his ribs, then strapped an ice pack to his side when Beck assured him he didn't have any cracked or broken ribs. They just hurt like hell. Beck held another ice pack to the back of his head where he'd been cracked in the skull with the gun when they kidnapped them.

Ashley allowed the other guy to take her blood pressure and listen to her heart. She settled her head on Beck's shoulder and whispered, "Thank you for saving my life. I love you."

He tilted his head, kissed her softly, and looked her right in the eye. "You saved mine the second you walked into my life. I love you, too, and I swear, I'll never let you go, and I will try every single day to make you happy."

Ashley brushed away the paramedic's unwanted attention, turned to Beck, and kissed him, her tongue sliding along his. He lost himself in her taste and the overwhelming sense that he got damn lucky escaping Brice and Guzman, and he wouldn't take a single day he had with her for granted. The kiss ended with them touching foreheads and looking into each other's eyes. He lost himself in the depths of love he saw in hers and the promise that she wanted to be with him forever. He'd have to make that promise permanent soon.

"How could you do this to me?" Brice bellowed from the gurney the paramedics wheeled him on toward the other ambulance, drawing their attention. "I love you. You're mine, Aurora. You're everything to me. Everything I did for you is because I love you. Don't you see? I did it for you. Please, Aurora, don't let them take me from you. I love you!"

Special Agent Bennett slammed the ambulance door

on Brice's next words and slapped the back, letting the ambulance driver know he could leave.

Ashley watched it go, letting out a heavy sigh of relief as Brice was finally taken away and out of her life. At least out of her sight for now.

Special Agent Bennett joined them at the ambulance. Caden stood with his shoulder propped against the door, watching over him and Ashley.

"Nice job taking down Guzman's men, Bennett, but you let that white-haired fuck get away with all the drugs." Beck shook his head, giving Bennett grief, but not really meaning it. "Thanks for saving my ass though."

"I really wanted to get the drugs instead," Bennett razzed him.

"Whatever." Beck rolled his eyes, still holding Ashley close.

"Miss Swan, I'm glad you're okay. Lucky for you, Trigger and King are the best snipers we have. I'm sorry to lose Trigger as an undercover agent, but I hope we can convince him to stay on in another capacity."

"I'm sure you can," Ashley said, no hesitation encouraging him in this way to stay with the DEA and in a job that would still be dangerous. She wanted him to be happy doing what he loved and trusted him to be careful and come back to her each and every day.

It meant so much to him to have her support.

"But Beck's leave of absence isn't quite over. I still need his help to make sure Brice gets what he deserves."

Bennett focused on her. "I think we can help each other."

Beck understood exactly where Bennett, King, and even Caden were going with this. He turned to Ashley and placed his hand on her shoulder and brushed her soft skin with his fingers. "We can use those files as leverage to get what you want and what we need to take down the rest of Guzman's crew."

"Okay, but . . ."

"Adam comes first." Beck finished her sentence, letting her know that Adam was his priority, too.

Bennett caught Ashley's attention. "I think I have a way to get you what you want and get King close to one of our major targets. Iceman took you two today. He's the one who took off in the truck. King went after him, but they had a hell of a head start. If King doesn't apprehend him today, I'll need your help to take him down."

"How?" Ashley asked.

Bennett and Caden laid out their plan, but it hinged on using the blackmail files Ashley wanted to keep secret because she knew what it was like to be targeted and exposed in the tabloids. She knew what it was like to have someone take control of your life.

In this case, Ashley would use the information to take down a very dangerous man and give a child a bright and happy life.

Beck hoped she understood and could live with the consequences of what she was about to do.

CHAPTER THIRTY-SEVEN

Ashley sat across from Sheriff Willis with the navy blue folder she'd brought lying across her lap. She didn't have to say what it contained. Sheriff Willis saw it, connected it to the folder she'd given him with all the pictures and SD cards containing the videos of what Brice did to her, and knew she'd come for a reason.

"So Special Agent Cooke is staying out of this."

She glanced over her shoulder at Beck standing outside the sheriff's office glass door making sure no one disturbed them.

"I thought you might like privacy for this meeting."

Sheriff Willis's eyes narrowed and his lips pinched together with frustration and anger. "There is nothing in those pictures that shows me doing anything illegal."

She agreed with him. And just like she did for Danny Radford, she came here to make things right for the sheriff. "Because you didn't do anything illegal. You simply found yourself caught in a situation you couldn't get out of without taking down a lot of people higher up than you."

Though he was innocent of what the pictures showed, he'd looked the other way when others had crossed the line.

"Senator Greer. Governor Ross. Judge Henry." He confirmed some of the men Beck helped her identify who Brice had forced her to watch through the two-way mirrors.

"Others who held high positions who couldn't afford to get caught with their pants down, so to speak," she added.

"I didn't sleep with that girl or do anything the others did," he bit out.

"But you didn't stop the others like you should have. *Sheriff.*"

His face reddened with anger.

She leaned forward. "Did you know I was in that house?"

"No." His immediate and emphatic answer rang with the truth.

She believed him. "Did you know what Brice was doing at that ranch?"

"Other than gathering an arsenal of blackmail material, no. I also had no idea why he needed it. As far as I know, he never used it. At least not against me, until Sergeant Foster brought him in for questioning and he tried to force me to dismiss your claims and charge you instead."

"But you refused to do it."

"I finally decided I'd rather take the fall for being star-struck than allow him to hurt another person the way he hurt you. The boy. Those other women." Sheriff Willis leaned forward and braced his arms on his desk. "What are you going to do with those pictures?"

They showed him sitting on the side of a bed, fully clothed, with a young woman standing naked in front of him. She looked to be barely eighteen. Brice offered to show him around the house, led him into the bedroom, and stood just out of frame of the hidden cameras he had in the bedrooms. He'd ordered the prostitute to give the sheriff anything he wanted. The sheriff had politely declined her offer and turned on Brice, furious for putting him in this position and threatening to arrest Brice for having prostitutes at his home in the first place. That's when Brice had held up the tablet, showing the sheriff the images he'd captured and used against the sheriff to keep him quiet and in his pocket. Ashley had watched the whole thing on the video that showed much more of the room than the camera.

"Nothing. In fact, now that I have my answers, I'll give them to you, so you can destroy them."

"In exchange for what?"

"Your word that when it comes to those men, you will not look the other way again."

"I promise from this day, I will, but you know Brice pissed off some powerful people. They want him to pay. They usually get what they want, and I expect they will in this case, too, one way or another."

That was Brice's problem, not hers. She was trying to do right by the innocent people caught up in his game.

"You should know Deputy Kent has been fired. Guzman used him to contact you and lure you away from Beck's place. He's facing charges for that and a number of other instances where he fed Guzman and his crew intel on drug busts."

"I'm glad you're tying up all the loose ends."

"To that end, I need your help."

She cocked up one eyebrow, completely disbelieving he'd ask her for something under the circumstances. "What do you want? Besides my turning over this folder to you."

"All but two of the women found on Brice's property have been identified. Given his . . . admiration for you, I would like you to ask him to identify the two women."

Her stomach dropped. The thought of seeing Brice again made her heart race. "You want me to go see him in the hospital."

"I want you to give two families who are probably missing these women the closure they deserve," the sheriff pleaded. "You're here to do the right thing. So help me do right by them. He won't speak to anyone without his lawyer present. I think he'll talk to you."

She didn't like giving Brice another moment of her time or a chance to hurt her more, but she'd do it for those women.

She set the blue folder in front of him to show that she had faith in him to do the right thing and fulfill the promise he'd made to her to never look the other way when someone needed help. "Let's go get those names from Brice."

Beck stopped Ashley outside Brice's room and cupped her face in his warm hands. "Are you sure you want to do this?"

She went up on tiptoe and kissed him softly. They'd spent the last two days since they were kidnapped by Guzman's men at home and mostly in Beck's bed. "It's not just for those women and their families. I want to close this chapter once and for all." Despite the ache in her stomach and fear coursing through her.

"It's done. He'll go to jail and die there."

"I know you don't want me to, but I have to."

Beck hugged her close, released her, and didn't stop her from going past the officer stationed outside Brice's door and inside to face the devil who tried to destroy her despite how much Beck wanted to protect her.

Ashley stared down at Brice's pale face, his arm held against his chest in a sling to immobilize his shoulder due to the chest wound.

She'd missed his heart.

Then again, he didn't have one.

"I heard you weren't talking to anyone without your lawyer."

"Aurora. I'd never refuse to talk to you, my love. I knew you'd come." Brice's breathless voice told her how much he'd wanted to see her again. His eyes shined bright with excitement.

She used that against him. "You failed me," she accused, letting her real anger infuse her words. "How could you just let me go after all we shared?"

Disbelief filled his eyes. He didn't understand her turn in attitude. "No. I tried to find you."

"You left me out there in the cold," she snapped. "I heard you calling for me." She pointed an accusing finger at him. "But you gave up. You went home and left me out there all alone."

"I begged you to come back. Why? Why did you run from me?"

"I had finally become the woman I always knew I could be."

"Yes. My Aurora."

"The woman worthy of your undying love and devotion." She filled her words with truth he believed beyond a doubt but made every cell in her body scream with denial.

"You have both," he assured her.

"But you allowed Darren to interrupt our beautiful dinner. You let him come between us and the night we were supposed to share. A night we were finally going to be together. A night more special than any we had shared."

Brice slid his free hand over his hard length under the blanket, rattling the chain on his handcuffs but not even thinking about them or the situation that put him in that bed.

Repulsed, she tried not to show it and held back the bile rising in her throat just speaking these words and putting on this act caused.

Brice raised his head. "Yes, Aurora, oh, yes. You have no idea how much I want you."

"You told me I was special." She forced tears to gather

in her eyes and made her voice crack. "That *I* was your one true love. But I wasn't."

He nodded vigorously. "Yes. You are."

"How many times did you show me your beautiful garden?" She clasped her hands together at her chest. "How many times did you make me look at the women you truly loved?"

"No," he shook his head rigorously. "They meant nothing. None of them were as worthy as you."

"I wanted to be worthy. I tried. I played your game. But you were always comparing me to them, weren't you? I wasn't enough." Her voice cracked again.

"You are. I love you. They meant nothing to me. They were just playmates. You are my one true love. You are the one I want to be my wife."

She narrowed her eyes and crossed her arms over her chest. "Who were these playmates?"

He saw her jealousy and tried to make it right. "No one. They meant nothing."

"What were their names?"

"It doesn't matter."

She let her fists fall to her sides and stood rigid. "Yes, it does. I want their names," she demanded like a lover scorned.

He rattled them off. All the names she knew and the two she'd been sent here to get. Rebecca Murphy and Angela Rodriguez. "That's all of them at the ranch."

Her stomach dropped and her heart stopped with that "at the ranch."

She kept her focus, stayed in character, and did what she had to do. "Let me guess, you have another garden that you covet."

"There is nothing I love more than you."

She remembered the parties she attended at his home in Beverly Hills. "The after-party for *After Midnight* at

your home—we danced under the moonlight in the court-
yard surrounded by roses."

His mischievous smile told her she'd hit the mark.

She jacked up the jealousy hoping it covered her shock
and horror. "How many others?"

"What does it matter? Young, eager women hoping for
a break in the business are a dime a dozen in L.A. and no
one misses them. You are special."

Easy prey. So many young women, including runaways
who might not be missed, flooded into L.A. hoping to
make their dreams of fame and fortune come true. Ashley
had been one of them once upon a time.

"Do you have any other gardens, Brice? Am I to dis-
cover more of your unworthy women?" She pouted out
the words like he'd broken her heart and not made her
sick with disgust and filled with sympathy for those poor
souls.

"No, my love. That is all of them. Well, except for
Mother. But I made that look like an accident."

Oh God, he killed his own mother.

"And Christy in college. They found her in the river,
but never connected her to me. That was an experiment
gone wrong. For years I got by with meaningless encoun-
ters with women who liked it rough, or just put up with it
because they wanted to be seen with me. A trip to Vegas
changed everything. Drunk, I took things too far with a
couple of hookers. I left them in Dumpsters where they
belonged." He spoke like he'd just told her he'd taken out
the trash, but these were people. Human beings who deserved better.

"I learned my lesson. Disposing of them exposed me.
I found a better way. A simpler way. But each time it got
harder to find the kind of satisfaction I craved. I needed
that rush."

Sex took a backseat to the pain he liked to cause to get off.

She shook her head. "Tsk, tsk, tsk. You've been very bad. Blackmail. Kidnapping. Torture. Murder. You had everything. Money. Fame. A grand life. Women who wanted you. Friends who adored you. Colleagues who looked up to you. But none of that made you happy."

"You made me happy, Aurora."

"My name is Ashley. Remember it. I am the one who is responsible for what happens to you next."

Brice smiled indulgently. "There is nothing you can do to me. My lawyer will make a deal. I'll be out sooner than you think. We will be together again."

"I will never see you again. You are going to pay for all you've done. Those women will be returned to their families."

"No. You can't destroy my garden."

"I will. I'm also going to ensure that Adam gets what you owe him for taking his mother away from him."

"She shouldn't have interfered. She didn't want me to be happy with you."

"You pretend to feel. But nothing makes you happy. Nothing makes you laugh. Nothing makes you sad. Nothing makes you regret. All you know is pain." She backed up toward the door. "Enjoy your stay here, Brice. Once they put you in a cell, this will look like the Ritz."

"I'll be out on bail soon and we can be together again."

She laughed. "Delusional much? You will never get bail. We will never be together."

"You don't mean that." Brice didn't want to hear the truth.

The officer opened the door for her.

"Where are you going?"

"Home. With Beck. The man I love. The man I will

spend the rest of my life with. The man who knows how to make me happy. The man who will raise Adam and our children with me. The man who gets what I never gave to you. All my love."

Beck stood in the doorway and glared at Brice, but said to her, "Let's go home, sweetheart."

Ashley dipped her hand down the front of her blouse and pulled out the wire the sheriff asked her to wear. "Be careful who you tell your secrets to."

She took Beck's hand and walked away from Brice.

"I'll kill you for touching her. She's mine. Aurora! Come back! I love you!"

The rest of his screamed threats faded as she stepped into the elevator and her future with Beck. She left her past behind.

Almost. She had a couple more things she needed to do before she truly moved on with her life.

CHAPTER THIRTY-EIGHT

Beck woke up with his ribs aching thanks to the beautiful, naked woman draped over him, her head on his opposite shoulder from where she lay down his side, one leg over his, her knee nudged up in his balls and her dark hair spilling over his stomach and arm. They arrived home last night after fighting their way past the horde of fans and reporters outside the hospital only to find the usual crowd camped out at the gate. He'd driven past them, despite his urge to drive right through them.

When they settled in last night with the chili and corn bread dinner he whipped together and turned on the TV, they found every station still reporting about Brice's arrest, Ashley's visit to the hospital, and their kidnapping by Guzman's men on the road after the paparazzi followed them.

That clip sent chills up his spine and he'd lived through it.

Ashley shut off the TV. They ate dinner together in the quiet, a fire burning and a light snow falling outside the windows. She stared at it for a long time, scaring him with how quiet and lost she looked. He could only guess her thoughts, but knew with Brice under arrest and facing life in prison, she could finally breathe and think about all that happened to her. He let her have the time and space she needed, held her close, and let his thoughts roam to that terrifying hour he thought Guzman might kill him, leaving Ashley at Brice's mercy. The man didn't have any. With Guzman gone, the threat against him eliminated, he gave himself time to think about what came next. After their visit to a certain judge and the state prison today, he'd be free to go back to work. They'd offered to put him in charge of his own team, or become a training instructor. He wasn't quite ready to give up the action, so decided running his own team might be the best fit. Though he'd worked alone a long time, it might be nice to be a part of a group.

He'd be a part of a family at home, too, with Ashley and Adam moving in here with him. They had a few more details to work out there, but in a few hours, he hoped to put Ashley's fears that she'd lose Adam to rest.

If this plan worked, they'd live their lives worry free.

Ashley didn't open her eyes, but mumbled, "Stop worrying."

He smiled and stared down at her pretty face. "I'm not."

"Are too. It's a prison. What could go wrong?"

"I don't know. I've never walked into a prison filled with men who haven't seen a woman in God knows how long with a super mega movie star. I think you might cause a riot."

She chuckled and hugged him tight. Still without opening her eyes. "Which is why we have an appointment with the warden."

"Which you got way too easily."

"Celebrity gets you in the door. It's what you do once you're in that makes the difference. How you treat people, the things you say, or don't, the things you do, or don't, those are the things that matter."

"I know you're uncomfortable with riding the line of right and wrong. I wish there was an easier way to get what we want without crossing over it."

"I'm finding that gray area that makes up that line is wider than I thought. That's all."

"If you want to back out, I'll go and meet with Adam's father alone. King and I can handle him."

"I know you can, but this is something I need to do. I owe it to Jackie to do the best I can for Adam. I need to convince his father, Scott, that I am the best choice for Adam."

"There's no doubt about it, sweetheart."

He just hoped her association with him didn't cost her the one thing she wanted. He'd do anything to make her happy, but he couldn't change who and what he was. He could do his best to prove to her and Adam's father that he'd be the best dad he could possibly be for Adam.

He didn't think about how fast he went from a broken man who'd escaped to his isolation as a means to cope with the things he'd seen and done to falling in love with a woman way out of his league, beautiful in body, mind, heart, and soul, and though broken in spirit like him, tougher than he'd ever thought possible.

She amazed him more each day. He'd been especially proud of the way she'd walked into Brice's room, faced her real-life demon, and played the part she needed to play. She got the information they needed to identify the women buried in Brice's yard and give their families the peace they deserved. He didn't know what it cost her to play pretend with Brice once again, but she'd done it because she had a kind and just heart.

She'd set the rest of this mess straight and finally have the time and space she needed for herself and Adam to heal.

Until then, he planned to do everything in his power to show her that love didn't always hurt. That kindness didn't have to come with strings attached. That when he wanted her, it came with all his desire to please her and no expectation of wanting anything she didn't want to give.

He slid his hand over her soft back, tracing the sunlight highlighting the slope of her hip. She snuggled closer and pressed a soft kiss to his chest. He slipped his fingers over the curve of her bottom and dipped deep between her legs, finding that sweet spot that made her sigh, then moan when he sent one finger deep into her soft center.

"How are you, sweetheart?"

"Warm. And floating toward heaven." Her soft husky voice amplified his desire.

He wanted to give her heaven. He wanted to give her everything. Anything she desired. And right now, that was him, judging by the hand that smoothed down his side, over his hip, and down his growing length. She stroked his hard shaft, her fingers curling over his balls and squeezing gently before her hand moved back up his cock and her thumb circled the head, driving him crazy.

She shifted on top of him, sliding the leg between his thighs over him, and settling on his lap. Her wet center rubbed against his hard dick from the bottom up to the top. She took him in and slid down his length and settled back with him buried to the hilt. She rose above him and sighed, her eyes closed, face soft, body warm over his. The bruises had mostly faded. She could breathe without her ribs hurting anymore, though they'd take more time to heal. All the good food he fed her filled out the hollows in her face and body and rounded her hips and breasts. Her hair hung over her shoulders in silky dark waves.

"God, you're beautiful."

Her eyes opened and she stared down at him. The hand she had braced on his shoulder traced over his skin and settled over the scar on his chest.

"You are so strong." Her other hand moved, her fingers tracing the scar on his side, then over his tight abs.

He reached up and lightly ran his fingers down her chest, over her soft breasts and peaked nipples, down her slender belly to her sloping hips. He grabbed hold and moved her over him.

"You helped me find the strength to be me again." He didn't know how to tell her how much it meant to him, but finding his way back, connecting with her, and reconnecting with his family had healed him in a way he never thought possible.

She planted her hands on both sides of his head and leaned over him, rocking her hips against his. "We did that for each other. And after we found ourselves again, we discovered we could love like this." She leaned down and kissed him, pouring everything into the sweet touch of lips as her body moved over his. The kiss remained slow but deepened as they moved together. They'd made love every night since that first time, sometimes more than once in a day, but this was altogether different as both of them had a need to show the other their deep and lasting love. It wasn't about reaching that ecstasy high, but when they did it felt more powerful than anything he'd ever experienced.

She collapsed on his chest, her head on his shoulder once again, her face tucked against his neck. Her soft breath fanned over his skin. Her fingertips tickled his shoulders and her warm body lay over his. He'd like to stay just like this forever. He'd die a happy man with the woman he loved in his arms.

But they had things to do, a few more tasks to finish before they could get on with living their lives.

He rolled her to his side and stared down at her pretty face and bright, happy eyes. "If we're starting our family today, I need to know one thing."

"What's that?"

"Where do you want to go on our honeymoon?" He

hadn't actually asked her to marry him, but he would. Soon. When the time was right and they didn't have all this other stuff cluttering up their lives.

Her eyes widened with surprise and filled with hope and joy. She didn't ask him if he was asking her to marry him. She simply answered the question he did ask. "Bora Bora?"

"I've never been there. Sounds good."

"I've never been there either, but I've always wanted to go on a tropical beach vacation and have a steamy love affair."

Beck smiled down at her. "I'm happy to oblige that sweet fantasy." He smacked her on the bottom, sliding his hand over her hip and back down. "Let's get going or we'll never get out of this bed."

"I'm okay with that," she purred.

He gave her another of those soft, lingering kisses they'd just shared, then rubbed his nose against hers and looked her in the eyes. "You're a temptation I'd like to indulge every second of the day, but we have work to do."

"I'd like a small wedding. Here. Elegant but simple. The only thing I really need is you. And Adam."

He nodded. "Okay. Then let's go get him."

CHAPTER THIRTY-NINE

Before they could pick up Adam and make a life together—the three of them—Ashley needed to right a few things and get what was owed to him. She stood in front of Judge Henry's desk, several of Brice's navy blue files in her hands in front of her, and stared down at the man who'd broken the law and had given Brice guardianship of a boy he abused.

"You want me to do what?"

"Retract Brice's guardianship and give it to me."

"He's in jail, facing serious charges. Adam is in protective custody. The courts will decide what happens to him next. Have your lawyer make your case and I'm sure you'll get what you want."

"I need it now. And you will give it to me for the same reasons you gave it to Brice." She held up the folder. "Would you like to see the photos? They're not pretty, but they are powerful."

"You don't want to play this game," he warned. "I'm not an enemy you want."

Beck stepped forward and folded his arms in front of his chest. "The last thing you want to do is threaten her."

"You're DEA. How can you stand by and let her do this?"

"Because the one thing I hate more than drug dealers is corrupt law enforcement. You're supposed to uphold the law. Instead, you let Brice get away with all his twisted games."

"He had me by the balls."

"Now I do," Ashley snapped. "You will do as I say, or I will publicly take you down. I won't stop until everyone knows the kind of sick man you are and everything that you've done."

"That's not fair. I never hurt anyone."

Ashley pulled out one of the photos. "This girl can't be more than sixteen. Do you think she grew up wanting to be a prostitute?"

"She never objected to being with me."

Ashley leaned over the desk and got right in the judge's face. "Doing what you're told for your survival isn't the same as giving consent."

"Yet, you're doing the same thing to me right now."

"Turnabout is fair play. And you're only getting fucked figuratively. If you end up in prison for your many crimes . . . Well, we know what will happen to you, a judge, in there."

"You're a real bitch, you know that?"

"I want what's owed. A safe and happy life for Adam. Compensation for the loss of his mother. And you off the bench and unable to twist the law to your liking."

"And you'll hold a gun to my head to get it. Figuratively," he added, using her term to get her attention, hoping it would make her back down.

She was doing exactly what he'd done. The thing is, it might be the same, but she had an altruistic reason for doing it and would take down those who had little or no care for the people they hurt.

She'd take the hit to her conscience for going about it this way.

The judge stared up at her for a good thirty seconds, then made up his mind and pulled up the files on his computer. He worked for nearly a half hour on the documents she needed, aligning everything with the signatures he already had on file from Brice. Once printed out, it all looked legit, even if the originals weren't so legit themselves.

The judge set the papers in front of her and Beck in stacks. "The order terminating Brice's guardianship. The order giving you both guardianship. And a revised will, backdated to the last time Brice updated it with his actual signature, naming Adam his sole heir." The judge signed off on all of them. "Anything else I can do for you," he bit out.

"Yes," she said cheerfully. "You can retire."

"What?"

"You have two weeks to get your affairs here in order, then leave the bench for good."

"I gave you what you wanted. You can't ask me to do that."

She picked up the papers in front of him. "I thank you for righting the wrongs you helped Brice perpetrate and ensuring Adam's future. But I won't allow you to use your position to help others commit crimes against anyone else. Retire with your reputation intact, or these photos and the recordings of you drunk, rambling, and spouting a whole bunch of bigotry and hate will go public."

"I think you might be worse than Brice."

"If you think that, then your compass is so far from north you need to leave this court and find the part of your soul that hasn't been corrupted by power."

"Get out!"

Ashley held the folders and papers he'd given her to her heart. The yucky feeling building inside her soured her gut, but she powered through knowing she'd done the right thing even if she'd done it the wrong way.

She and Beck walked to the door. Beck held it open

for her, the judge's assistant's and office staff's attention on her, the movie star. She used that to her advantage. "Thank you so much for all your help, Judge Henry. And good luck on your retirement next month." She spotted the mounted fish over his head. "You'll finally have all the time you want to go fishing."

The judge glared so hard at her, she half expected the hate coming at her to hurt. It didn't. He deserved everything he got.

She spun on her heel, smiled brightly for everyone in the office, even signed a couple of autographs on her way out, and finally breathed easy when Beck helped her into his truck and they drove away, off to their next appointment and one step closer to being a family with Adam.

CHAPTER FORTY

Beck stood outside the jail cell of a man he'd helped put behind bars several years ago. A man Beck needed to do something for him now. A man who'd thought him a friend until Beck turned on him and took him down.

Two guards stood beside him. King lounged on the top bunk, looking relaxed and indifferent, despite the black-and-blue shiner, cut lip, and swollen knuckles, keeping up appearances as just another inmate. He was anything but. King's eyes darted to the wall beside Scott Lewis. Beck stepped to the side so he could see what King wanted him to see. Beck's heart beat faster when his gaze landed on the colorful drawings taped to the wall. Ones he recognized as Adam's art.

"Trigger? Is that you?"

Beck purposefully left his jacket in the warden's office with Ashley and pulled up his sleeves so Scott would see his tattoos and recognize him.

"Hey, man."

"What the fuck are you doing here?" Scott's angry gaze narrowed with rage.

"We need to talk."

Scott spoke over him. "I don't have anything to say to you."

"About Adam," Beck finished.

Scott moved to the bars, clamped his hands on them, and leaned his face between them. "What about my son?"

Beck nodded toward the officers to let him out.

"Step back," one of the officers ordered.

Scott did as he was told, but his sharp gaze never left Beck's.

"Open ten," the guard spoke into his radio. The bars slid open a moment later.

Scott held his fists at his sides, but didn't move to leave his cell.

"The warden wants to see you." Beck waited.

"I want to know about my boy."

"Come with me, and I'll tell you everything."

Scott glanced at the wall beside him. "I haven't heard from his mother in almost a year."

"I will tell you why."

"Is he dead?"

"No. But he is in protective custody."

Scott hung his head, understanding what Beck didn't say. "Jackie." Scott understood she was dead. He finally walked out of his cell and stood on the white line in the alleyway between the two officers.

"You, too." The officer waved King out of the cell.

"What the fuck did I do?"

"Started a fight in the mess hall. Now you get to clean it up."

King fell in line behind Scott, moving a bit slow after taking down a rival to the band of misfits Scott ran in this hellhole, his swollen face a mask of barely restrained rage. Beck gave him credit for playing his part. He just might make it through this dangerous situation that even Beck would have balked at taking.

Beck hoped to make things a bit easier but no less dangerous for him with this talk with Scott. Beck pulled his sleeves down, hoping no one else recognized him with his hair cut and arms covered. He stared straight ahead as they walked out of the cell block to mean taunts and bawdy and unwanted requests that sent a chill up Beck's spine.

Beck opened the door to the warden's office and let Scott and King walk in ahead of him. The two guards stood outside after Beck closed the door.

"Holy shit, you're Ashley Swan." Scott stared at her, his jaw open.

Ashley walked away from the window she'd been staring out and went to Scott. She held out her hand. "Scott, it's so nice to meet you."

He stared at her hand for a good five seconds, then wiped his hand on his red jumpsuit, and took her hand, shaking it softly. "It's nice to meet you. What are you doing here?" The disbelief that she'd be here of all places filled his voice.

"I came to talk to you."

"Let her go and take a seat," the warden ordered Scott.

He let Ashley loose and did what the warden said.

Ashley turned to the warden. "Thank you for setting up this meeting. I appreciate it. If you don't mind, what I have to say to Scott is personal and between us."

"I'm not leaving you in here alone with two unrestrained inmates."

Ashley smiled at Scott and King, then back at the warden. "I'm positive they'll behave themselves."

Beck stepped forward and laid a hand on Scott's shoulder, giving him a hard squeeze, mostly to appease the warden, but also warning Scott to be good. "I've got this, warden. There are some things you don't want to be privy to. Plausible deniability and all that."

"Special Agent Cooke, I leave her safety in your hands and hold you personally responsible if this goes south."

"It won't. Her safety means my life."

The warden reluctantly left them alone, though Beck had no doubt the two guards remained by the door. Just in case.

King rose and went to Ashley, hugging her close. "You're a sight for sore eyes, beautiful."

"What happened to you?" Ashley gently touched King's battered face.

King cocked his head toward Scott. "I saved his ass this morning."

Scott eyed them. "What the hell is going on? How do you"—he pointed to King—"know her?" His gaze shot to Ashley, suspicious of them both.

Beck moved behind Ashley and sat back against the warden's desk. "You know I'm DEA."

"Yeah, I figured that out when I got arrested and you were the only one besides me who knew where and when that shipment would be delivered."

"You arrested him?" Ashley turned, disbelief in her eyes. "Why didn't you tell me?"

"Because I didn't want to squash your hopes that Scott would turn you down outright when he found out what you and I want." He turned his attention back to Scott. "I'm a cop. You're a drug dealer. You're facing a long sentence because of what you did, not because of who I am. I hope you can keep that in mind."

"I still have no fucking clue what is going on here." He turned to King. "Are you a fucking cop?"

"DEA. I work with him, and we need your help."

"Like I'd fucking help either of you." Scott put his hands on the chair arms and went to stand.

Ashley put her hand on his shoulder and pushed him down. "I hope you'll change your mind." Ashley took the seat beside him and turned it so she sat facing Scott. "I'm not sure how much you've seen on TV about what happened to me."

"The two of you getting taken down on the road by those men was really cool."

Beck shook his head. "Yeah, loads of fun."

"Looked just like one of the movies you've been in," he said to Ashley, then turned back to Beck. "I didn't make the connection between that guy with her and you."

Beck tilted his mouth into a lopsided frown. "Too bad Guzman did, though I put a bullet in his head after he sold Ashley back to Brice and before he kidnapped your son again."

"Again?" Scott moved to the edge of his seat. "What the fuck are you talking about?"

Ashley laid her hand over the scorpion tattoo on Scott's arm. A symbol many of the men in Guzman's organization wore. "Did you know Jackie worked for Brice?"

"No. She sent me letters about Adam. Pictures from him, but she kept the details about their life to a minimum. I didn't want anyone knowing where my son was. Just in case."

In case someone wanted revenge and went after his kid.

"She worked for Brice at his ranch. They had a relationship."

"I heard what he did to those women. The ones they found buried in his yard. Are you telling me she was one of them?"

Ashley had asked the sheriff to hold off notifying Scott about Jackie and Adam, so she could do it herself. "Yes."

"That bastard tortured her to death?"

"Not exactly. When I met her, they were having an affair of sorts. She warned me away. When I couldn't escape, she pleaded with Brice to let me go. For going against him, for not following his rules, he killed her."

"Are you saying she's been dead for nearly a year and that's why I haven't heard from her?"

"Yes."

Scott sat quietly for a moment, absorbing the news and holding back the grief Beck saw in his eyes, but Scott didn't let out. He couldn't. As an inmate for the last several years, he'd learned never to show emotion or any sign of weakness.

Scott finally spoke. "What happened to Adam?"

"Adam remained at Brice's house, mostly hidden away in a room all alone, barely fed, beaten when he disobeyed." Beck hoped Scott thought about his own circumstance living here in a cell at the mercy of his jailers.

Scott's hands fisted on his thighs. "Is he okay?"

"At first he barely spoke. He shied away from everyone." Beck thought back to those first few days. "But he saw me as a protector and showed me more and more the bright, happy little boy he'd had to hide away from Brice. He feared being punished for the simplest thing, like spilling crumbs on the floor. He got over that with me when I showed him that not all men are mean." Beck kept his gaze locked with Scott. Yes, he was the man who'd taught Scott's son to trust again. "He loves sweets and *Scooby-Doo* and Ashley. When Ashley finally had an opportunity to escape, she didn't hesitate to take Adam with her. She carried him for miles in four-inch heels and a ball gown three sizes too small for her with four cracked ribs and lash marks up and down her thighs. You want a mother for him who will protect that boy, love him, put their life on the line for him—she's proven she'll do all that and more. Hell, she blackmailed a judge to change Brice's will so his entire estate goes to his one and only heir—Adam."

Scott slapped his leg and gaped at Ashley. "Damn, you don't play."

"Brice owed him a debt and I made sure he'd pay up for taking Adam's mother away from him."

Fury flashed in Scott's eyes. "Oh, he'll pay."

Beck exchanged a look with Ashley, reading the threat of revenge in Scott's eyes. With Brice in the prison infirmary recovering from his injuries, and word spreading fast that he was here, it was only a matter of time before Brice and Scott crossed paths. Beck wouldn't want to be Brice when he faced off with Adam's father.

Beck couldn't help thinking that Brice and Scott ending up in the same prison had something to do with the powerful people Brice pissed off. Beck smelled a setup, but couldn't prove it or do anything about it.

"Where is Adam now?" Scott demanded.

"Protective custody with my brother and his fiancée. Caden is also with the DEA."

Scott nodded, taking a moment to absorb that, too.

Ashley held out the papers she'd been holding. "I had a busy morning. In addition to getting Adam's compensation . . ."

"You make it sound like you got him an insurance settlement." Scott shook his head and smiled, admiring Ashley for her ingenuity.

"I also got the judge to give me and Beck guardianship over Adam so he doesn't end up in foster care."

Scott's eyebrows went up as he stared at Ashley. "Aren't you the badass."

"We only get to keep this so long as you don't ask a judge to revoke it and send Adam to his grandmother in Florida. She's raising Adam's cousins down there, and they'll probably end up in a place like this in the next five to ten if they keep on the path they're headed down right now."

Scott scrubbed his hands over his face and head. "I don't want him in foster care or in Florida, so what do you want from me? He's my son. I thought Jackie was taking care of him. Instead she's fucking a psychopath and allowing that sick fuck to hit and terrorize my kid."

"I want you to sign over your parental rights and allow Beck and me to adopt Adam. We will raise him as our son."

Scott fell back in the chair, his mouth open, eyes filled with disbelief. "You want me to just give him up?"

"You aren't getting out of here anytime soon." Ashley gave Scott the cold hard truth. "Do you want him to end up at his grandmother's where at best he'll be taken care of but allowed to run wild like his cousins, or put in the foster care system where God knows what will happen to him? Beck and I want him. We'll give him a good life. I promise you that."

"He's my son, and you just want to take him from me because I'm in here."

"We want to give Adam the life you can't." To help him make his decision, Beck took out his phone and called Caden, who was expecting the Skype call.

Beck smiled at Adam when his cute face appeared on-screen.

"Beck." Adam's smile and joy at seeing him warmed Beck's heart.

"Hey, buddy. What are you doing?"

"Making peanut butter cookies with Aunt Mia."

"Are you going to save one for me?" Since Brice's arrest, he and Ashley went to see Adam every night. Now, they wanted to take him home.

Adam stuffed half a cookie in his mouth, smiled around it, then mumbled, "Maybe."

Beck laughed. He loved seeing Adam so carefree. "I miss you."

"I miss you, too. When am I coming home?" He asked that every time he talked to him or Ashley. He really did think of Beck's place as home and Beck and Ashley as the ones who'd take care of him for the rest of his life. "Soon. I'm trying to work that out right now. Do you remember your dad?"

"Kinda. I make him pictures."

"He keeps them on his wall." Beck glanced at Scott watching him back. "Do you want to talk to him?"

"I guess so."

Beck felt for Scott and the sadness in his eyes. His own son didn't know him. Not really. Not as anything more than an absent father. "Here he is."

Beck turned the phone to Scott and handed it over. Scott held it reverently and stared at his son, probably for the first time in a couple of years. The guy who had to hold everything inside and be tough as nails and cold-hearted to survive jail teared up at the sight of his son. "Oh man, you got so big."

"I can read. Aunt Mia helps."

Choked up, Scott said, "She does. That's real good, Adam. You keep at it. You learn as much as you can."

"I want to see Ashley."

"She's here with me. You like her a lot."

"Yes. She saved me from the bad man. Are you a bad guy?"

"I'm trying not to be," Scott answered, looking up at Beck. "I heard about your mom, buddy."

"The bad man hit her. She went to sleep. I tried to wake her up. He took her away. I don't think she's coming back."

Beck shared a look with Ashley, silently letting her know they'd do everything they could to help Adam understand what he'd seen and cope with what it meant.

"She's not coming back," Scott confirmed for Adam.

"Are you coming back to take care of me now?"

Scott leaned his elbows on his knees, held the phone in one hand so Adam could see him, and scrubbed his hand over his mouth and jaw. "I'm sorry, son. I can't come home." Scott looked from Beck to Ashley, then back to his son. "Do you want to stay with Beck and Ashley?"

"I'm going home with them soon."

"Are you happy at home with them?"

Adam nodded. "Beck lets me sit on the horse. I help him exercise. He's like a big ride."

Scott glanced up at Beck.

"He likes to sit on my back while I do push-ups. I carry him around on my shoulders so he thinks he's a giant. Stuff like that."

"We're going to make a snowman," Adam added. "He promised. I told Uncle Caden we can't because I have to do it with Beck."

"Are you having fun with Uncle Caden and Aunt Mia?"

"She cooks real good and hugs nice. I beat Uncle Caden in the car race again last night."

"Sounds like you like it there."

"Yeah, but I want to go home."

"Home with Beck and Ashley?"

"Yeah. She needs me. I make her smile. She only smiled when I snuck out and she saw me. The bad man broke her arm when she stopped him from hitting me."

Scott turned to Ashley and saw the tears slide down her cheeks.

"Daddy, can I read you my book?"

Scott turned back to Adam, who read him *Goodnight Moon*, not missing or stumbling over a single word.

Scott wiped away another tear. "That was so good, Adam. You are so smart."

"I know. Ashley told me."

That made Scott smile. "Would you like Ashley to be your mom now?"

Adam sighed and nodded. "I hope so."

"What about Beck? Do you want him to be your dad?"

"I thought you were my dad?"

"I am. I will always be your dad. But I can't be there

for you right now, so maybe Beck can be your dad for a while."

"I can have two?"

Scott swallowed hard. "Yes. If you want that."

"I like him a lot. He's strong. He can keep the bad guys away. But not you. He'll let you come see me."

Scott glanced up at Beck. "Is that right?"

"You will be allowed to Skype Adam once a month. More often when he's older and wants to talk to you," Beck confirmed.

"I will send you letters detailing what we're doing, how well he's doing. I'll include any pictures or other things he wants to send you, just like Jackie did," Ashley assured him. "We don't want to take him from you—we want to be the family he deserves. And that includes you."

"How do I know you'll keep your word?" Scott eyed Beck, telling him without words that he'd trusted him once and been betrayed.

"Say goodbye to your son, then we'll talk."

Scott waved to Adam. "I have to go, son, but I'll talk to you soon."

"Bye," Adam's voice still held all the joy a little boy should feel.

Scott handed Beck his phone, then fell back in the chair. "He really wants to be with you guys."

"We want him," Beck assured him. "You have no reason to trust me, but I swear to you, I love that little boy. I will raise him as my own. And I will let you see him, so long as you don't allow the world that led you here to ever touch him."

"I worry that my life will make him a target. I guess the best place for him, the safest place, is with a DEA agent who knows this world and can protect him."

"I'd lay down my life for him."

Scott folded his arms over his chest. "And you'll keep your word. I get to see him once a month."

"Yes. But I want something in return."

Scott turned to King, who'd sat quietly through this whole thing, then turned back to Beck. "I'm not a snitch."

"That's not what we need," King spoke up. "I saved your ass this morning."

Scott's mouth drew into a tight line. "A calculated move on your part, I take it."

"I get in with your crew here I have some credibility to go with my incarceration for possession with intent to sell."

"So? That'll only put a target on your back from my rivals here."

"Exactly. And for the next six months, I'll watch your back and you'll watch mine. And when I get out, you'll vouch for me."

Scott laughed. "Vouch for an undercover DEA agent. You must be smokin' somethin' you shouldn't, man."

"Do this and I will bring Adam here to see you once King is set up in Iceman's crew," Beck promised.

"You think I want my son to see me in here? After he witnessed his mother's murder, you think I want to traumatize him more by subjecting him to this place? He already thinks I'm a bad guy—I don't want him to see the kinds of people I'm with in here and make him believe I don't have anything good to offer him."

"Then what's it going to take to get you to cooperate?" Beck didn't back down.

Scott turned to Ashley. "Every year on holidays and his birthdays, I'll pick something I want you to get him. You'll buy it and give it to him from me."

"I'd do that anyway," she said, giving Beck no leverage to use there.

"Rich girl like you, I'm sure you would."

"You want to show Adam you have something good

to offer, then do the right thing. Help King infiltrate Iceman's crew. All you have to do is vouch for him. Keep your record inside clean, show us in the calls and your letters to Adam that you want to be a positive influence in his life and Beck and I will speak at your parole hearing. When you get out, we will help you get a job and find a path that keeps Adam in your life."

Scott eyed King. "Are you prepared for life inside for the next six months as my new best friend?"

"Whatever it takes. Iceman knows Beck took out Guzman and why. He may even know Adam's connection to you, Brice, and now Ashley and Beck. The sooner we take him down, the sooner we eliminate a potential threat against your family." King meant Adam, and now Ashley and Beck, too.

Scott glared at Beck. "You're a real pain in my ass."

"You're not the first to say that," Beck confirmed.

"Iceman is not a man you cross. If he knows about Adam, or has targeted you"—he shook his head at Beck, who he probably thought deserved what he got—"he's a threat, and we don't have six months. We're going to have to get you set up and out of here on good behavior." Scott stared out the window lost in thought for a long moment. "Did you know Iceman has a daughter?"

"No," King and Beck said in unison.

"She hates him, but she may be your safest way in. She hires ex-cons and helps them get back on their feet if they prove to her they really want out of the life. Iceman stays close to her. She knows who and what he is. They have this strange love/hate thing. You might be able to use that because getting out of here and going right to him or someone in his crew isn't going to work. He's too paranoid. With Guzman out of the equation and him taking over or at least rising in the ranks, he'll be even more suspicious and dangerous."

King tilted his head, his eyes filled with doubt. "Why are you helping me like this?"

"Beck may have gotten me arrested, but he saved my life."

"You did?" Ashley asked him.

Beck shrugged it off.

Scott didn't let it go. "He grabbed the gun out of my hand seconds before the cops busted in to take us down. He claimed he was a better shot and would protect me. He was really making sure I didn't shoot at the cops and get killed. He protected them and me." Scott shook his head. "Even if he doesn't want to take credit for it, I pay my debts. So if this eliminates Iceman as a threat against him and my son, I'll give you all the information I have on the guy."

Scott took the papers giving up his parental rights from Ashley along with the pen. "I guess I owe you another debt for taking care of my kid."

Beck shook his head. "You don't owe me anything for that. Not when I get the better end of this deal."

Scott nodded knowing Beck meant it, because he'd get to be Adam's dad and enjoy all the moments big and small Scott would miss in Adam's life.

He went to sign the papers, then stopped. "Are you going to turn my kid into some spoiled, messed-up child star?"

Ashley laughed. "No. We're going to live here in Montana and give him the most normal life he can have with me as his mother."

"He's lucky to have you. Anyone who can survive what that asshole put you through has more strength than most of the guys in this place." Scott signed the papers and handed them back to Ashley, but held tight to them when she took hold of the other side of the papers. Scott looked her dead in the eye. "He won't get away with hurting you or my son."

Ashley's eyes softened. "Scott, please, don't do anything that will get you into more trouble."

"How could I? I've got a DEA agent for a bunk mate." Scott stood and held out his hand to Beck.

He took it, held tight, and spoke first. "Thank you for allowing us to raise Adam. It's an honor I take seriously and will wholeheartedly do my best to see him healthy and happy."

"I believe you will. Above all, protect him. Make sure he never ends up like me."

Beck shook and released Scott's hand. "We'll be in touch. If you need anything, you can contact me through the warden at any time."

Scott turned to Ashley. "Buy him a bike for Christmas. A red one. He should know how to ride more than a horse." The sheepish smile made Ashley laugh.

Ashley smiled up at him. "A perfect choice. It will be under the tree on Christmas morning, I promise. I'll put some money in your account here as well before I leave."

Scott chuckled. "Thanks. It's like having a fairy godmother, or something."

"Don't think you'll get anything out of her," Beck warned.

"All I want is for her to be the mother Adam needs and deserves. He comes first."

"Always," Ashley and Beck said in unison.

Beck pulled her up out of the chair and into his arms, and they smiled at each other, so happy they'd gotten what they came here for—their son.

"You guys are making me sick," King said. "All this love and sex dripping off you guys and you're leaving me in here with this asshole."

Scott eyed Beck and Ashley. "You two will show Adam that a man and a woman can be good for one another. Maybe if I'd put Jackie first when she was pregnant, I wouldn't be here. Maybe I wouldn't have lost both of them because of that bastard."

With that, Scott went to the door and opened it. One guard took his arm and led him away.

The other grabbed hold of King. "Let's go. There's a bucket and mop waiting for you in the dining hall."

King glanced over his shoulder. "Lucky me."

Beck waved goodbye to his friend, hoping Scott kept his promise, and he saw King again. One word from Scott in here that King was an undercover DEA agent and King would be dead.

Ashley hugged him. "He'll be okay."

The warden walked in and caught them kissing. "I hope you got what you came for, Miss Swan."

"I did." Ashley smiled and went to the warden, taking his hand and holding on to it. "I can't thank you enough for indulging me. You are just so sweet."

"Happy to help," the warden assured her, eating up her undivided attention. Beck held back rolling his eyes at how she managed to turn every man into her devoted fan when she turned on the charm.

She gave the warden an even bigger, brighter smile. "I'll be sure to tell the press when I leave what an impressive facility you run and that the people of Montana can feel safe and assured that monsters like Brice are safely locked up." She picked up her purse and folders, then turned back to the warden with a pouty frown. "Oh, I do hope nothing bad happens to my new friends."

"While this is a very safe facility, Miss Swan, bad things do happen between inmates. As you saw, one of your friends was involved in an altercation."

"Yes, well, I do hope your guards will do their best to

make sure that doesn't happen again. I don't want anything to happen to my friends. If it does, I'll be back to check on them." She frowned again. "I know that's not easy for you and your staff, what with all the press I bring with me." She blew out an exasperated breath.

The warden's eyes widened with dawning understanding of what she meant. The warden appreciated the good press, but anything negative reflected directly on him.

"Come on, honey, it's been such a long day. Let's head home."

Beck took her hand. "Anything you want, sweetheart." Beck gave the warden a knowing look, telling him without words that he better give her what she wanted to keep her happy and away from here with all the press who followed her.

CHAPTER FORTY-ONE

Brice hated his tiny cell, his lumpy bed, the incessant noise, the stares, the threats when he walked down the corridors, the guards who watched his every move, the food, the smell of this place—everything. He couldn't escape Ashley's name or the fact that every man in here was a fan and despised him for what he'd done to her.

The guards kept a close watch on him, but that wouldn't last as his time here stretched into a long and bleak future. His lawyer tried to cut him a deal, but that bitch Ashley had already tricked him into revealing the names of the two girls they hadn't been able to identify at the ranch. Once they desecrated his Hollywood garden and discovered the other eight girls and ID'd them, he had nothing to bargain with and they'd charged him with the maximum on all counts. After all he'd done for her she turned her back on him. He hated her. If he ever got his hands on her again, he'd strangle the life out of her. Slowly. He'd take his time, reviving her again and again. He fantasized about all the time they spent together, and what he'd do to her before he finally extinguished the light he saw in her.

All he had left were his fantasies.

They'd been enough once. They'd have to be enough again. At least for now.

The few men entering the shower with him were like him, segregated from the general population, kept in isolation for their protection for one reason or another, and not likely to cause trouble. They were brought to the showers in small groups. They usually kept to themselves, but today they outright avoided eye contact and kept their heads down.

Something seemed off, but Brice shook off the warning chill up his spine.

Brice got down to business, this being the only time he actually felt clean in this place. He dropped his towel and took the bar of soap he'd purchased at the commissary with him. He missed the expensive French soap he used back home with its thick lather and fresh woodsy scent. What Brice wouldn't give to be out on his patio looking at his garden and enjoying the beautiful land.

Standing under the shower, ready to turn it on and have just a few minutes in the heat and massaging spray, Brice swore under his breath when yet another commotion outside made the guards order, "Everyone line up against the wall."

Brice went to grab his towel, but someone grabbed him around the waist and dragged him back behind a low wall. Before Brice could scream, the man covered his mouth and nose, cutting off his air and his ability to call for help.

"March it out into the hall," the guard ordered the other six men. "We've got a situation."

"It's taken three days to finally get you alone," the man said at his ear as Brice struggled to breathe. "We don't have much time. Lucky for you. Because I would love to torture you for hours, days, weeks, months, a year, the way you did to Ashley and those women. The way you tortured my son."

The jolt of awareness and adrenaline that shot through him stilled him. Then the need to breathe before the blackness closing in on the bursting lights in his eyes overtook him again. He pulled at the guy's strong hand at his mouth, but didn't budge it.

The man finally let him go, throwing him to the side. Brice gasped for a breath, but the guy kicked him in the stomach, making him vomit and cough for air that just wouldn't fill his aching lungs.

Brice looked up at the naked blond man with the scorpion tattoo on his arm, an array of other tattoos on his toned body, including Adam's name scrolled over his heart.

"Why are you naked?"

His prison jumpsuit and shoes sat atop the wall behind him.

"Because you'll be a bloody mess before I finally kill you."

The promise in those words sent a bolt of fear through Brice's system that made him shake. Brice tried to get up and run, but the guy kicked him in the gut again, sending him back to the floor in a heap of pain.

"Is that what you did to my boy? Did you toss him down, then kick him? I bet you did, you fucking coward. You pick on people smaller and weaker than you. When they don't start out that way, when they pose a real threat, you starve them until they're so weak they can't fight back. That's what you did to Ashley, isn't it?"

Brice finally sucked in a lungful of air and held his hand up to stop the man. "You don't understand."

"Oh, I understand. You like pain. Well, I'm going to show you the kind of pain you inflict on others. But don't worry, you'll get off easy, because I don't have much time. But you'll get my point."

"I never hurt Adam. Only the women."

"You killed his mother." The man kicked him again.

Brice curled into a ball and held his aching stomach and ribs. "Stop. Please, stop."

The guy laughed. "I bet you got off hearing all those women beg you to stop." The guy reached up, unscrewed the showerhead, then stuffed it down a sock. He swung it back and forth, then over his head and down on Brice's thigh. "Did you stomp on my son's leg after you knocked him to the ground?"

Brice held his thigh, the excruciating pain radiating up to his hip and down his leg. He scuttled backward, but came up against the cold tile wall. No escape.

The man swung again, hitting his forearm. The bone snapped with the impact.

"You broke Ashley's arm when she tried to help my son." The man swung again, hitting him in the back, once, twice, three times, again and again until Brice felt like a tenderized piece of meat, his voice ragged and cracking from the screams he could barely get out anymore. Blood oozed over his skin and sent a metallic scent into the air to go with the sour smell of vomit. He could barely breathe; now that his back and ribs throbbed so bad moving hurt too much to bear.

"Hurts, doesn't it? All you want is for it to stop, but you know it won't, because the person doing it wants to make you feel the pain." The guy grabbed Brice's hair, pulled, and lifted his head. "Do you like it now?"

"No. No. Please. Stop. I can pay you. I've got money."

The guy smiled. "No, you don't. That money belongs to my son. Compensation for you taking his mother from him."

Brice shook his head, though he could barely move with the guy ripping out his hair as he held his head up. "No. It's mine."

"That's what you think, but you fucked with the wrong woman. You thought you could break her, but you couldn't. That's why you kept her so long. She lasted longer than the others because deep down that woman is stronger than you will ever be."

"I loved her."

"I bet you did, because she took it and took it and took it. And the more she did, the more you wanted to punish her, to see her fall apart. Well, let me tell you something about people like her—they live to get their revenge. She blackmailed that judge you coerced into giving you guardianship over my son and made him change your will."

"No, she can't do that."

"She did. Adam gets everything. So if you think I'll let you live and squander away that fortune on some pathetic attempt to defend yourself and line those fancy lawyers' pockets, guess again. I may not be able to raise my son, but I can ensure he gets every dime coming to him for what you did." The man glanced down the length of his bruised, battered, and broken naked body. "You're pathetic. Fat. Old. Weak. The only thing you're good at is running your mouth. You can't wait to get in front of those cameras and give your jailhouse interviews, telling anyone who will listen some sob story you think will excuse what you did. The only headline left to splash across the screens and pages is that you finally got what you deserved."

SCOTT STOOD BACK, his breath heaving in and out, the showerhead stuffed in a sock hanging from his hand dripping blood. He didn't know exactly when Brice finally died. He didn't much care. He didn't feel anything but a sense of relief that this man would never hurt his son, would never hurt anyone, ever again. Not with his voice on the radio spouting lies, his face on the TV, pleading with people to sympathize or telling his version of what happened in that house.

Scott had come into this place a drug dealer. He'd been in his share of fights and left others damaged but never dead. He didn't think he had that kind of violence inside him. But for Adam, for Jackie and those other women, and the one who swore to raise and love his son, he'd done the right thing and sent that monster straight to hell. Maybe one day he'd join him there, but Scott swore from this day forward he'd do everything in his power to be a good and decent person, someone his son would want to know one day. And maybe even be proud to call him dad.

Until then, he'd serve out the rest of his time as a model prisoner.

He took the showerhead out of the sock, turned on the water, and rinsed it in the stream. He turned off the water, replaced the showerhead, turned it on and rinsed himself and the sock off.

The fight he'd set up outside would be resolved soon. The other inmates would be back to shower once the guards got everything under control again. He needed to hurry and make his escape before he got caught.

He dressed quickly and didn't even look back at the pile of shit he'd left on the floor before he went out the door he came in to retrieve the towels for laundry service. He pushed the cart he'd left outside down the hall in the opposite direction from where the guards held three of his buddies and the other men who'd come to shower on the floor with their backs against the wall. No one looked twice at him as he walked away, leaving Brice dead on the floor with the hot shower beating down on him, washing away any trace of Scott ever being there.

He left the cart in the laundry for the others to empty and load in the washers, went to the sink where they soaked items in bleach, dropped in the bloodstained sock, pushed it to the bottom with a scrub brush, and walked out with the others who finished their shift.

Scott sat on his bunk and laid his fisted hands on his knees and stared at the wall, letting the adrenaline wear off.

"You all right, man?" King, now Flash to everyone on the block, stared down at him from the top bunk. Scott gave him the nickname for his quick reflexes and the scar on his arm. And so he didn't slip and call him King in front of anyone.

"Fine."

The alarm sounded and guards rushed to get everyone in their cells for a full lockdown.

Scott lay back on his bunk, hands behind his head, and waited. It didn't take long for word to spread about why they'd been confined to their cells.

"Someone fucked Brice Mooney up in the showers," an inmate yelled down the block.

Flash bent over the side of the bed and looked down at him. "Do you know anything about that?"

"Nope."

Flash frowned, stared at him for a long moment, then said, "You seem to be missing a sock."

Scott stared down at his shoes and his one bare ankle.

"It got lost in the laundry."

Because the walls had ears, Flash didn't voice his suspicions. Because that's all Flash had on him. He couldn't prove anything. And if he opened his mouth, Scott would yell to the rafters that he was an undercover DEA agent. He wouldn't get off the block alive.

Flash wanted his big bust. To make a name for himself in the DEA. Scott would give him that chance because taking down Iceman would ensure his family's safety. And yeah, that family included the DEA agent raising his boy.

CHAPTER FORTY-TWO

Ashley pulled her little 4x4 Jeep into the driveway. She loved it and the home she'd made here on Hope Ranch with Beck and Adam. She'd found exactly what she needed here with them. Peace. Quiet. Love. Family. Time to find her way out of the darkness Brice brought into her life and find her place in the light again and be happy and healthy in body, mind, heart, and soul. She didn't want what happened to her to ruin the rest of her life with her inability to trust others, but she found the longer she spent with Beck and Adam, the more good she saw in them and their open hearts, the easier it was to trust. That trust extended to Beck's family and her mother. She slowly let the people she used to work with and old friends back into her life.

Four months of weekly sessions with Dr. Lanning helped her talk about what she'd been through, put her feelings and anger into perspective, and believe that what happened wasn't her fault and didn't have to become the whole of her life. She could let it go. She could move on, stronger as a survivor, knowing she'd done everything possible to take Brice down and make amends to others he'd hurt.

Like Adam. He was the light of her life. When the past encroached on her happiness, Adam pulled her into the present with his sweet smiles, enthusiasm for life, and absolute joy in school and ranch life. He loved the horses and had become quite the rider. But nothing made him happier than spending time with his real-life hero, Beck.

What a fantastic father. Seeing him with Adam always made her heart melt. She loved him so much for taking this journey with her. From the moment he'd found them, he'd been her partner in everything. He made it clear every day how much he loved them and wanted them here with him.

Just like after every session with Dr. Lanning, she couldn't wait to see him and share how well it went, how much better she felt about her life and future, and how grateful she was for his unwavering support. She exited the car and walked up the porch steps, expecting Beck to open the door, anxious to see her as always. Instead, she found a note taped to it.

Meet me at the river.
I Love You, Beck

Ashley went back down the stairs and around the side of the house to the snowplowed path Beck cleared to the river for her because he knew how much she loved it down there. It had become her place to think and enjoy the quiet. Beck sometimes came looking for her when she was away too long lost in her head. He never made her talk when she didn't want to, but held her in his arms and stared at the water, letting the solitude and their connection surround them. They didn't need to say anything; they read each other so well.

Their love may have blossomed out of dire circumstances, but it had taken root and grown strong these last four months. They'd had some tough days when everything settled down and reality hit her hard about all that happened to her. Through it all, Beck's patience and understanding never wavered. He loved her through the hard times.

She encouraged him as he settled into his new role with the DEA. He loved his job, but the slower pace and bureaucracy frustrated him. He was used to working mostly alone, but he'd settled in with his team and with her and Adam.

She approached the river and saw Beck walk out of the trees to meet her. Her heart skipped a beat, then sped up in her chest as the thrill of seeing him rushed through her. God, he was so handsome. And hers. And that bright smile that came so easily to him now melted her heart.

He didn't say anything, just came to her, slipped his hand beneath her hair, and drew her in for a soft kiss. "I missed you today."

He'd left for work early this morning before she woke up and returned while she was at her session.

"I missed you, too. Where's Adam? Still with the sitter?"

"He's spending the night with Caden and Mia."

She gave him a seductive smile. "Really. You and me and the house to ourselves. I love it." She rubbed her hands up and down his chest.

"You and me in front of a blazing fire just like the first time we were together."

"I can't wait." She pulled back to walk to the house with him, but he held her still.

"I love you."

She smiled up at him wondering why he looked so nervous. "I love you, too."

His fingers brushed softly against her neck. "You've come so far. All I want is for you to be happy."

"I am. Here with you. What we have is more than I could have ever hoped for or dreamed possible."

"It's real, Ashley. For both of us. You make me so happy. You're smart and beautiful and kind and generous and sexy and you love me in a way that fills me up so much I don't know what to do with all you make me feel."

"I feel the same way, Beck."

He dropped to his knee, took her hand, and held up a diamond engagement ring.

She gasped, completely taken by surprise.

"I will spend the rest of my life making you happy, sweetheart. If you promise to spend the rest of your life with me, I will love you the best I can every day. Will you marry me?"

Her heart overflowed with so much love she had a hard time getting the single word out. "Yes."

Beck came up and kissed her, wrapping her in his arms and holding her crushed to his chest. He kissed her again and again, then leaned back and swiped the happy tears from her cheeks. He laid his forehead to hers. "I love you so much."

"I love you, too. I can't wait to be your wife."

He leaned back, took her hand, and slipped the ring on her finger.

"It's beautiful, Beck. I love it." She held her hand up and admired the sparkling diamonds and antique setting. Gorgeous. Classic. He knew her so well he'd picked the perfect ring to suit her.

She went into his arms again as they held each other close and stared at the rippling river and the beautiful white winter landscape spread out before them, happy and content and wrapped in their love.

"This is so much like the river I used to go to in my mind."

Beck stared down into her eyes. "I'm glad you've found your peace here."

"In that dream, there was a dark-haired man who stepped out of the trees. I tried so hard to get to him. When I escaped, I found you, here by the river."

"I was waiting for you."

EPILOGUE

Tonight at eight on Celebrity Centerfold *with Sharon Waters, as the one-year anniversary of Ashley Swan's courageous escape from Brice Mooney's house of horrors approaches, we'll look back at the crimes and victims. What is life like for Ashley Swan now?*

Pretty damn good, in Ashley's opinion.

She shut off the TV in the suite, not wanting anything from the past, not even a promo for a show she wanted nothing to do with, to touch her today. Her wedding day.

The diamond engagement ring Beck gave her by the river winked on her finger now as she stared at her reflection in the mirror and admired the beautiful and simply elegant white gown with the deep V in front, beaded belted waist, and flared skirt that softly draped to the floor. Beautiful beads and crystals created a vine and flower pattern that went from her shoulders, down the bodice, and wove out over her hips in different lengths down to her thighs, leaving the bottom of the skirt in pristine white. So feminine and pretty. She felt like a princess.

"Oh my, you're gorgeous," Mia said, coming into the room with Beck's sister, Alina, and Adam.

Ashley sent her mother, hairdresser, and makeup artist out so she could have a few minutes alone with Mia and Alina before the ceremony started.

She admired Mia in her pretty navy blue matron of honor gown. "You're beautiful, Mrs. Cooke."

Mia beamed a wide grin, pleased to hear her new name. She and Caden were married yesterday. All of them had rented out the rustic chic lodge for the weekend for the double wedding. Mia and Caden tied the knot yesterday afternoon with Ashley and Alina serving as Mia's maids of honor. Mia and Caden spent the night in the honeymoon suite and planned to leave tomorrow on their honeymoon to Hawaii after their family breakfast. She and Beck couldn't wait to spend some time alone in Bora Bora. But not before they got married in the garden under the trees in just a few minutes.

Mia and Caden would stand beside them as she and Beck did for them yesterday. They'd become a very close family these last months. Ashley adored her new brother and sisters, though they didn't often see Alina, who agreed to babysit Adam while they escaped to their honeymoon hideaway.

"Mommy, you're so pretty." Adam hugged her legs.

She brushed her hands over his golden hair. "You're so handsome." Adorable in his tiny black tux, he smiled up at her.

"Daddy can't wait any longer. He said 'Hurry it up.'"

Adam so easily let the past go and settled in to being with her and Beck and accepting them as his new mother and father. He spoke to Scott once a month. Ashley kept her promise and sent Scott pictures from Adam and a letter filled with all the little details he missed in his son's life.

They never spoke about Brice's suspicious death. No one had ever been found responsible. Scott promised his son would never have to fear that man again. If Scott made sure that never happened, he'd done her a favor, too. She slept easier knowing Brice no longer walked this earth.

But she hated that Scott had to carry that burden, though it didn't seem to be weighing him down. He smiled and laughed with Adam and thanked her and Beck all the time for taking such good care of their son. Because Adam belonged to all of them and deserved to have all the love they showered on him.

"Beck is impatient to get this done." Alina shook her head. "Once those guys set their minds to something, they want to get it over with immediately."

"Caden sure did look relieved when you said 'I do' yesterday," Ashley pointed out to Mia.

"Like I'd say no to that man." Mia's bright smile matched the happiness in her eyes.

"Let's not keep Beck waiting." She bent and looked at Adam. "Do you have the rings?"

Adam pulled them out of his coat pocket. "I got this, Mom."

So confident. He got that from Beck.

"I know you do." She kissed him on the cheek, stood tall, not an ounce of nerves fluttering in her belly, and walked with them to the door, ready to go downstairs and marry the man she loved more and more each day.

Bᴇᴄᴋ sᴛᴏᴏᴅ ᴀᴛ the front of the aisle, the justice of the peace behind him, and his brother, Caden, beside him. He breathed a sigh of relief that he didn't spot a single helicopter overhead. Not one reporter or fan had discovered them at the lodge. They'd somehow managed to keep this wedding a secret from the press. Thank God.

This was their day to celebrate with family and friends.

Ashley's mother smiled at him from the front row, probably thanking God he'd covered up his tattoos today. Except the new ones on his hand. Like the scrolled *A* on his ring finger where he'd wear the wedding band he couldn't wait for Ashley to put there. If she'd hurry up. And Alex's name on the side of his index finger. He couldn't wait to add the names of the children he couldn't wait to have with Ashley. When she was ready.

She loved being Adam's mother and needed these past months to let go of the past and find herself again. She'd rebuilt her confidence and discovered what was really important to her and what she wanted for her future.

Which led him to the two guys sitting together in the second row. Danny Radford and Ashley's manager, Stuart, sat together, looking like good friends in front of the other guests, but Beck knew the two had a close, loving relationship that for Danny's own reasons they kept private. With so little about Danny and Ashley private in their very public lives, Beck understood why the movie star wanted something special for himself.

He and Ashley were doing their best to keep their relationship theirs, and not everyone else's.

At least he didn't have to worry about the leading man in her next movie hitting on her. He couldn't be more proud of her for accepting the movie deal to work with Danny. A dream come true for her to work with him, but also a way to get back to doing what she loved with a friend who'd look out for her. It couldn't be easy for her to play another role, but she looked forward to the challenge and overcoming the anxiety of pretending to be someone she wasn't again.

He had complete faith in her.

And more than anything, he wanted her to be happy doing what she loved.

He'd settled into his new place in the DEA, running his own team and training others going undercover, including overseeing King's op. He even consulted on cases with Sheriff Willis.

Adam ran down the rose-petal-strewn, white-draped aisle and smiled at his grandparents. Beck's mom and dad and Ashley's mom spoiled him rotten. Adam launched himself into Beck's outstretched hands. "She's coming! She's finally coming!"

Beck smiled and laughed. He did that a lot these days. Adam gave him so much joy.

Ashley had taken control of Adam's massive inheritance from Brice and had done some good things. Like demolishing the burned-down ranch and the house in L.A., taking away the opportunity for people to indulge the gruesome curiosity that drew them to these places for strange reasons. She'd help Adam rebuild his own place when he was old enough, or sell the properties outright.

She compensated each family of the deceased women found in Brice's gardens, as well as Sergeant Foster after Brice brutally attacked him.

She had such a good heart, and it belonged to him.

Music started playing, letting the guests know the ceremony was about to begin. The photographer took several shots of him holding Adam.

Beck shook off his dark thoughts and concentrated on the five-year-old in his arms. "Are you ready?"

"Yes!"

Beck set Adam down. "Go get her and bring her to me."

Adam ran off to do his very important job and walk Ashley down the aisle.

"Are you ready?" Caden asked him.

"At this point, I consider her my wife already."

Caden slapped him on the shoulder. "Well, let's get the formality out of the way."

Beck backhanded his brother's chest. "Check out your wife." Beck stared at Mia walking down the aisle, beautiful and glowing like any newlywed woman should in her dark blue gown, holding a bouquet of white roses.

"Damn. I love that woman." Caden winked at his wife. They both smiled as Alina walked down the aisle and winked at them. He hoped someday soon their little sister found the kind of love he and Caden had found.

Alina darted a glance at his buddy, Special Agent Bennett, who stared hard at her, then she faced front again avoiding Beck's and Caden's gazes. They exchanged a look wondering what the hell that was all about.

Beck's gut tightened with anticipation. He didn't have long to wait for his beautiful bride to appear at the end of the aisle. A soft gasp went up from the crowd of their friends and family. He knew exactly how they felt. She took his breath away.

Lovely with her dark hair swept up, her makeup subtly highlighting her beautiful green eyes so filled with love and anticipation as her gaze locked with his. Her pretty smile undid him. It came so easily these days, especially for him and Adam.

Adam held her hand and walked her down the aisle. She took her time, smiling to their guests, but always looking back at him, making sure he was there and getting closer. The photographer snapped several photos of her in that dress. He loved it. For the longest time, and partly due to the cold winter, she'd kept herself completely covered, cocooned in layers of clothes. But slowly as she healed, she'd found confidence in her appearance and the anxiety that someone's appreciation of all that beauty would turn ugly had faded. Today, her confidence was on display. She knew she looked good in that gown. To him, she always looked stunning.

She finally stood beside him. He stared into her bright green eyes, took her hand in one of his, and held Adam's in the other. They stood before the justice of the peace, hands joined in a circle. The three of them connected. He and Ashley more than ready to make their promises and seal their bond with this ceremony.

"We are gathered here today to celebrate the joining

of two lives in matrimony. Beck and Ashley arrived here today having shed their roles of the past, ready to stand together as their true selves to create a bright and happy future together with Adam. Though they have both traveled rocky roads to get here, their love has set a clear path ahead they will walk together, meeting any challenges or obstacles as one."

Beck squeezed Ashley's hand, letting her know she'd never be alone again. She had him. They had each other, because with her beside him, he could face anything.

They recited the standard vows, but took a moment to speak from their hearts and make their promises as they exchanged rings.

"I have them." Adam took out the thick gold band Ashley got for him and handed it to Ashley.

She took his left hand and slid the ring into place over the scrolled *A* tattoo on his finger. "With this ring, I promise to be your unwavering partner and to love you wholly and unconditionally, now and forever."

Working undercover meant being left to work the case mostly alone. Now he'd always have her by his side. His partner in life.

Beck took the three-stone diamond ring that complemented the engagement ring he'd already given her from Adam's hand.

He slid it on Ashley's left hand over the scrolled *B* she'd had tattooed there when he got his new ink. He just wanted her to come with him. He never expected her to get one, too. But she did and added one to the inside of her wrist. An infinity symbol with *Beck* written in one loop and *Adam* in the other. He brushed his thumb over it now.

"With this ring, I promise to be the leading man who makes you happy for the rest of our love story." He gave her back the promise she'd made to him. "I will love you wholly and unconditionally, now and forever."

She took his hand again and squeezed it. "We will be the stars of us."

And so they were from that day forward, living their lives the way they wanted, out of the spotlight in Montana, only venturing into the limelight when Ashley had a new blockbuster movie come out or received yet another award for her outstanding work. Otherwise, they were happy to live in peace, surrounded by the love they shared with Adam, their daughter, Juliette, who arrived just over nine months after their wedding when Ashley was up for yet another Oscar for the movie she did with Danny Radford, and their son Tucker, who arrived two years after his sister.

Together, they lived and loved on the ranch where he and Ashley made a home for themselves and their children and the life they both wanted, filled with laughter and more love than either of them ever thought possible.

Continue reading for a sneak peek at
Jennifer Ryan's next Montana Heat novel

MONTANA HEAT: TRUE TO YOU

On sale February 27, 2018!

PROLOGUE

15 months ago . . .

Two men faced off in the middle of the warehouse. Rivals with a deep hatred that boiled over from time to time and ended in bloodshed between the opposing drug cartels. Guzman's man held his ground. Iceman, by far the deadliest lieutenant in Guzman's crew, didn't know how to do anything else. Cool, calm, unfeeling, the perfect embodiment of his nickname.

Which is why Guzman sent his number one enforcer to meet Manuel "Manny" Castillo to broker a truce between the two outfits. The last time things got this hot between the two rivals, twenty-three men lost their lives in five days. Judging by the hostility filling the massive room today, they wouldn't settle anything any time soon.

"You crossed the line, Castillo. I'm surprised a cowardly piece of shit like you showed."

DEA Special Agent Dawson King—just King to everyone who knew him—held both men in the crosshairs of his sniper rifle scope. He'd been lying in wait for more than ten hours. He'd watched both cartels' men come in and search the building—missing King, thanks to his stealth—and give the all-clear to their respective leaders. Neither side trusted the other.

Iceman had a man covering his back two rows over on the east side of the building. Manny had a man on the west. None of the men in the building knew King hid in the shadows, perfectly still, concealed, and ready to strike when he gave the order for the raid.

Meetings like this were usually held out in the open in some remote place, making an ambush impossible. Why take the risk of meeting in an enclosed warehouse? He tried to stay focused on them and not their stupidity.

Castillo's smile didn't inspire one to believe he wanted peace. His words backed that up. "You come after me and mine, you can bet your ass I'll go after the one and only person you love."

King had no idea what the two evil bastards were bitching about, especially since neither had a conscience or a soul. Not when they both went after what they wanted and didn't care who they took out or hurt in the process.

King wondered if Iceman knew Castillo was packing. Iceman's guy patted Castillo down, but King would bet his left nut Castillo had a small gun tucked in his heavy jacket that the guy missed in his cursory search. King couldn't believe Iceman let his guy get away with such an inept job. Why hadn't Iceman ordered Castillo to discard his jacket at the door like Iceman had done, showing good faith that he'd come to this meeting unarmed?

It didn't add up. King didn't like it when things didn't make sense. It sent an icy chill up his spine.

"Ready, one?" Special Agent Griffin's voice filled his ear through his com. He'd requested King for this op when his team intercepted a coded message. He wanted the best sniper the DEA had in Montana. Since his counterpart, Trigger, was out of commission after taking out Guzman's cousin Marco and getting shot in the process, that put King in his perch and these men in his sight.

He and Trigger had a friendly rivalry on the shooting range. Trigger bested him most of the time, but he made King work that much harder to kick Trigger's ass.

King listened as the three teams checked in, everyone ready to end this on King's call.

Any time now.

He tensed his thighs and calves, trying to get his blood flowing after lying in one position so long. He kept his aim and his eye on the two men facing off, talking about some personal beef instead of the business they were here to work out to stop the bloodshed between the two groups.

Neither thing mattered because they weren't going back to deliver the terms of the ceasefire to their bosses. They were headed straight to jail on a list of charges that would keep them behind bars the rest of their lives.

"You won't have time to regret what you did," Iceman warned. "Payback is a bitch."

An egomaniac like Manny overreacted to taunts like that. King didn't know why Iceman, a guy as cold and calculating as his name implied, goaded the other man rather than sticking to business. He had to know Manny would push back.

And in a split second, he did, pulling the small pistol from his jacket.

Iceman stood with his back to King. He couldn't see Iceman's face, but the man went stock still and spread his hands wide and held them out at his sides.

"I'll fucking kill you right here, right now, asshole." Manny practically spit out the words, pointing the gun right in Iceman's face.

"Go," King ordered into his mic. They needed to use this distraction to their advantage and get these two in cuffs before Manny killed Iceman and the DEA lost its chance to get the goods on Guzman's crew.

"No, you won't." Iceman's words boasted confidence. Too much.

A chill danced up King's spine.

Manny's eyes narrowed.

King knew exactly what was coming and made the split-second choice. He fired to Iceman's right, hitting the cement floor, kicking up chunks, and predictably making Iceman step to his left. Manny froze, surprised by the shot. King pinned Manny in his sight and fired, killing the man before Manny shot Iceman.

Iceman spun around. Even though he couldn't possibly see King, he smiled and gave King a two-finger salute.

DEA agents poured into the building on both sides.

Manny's man started firing, drawing agents in his direction. It gave Iceman's man the few seconds he needed to toss out two smoke bombs.

Visibility obscured, King didn't have a shot at Iceman. He couldn't take out the unarmed man anyway.

He swore, shifted focus, and took out Manny's man as he fired at and held back the other agents.

What should have been an easy takedown turned into a fucking mess.

And Iceman got away.

King swore when he spotted the open window that had originally been blocked by a heavily laden rack of boxes. A window King didn't see behind the obstacle that he now realized was on wheels and shoved aside to provide the perfect escape. King hoped one of the agents left to cover the building outside intercepted Iceman, but the sound of two motorcycles indicated the men had found an easy escape. Too easy.

The DEA had been played.

The intercepted message nothing but a ruse to get the DEA here.

On a much more disturbing note, Iceman set King up

to make the kill. He'd wanted Manny dead and used King to do it for him, knowing Manny would come armed. That inept search by his man had been on purpose. Iceman had led Manny to believe he had the advantage, all the while Iceman coldly planned and executed his death without firing a shot himself.

Iceman set King and the DEA up as the scapegoat so the Castillo family didn't go after Guzman for Manny's death.

King let loose a string of curses, laid down his rifle and his forehead on his hands and vowed he'd get that bastard if it was the last thing he ever did.

CHAPTER ONE

15 months later . . .

King limped down the path, chain-link fence topped with razor wire on both sides of him and an armed guard at his back. He wanted to run from this place and never look back. He'd hated every second he'd spent behind bars. Although he hadn't broken the law to get here, a part of him believed he deserved the last one hundred and fifty-three days in jail for what happened to Erin long before he ended up locked in a cell.

He shook off those dark thoughts, buried his guilt once again, and concentrated on the man standing outside the gate ahead. He stopped in front of it and gave his DEA counterpart, Trigger, an irreverent grin.

"You have no idea how much I want to tell them to keep your ass locked up." Trigger stood with his arms folded over his chest.

"How will you win back the title if you don't let me out of here?" A mocking smile tugged at King's lips. He'd won the last shooting contest, stealing the title of best shot from Trigger. His last many months undercover in the state prison had him out of practice. He'd be no match for Trigger right now.

Trigger signaled for the officer at King's side to go

ahead and let him out. Before he stepped past, the officer held out his hand. King took it and held firm while the guy found the words so obvious in his gratitude-filled gaze.

"Thank you for saving my life, Flash."

His cellmate Scott gave him the nickname because of the lightning bolt scar on his arm. He'd used it instead of the fake name he'd been booked under—Chris Hickman. As far as the guards and everyone but Scott in the prison knew, he was Chris, aka Flash. No one, not even the warden or the guard shaking his hand, knew he was undercover DEA.

King nodded to the guard, not saying anything. He'd done what he had to do during the fight that broke out in the prison yard three days ago. It became the perfect excuse to get King out of there on good behavior without serving the rest of his six-month sentence for drug possession with intent to sell. He'd gotten in good with Scott Lewis's crew and put himself in a direct line to Iceman, though he planned to take an indirect route to Iceman's demise.

The officer released his hand and waved him out the gate. Guards in the tower watched King leave and gave him a salute. He'd saved several people's lives in addition to the guard who locked the gate behind him. If he hadn't stopped that fight, it might have turned into an all-out riot.

He appreciated their gratitude, but he didn't want to see them or the inside of this place ever again.

The clink of the gate behind him echoed through his ears. He raised his head and looked up at the dark sky and stars and breathed in his first real taste of freedom.

"You okay?" Trigger asked, concerned by King's unnatural quiet. Normally he'd be the guy cracking jokes and flirting with the gorgeous woman leaning against the Camaro behind Trigger. He didn't have it in him at the moment. Not because it was just after three in the morning and he hadn't slept. Hell, he'd barely slept at all in the noisy jail. But as the days went by and he'd put his life on the line more than once in that hostile environment, he'd started to wonder if it was worth it. Was what he was doing going to make a difference? Would it lead to Iceman spending the rest of his life behind bars where a man like him belonged?

King wasn't so sure anymore.

Worn down and out, he wanted to step back and take a breath. Not going to happen. The next step in his assignment started now.

"King, if you're not ready . . ."

"I'm ready," he lied, though not convincingly if Trigger's narrowed gaze was any indication. "What do you have for me?"

Trigger motioned him to walk over to the car.

King stepped up to the woman who walked toward him with her arms out. She embraced him in a hug that he returned with a soft squeeze because damn it felt good to feel a beautiful woman pressed up against him again, even if she did belong to another man. She smelled like flowers. He inhaled, hoping to erase the acrid stench of too many men crammed together in a tight space mixed with the awful food they served and inmates who liked to throw their urine and feces at the guards to fuck with them.

Ashley Swan, movie star and Trigger's fiancée, pulled back and looked up at him. "You don't look so hot."

"You're gorgeous as ever. Ditch the dirtbag and run away with me. I haven't had sex in months. The first time will be fast, you probably won't even notice, but after that, I swear I'll treat you right." Flash found his smile when Ashley giggled.

"With your tiny pecker, no woman would notice, no

matter how long it took you to get your rocks off. Now unhand her or I'll shoot you." Trigger might be joking about his "tiny pecker," but not about shooting him if he didn't hand his fiancée back. After all they'd been through together after Ashley escaped her year-long captivity from a psycho serial killer, King understood Trigger's protective streak. Trigger had almost lost Ashley when Guzman struck a deal with that psycho to not only kill Trigger, but sell Ashley back to him for the price of the drugs Trigger cost Guzman during another raid.

Now Trigger and Ashley were happily living on their ranch with the little boy they saved from the same man who tried to kill Ashley. A boy who was actually King's ex-cellmate's son, and King's way in with Iceman's crew.

Trigger gave up the undercover work, but was here to give him any new intel on Iceman and his crew who had taken up where Guzman left off after Trigger killed him.

Ashley ignored Trigger and held King at arm's length. "How bad are you hurt?"

"A few nicks and scratches, nothing serious," he lied again.

Trigger eyed him, then pointedly dropped his gaze to King's thigh where he'd been shivved by an inmate hell bent on taking out one of Scott's crew but only ended up shot dead after he stabbed King. Luckily, King saved that other guard and put his hands up before the crack-shot guard took him out, too.

Ashley touched the bruise on his jaw where he'd been sucker-punched during the fight. "I probably don't want to see what the rest of you looks like, right?"

"You want to see it, honey, I'm happy to show it to you." King liked to razz Trigger by flirting with his girl. It actually made him feel a bit more like himself to let his guard down and fall back on old habits.

"Enough." Trigger pulled a stack of folders out of the car through the open window and set them on the hood. "Here's what we know about Cara Potter."

"I still don't get why I had to serve time to get close to her."

"You're the one who set up the plan to get in Iceman's crew," Trigger pointed out.

"Yeah, but the second we found out we could use her, why didn't we go after her?" After months in jail, King could no longer see the reasons for it if they weren't going directly after Iceman.

Trigger sighed. "You know why. She takes one look at you, she won't believe a guy like you would want to work in a coffee shop."

"What's wrong with the way I look?"

"You're a little banged up now, but you've got military stamped all over you with the way you carry yourself. You open your mouth without all the joking and sarcasm and she'll hear your intelligence. What we don't want her to guess is that the military led you to law enforcement and straight to her father. She's got a weakness for ex-cons trying to better themselves. We're exploiting that to our advantage. What you look like and where you come from won't matter as much to her as the story you're building that you've hit rock bottom in life and want a fresh start."

Trigger laid it out for him without any animosity. Undercover for long periods of time, even Trigger had needed reminding sometimes about why they did what they did and the ultimate objective that sometimes got obscured by all the bullshit along the way.

Refocused, King hobbled over to the car and stared down at the five-by-seven photo of his target. Taken off guard by Cara's delicate beauty, he stared at her porcelain face, pale blonde hair, and haunting blue eyes. He saw her father's strong features in the stubborn set of her chin and her direct gaze. Something in her eyes spoke to a hard life that didn't match her fairy-like features.

Trigger ran down the info. "We've had eyes on her for the better part of a month leading up to sending you in. Iceman dropped in to see her a couple times at the place she runs. It's outside town at an intersection where gas and food are the last place to get them for about fifty miles outside heading back into town. Locals love her place. Long haulers are regulars. According to our guys, the homemade doughnuts and fresh-brewed coffee are worth the drive. Every man that goes into that place is in love with her."

"Living with her will be a hell of a lot easier on the eyes than living with Scott, that's for damn sure."

Trigger gave him a look that said, *Hands off.*

King got it. She was a job. Nothing more. But give a guy a break. He'd been locked up in a sausage factory for one hundred and fifty-three days. Too long for a man who liked companionship with the fairer sex, even if it only consisted of sharing a few beers at the bar. Work consumed his life. He didn't have time—or make the time—for relationships.

"On the surface, she appears to be a do-gooder. Takes in strays on probation or with a record that keeps them from getting gainful employment, so long as they swear they've left that life and want to remain on the straight and narrow. She doesn't give second chances if they break the law."

"She is their second chance," King guessed. "I'll bet she's loyal to them so long as they are to her."

Trigger pointed to a map. "That's how it seems. She's got a large piece of property. Mostly open land. She lives in the main house. She converted the barn into a kind of communal housing unit with four rooms, a large living space, and kitchen area. Right now, only one guy is living there. Ray McDaniel. Sixty-four. Lifetime criminal. Mostly drugs and minor assaults that amounted to nothing more than bar fights. One sexual assault charge, dismissed due to lack of evidence. He'll be your roommate if she lets you stay."

"She will." To end Iceman's rein in the Guzman cartel, he'd do anything to get Cara on his side.

"She doesn't just let anyone stay there. The people who work for her have been with her for years."

"Seems like there's space for me at her place if only one guy is using those four rooms."

Trigger opened another file. "Tandy is Cara's best friend and works for her as a waitress. She stays in the apartment above the restaurant. Her rap sheet includes possession, pandering, and prostitution with one assault on a broke and doped-up john who couldn't take no for an answer. She stabbed the guy and was kicking the shit out of him when the cops arrived. She was in and out of jail from sixteen until three years ago when she went to work for Cara."

"What about the coffee house?"

"Crossroads Coffee."

"So, not just where the place is located on the map, but a place for people who are at a crossroads in their life. Stay on the straight and narrow, or take another path."

"I hadn't really thought about it, but maybe that's exactly why she named it that." Trigger closed the file and stacked it with the others. "Everything we've gathered on her and Iceman and his crew over the last few months is in these files. Don't get caught with them."

King took the stack of papers.

Trigger pointed to the battered pickup parked behind the Camaro. "Ashley and I went to your place, cleaned out your fridge, and packed you a bag. The truck title says Chris Hickman, but trust me, it will be easier if you stick to everyone calling you Flash from now on. One person calls you Chris and you don't answer, it could raise suspicions with Iceman. You don't want him digging too deep into your cover."

King took the advice. Trigger had spent far longer and deeper undercover than King ever wanted to go, but he wanted to see this case against Iceman through to the end.

"I left directions inside the truck cab for a motel on the outskirts of town. Get some sleep, your head together, and eat a decent meal."

King needed it. He'd bulked up thanks to the hours working out in the prison yard with Scott, but the food sucked and he'd leaned down.

"Head over to the coffee place this afternoon when the morning crowd thins out. You shouldn't have a problem getting the job. She's down two employees."

Suspicious. "Two? Why?"

"They eloped in Key West and decided not to come back."

King tilted his head. "Did the DEA help out there?"

"No. Love and sex on the beach had everything to do with that. It worked in your favor."

"A love story for the ages." Ashley rolled her eyes and yawned.

"I can't believe you guys drove all the way here to see me off. One of the guys from the local office could have left me the truck."

"I wanted to see for myself that you're holding up after being in there." Trigger notched his chin toward the prison at King's back. Exactly where he wanted to keep it from now on. "Ashley wanted to see you and check in with Scott. Plus, she refused to let me come alone, too afraid I'd fall asleep at the wheel."

"Sweet." King pretended to gag. "You guys make me sick with all your love and happiness. I just got out of jail and you flaunt your gorgeous fiancée and how concerned she is with you. You're a jerk, you know that, Trigger." For all his teasing, he kind of meant it, mostly because he didn't have a woman welcoming him into her loving arms when he walked out of those gates. Trigger had been through hell this past year and ended up with an angel in his bed, his heart, and in his life, *forever and ever, Amen!* as the Randy Travis song goes.

"Sorry I'm going to miss the wedding."

"Agent Bennett will be available while I'm on my honeymoon."

"You guys have fun. I'll just be here taking down the bad guys."

Trigger deserved all the happiness in the world.

King just wanted a little piece of it before he went back undercover again for God knows how long. Judging by the fact that Trigger showed up here and sprung him in the middle of the night to give him all this information, he wasn't going to get any downtime before he headed straight for Cara Potter. And Iceman. He had some payback to dole out to that guy.

But first he needed to get in with his daughter.

THE MONTANA MEN NOVELS

AT WOLF RANCH
978-0-06-233489-3

WHEN IT'S RIGHT
978-0-06-233493-0

HER LUCKY COWBOY
978-0-06-233495-4

STONE COLD COWBOY
978-0-06-243532-3

HER RENEGADE RANCHER
978-0-06-243535-4

HIS COWBOY HEART
978-0-06-243540-8

JRY 0717